STORMGATE PRESS

CHARLES F. MILLHOUSE PRESENTS:

| Number 2 | CHARLES F MILLHOUSE Publisher | Summer 2021 |

EDITED BY: CHARLES F. MILLHOUSE - ROSE SHABABY & MARY ANN MILLHOUSE

IN THIS ISSUE...

ISBN: 9798736149599

Imprint: Independently published

COVER ART BY: Clayton Murwin

CAPTAIN HAWKLIN COPYRIGHT ©2021 CHARLES F. MILLHOUSE

PULP PONDERINGS

Welcome to the second issue of Pulp Reality. With the huge success of the first issue, we had to do a second one, (which was always my intent). With this outing, Pulp Reality is now a series.

What better way to celebrate then to make the second book, bigger and better than the first one? I mean we have to go up... right?

In this issue, we have Pirates, PI's, Apparitions, vigilantes and much, much, more. With stories from returning authors, Kellie Austin, Bobby Nash, Brian K. Morris, Clyde Hall, and myself. As well as new writers joining Stormgate's fold, Amy Hale, Ron Fortier, Scott Donnelly, and Marlin Williams.

Let's not forget the artists, whose tireless efforts bring life to our stories. With talents like Clayton Murwin, (this issue's cover artist), Damian Aviles, Stephen Burks, Candice Comelleri, Erikius Castro, Ted Davies, Rob Davis, and Jeffrey Ray Hayes.

Another way Pulp Reality 2 is bigger and better is Special Features!! Much like a Blu Ray, PR2 offers videos spotlighting our creative talents. You'll be able to access them with the QR code here on this page. Check out the videos there and learn about our creative talents.

CONTRIBUTORS

WRITERS

KELLIE AUSTIN

SCOTT DONNELLY

RON FORTIER

AMY HALE

CLYDE HALL

CHARLES F. MILLHOUSE

BRIAN K MORRIS

BOBBY NASH

MARLIN WILLIAMS

ARTISTS

DAMIÁN AVILÉS

STEPHEN BURKS

Erikius Castro

CANDICE COMELLERI

TED DAVIES

ROB DAVIS

JEFFREY RAY HAYES

CLAYTON MURWIN

**121 EAST SYCAMORE
KOKOMO, INDIANA
46901
(765) 450 4126**

1

NEW FLESH ON OLD BONES

BY MARLIN WILLIAMS

ART BY JEFFREY RAY HAYES

NEW FLESH ON OLD BONES
Marlin Williams

By nightfall, the surface of the West Indies waters had turned into a tempest. As the wind screamed around them, torrential rain pelted the deck and crew. Lightning repeatedly flashed and thunder shook the vessel. A thirty-foot swell of churning sea slammed against the wooden hull of the Defiance. The square rig, three-mast vessel that Lefleur had pillaged from the British Royal Navy now sailing under the flag of skull and crossbones rocked, rose, and fell as the raging sea continued to toss it around. The small crew of men manning the deck slid across the wet planks while grasping for anything that would keep them from slipping over the edge.

Captain Lefleur's ability to maintain the balance of his tall frame during the tumult seemed almost supernatural. He lifted the customary eye patch he wore over his left eye and peered through a spyglass. The torrential rain obscured his quarry that bobbed about a hundred yards off the port bow. A flash of lightning lit the other vessel as it disappeared behind a mountain of water. Several days ago, they had found the Catholic sailing vessel anchored off the island of Tobago. Ringed by blue water and white sandy beaches, the port was a pocket carved into the jungle wilderness thriving with the homes and businesses of wealthy merchants. The vigorous trade marketplace was well guarded by a battery of heavy cannons and English mercenaries. Lefleur and his crew dared not get too close since any attempt by the pirate ship to approach would be enough cause to be fired upon. Instead, the Defiance anchored a mile off the southern tip of the island in waiting. When the Catholic ship got underway to the Vatican City, Lefleur and his crew gave chase, but the storm had turned their mission askew.

Lefleur broke away from the spyglass and turned to Tieg. Raising his voice above the wind, he shouted, "Summon the three masts' captains and their crews to the main deck!"

Tieg stood at his captain's side clinging to a rail with one hand and awkwardly gripping a trumpet in the other. A bolt of lightning frolicked next to the ship and illuminated the terror in the boy's green eyes. Lefleur had discovered the orphaned boy loitering around the docks in Clew Bay, Ireland and afraid he would fall prey to unsavory characters, the pirate captain had taken him under his wing. The inexperienced cabin boy had been unceremoniously promoted to first mate just an hour before when the original seasoned deck officer had been crushed beneath a collapsed rigging while dousing the sails preparing for the storm. Other qualified crewmen who would be next in line were either manning their stations or dead themselves.

Tieg raised the trumpet to his lips, but the forceful wind ripped it from his grip. It quickly sailed out of sight.

"Take the message to the quartermaster yourself and be lively about it!"

Tieg gave a nod. He turned to leave.

"Mister Tieg!" Lefleur called out.

The first mate wheeled around.

"Tell Mister Suggs that we are raising full sails and giving chase."

Tieg thought the decision was unrealistic, but out of deference, he held his tongue.

"And we'll need to lighten the load for more speed. Tell the quartermaster to order the men to toss the barrels of food and water overboard." A loud peal of thunder punctuated his command. "And the cannons."

Tieg's common sense balked. If they survived the storm, those necessary supplies to sustain the lives of the crew would be gone, and without heavy artillery, they would become easy prey for other pirates that roamed these waters.

"Do as I say," shouted Lefleur, still holding an awe-inspiring stance on the poop deck, "and carry out your duty!"

He had no idea where to look for the man. For all he knew, by now, the quartermaster could have been washed over the railing.

Tieg tarried too long. The captain's seething dark eyes set him into motion. With the aid of the handrails, he succeeded in laboring down the steps, but as he set one foot on the main deck, a juggernaut slammed the Defiance. The impact tilted the ship to one side. As it did, a neighboring surge collapsed and caught the head of the center mast in its grip. The vessel was suddenly in jeopardy of capsizing. As the ship listed, water washed across the working area. The crewmen struggled in a swift current of knee-deep water. A few cried out for God, others, to the deities they worshipped.

The sudden shift threw Tieg into the rail. He latched on tight. He squeezed his eyes shut, and in his thick Irish brogue cried out, "Sweet Mother of God!" He freed a hand and clutched the cross bound around his neck by a thin leather cord. At the last second, the mast broke free, and the abrupt release sent the ship rolling in the other direction, but by what seemed a miracle, the Defiance righted itself.

Tieg stumbled through the strobing darkness and managed to locate the battened doors of the main hatch. He opened one and clamored down far enough to close it. His surroundings went from dark to pitch-black. The eerie atmosphere weighed heavy around him as he plunged deeper into the bowels of the rocking vessel, shouting the quartermaster's name as he went. On the third level, he made a stop.

He opened the door to his closet-size room. The glowing green fungi, growing in the cavity of a small rotting log, washed across his face. He had discovered the rare natural phosphorescence while filling barrels with fresh drinking water on a deserted island they had recently docked. He grabbed the Foxfire from the shelf.

With the mock flame in hand, he continued his trek. En route, his light set aglow the terrified eyes of crewmen intoxicated with fear. They had shirked their duties to hide below. If Suggs found out, he would string the cowards up and castrate them. They begged Tieg with their eyes to keep their insubordination a secret.

Tieg crept past the iron bars that caged the wild creatures that Lefleur had recently acquired on the coast of Gabon. To him, they were strange and unworldly, and when his duties didn't require him to feed or clean, he gave the large cage a wide berth. He felt their eyes on him as he passed. He quickened his pace and continued down.

The steps delivered him to the bottom hold where he was met by the heady aroma of stale air, sweat, sewage, and the sweet scent of rum. A single lantern burned. Open flame on a wooden vessel, especially one carrying dry powder, was a major hazard, so a man was tasked to hold the light source. Crewmen glistening with perspiration stood knee-deep in rank water as they took turns cranking the wheel of the bilge pump.

The quartermaster, Suggs, sat atop a barrel overseeing the operation. He was an oafish looking man with a pop eye nestled beneath a bushy eyebrow. An elongated tooth jutted from his bottom gum and overlapped his top lip. The tip of the jagged canine rested just below his left nostril. He stopped barking orders long enough to glare at Tieg with his pop eye. "Well, what do you want, boy?"

Tieg parted his lips to speak, but his response was cut short by a loud groan followed by a rapid succession of creaks and pops. Work ceased; all eyes were on the hull. It bowed in, and for a few anxious seconds, it seemed the vessel would crack like an egg and let the sea pour in. They held their breath and waited to embrace death. Sighs of relief came when the wood relaxed and assumed its designed shape.

"What's the matter, bilge suckers?" Suggs' eye was on the flustered crewmen. "Get back to work or there'll be the devil to pay!" He turned back to Tieg. "Hurry it up, boy. I ain't got all day."

"I came to give you orders."

Suggs usual vinegary disposition soured even more as he narrowed his eye at the lad. "I don't take my orders from the cabin boy. Get on wi' ya, or you'll get the back of this." He lifted his hand and cocked it back to strike.

"I'm first mate."

Suggs lowered his hand and grinned. "Don't be runnin' a rig on me, lad."

"This is not in jest."

At first Suggs looked taken aback, then he laughed. The others joined in. "Shut your mouths!" cried the quartermaster. "Or, I'll have every last one of ya keelhauled!" He turned to Tieg. "You had better be speakin' the God's honest truth, lad." He slipped off his perch and sloshed through the water to grab a handful of Tieg's fiery red locks. The quartermaster looked him straight in the eyes. "Or I'll keelhaul your sorry carcass as well."

Tieg shuddered at the memory of one poor wretch's head and upper chest with webs of veins and sinewy tissues of his innards dangling from the open cavity. He could almost feel the ropes bound around his wrists and the sharp barnacles on the bottom of the ship slicing his skin like razors as he fought off sharks attracted by his blood. That's if he could hold his breath that long.

"Well," said Suggs.

Tieg purged his anxiety with determination. "I speak the truth." He pulled free of Suggs' grip and took a step back. "I swear on my oath of allegiance and honor to my captain and crew."

"You're the quartermaster," one of the men told Suggs. He pointed a finger at him. "You should be first mate."

Suggs mulled it over for a second. "Well, it appears that ain't the way of it." He turned to Tieg. "What be the captain's orders?"

"The captain wants all mast crews topside."

A man wrinkled his brow at Tieg. "Why in blue blazes would he have need for the mast crews in this storm?"

"We're going to hoist the sails and give chase to the Holy Cross."

Grumbling broke out.

"His obsession will be the death of us all!" cried one of the men.

"The masts won't take it!" exclaimed someone else. "They will snap!"

"And we are to throw the barrels of food and water over the rails," said Tieg.

Everyone except Suggs stared in disbelief.

"And the cannons," Tieg added.

"He's mad!" yelled another. "The ship needs a full belly if we're to stay upright."

"And so do we," replied one more.

The majority speculated the captain had taken leave of his senses. They quickly decided that a mutiny was in order.

Suggs drew his knife, whipped around, and pressed the tip to the belly of the closest man. "You heard the captain's orders." He skimmed his gaze across every man. "Any mutiny from any of ya and I'll fill yer belly wi' my blade!" He withdrew the point from the relieved man and faced Tieg. "Tell the captain, aye—aye."

Tieg quickly took leave of Mister Suggs and the others. He hurried up the stairs and restored his precious foxfire to the shelf before he returned to the deck.

A bolt of lightning split the darkness. He caught a glimpse of Lefleur still standing on the poop deck. The tails of his coat slapped furiously in the wind. A gust suddenly ripped the leather tri-cornered hat from his head and flung it into the sea. Now bareheaded, the long locks of his dark hair whipped violently in the tempest.

Lefleur sensed the boy's presence. He turned his head to look at him.

There was something in Lefleur's dark eyes that made Tieg tremble. He thought the others might be right: the captain was driven by madness.

"Come up here," Lefleur shouted.

Like a shot, Tieg was at his side.

Lefleur pointed at the other ship. "They've tossed something over the side." He extended the spyglass to Tieg. "Have a look and tell me what you see." Lefleur knew that his first mate's green eyes were keen. From the perch of the crow's nest, the young lad could spot a small school of fish a mile away.

Tieg took it and pressed it to his eye. He had to wait for a bright flicker of lightning to illuminate the surroundings. When it finally came, Tieg lowered the spyglass and with a concerned look on his face, turned to his captain. "Looks like a woman!" The wind carried a high-pitched scream to their ears.

Lefleur took the spyglass from Tieg and peered out again. A flicker of lightning lit the speck bobbing in the swells and the ship that had slipped further away. He lowered the spyglass, reached into the hip pocket of his breeches, and felt down for the rosary beads that he kept tucked there. He ran a finger across the engraved name on the back of the cross and weighed his choices. If he stopped his pursuit, he would risk losing his prey, but if he continued on, the girl would drown. He turned to Tieg. "Rally some of the men and have them lower a longboat to fetch her."

The look of concern on Tieg's face shattered and turned to shock. Dropping a small vessel into the raging sea would be certain doom for the men manning it. Another swell rocked the square-rigged vessel.

He narrowed his eye at Tieg. "Do as I command."

Caught between the backlash from his captain if he did not follow orders and the hostile recoil from the crewmen, Tieg stood in place.

"You'd better get a move on, Tieg, or you'll join the female."

He turned and raced to find Suggs. Tieg found him and a handful of crewmen on the second deck fighting to maintain balance while gathering barrels. He managed to stammer out, "They threw a woman over the railing of the Holy Cross!"

Suggs spit. "Damn Catholics."

"The captain says to launch a longboat and fetch her."

"Enough!" One of the other men gritted his teeth and narrowed his eyes. "This is beyond madness!" He slammed his fist against the hull. "Bringin' a woman aboard—" He shook his head. "It's bad luck that's what it is." He turned to the others. "I say we heave the captain over before he calls down the wrath of the gods on us!"

Suggs narrowed his eye and turned it on the men. "If any of you buck the captain's orders, you'll suffer the whip." His threat drew silence. "Now, choose four amongst yourselves and carry out the orders."

"Four?"

Suggs nodded. "Two to bail water and two to row."

They drew straws. The four losers grudgingly went topside and braved the storm. Suggs supervised the launching of the longboat and saw the fear in one of the men's eyes. Suggs took him by the arm. "Keep ya wits about ya or the storm will get the best of ya." The man nodded and drew a deep breath. He climbed in, and using the guide ropes of the davit, the four lowered the small craft down into the tumultuous water. The boat bucked in the waves. The four men scrambled into position. Two men grabbed the long-handled oars and began to row. As quickly as the other two scooped water from the bottom, more poured in over the sides.

Despite the tossing of the sea, those crewmen able to take leave of their duties congregated at the railing to watch the rescue, including Tieg and Lefleur. Some were certain it was a doomed effort. Others hoped for luck. Normally, wagers as to the outcome would be made, but an arrogant display such as that tempted fate and would have brought a slew of bad luck to the ship. Coins remained in pockets.

Time had seemed to stretch into infinity until the longboat returned carrying the rescued female. The crew rallied to hoist the longboat from the water. When safely aboard, the four men jumped onto the planks of the deck and fell to their knees in praise.

Lefleur helped the female out of the boat. The men stared wide-eyed at the woman as she set foot on deck. She was pale and shaking.

"Sweet Mother of God!" One made the sign of the cross over his heart. "She's a nun!"

Her headwear had been claimed by the sea, so all that remained of her uniform was the tunic. She stood shivering while clutching a set of rosary beads in her hand.

A bolt of lightning struck the center mast in a bright flash and a loud CRACK of thunder shook the ship.

All but Lefleur crouched and instinctively covered their heads as sparks rained down, danced briefly on the wet planks, and winked out.

"See!" one man shouted. He pointed a finger at the young woman. "She is the one that has brought about this tempest. Heave 'er o'er the side and appease the gods afore we sink!"

Their decision came in unison as they shouted, "AYE!" They advanced toward her.

Lefleur stepped between the nun and his men. They stopped and fell back a step. He turned to the nun, grabbed her robe by the collar, and ripped the material down past her navel.

The unexpected display of feminine flesh brought a mixture of responses from the depraved seamen from openly ogling and leering, to shy surreptitious glances. The terrified woman gasped as she covered her bare breasts with her hands.

Lefleur placed the palm of his hand on her swollen belly. "Have mercy! She has a child in her womb."

"The pious woman has sinned! It is her and her unborn child that God seeks to punish, not us! If we stand in God's way He will surely destroy us all!" The man had fire in his eyes. He stepped up to Lefleur. "Stand aside, Captain."

One man continued to gaze up at the mast. He raised his hand in the air. "An omen!"

They all looked in the direction where his grimy fingernail pointed. Green balls of light danced along the rigging.

Men who followed the Christian faith fell to their knees. One said, "Glory to the patron Saint Elmo!" He pushed aside the crewmen. "Leave her be!" He pointed to the ebbing balls of fire. "It's a sign! She stays."

The nun's eyelids flickered; she sagged at the knees then crumpled onto the deck face up. The rain poured down on her.

Lefleur turned to Tieg. "Take her below and strip her of the wet clothes and put her in my bed. Then return to your duties."

Tieg nodded, scooped her up in his arms, and whisked her away.

As Lefleur parted company from his men, they divided and let him pass. He returned to the poop deck, raised the spyglass to his eye, and scanned the waters. A swatch of lightning confirmed his fears. The Holy Cross was nowhere in sight. Either the storm had claimed her as one of its victims or the ship had broached and been driven off course.

He spent the night searching the waters to no avail. By morning, the swells were in their final throes of passion. The winds had calmed and the clouds were breaking.

Lefleur tossed the spyglass to the raw-boned man of dark color. "Up you go."

The man scaled up the rigging like a Bolivian spider monkey. From the crow's nest, Sims called out. "She's nowhere in sight."

"Come down, Mister Sims."

"Aye, aye!" The man scrambled down.

"Follow me, Mister Tieg."

They left the rear quarterdeck and made their way to the Captain's Quarters. Lefleur only gave the slumbering woman a glance as he walked past the bed. He approached the back wall of cherry wood panels, stopped, grabbed a corner section, and pulled a hidden door open. It rasped sharply against the jamb. The light from the room rushed in, quickly fusing with the darkness, creating a hazy gloom.

Tieg strained to see, but the abysmal darkness refused to yield its secret. "Shall I wait here for you, Captain?"

Lefleur shook his head. "Come." He stepped inside and lifted the patch that protected his left eye from the light; it was already accustomed to the darkness.

It took a moment for Tieg's eyes to adjust, but as they did, the smoky outline of a robed man stood in the back of the compartment. At first, Tieg looked bewildered, but he had long suspected that someone or something besides the captain dwelled in his cabin. Tieg's responsibility as cabin boy of delivering meals and picking up the slop bucket from the Captain's Quarters had been causing him double duty.

"This is my brother," said Lefleur. "His name is Caba." Caba was the natural born son of the voodoo priestess that had fostered Lefleur from infancy after the death of his own mother.

The robe-clad figure stepped forward and lit the candle sitting in the middle of the table. The small flame dancing on the tip of the wick created a circle of light, but the hood he wore shrouded his face in shadows. "As-Salaam-Alaikum, my brother." The Ethiopian tilted his head to one side with curiosity. "Why have you brought the cabin boy?"

"First mate," Tieg countered. He lifted his chin and squared his shoulders.

"If I should fall," said Lefleur, "he will assume command."

The thought of stepping into such a large role terrified Tieg. He hoped that he wouldn't be called upon to fulfill the task.

Caba nodded. "Have you come to seek my counsel?"

"Yes," said Lefleur.

Caba pulled back the hood. The material settled on his shoulders. Cryptic tattoos covered the dark skin of his face and shaved head.

His appearance shocked Tieg. He took a step back.

One eye was dark and peered at the first mate with crystal clarity. The other, filmed over and sightless, gazed into the ether.

Lefleur draped an arm reassuringly over the lad's shoulders as he replied to the mystic. "I lost sight of the ship in the storm."

Caba gave a knowing nod and positioned himself in front of the candle then sank to his knees. He closed the eye with sight and directed his god-eye at the flame.

In the minutes that passed, the air inside the compartment seemed to charge with electricity. It crawled across Ticg and prickled his skin to the point that he grew uncomfortable and restless. The candle's flame wavered in a phantom breeze. The air chilled.

At last, the oracle opened his eye and stood. "The ship is not far. Sail thirty degrees west and you will intercept her."

"And what of the man I seek?" asked Lefleur. "Did he survive the storm?"

For a moment, Caba's dead eye stared beyond the thin veil of forms and into the unfathomable zone of spirit. At last, he nodded his head and replied, "Yes. The man you seek has gone into hiding. Find the Talah and you will find him."

Lefleur thanked him and readied to leave.

Tieg anxiously made his way to the door.

"Wait!" Caba grabbed Lefleur by the arm. "Aboard the Holy Cross awaits death."

The man's words stalled Tieg. Uneasiness settled in his bones. He stopped and waited to hear more.

"I see the fall of many," said the Ethiopian, "but one man shall emerge victorious and the other is doomed."

"And who is the man that will emerge victorious?" asked Lefleur.

Caba shook his head. "I can only tell you that both men are hiding their true purpose. One seeks to hide his sins."

Lefleur instinctively sought the rosary in his pocket.

"The other seeks revenge," continued Caba. He released Lefleur's arm. "Be careful, my brother."

The captain agreed with a solemn nod and left.

Outside, Lefleur closed the door. "Caba can foretell the future and see into the unknown. But whatever he shares with us should never be repeated. Do you understand?"

The captain did not need to explain. Tieg was well aware the crew was superstitious and they might perceive the mystic's prediction's as a blasphemy. Ticg nodded.

Lefleur peered at the sleeping girl. Her bare arms were above the covers. One hand at her side, the other hand holding the rosary beads rested across her chest. Lips, slightly parted, her chest gently rose and fell with each breath. The cords of her long dark hair spread out haphazardly across the pillow like the tentacles of an octopus. Her looks were exotic.

He walked over to her and gently lifted the cross. Engraved on the back was the girl's name. He eased it down and turned to Tieg. "Place dry clothes next to Maria so that she has them when she awakens."

He turned to gaze at his own disheveled appearance in the looking glass hanging on the wall. A two-week growth of beard shadowed his strong jawline. The tempest had scattered the long locks of his dark hair in every direction. He pulled the tresses into a ponytail that cascaded down his spine and then topped his head with the Cavalier hat that he had stowed on the shelf above the bed. He gathered his two pistols from the nightstand and stuffed them in his sash. His cutlass lay on the floor; he scooped it up and slipped the blade into a metal ring attached to his leather belt. Lefleur turned to leave, but hesitated. He turned back to Tieg. "I have something for you." He opened the lid of a chest at the foot of his bed.

The first mate watched with great curiosity as his captain dug through the contents.

Lefleur dredged up a horn. He handed it to Tieg. "This was mine when I was a first mate."

Tieg took it. Speechless, he watched the captain as he left the room.

Lefleur returned to the deck where he gave the helmsman new coordinates. Once they were on course, the crew tended to restoring order to the deck, rigging, and caulking leaking seams down below.

Half the day passed before a crewman suddenly cried out, "Sail ho!" A ship sat in the far-off distance.

"Mister Sims!" cried Lefleur.

The raw-boned man hustled over to him. "Aye."

Lefleur tossed the spyglass to him.

Sims scrambled up the rigging. "It's her!" he called down. "She's sitting dead in the water."

Tieg stood at his captain's side awaiting orders.

"Sound the order for half sails," Lefleur told him. "We go in slow."

Tieg piped out the order.

"Half sails!" echoed across the deck

The well-practiced crewmen of different ages and nationalities quickly collected on the main deck. Barefoot and bare-chested they scrambled to carry out their assigned duties of scaling mast, pulling rope, hoisting and lowering sails for balance and reduced speed.

In a matter of moments, the deck planks beneath the boots of Captain Lefleur shuddered as the helmsman wheeled the sailing ship into position.

Lefleur and Tieg maintained a vigilant watch on the other vessel. With every nautical mile that lay in their wake, the clearer the details of the Holy Cross became. The ship was outfitted with two decks of cannons of what appeared to be eight pounders. It was not uncommon for a Catholic ship to be heavily armed since many of them carried a belly full of gold.

When the gap between the two ships narrowed to a mile, a white makeshift flag with black skull and crossbones climbed the center mast of the Holy Cross. Once at the top, it flapped furiously in the wind.

Tieg stared in disbelief. "Are they asking for—?"

"Parley," Lefleur nodded.

Tieg knew the meaning of parley, as did every other pirate. The Pirate Lords, Morgan and Bartholomew, had set down the rules of parley in the Pirata Codex long ago. The pact allowed any person to invoke temporary protection brought before the captain to negotiate, without being attacked, until the parley was complete. "How can we trust them to honor the Code of the Pirate Brethren?"

"We don't." Lefleur lowered the spyglass. "I suspect a trap."

"What should we do?"

"We maintain present course and speed."

In a short time, the Defiance approached its prey. She loomed off the port bow. Lefleur ordered Tieg to signal the helmsman to turn the ship into the wind and for the crew to drop sails.

Canvas quickly came down. The Defiance came abreast the Catholic ship and grated along the upper deck. Both ships trembled under the stress, but quickly came to rest. The two vessels, almost identical in size and design, bobbed next to each other. With an air of anticipation of what would happen next, the crew of both ships locked eyes and stared across the narrow gap of sea and wind that divided them.

"Tie off!" rose the command from the quartermaster aboard the Holy Cross.

In a cloud of murmuring voices, the crew quickly busied themselves with the task of securing ropes to the railing of their own ship and then tossing the loose ends across the divide. Once the crew of the Defiance secured the binds, the parley flag came down and a Red Duster, a British Naval flag, crawled up the center mast of the Catholic ship.

Tieg narrowed his eyes at the Royal British Navy officer that suddenly appeared and was now strolling across the deck. Tieg laid a hand on his primed pistol stuffed in his sash.

From the corner of his eye, Lefleur caught the infraction and frowned down on his first mate. "Hold."

Tieg let his hand slip from the wooden handle.

The British officer now stood at the railing. His tall stature was topped by a Bicorne hat and traditional powdered wig. "I am Thaddeus Beaumont, Captain in the King's Royal Navy." He squared his shoulders. Through a pair of close-set eyes, he stared down his long nose. "Captain Gosson Lefleur, as gentlemen, it is my hopes that you and I may discuss terms of surrender."

"Mine or yours?"

Beaumont frowned. "Do not mock me, sir. Surrender and you'll be taken back to England for a fair trial."

"I've heard tales of the king's fair trials."

"Do not dare scorn the king's generosity."

"I suppose your king, as well as the Pope, have extended their generosity to you," Lefleur replied.

"I don't know what it is that you speak of."

"Now it is you, sir, that mocks me," answered Lefleur. "I am well aware of the bounty placed on my head by your king and by the Pope. A prize such as myself, along with the return of the Defiance to your king, will fetch a handsome reward and hasten a commission in rank."

"I do it because it is my sworn duty, not for personal gain. However, Mors tua, vita mea."

"Mors mihi lucrum," Lefleur responded.

"Ah!" Beaumont smiled. "You are an educated man, Mister Lefleur."

"Oxford."

"My opinion of you has slightly elevated." His smile suddenly collapsed under the weight of a frown. Beaumont growled out his words, "Moreover, I say to you, surrender or you and your crew shall die."

Lefleur nodded. "It seems that I have no other choice." At his back, the crew of the Defiance whispered in voices that articulated concern. "These are my terms: Stand on the bow of your ship, unbutton your breeches, and piss into the wind. When you're done go back to England and tell your king to kiss my arse." His words stirred whispers from the crew of the Holy Cross. Lefleur's crew laughed.

Captain Beaumont narrowed his beady eyes and gritted his teeth.

"After you have completed my terms," said Lefleur, "return here and I will surrender." He grinned.

Beaumont ground out his words through his gritted teeth. "Insolent bastard!"

"Oh, I'm not the bastard. Your king is. He has twisted the truth. Anyone that has spoken against him has summarily been put to death. He has taken the lives of innocent men, women, and children that have totaled into the thousands. I, sir, am a saint compared to the ruler of England."

"Enough of your patronizing sermon!" Beaumont glared then drew his sword. Thrusting the tip high in the air, he bellowed out, "MUSTER!"

In tandem, the mast captains echoed the word. The command summoned armed uniformed soldiers from every outlet. In an orderly fashion, they assembled on the deck. All were ready fighting men. After the thunder of feet had ceased, Beaumont said, "No doubt, Gosson Lefleur, once I return to England, our encounter will become a tale that will regale my dinner guests for years to come."

Lefleur stared at the congregated soldiers then turned his eye on Beaumont. "I suppose I should be astonished by your resourceful cleverness."

Beaumont smiled back. "Along with my tactical military skills for war, I am a compassionate man, Captain. That is why I feel compelled to offer you one last chance to surrender yourself and the Defiance."

"And my offer to relieve your bladder into the wind still stands." Lefleur's crew laughed.

Beaumont narrowed his eyes. "Don't be a fool. Your crew is no match for ball, black powder, and the sharp edge of a sword in the hands of a hundred and fifty of the king's trained soldiers."

"Your assumption is well-founded," Lefleur replied. "My crew is no match for your men." He turned to Tieg. "Sound the horn."

The first mate raised the horn to his lips and sounded three long blasts.

Two of Lefleur's crewman raced to the double doors of the quarterdeck.

Beaumont stood dumbstruck for a moment, but quickly recovered. His traditional military training became fluid once again as he raised his sword and shouted. "READY!"

The two men aboard the Defiance flung the doors open.

"AIM!" Beaumont's eyes locked on the small figures gushing from the threshold. "FIRE!"

The soldiers' eyes filled with terror as they shrank back without a shot. Dark-skinned, wild-eyed pygmies stared back. The blunt features of their faces were disguised beneath painted death masks of white skulls. Bone piercings jutted from their noses and ears. Their bodies would have been bare, but for the strips of animal skin concealing their genitals.

Beaumont spun around. "Hold your ground for God's sake! You are trained fighting men not frightened little children!"

The sailing crew of the Holy Cross began to abandon their posts. One happencd to bc a frcsh-faccd young lad of about thirteen years of age. As he tried to rush past Beaumont, the infuriated officer thrust his sword into the boy's chest. The lad's eyes widened with disbelief and horror as he screamed out in pain. His eyes rolled back. He slipped from the blade and collapsed onto the

deck. Beaumont turned to the panicked crew and thrust his bloodied sword into the air. "Anyone else abandons your post and you will face my wrath!" The retreating mob came to a halt and silenced as they watched fresh blood drool down the blade of the cutlass and onto the fluted cuff of Beaumont's white shirt. He lowered his cutlass and turned back to the matter at hand.

With their knees bent and their bamboo sticks poised the pygmies stood ready for assault. Lefleur stood tall with his arms folded across his chest and glaring dangerously.

Beaumont met his stare. "It appears that your startling exhibit has boggled the minds of my men and struck fear into their hearts, but their fright shall wither beneath my leadership." He looked back over his shoulder. "Bridge the gap!"

Four soldiers carried a long flat timber between them. They rushed forward and quickly linked the two ships. The rest drew swords and pistols as they readied to charge the Defiance.

"Seize him!" cried Beaumont. Still clutching the sticks, the pygmies scurried up the ropes with adept speed. Beaumont turned to his hesitant men. "See, even the savages fear the king's soldiers." He snapped to attention. "ATTACK!"

The timber bowed and shuddered under the weight and rapid advance of the soldiers.

Lefleur clamped his hand down on Tieg's shoulder. "Sound the order."

He sounded three short blasts on the horn.

One of the pygmies raised the bamboo stick to his lips and blew.

The lead soldier on the plank flinched and stopped. Dazed, he pulled the wooden needle from his neck as the others, engaged by the incomprehensible phenomenon, watched.

Beaumont screamed from his post, "Advance! I command you!"

The baffled soldiers watched in horror as frothy red foam formed on the man's lips. The pain-filled look on his face became a glassy-eyed stare. His eyes rolled back in his head. He buckled at the knees, collapsed on the narrow plank, and began to twist and wither like a freshly unearthed worm. He tumbled into the water with a splash.

A voice filled with fear cried out to retreat. A moment later, scores of darts whizzed through the air and struck additional soldiers.

Beaumont turned to the soldiers on deck armed with long rifles. "Fire!"

They stood frozen by horror as they watched their brethren collapse, twist about and wither.

The veins on Beaumont's neck stood out. Red-faced, he screamed, "Discharge your weapons!"

On the brink of abandoning their post, the small band of infantry remaining raised their rifles with indecision. More poisonous darts sailed through the air, struck, and men fell, writhing in pain. Emotionally charged by panic and fear, the standing soldier's orderly formation quickly collapsed into disarray.

Beaumont pointed his sword at them in anger. "Stand firm, or I will have you all court-martialed!" He wheeled back around. "March forward I say!"

Instead, they turned to run. As they did, well-aimed darts struck them in the back of their necks.

One by one, they began to drop.

"On your feet! I command you!"

Their deaths drew cheers from the deck of the Defiance.

Beaumont looked astonished by the unprecedented defeat.

"Perhaps this wasn't the grand affair of sweeping victory that you had planned," piped Lefleur.

Beaumont staggered. He doubled his fist and scowled. "This isn't over!" He raised his flintlock and turned the open bore upon Lefleur. "It was the king's wish to bring you back alive, but your dead rotting corpse will have to suffice." He fired. The discharge came with a loud crack and fire. The ball missed its intended target by a narrow margin. Fear festered in Beaumont's eyes as the savages turned their blowguns on him. "You cower behind your savages."

Lefleur turned to the pygmies, speaking their native tongue he ordered them back below then drew his cutlass and stormed across the plank and onto the deck of the Holy Cross. Lefleur weaved through the dead. He gritted his teeth as he stepped over the body of the dead boy that mirrored Tieg in age and stature.

Beaumont raised his blade and poised for a duel. He looked back over his shoulder. The crewmen stood frozen in place, watching. "Protect me!"

With the threat of the pygmies gone, the crew aboard the Holy Cross armed themselves and began to advance.

Suggs nudged Tieg in the side with his elbow. "You'd best lead the men in an attack."

Tieg shook his head. "I can't. You lead. You should be the first mate."

"As I said before that ain't the way of it." He jammed the tip of his thick finger into the boy's chest. "Once the captain set foot off this ship, you assumed command."

Tieg looked uncertain. He shook his head.

Suggs nodded. "Find your grit, mate, and storm the deck of the Holy Cross afore it's too late."

Tieg swallowed hard. He drew his pistol and turned to the men. "Follow me!"

They all looked to Suggs.

He lowered his bushy eyebrow and narrowed his pop-eye at them. "You hcard thc captain!"

Their cry rose in unison as they stormed the deck of the Holy Cross with Tieg in the lead. The unharmonious din of calamity filled the air as the two waves clashed: blades met, shots fired, and men wailed in pain.

Lefleur and Beaumont were already locked in mortal combat of swift footwork and clashing swords. Each matched deathblows and thrusts of the other. The chaotic clanging became jarring death music. Minutes passed. Neither had drawn blood, but both glistened with sweat, their chests heaved.

Beaumont used his hand and beckoned to stop.

Breathing hard, Lefleur nodded and took a few steps back.

The Englishman bent at the waist, planted a hand on his knee while using the cutlass in the other hand as a prop. He panted. It took a moment for him to catch his breath. He looked up. "You may believe that you are well versed in the art of sword fighting," his tone became arrogant, "but your awkward brawling will prove to be no match for my capable skills. I shall emerge as victor."

Lefleur raised his cutlass. "Your hubris shall be your downfall."

The Englishman narrowed his eyes. His cheeks flared red and his knuckles whitened as he tightened his grip on the hilt of his cutlass. He swung.

Lefleur countered with a powerful downward blow. A loud metallic clang rang out as the English captain's blade snapped. The sharp tip of Lefleur's blade sliced through the breast of the officer's coat and met skin. Terror swept across Beaumont's face as he watched red spread across the material of his jacket.

Lefleur hiked his foot into the air and served a hard blow to the surprised man's chest.

The impact sent Beaumont sprawling back. He struck the planks and stared up at Lefleur in disbelief.

The pirate captain swiftly deposited the tip of his cutlass to the soft pocket of Beaumont's throat.

A crewman of the Holy Cross witnessed the incident and cried out, "The

Captain has fallen!" loud enough to be heard above the racket.

Immediately, the din of battle ceased. Heads turned, but the opponents remained composed, ready to resume the fight.

"You are beaten!" Lefleur told them. He pointed out the scarce numbers of the rival crewmen. "Surrender or die!" Lefleur called out. Their resolve came with a resounding clatter of weapons striking the deck. The men stepped back. Lefleur looked down and stared into Beaumont's beady eyes. "Tell me where to find the Talah."

The Englishman chuckled.

"Take heed, Captain. You don't seem to understand just how dire your state of affair is."

"Kill me and you'll never find it."

Lefleur responded to the officer's remark with a self-assured smile. "I'll find it even if I have to drag this ship to a nearby shore and dismantle it one plank at a time." He applied pressure to the hilt of his cutlass. A depression formed where the tip of his blade met flesh. A pool of red filled the cavity.

Beaumont lost his grin. "Do it, Lefleur! I am a soldier, and I have always been prepared to die in battle."

"There may be another way that I can loosen your tongue." He turned to his crew. He pointed out two men. "Find rope." Coupled by their mission the men simultaneously nodded and hurried away.

Beaumont laughed, "Hang me and the king shall hunt you down. You'll never find rest lest you give yourself up."

"Hanging would be merciful compared to what I have in store for you." He took a pause. "One last chance, tell me where to find the Talah or the sharks will dine on your flesh!"

Beaumont clamped his jaw shut.

The two men returned. One had a coil of rope slung over his shoulder.

"Bind him," Lefleur ordered.

The men busied themselves with the task of twirling and knotting the rope around Beaumont's wrists. After his fetters were applied, Lefleur tested the security of the knots. Once he was satisfied, he ordered the same two men to ready one of the longboats. He turned to Tieg. "Fetch the hourglass from my quarters." The first mate quickly departed. Lefleur grabbed the trailing end of the rope. "The sharks shall see to it that your glory and honor as a soldier dying in battle is stricken." He callously yanked Beaumont. The Englishman fell to his knees. Both kneecaps quickly bloodied on the rough planks as Lefleur forced him forward.

"I am a highly valued officer of his majesty's service," Beaumont cried out. "The king will stop you!"

Lefleur laughed. "If your king is to do that then he'd better sprout wings and hasten here." His remark brought laughter and jeering from the crew. "Come take him away," he told them,

Two men stepped forward and one flanked each side of Beaumont; grabbed an arm and jerked him forward. He tried to dig his heels into the planks as they dragged him along. His leaking wounds left behind a trail of blood. At the boat, the men picked him up, harshly tossed him in, and then followed. Using ropes attached to the davit, they lowered the longboat.

Tieg returned breathless.

Lefleur took the hourglass from his hand and strolled to the ornately carved rails. He leaned over. "I will give you the hour. If you survive, I will set you free." He flipped the timepiece over. "Or cry out for mercy. You will be brought aboard the ship."

Beaumont called up, "I will rot in hell before that happens."

A few armed men guarded the remaining crew of the Holy Cross and the others gathered along the rails. Wagers were quickly made. One man shouted, "I wager my shilling on the sharks!" Laughter and swearing followed. One man brought bottles of confiscated rum from below to distribute amongst the festive spectators.

The longboat settled onto the water with a splash. It rocked a second before stabilizing. Each man took an arm and hoisted Beaumont up. He squirmed in their grip. One of the men balled his hand into a fist and delivered a hard jab to his ribs. Air fled his lungs. Momentarily paralyzed, Beaumont was unable to fight and they easily tossed him over the side. He broke the water with a loud splash and began to sink but managed to kick his way to the top. He gulped in air and bobbed beside the boat.

The salt water stung the wounds on his chest and knees. The blood-soaked material began to release its bounty into the water. He looked around. Beaumont's heart filled with fear. It would only be a short time before sharks picked up his scent.

One of the crewmen managed the tension on the rope as the other rowed. The longboat slipped through the water. The slack line tethering Beaumont to the stern grew taut. He jerked, and now on his back, his body planed out, and with his hands high above his head, he glided through the chop. He fought to remain face up while moving his head to and fro looking for the carnivorous killers. He spotted one. Off to the left a large fin sliced the water as it closed in on its prey.

Pent up lust and male aggression was released as the crew of the Defiance cheered.

The creature smashed into his thigh. The impact sent a shock wave of excruciating pain through Beaumont's leg and rolled him onto his belly. Facing down, he stared into the blue haze. The salt burned, his eyes were on fire, but he dared not close them. The monster wheeled around. It whipped its tail as it shot toward him at blinding speed. The shark was coming in high on his left side. Beaumont tried to maneuver his body into a position that would allow him to deliver a kick, but the drag of the moving boat prevented the action. As it neared, he looked into the thing's soulless eyes, the deep, dark, fathomless pits of a killing machine. The creature opened its mouth. Rows of sharp serrated teeth capable of ripping chunks of flesh from bones were dangerously close.

Suddenly, he felt a tug as the crewman managing the rope reeled him in. The unexpected acceleration caused the shark to miss him by inches. Then the line went slack and he treaded water to stay afloat. The one manning the oars stroked the water furiously. The rope went tight again. Beaumont jerked and planed out on his back again as he glided behind the boat. He realized they were toying with him for their own sadistic pleasure. He looked around. The fin was nowhere in sight. He rolled back onto his belly. Eyes burning, he searched the blue abyss. He spotted the thing.

Determined not to be cheated out of its meal, the creature had swung around. It zipped toward his feet. Beaumont cocked a foot back. The man working the rope began to reel him in again. The gap between Beaumont and the creature widened, but if the man were to let go of the rope, then Beaumont would be deposited directly into the things open mouth. Instead, his head bumped against the boat. Hands grabbed hold of his arms and jerked him from the water. He lay on his back staring wildly and gasping for air. Beaumont had lost his hat and powdered wig. The few sprigs of hair that he owned, clumped, and stood on end. His uniform clung tightly to his thin frame.

One of the crewmen, a leather-faced man with a deep scar across his cheek, leaned over him and stared down through a pair of already blood-shot eyes. "He looks like a drowned rat."

The other seaman grinned big and displayed a chasm of rotten teeth. "Are ya ready to go back in? Ol' Mister Shark is waitin' for ya."

Beaumont coughed up seawater and blinked it from his eyes. Spent, he managed to shake his head and give a weak reply. "Mercy."

"He's ready to talk," said the mate. "We take him back." He picked up an oar.

"I don't believe this son of a whore." The other man looked down on Beaumont. "He's shifty. I say we heave him over the side and make another run."

"The man asked for mercy," replied the other.

"I'd druther take my chances sitting on the poisonous quills of a puffer fish before I would believe the likes of him." He grabbed the Englishman by the arm. "Another go with the shark will prove his words to be ripe with truth."

The other man conceded to the sound reasoning with a thoughtful nod.

Beaumont's eyes filled with terror as they lifted him. The water muffled his feeble cry as he broke the surface. His eyes frantically darted around as he searched out the predator. The shark loomed nearby hunting for its prey. Another shark appeared out of the haze. The pair of man-eaters were on course for him.

Beaumont's lanky limbs barely held enough strength to fend off one shark, much less two, but he summoned new power from somewhere inside. Like a dragon warrior from the Far East, Beaumont used his feet to deliver kick after kick. Each blow temporarily warded away death as the sharks darted out of sight only to return for another try. Finally, using a pair of already overtaxed lungs, Beaumont garnered enough strength to scream,

"MERCY!" The word traveled across the water to the decks of the Defiance and Holy Cross, to the ears of the crews and the pirate captain.

The two disappointed boatmen reeled him in.

When they delivered Beaumont back on the deck of the Holy Cross, coins exchanged hands as they drug the captain's limp body across the rough planks. Losers cursed his performance with the sharks while others praised him. The two men deposited him face down at Lefleur's feet. He gave the Englishman a nudge with the toe of his boot.

Beaumont managed to lift his head and cracked the lid of one bloodshot eye to peek at the hourglass in Lefleur's hand. Only a scant half hour had passed on the deck of the Holy Cross. For Beaumont it had seemed hours. Exhausted, he planted his face on the planks and closed his eyes. He let out a groan.

Lefleur used the toe of his boot to roll Beaumont onto his back. "Where is the Talah?"

Beaumont remained silent.

"Take him back," Lefleur told one of the men, "and this time come back without him."

A look of sheer terror filled Beaumont's face as he moaned and shook his head.

"Where is it?"

The Englishman tried painfully to strain words through a throat swollen by saltwater.

"Very well," Lefleur drew his dagger from its sheath. He grabbed Beaumont's hand and raked the sharp edge of the blade across the man's finger. Blood poured from the wound. "Write it." Using his foot again, Lefleur rolled the man back onto his belly.

With a shaky hand, Beaumont managed to scrawl one word: bilge.

"Mister Suggs." Lefleur turned to his quartermaster. "Gather a few men. Quickly."

"Aye, aye, Captain."

While Suggs quickly made a selection from the men loitering nearby. One of which wore a billowy, white linen shirt with a hood pulled up over his head.

Lefleur looked down on Beaumont. "If you speak the truth, I will hold to my promise to set you free."

Beaumont passed out.

"Come," Lefleur told the men. Their route took them across the deck littered with dead bodies. The crewman beneath the hood respectfully made the sign of the cross over his chest.

At the ship's midsection, they came to a small structure that housed the stairwell leading down into the bowels of the vessel. Lefleur stopped. He ordered two of the men to open the double doors. Lefleur and the other men stood aside. They raised their blades, in case a trap lay in waiting.

Sunlight spilled down the stairs but quickly stalled. Lefleur's cutlass led the way as he crept down the steps. The others followed him down the narrow passageway. If a trap did lie in wait, the sound of water lapping against the hull, along with the constant groan of wood and squeal of stretching rope, would mask their approach.

They clambered to the bottom of the steep stairs. Lefleur stopped. The dank smell of ocean and damp wood filled his nose. He lifted his patch. The eye, accustomed to the darkness, allowed him to peer into the almost nonexistent light. In the heavy shadows, dark shapes loitered along the aisle. Crates and barrels quickly took form. Undaunted, he waded a few feet further into the darkness. The others filtered down and flanked him, two on each side.

Suggs stood on Lefleur's left. His pop eye seemed to possess the magical ability to cut through the gloom. He quickly pointed out the stacks of powder kegs. He leaned over and brought his lips close to Lefleur's ear. "If you set the Englishman and the crew free what's to stop them from turning their cannons on us?" He didn't wait for an answer. "If you don't mind me sayin', we need to break every last keg open and spill the gunpowder, and it should be done afore we go any further."

Lefleur nodded. He turned to the man standing on the opposite shoulder from the quartermaster. "You," he said as he planted a finger on the man's chest. "Go and fetch axes and return here."

The crewman nodded and spun around.

"And find Tieg," said Lefleur. "Have him bring his foxfire."

The barefoot man stole silently up the unlit stairwell. The other two crewmen hovered nearby. The hooded one stole silently down the narrow aisle and quickly dissolved into the darkness.

The heavy atmosphere seemed to stifle conversation, but the familiar tune of the ship's song, playing like a sweet, soft melody seemed to bring some comfort in the minutes that passed. However, Lefleur grew anxious. He drifted away from the others and despite almost completely blinded by the dark; he began to carry out the search for the Talah.

The rapid succession of footsteps thundering down the stairs interrupted Lefleur's hunt. The crewman sent on the errand had returned. Two of the men gathered around him. The other hooded one remained missing. Lefleur searched the darkness for the deserter, but his effort was in vain. His suspicion immediately grew.

The man holding the axes distributed them. He lay the fourth aside. The three wasted no time hacking into the kegs. After each strike, the crack of wood and flying splinters followed. The granular contents of the barrels spilled across the floor like sand. Breathing hard from their labors, they stopped to wipe the sweat from their brows.

The sound of shuffling footsteps whispered down the stairs. They all turned. An eerie green glow filled the stairwell. A light appeared and bobbed down the steps and stilled at the bottom. A face floated behind it. It was Tieg.

Lefleur extended his arm and opened his hand.

The first mate brought the foxfire to his captain.

Using the gift of the organic light, Lefleur slowly passed it over the crates and barrels as he walked, but his progress was limited to a crawl. With axes still in hand, the others stayed close at his side. The green glow washed over a small chest hidden in the shadows.

Suggs moved it closer. "What's this?"

Lefleur stood over it and leaned down. The leather covering the chest was wrinkled and darkened by age. Across the top, the words Sanguis Christi were embossed in the withered material. The inscription led him to believe the Talah could be inside. Caba's words came flooding back to him: Find the Talah and you will find whom you seek. Lefleur's gaze moved to the unlocked hasp. He slowly raised the lid. Anticipation of what lay inside stirred whispers as the dim light spilled into the deep cavity. At the bottom, something boiled in the shadows.

Like a demon summoned from hell, a serpent sprang up. With blinding speed, it spread its hood and struck. Its venomous fangs sank deep into the sleeve of Lefleur's coat, barely missing the flesh of his arm. He quickly seized the snake around its neck and yanked it free. The cold-blooded reptile whipped its tail and wiggled as it tried to liberate itself from his grip. The only way for Lefleur to unshackle himself and the others from harm, he would have to sever its head. He tossed the thing to the floor and drew his cutlass, but before he could act, the cobra quickly slithered beneath the stairs. A cry of terror rose from beneath the risers, and a robe-clad priest frantically fled the sanctuary of his hiding place. His eyes flitted uncontrollably as his gaze darted randomly from man to man. He clutched the Talah tightly against his chest.

Suddenly, like a vengeful ghost, the hooded person appeared out of nowhere and pressed the blade of a dagger against the priest's throat, but before the sharp edge could slice into the soft folds of flesh, the priest stumbled backwards. His feet tangled and he crashed into a stack of barrels that toppled and settled.

The assassin raised the weapon to strike the prone man.

Lefleur recognized the knife by its handle. It had come from his quarters.

Lefleur bound into action, freed the weapon from the killer's hand, and then yanked the covering from over the person's head.

The reverent man, lying in the rubble, made the sign of the cross.

The young nun's face twisted with rage as she tried to pry the knife from the tight grip of Lefleur's fingers.

He yanked his hand away and threw the dagger. The tip struck one of the ship's beams and the blade sank deep into the wood.

She spun and futilely tugged at the handle.

Lefleur grabbed her arm and pulled her to him.

Red-faced, and with anger still blazing in her dark eyes, she pointed to the priest. "Monsignor Bastrop deserves to die!" She spit at him. "He violated me! And to hide his sin, he tried to kill me!"

Lefleur nodded at Bastrop. "Take this piece of filth to the main deck!"

"And what of the cross?" asked the same man.

Lefleur stooped, pried the Talah from the terrified priest's fingers, and tossed it to the floor. "Leave it."

The others watched in astonishment as the priceless relic struck the floor with a solid thud.

"Here! Here! What manner of madness is this?" asked one. They all fell to their knees, and in a frantic tangle of arms and hands, each scrambled to gain possession. Shouts, rants, threats, and curses rose.

Angered by the bedlam unfolding at his feet, Lefleur drew his cutlass. "Cease your foolishness!" He swung. The sharp edge passed inches above their heads. "Or I will have all your noggins on a stave!"

As quickly as the turmoil began, it ended the same way. Now silent, they climbed to their feet. The expressions on their faces conveyed the look of reprimanded children. As an appeasement, the man holding the cross held it out to Lefleur. He snatched it from the man's fingers. "Take the priest up!"

With their minds now occupied with a new mission, they quickly forgot their squabbling as they jumbled around the man and hoisted him to his feet. With their prisoner securely in hand, they awkwardly clumped up the narrow staircase.

The nun tried to follow them but Lefleur grabbed her by the arm. "I'll see to it that punishment is carried out."

She yanked free. "I should be the one to serve it." Maria planted a foot on the bottom riser.

Lefleur stopped her. "Why would you fall to temptation and break your sacred vows?"

"Perhaps this is a call to truth." She looked up at him. "Possibly this is no longer my calling." She cast her rosary beads to the floor.

"Your unrestrained feelings cloud your judgment."

He placed a hand on her belly. "Your calling is to sanctify this life."

"What about you?" she asked.

"I am a heathen." He wheeled around and clumped to the top.

Already topside and dragged halfway across the deck, the priest's captors released him. His head struck the wood with enough force to tremble the planks.

Lefleur emerged on the deck and marched over to him. "It was you that threw the woman into the sea."

Bastrop lifted his head. Blood trickled from the wound hidden within a jungle of gray hair. He squinted against the sun. "Sister Maria broke her sacred vows with God. She became disheartened for what she had done and flung herself into the tempest."

"You tossed her over to silence your wicked deed."

"Wicked deed?" Bastrop huffed.

"It is your baby that she carries in her womb."

"She lies!"

"How many others have paid for your sins with their lives?"

"How dare you accuse me of such atrocities?! I am a man of God!"

"You are the devil himself."

"Blasphemer!" cried Bastrop.

Lefleur reached into his pocket, retrieved the rosary beads he kept there and tossed them to the planks next to the priest's head. The sun winked off the silver skin of the cross. "Pick it up," Lefleur commanded.

Bastrop shook his head.

Lefleur delivered a swift kick in the Monsignor's side.

Air gushed from his lungs. Bastrop grimaced. He tightened into a ball and clutched his ribs. "You will pay for this."

"Pick it up!"

Bastrop freed one of his hands from his aching ribs, and with a shaky hand, he slowly reached out and retrieved the rosary.

"Turn it over."

The priest used the tips of his thick fingers to spin the cross. A smudge of reflected sunlight settled on his cheek. Bastrop's eyes grew intensely wide. The cross slipped from his fingers and tumbled to the deck. He looked up. "She fornicated with Satan!"

"That is a lie, Monsignor Bastrop. You forced yourself upon her." He gritted his teeth. "After the baby was born you had the mother hung."

"It was the decision of the council!" shouted Bastrop. "She had to be punished!" He suddenly looked dumbfounded. "How do you know of this woman?"

"She was my mother."

A look of surprise sprang up on the priest's face. "Impossible! I had that baby..."

"Destroyed?" Lefleur shook his head. "The voodoo priestess you gave me to did not kill me as you had thought. She raised me, and when I

became old enough to understand, she gave to me my mother's rosary beads and told me everything about you."

"I don't believe you!"

"Believe, Father." He nodded. "I am your son."

"No!" Bastrop wadded his hand into a fist and gritted his teeth. "You are a bastard child!" He looked up into Lefleur's eyes. "When you die the gates of heaven will be closed to you." He spit on the toe of Lefleur's boot. "And your wretched soul will suffer eternal damnation."

Lefleur turned to the four men who had accompanied him down into the hold. Remaining true to his promise, he said, "Release Captain Beaumont."

They questioned him with their eyes.

"And use the rope to lash the priest to the mast."

Their puzzled gazes remained steadfast.

"Be quick about it!" Lefleur snapped.

One of the men pulled his knife, hurried over to the still unconscious Beaumont, and stooped. The act of sawing through the bindings jostled the Englishman. He cracked an eyelid. His face was near the crewman's bare feet. They were coated with gunpowder soot. The man stopped sawing and stood. Beaumont snapped his eyelid shut. The pirate gave the Englishman a nudge. Satisfied Beaumont still lay unconscious; he delivered the recovered rope to the place where the others waited.

"Get up," said one of the men. He reached down, slipped a hand under

Bastrop's armpit. One of the other men did the same. Together, they hoisted him to his feet and pinned him against the mast. They held the priest in position as the others wound the rope tightly around his body and tied off.

Lefleur strolled leisurely across the deck. He stopped.

"I can't breathe." Bastrop wheezed, and then coughed.

"In a moment you won't have need of your breath." Steel whispered as Lefleur drew his cutlass from the metal ring.

Mesmerized, all gazes fixed on the spectacle.

Bastrop's eyes now filled with terror as he stared at the blade. He paled as Lefleur planted the sharp edge against his throat. "Spare me. Please, I beg you!" He began to weep. "My son."

"I shall enjoy watching you die."

"Gosson Lefleur!" The man's voice came from behind.

Lefleur spun around.

Captain Beaumont stood with his back to the open doorway of the shelter housing the stairs. In one hand, he held a lit torch. He stretched his arm back into the cavity.

Lefleur remembered the broken kegs of gunpowder.

The crew of the Defiance aimed their weapons.

"If I die, the torch falls and you shall all die as well!" Beaumont cocked his arm back a little further and uncurled a finger from around the torch.

The hush ripened with tension. They held their ground.

"Very well." Beaumont glared at Lefleur. "Your men have sealed our fate." He whirled around to deliver the torch, but was met by the hooded figure. Sunlight winked off the dagger as the nun plunged the blade deep into Beaumont's chest. The look of surprise on his face turned spiteful as he used the last few seconds of his life to toss the torch into the hole. As it sailed down the stairs, Beaumont's eyes rolled back. He slipped from the blade and crumpled at her feet.

Below, the dry tender quickly burst into flames. Dark smoke rose from the stairwell and spilled into the air.

A terrified cry to abandon ship filled the stunned silence.

There came the clash of voices filled with terror, mixed with thundering footsteps, as both crews charged across the deck and hurdled over the railing to the deck of the Defiance. Most succeeded in clearing the gap, but many failed. The ones that didn't make it splashed into the water, heads bobbed. The sharks began to strike. Screams and curses rose into the air.

"Cut the ropes!" Lefleur charged the order with a high sense of urgency.

Men frantically sawed through the ropes. The ships began to part.

"Hoist sails!"

Eager to birth a wide gap between the ships, the crew worked diligently to raise the sails. Lefleur raced to the poop deck and found Tieg already there.

"The nun is still aboard the Holy Cross," the lad stated.

Still wielding the dagger, she stood next to Bastrop as she watched blood pour from the slit in his throat.

Lefleur's gaze pivoted to the stairwell. Black smoke boiled from the opening.

He raced down the steps leading to the main deck, rushed to the forward mast, and quickly scaled halfway up. The gap between the ships grew wider. Lefleur grabbed the rope attached to the end of the yardarm and swung out.

He made a sweeping downward arc that ended just shy of the Holy Cross. He released his grip on the rope, but momentum quickly spent itself. Instead of the brazen exploit depositing him on the deck, a force of nature grabbed hold and tugged him down. As he skimmed down the side of the vessel, Lefleur latched on to the edge of the deck with his fingertips. He jerked to a stop. He looked below. Sharks were manic in their feast. He began to lose his grip. Lefleur mustered his strength. His arm muscles strained as he hoisted himself up to the railing and over. He flopped down on the deck, but quickly popped up and raced to where Maria stood. She stared into the lifeless eyes of Bastrop. Lefleur shook her from her reverie.

She blinked.

"We must go." He pointed to the dark smoke coming from the stairwell.

She looked. The opening vomited fire.

"Now!" he cried. Lefleur grabbed her arm and spirited her to the rails. Instead of jumping, they both came to a grinding halt. The Defiance was quickly slipping away. More wails and cries rose from the deadly waters below. They looked. The sharks continue to ravage the crewmen floundering in the water. The scent of blood had drawn more.

The shocked nun took a step back as she turned her head away from the ghastly scene.

"Jump!" he told Maria.

She shook her head and turned to run.

Lefleur latched onto to her arm and reeled her back. "It's our only hope," He pushed her over the rails and dove in after her.

They struck the water and feverishly kicked their way into a dive down. A shark zoomed toward them. In seconds, the jaws of death would be upon them.

Suddenly, an explosion shook the ocean. The shock wave sent both Maria and Lefleur tumbling head over heels beneath the water and the sharks fleeing.

Above, chunks of burning wood sailed through the air, some landing on the deck and rigging of the Defiance. The crewmen scurried up to the canvas sails and put out small fires with their bare hands. Others stamped out the burning chunks of wood scattered across the deck with their bare feet.

Tieg maintained his watch from the poop deck with the spyglass. To his relief, Lefleur and the nun popped up and bobbed in the water, but his joy was short lived. The sharks had returned. He lowered his spyglass. "Mister Suggs!" The quartermaster raced over to his side. "Launch the longboats and rescue the survivors!"

"Aye, aye, Captain!" He hurried across the deck calling out names. Each man joined the quartermaster at his side as he continued at a brisk pace.

Tieg raised the spyglass back to his eye. Fins sliced through the water. Lefleur tried to help the girl as she struggled. "Mister Sims!" Tieg kept his eyes to the monocular.

The man raced over to him and awaited orders.

"Get every man with a long rifle to the railing. Quickly!"

The man nodded and raced away.

Tieg watched helplessly as Lefleur and the nun warded off their attackers. The fins veered off, but the man-eaters returned, Lefleur remained persistent in hampering their attacks with more kicks and punches. Nearby, the less fortunate screamed out in pain before disappearing beneath the water. Blood rose to the top and pooled on the surface.

"Guns!" cried Tieg. He turned his head away from the spyglass and looked back over his shoulder. "Where are the rifles?"

The rescue boats came around the bow of the Defiance as the men rowed furiously toward the couple. The man standing at the bow held a long rifle. There came a flash of fire followed by a puff of smoke. One of the sharks flinched and thrashed. The crack of the discharge lingered across the water.

On board the Defiance, men with long guns charged the railing, took aim, and fired. A hail of balls pelted the water. The hits were marked by spurts of blood. The surviving sharks swam away, but in seconds, they returned. The men with the rifles feverishly reloaded their weapons. Once done, the

earsplitting crack of disjointed gunfire sounded. More sharks thrashed and sank, the wounded predators deserted, and the success brought hurrahs from the crew. The rescuers hauled the ones spared from death out of the water, and returned them safely.

Suggs watched as the terror-stricken survivors filed out of the boats and stood on the deck of the Defiance. His gaze drifted from the sight and settled on Captain Lefleur. "What'll we do with the crew of the Holy Cross?"

He laid a hand on his quartermaster's shoulder. "We drop them at the next port."

Suggs stared after the man as the captain sauntered away leaving a dripping trail of water behind.

Maria caught up to Lefleur and latched on to his arm. He and the nun joined Tieg on the poop deck and watched the remains of the burning vessel sink.

The Talah, the cross that was fashioned from two of the nails used in the crucifixion of Christ and believed to have mystical powers, spiraled to the ocean floor.

Lefleur turned to the helmsman and issued new coordinates. The ship turned toward the setting sun. As the last of it dipped beneath where heaven and earth met, a sudden flash of green sparked the horizon—in the shape of a cross.

***

Marlin Williams grew up in a small town in Texas where the prairies were big, the grass grew tall, and the imagination ran wild.

2

There was on average sixty-two crimes a day in New York City in 1938, according to the district attorney's office almost six-hundred and thirty in a week. Of those, there were eighteen murders. Statistics that go unnoticed by the city's unsuspecting population, until their lives become just another number in the ever-growing list of victims.

NIGHTVISION: MURDER AFTER MIDNIGHT

Charles F. Millhouse

PART I

Darkness surrounded her, fear entangled her, and she ran, she ran as if her life depended on it, because it did. Her heart pounded in her chest like a sledgehammer – her legs weighed heavy as if chained to cinderblocks and her eyes were blinded by tears. Death loomed over her, as certain as if she knew her own name – but she ran anyway.

Darting through Central Park, she hoped the well-lit sidewalks would give her an advantage. She slowed her pace, keeping a cautious eye behind her, certain her pursuer would emerge at any moment.

She brushed a strand of her blond hair out of her waterlogged eyes and stilled her nerves. A streetlight engulfed her and for a moment she thought herself safe.

She was a lovely woman, in her mid-twenties, her classic features reminiscent of a silent movie star, slim and elegant. Her skin was unnaturally light, as if she hadn't spent a lot of time in the sun. She wore a gray-blue dress, with a black collar, and a thin strand of pearls. She clutched a small handbag in her left hand. Her feet were bare, except for her dark silk stockings, her high heal shoes abandoned several blocks back for better mobility.

A trash can toppled in the distance, and she spun around on the balls of her feet. The shrill of a cat, drew her attention – then it appeared out of the dark. A black mass of *something*. It was too bulky to be a man – it was something more – purely evil.

The woman stumbled backward, her feet slipped out from under her and she fell to the concrete sidewalk with a thud; her handbag flung from her grip. A sharp pain cut through her body, but she didn't cry out or make any sound.

Scrambling to her feet she did not run. The black mass filled her vision – she focused on it, prepare to meet death on her terms.

When the unwavering mass moved closer toward its victim, its bulky form transformed into another shape. Less cumbersome, yet just as evil. The linear form slithered ahead and struck as fiercely as a snake. The woman gasped when the blade of a knife sliced into her midsection, the look of astonishment twisted her features and a single tear streamed down her cheek. She slid off the blade and folded to the sidewalk with a gruesome thud.

The dark mass of evil stood there, studying its victim as an artist would a sculpture, proud of its work.

Suddenly the black mass turned, its sharp silver eyes seething with hate, and hissed, *"I see you..."*

Simon Rook came out of the vision in a cold sweat, coming to his feet he steadied himself with the edge of his large mahogany desk, unable to get the piercing cold stare of the killer out of his mind. His visions had always been intense, ripping away a part of his soul. In the years since his visions began, none of them ever communicated with him. It was as if the killer knew he was there. *That's not possible,* he thought. He rubbed his eyes and brought them into focus. He stood in his dimly lit room, trying to get his heartbeat under control and shake off the foreboding feeling that came with this vision.

Simon's visions had been a part of his life since he was sixteen. It wasn't until his early twenties that he understood what the visions were. Murders, and crimes that would happen that night. He tried to tell the police, but they laughed at his warnings not taking him seriously. He could not allow harm to come to these people, so he decided to take matters in his own hands.

If the people who knew him, knew how he spent his nights, dressed in a mask and hood protecting the innocent, he might find himself in a Psychiatric Ward somewhere. Simon understood the risks, but he was compelled to help. He considered it more help than he received growing up with an abusive father.

"Professor, Professor Rook," a knock came to his office door. "Are you alright, Sir?"

Simon steeled his nerves, and said, "Yes Lori, I'm alright, you can come in."

Lori Gail was a slender middle-aged woman with shoulder length corn silk hair and big round cobalt eyes. She came to work for Simon at the beginning of his tenure at the university, and he came to relied on her. Lori watched out for him in a motherly fashion, and that's how Simon looked on her. Sort of a mother and a wife rolled into one.

"I heard you call out. Are you sure you're alright? You're as white as a sheet."

Simon put a hand up, and replied, "Yes, yes, I'm fine. I had a bad dream is all."

"You were sleeping? You have class in ten minutes."

Simon focused on his wristwatch, and scooped up his tweed jacket off the back of his desk chair and said, "You have the list of students?"

Lori pointed at the large desk and said, "I put it there last night, don't you remember?"

"Yes, of course. I was out late last night and forgot to take it home with me."

"You're out late every night. You need to slow down a little. It's dangerous out there, what with sightings of that ghost."

Simon blinked a couple times, and asked, "Ghost?"

"He's all over the news on the radio and in the papers. It gives me the willies."

Simon smiled. Seems his appearances in the city hadn't gone unnoticed as he hoped. His missions into the night to fight for those in danger were not for accolades. He simply wanted to help.

"Here, you'll need these," Lori said picking up a pair of prescription sunglasses and handed them over.

Simon hitched a smile and put on the special lenses. He suffered from a unique form of day blindness. Bright lights rendered him blind, an abnormality brought about from his father's constant physical abuse and strikes to Simon's head. Though there hadn't been a reason for it, Simon was sure the beatings he received from his father also brought about his visions. Visions of crimes that would happen that night.

He picked up his attaché case and a walking cane and brazened out of his office as Lori reminded him, "You have a meeting this afternoon at three o'clock. Try and remember."

"Have I ever been late for a meeting?" Simon asked.

"All the time," Lori said as the office door closed behind him.

Simon walked outside onto the campus of New York University, where he had been teaching economics since nineteen thirty-five. With four years behind him, he strived to mix his teaching with his increasing night life. No matter how hard he tried, he was compelled to go out each night in an

attempt to stop the crimes from his visions, each ending in various different degrees of success.

His visions always came during the day and without warning. They came on quickly and ended the same way – leaving him cold and distant as if he lost a piece of his soul. The death of the woman from his vision today, was now a part of him. He could no more forget her face, than he could his own.

Some visions were simple muggings, or break ins. Then there were the ones like today. Brutal murders, and attacks. If he was lucky, on most days he would receive one vision, but on rare occasions he would have multiple premonitions, and like some sick game, he had to determine which were the more important. Who would he save, and who would he not?

As per his contract, Simon's classroom faced away from the mid-morning sun, and all of his classes were scheduled to finish before mid-afternoon, with the occasional evening classes.

"Good morning," Simon said upon entering the class. He strolled past the first row of desks and went to the windows pulling down the blinds, darkening the room. The students were aware of his handicap on enrolling, and no one complained about the dim light in which to work.

His desk at the front of the room was not as ornate or lovely as his large mahogany, but it was sufficient. He placed his briefcase atop it, and pulled out his list of student names, and began to match the names to the faces in his room. He stopped when he came to an empty seat, third row back. "Seems we have someone tardy," he said. "Does anyone know a Miss Natalie Green?"

No one replied, and Simon continued to go through his list of names, finding the remainder of the class in attendance.

"Alright, if everyone will take out your notebooks, we will begin the spring semester by talking about businessmen of the twentieth century, starting with the success of Captain Steven Hawklin and his impending trial in Crown City and how that will affect his notoriety and..."

The classroom door opened, and all eyes turned toward the lovely woman coming into the room. She was of mid-height and wore a gray-blue dress, with a black collar, that cut off just below the knees – dark silk stockings ran the remainder of her legs.

"I'm sorry I'm late Professor," she said in a silky tone. "I got turned around on campus."

Simon drew a breath to reply but held it when the woman's face came into view. It was the woman from his vision, right down to the strand of pearls around her neck. It took him off guard. He'd never come face to face unexpectedly with a victim from his visions beforehand. He studied her, having only seen her in the clouded mist of his mind. She was even lovelier in person. Her soft white milky skin and subtle hazel eyes were simple, yet pleasant to look at.

Someone coughed, and Simon realized everyone in the room was looking at him. He cleared his throat, and said, "That's quite alright, Miss Green.

Please don't make a habit of it. Take your seat."

After a long lecture, and conversation that distracted Simon, the bell rang, and the students poured out of the room in a rush, as Simon reminded them, "Have a ten-page summary of Steven Hawklin's strengths and weaknesses on my desk by Friday morning, and make sure to include a program model of how he should diversify moving into the new decade, and how his trial will affect him."

As Simon gathered his things, shoving papers and notes into his briefcase, he glanced a shadowed movement. "Miss Green," he said seeing the young woman lingering near the desk. "Is there something I can help you with?"

"No Professor," she said in a soft tone. "I just wanted to thank you for understanding my tardiness."

"As long as you don't make a habit out of it, we won't say any more about it," Simon said refraining from saying anything more. Unsure what prolong contact with a victim would do to the outcome tonight. His visions came and went without warning, and he filed them in categories, from least important, like break-ins and vandalisms, to most important, like attacks and murder. Natalie Green was in the most important category – having seen what very well could be her death. The last thing Simon needed was to become too attached to her. *That's the problem*, he thought. *I already am.*

Natalie offered a worrisome smile and continued to loiter. Her soft expression hardened, and she kept her fingers to her mouth, chewing on them nervously.

With his personal affects gathered, Simon stopped short of the door and turned. His inaction, or lack of concern for Natalie's apprehension might be a factor. *If I say or do nothing....* He drew a breath, and said, "Is everything alright Miss Green?"

"You might think I'm silly, Professor, but I've had this peculiar feeling that I've been followed all day. I was late to class because I was trying to make sure I wasn't being followed."

"And where you?" Simon asked.

Natalie hitched a smile, and said, "I don't know."

Again, Simon wasn't sure how to react. He could do the simplest thing and offer her a ride home, wherein she wouldn't encounter that thing in the park, but Simon wasn't sure what would happen. If he changed his vision, he would be changing the future and he'd never done that before. *What would be the implications?* he wondered.

"Can you call someone?" he asked.

Again, Natalie offered a worrisome smile. "There's no one to call," she said.

"I see, well..."

"It's alright Professor. I'm just being a nervous nelly. I'll be alright."

Against his better judgement, and even after telling himself not to, Simon said, "Let me offer you a ride home at least."

Natalie's expression brightened a bit, but quickly dulled, and she said, "Thank you, but no Professor, that wouldn't be proper."

Simon swallowed, and drew a hesitant breath, and said, "No. Perhaps you're right." All the while wishing he could do or say something to prevent her inevitable future. This was an opportunity never offered him before. Even with his prescient abilities it seemed he couldn't change things to come. He always thought his visions were a gift, and in many ways they were. Yet at that moment he realized they were also a curse.

The next class began to amble into the room. Simon looked at the time and remembered his scheduled meeting. He focused, as Natalie shuffled her way out of the room amid the arriving students.

Simon gathered his belongings, and chased after her, only to lose her in the flow of people in the corridor. He paused, bumping into a student or two, who apologized as Simon brushed past them, swimming upstream in an attempt to get out of the building.

Outside, the quad bustled with activity, and the bright morning sun shocked Simon's senses, as he dug his special sunglasses out of his pocket and shoved them on his face. Despite the protective lenses, the bright glow washed his vision, and even though he saw the mass of people in front of him, their forms were sluiced, their features masked. *I've lost her...*

"There you are Professor," Lori said when Simon entered his office. "Your appointment has been waiting."

"Cancel it," Simon replied.

"But he's already in your office," Lori said. "I sat him in there with a cup of coffee nearly twenty minutes ago."

Simon stepped further into the outer office, and said, "Call Atticus and have him pick me up please."

"But your meeting," Lori huffed.

Simon released a breath, "Alright, I'll see him. But please call Atticus."

Lori scooped up the phone receiver in her hand, as Simon stepped into his office and closed the door. His vision equalized in the dim light, and he glimpsed a form sitting in the chair near his large desk.

"My apologies," Simon said. "It's a bit of a hectic day."

"That's quite alright Professor Rook," the man said in a thick New Hampshire accent. He stood and turned toward Simon, holding an oversized portfolio in his right hand. "This interview won't last long."

Simon crossed to the other side of his desk eyeing the tall stocky man. "I'm afraid I haven't been briefed about this meeting mister...?"

"Payne. Morgan Payne."

"Mister Payne," Simon said motioning for Morgan to sit, as he lowered himself into his desk chair. "Why are you here exactly?"

Morgan Payne reclined in his chair and regarded Simon for a moment. Payne's long narrow features were stolid, regal, and menacing. "The university is conducting a research study on its faculty, and I'm afraid it's your turn," he said with a dark smile.

"What kind of research?" Simon inquired skeptically. He wasn't aware of any interdepartmental research study.

"Nothing too intense," Morgan replied. "They want to know a bit more about who teaches at the university. To better evaluate just who you are."

"So, this is a psychiatric evaluation?"

"Of sorts, you understand."

Simon sat forward, and with his hands flat on the desk, said, "No, I'm afraid I don't. This feels like an invasion of privacy."

Forgoing more preamble, Morgan opened his portfolio, skimmed his long index finger down a page and said, "You were orphaned."

"No," Simon replied. "My mother died when I was young. *My* father was charged and sentenced with her death. He's been sitting on death row ever since. *I* really don't see what this has to do with my teaching ability."

"You are resentful."

"I'm sorry was that a question or a statement?" Simon asked.

"For the death of your mother," Payne pressed.

With tension in the air, Simon held a tight breath in his chest, and said, "My father is a loathsome man, with nothing but hatred in him. He hated me, and to tell the truth I'm not sure he ever loved my mother."

"How does that..."

Simon went to his feet and he fisted the top of the desk. "My father would beat me, slap me around every chance he got. My mother would take the brunt of my beatings herself, to spare me. By doing so, it drove her to her grave, and left me with this damnable day blindness because I took one too many hits to the head. If my father had his wish, I'd be in a plot next to my mom, and he wouldn't be sorry for either of our deaths."

"Yes, but how does that make you..."

"I hate him, Mister Payne. Is that what you want to hear me say? Well, I'll say it again. I hate him. This interview is over, good afternoon, *Sir*." Simon rounded the desk, and held the office door open, waiting for Payne to stand.

"You have a hatred in your heart too, don't you Mister Rook?"

"The only hate I have is because I have to suffer through an interrogation such as this, and I... I..."

Payne stood slowly from his chair, his hands shimmered a bright orange, and he said, "Is there something a matter, Mister Rook?"

The vision came on without warning, like they always did. Simon found himself transported through space and time. Night loomed upon him like a blanket of pure evil, as images tunneled around him. To be transported yet again, to witness another crime was unbelievable, yet there he was staring at the victim of a brutal beating only inches from him. The body was mulled – not an inch of the corpse was untouched. The victim was a woman and for a handful of heartbeats Simon thought it might be Natalie, but the body configuration didn't match his student's slender form. Her face unrecognizable, her clothes drenched in dark amber, the odor of copper lingered on the air.

The heinous crime looked more like an animal attack than something done by another human. Then Simon saw them, footprints in the blood, and beyond that the image of... something.

He squinted to get a better look, but the form was nimble, and masked itself in the shadows.

"*I see you,*" the insidious voice growled, and Simon screamed.

PART II

Simon came out of the vision gasping for breath.

"Professor, Professor," Lori called. "Are you alright?"

Simon took inventory of his surroundings before regarding Lori. He drew his tongue over his lips, feigned ignorance and said, "What happened?"

"I was about to ask you the same thing," Lori replied. She was his personal secretary. Privy to many aspects of his life at the university, though Lori knew nothing of his visions. That secret was closely guarded.

Simon cleared his vision, scoured the room, and asked, "Where is Mister Payne?"

"He took out of here in a rush," Lori said. "He didn't say a word."

Simon stepped back into his office, glimpsed the clock on the wall, and turned. "Has Atticus arrived?"

"He's out front, waiting," Lori said, and questioned, "Are you alright. You gave me a start."

"It's just been a long day. Too much of the sun, I suspect," Simon said, hoping his lie wasn't prevalent.

Lori's brow tightened, but she didn't reply. Simon could tell by her wan expression she didn't believe him.

Scooping up his jacket, Lori helped Simon slip his arms into the coat without a word, as he fisted his briefcase and headed toward the door.

"Professor."

Simon turned back and offered Lori a congenial smile.

"Try and get some rest," she said.

Simon replied with a nod, before exiting the office.

It was still high sun when Simon slid into the backseat of the Chevrolet Master Deluxe sedan with special blackened windows. Atticus Harper sat behind the steering wheel. "Where to?" he asked.

"The Tower," Simon said. "Be discrete."

"Aren't I always?" he asked. Atticus Harper was a brawny man in his late thirties with a thick black beard, that partially hid an aged knife scar that came across his right eye and trailed down to the bend of his neck. He wore a bracelet on his left hand. The all-seeing eye. Over the years many others join NightVision's Watchmen, but Atticus was the first.

Simon met Atticus while in college, having saved him from death at the hands of a mob boss on the east side of Chicago. His vision of Atticus' murder was one of the first he ever thwarted. He found a friend in Atticus who repaid him by becoming Simon's private chauffeur, though at the time Simon could barely buy food, but Atticus considered it repayment for his life.

"You seem troubled."

Simon pinched the bridge of his nose with his thumb and index finger. "I had a second vision today," he said.

Atticus' eyes furrowed in the rearview mirror and he said, "A second... that doesn't happen a lot."

"There's something else," Simon said in a wrenched tone.

Atticus glanced at the road, and then back to Simon without a word.

"The body in the second vision was already dead. In all my visions, the victim has always been alive, with the action of the crime part of the prophecy."

"What's it mean?"

Simon recounted his predictions, making sure to tell his friend of the first victim, *his* student, and his strange encounter with something lurking in both of his visions.

"It communicated with you?" Atticus asked.

"It was watching me, but I don't know who it was."

Atticus held his breath and returned his eyes to the road in front of the car.

In the six years since he and Atticus decided to do something about his visions, nothing ever happened remotely like this. There were strange cases. Devilish, heinous crimes committed by normal everyday people, but nothing on this scale. It was almost as if, all the cases, the people they saved over the years were nothing but a warmup for something grander, and more aligned with Simon's powers.

Am I ready for this? Simon wondered. *Is NightVision ready for this?*

NightVision grew out of desperation. On one hand Simon wanted to stop the crimes his visions presented him, but in turn he wanted to have some kind of normal life. The idea of the mask still seemed silly. What grown man would hide his face to deal out justice? Every time he pulled the cowl over his head, Simon wondered if it would be the last time. If he were to die wearing the hood and mask, how would his acquaintances deal with the fact that he was a masked vigilante? Would they even care? His only true friend was Atticus, and Simon believed that whatever happened to him, Atticus would share in that fate.

The sedan pulled up to an abandoned fire station on Manhattan's east side. The hulking Behemoth of a building sat unused for nearly a decade. In the center of the large structure was a massive tower – the original bell still hung in the top of the construct and Simon spent many of his nights staring out at the city before he went off to prevent whatever his visions showed him. In many ways he was more at home in the firetrap, than at his actual home.

Atticus drove the car through an oversized door, once reserved for the old horse drawn firewagons, and turned off the engine and checked his wristwatch. "It's still several hours before sunset. You have any idea what you're going to do?"

Simon slipped out of the backseat and came around the front of the car. Atticus climbed out of the car and watched Simon but didn't say anything else.

Simon stopped and turned to Atticus. "I go with my initial vision. I know where Natalie will be and what time."

"And what of the other victim?"

Simon rubbed his face and put his hand to the back of his neck. "I don't even know who she is, or where she was in my second vision. Even if I wanted to prevent her death, my vision didn't show me anything concrete."

"Maybe we should call the police."

"And tell them what?"

Atticus winced. "I get your point."

"We go after Natalie. It's all we can do."

"And what if it isn't?" Atticus asked. "We've never faced anything like this before."

Simon didn't have an answer and he wished he did. Ascending the staircase into the tower, he fought with memories long since buried. Memories brought back to him after the visit by Morgan Payne. Simon lived with constant agony, both physical and mental at the hands of his destructive father. Ice chilled Simon's blood as he fought the painful memories.

"We do what we always do," Simon said. "We protect those who can't protect themselves."

"But if someone is going to die..."

Simon thought a moment, and said, "How many murders happen in this town in a week? In all those deaths we are shown maybe one, or two. People die, Atticus we can't stop them all. We're going to fail someone tonight, but we will save someone too."

***

The idea of NightVision came out of a need to save people. The mask and hood were to give Simon a sense of normalcy, though Simon's life was anything but normal. In the weeks after his decision to become a barb of justice, Simon took his licks. In many cases his sense of duty led to many failures, having taken the brunt of the battle – being beaten near death many times, he refused to give up. He refused to allow one person to die, and in the six years the crimes Simon thwarted, all ended with him as victor, and the murders he'd envisioned, ended with the people being saved.

In six years, his fighting skills improved, even though his impediment was a hindrance, he took precautions, fitting his mask with special light reflecting lenses, that prevented bright lights from blinding him. He carried a Browning Auto-Five shotgun for those times when accuracy wasn't possible and he wore a utility belt filled with extra ammunition, smoke bombs and garrote wire.

"Are you ready?" Atticus asked when he stepped into the weapons room.

Simon turned, dressed in his protective grey suit, he snapped his belt in place. "Ready," he said.

Atticus stood quiet for a minute. His face tight with apprehension.

"You have something to say?" Simon asked.

"I've got this funny feeling about tonight is all."

Simon didn't reply with words of reassurance, the thought of easing Atticus would do nothing for his own self-doubt. The idea that tonight could be the end, never crossed his mind, but it loomed over him as an inevitability. "We do this by the book," he said.

Atticus nodded, though it seemed like he wanted to say something, he didn't.

"You drop me off on the north end of the park and pick me up on the south end."

"It's what happens between point A and point B that has me worried."

"You're never a nervous nelly," Simon said with a smirk.

Atticus laughed, and shook his head in response, even with a cloud of gloom in the air.

The drive from the tower went in silence. Simon sat in the backseat, hunkered in the dark to mask his presence from others. Atticus never once looked back at him in the rearview mirror, but Simon watched his friend's eyes when a streetlight or passing car highlighted them. They were full of worry and desperation. For a passing moment, Simon considered turning around, and allow things to playout normally – he thought otherwise. Living with that decision would haunt him for the rest of his life. However the cards fell this night, he would face them eyes forward, and ready.

"See you soon," was all Atticus said when Simon stepped out of the car as NightVision, replied, "Soon."

NightVision took to the shadows of the park, keeping off the beaten path so park strollers wouldn't see him. The trollop of a horse and buggy crossing along the thoroughfare filled the night and the sound of an accordion and applause came from a tiny cropping of people in a small clearing.

This isn't where it happened, NightVision thought and he moved further away from the populated areas. He'd recognize where the attack would happen when he saw it.

Deeper into the park he traveled, and soon he was alone. That's when it came upon him. A sense of cold filled the air. The spring night quickly turned bitter, which wasn't unusual in New York, but this kind of cold bit at him, seeping into his skin and chilled his bone. The presence of another being stirred somewhere nearby and NightVision hunkered in the bushes, watching, waiting.

Moments later, the sound of footfalls filled the night and he peered over the bushes to find Natalie Green, just like it was in his vision. Scared, confused, and running for her life.

NightVision fought the urge to spring from his hiding spot even though every passing moment brought his student closer to death, but he waited for the perpetrator to show himself.

The air became colder, and NightVision's hands trembled as he held onto his Browning. Preparing to spring from his spot, NightVision froze, when a black-clad form came out of the night. Natalie stumbled backward, losing her footing she fell back onto the concrete sidewalk and screamed.

NightVision broke cover – his finger tightened on the trigger of his shotgun, but he hesitated, narrowing his sights down the barrel of his gun. "Stand to," he ordered, but the black form didn't move. "I said, stand to."

Without warning, the form turned holding something in his hand, instantly NightVision's sight blurred and he dropped his shotgun to the pavement, it made a clatter on impact.

With the crook of his right arm over his eyes, and his left hand shoved in front of him in a vain attempt to push back the blinding light, NightVision dropped to his knees. The cackle of his attacker filled the night, and then a sharp dazzling light came to the back of NightVision's eyes, and he toppled to the ground in a pool of black.

PART III

The flash of dim light sent a piercing hard stab into the back of NightVision's head when he opened his eyes. Sharp pricks of needles burned his arms when he woke – they held the brunt of his weight as he dangled from a support beam above. He surveyed his surroundings, bright light washed his vision, but he managed to make out the form of Natalie Green crumpled on the floor near him. Motionless, he feared the worse until he saw the slight heaving of her chest moving up and down. She was breathing, *she's alive,* he thought.

Shifting his body, NightVision managed to put his weight on his legs, as he found his footing and stood. The rope was taught, and it sliced into his flesh cutting off the circulation. *Just a flick of the wrist,* he thought trying to activate the spring in his gauntlet and produce the hidden blade within. *Come on, come on. Damn it.*

"You're awake," a voice from the shadows called out.

NightVision didn't respond. Instead, he scoured the area where the voice came.

"I didn't think you would be that easy to bring down," the faceless voice said. "Evidently I was wrong."

NightVision tightened the muscles in his arms and leaned toward the voice, the voice he recognized. "Show yourself."

"The papers paint you as some kind of Street level Messiah, and clearly you do have a god complex, otherwise I wouldn't have been able to bring you down so easily. Know thine enemy."

"Am I supposed to be impressed?" NightVision asked.

"Please," the voice said. "Don't act as if you don't know who I am." The form manifested from the shadows, and Morgan Payne came into view.

"You don't seem surprised," Payne said.

"Should I be?"

"Considering I was in your office this afternoon. You should be a bit more shocked that I'm here... yes."

Damn it, NightVision grimaced. *He knows who I am. Or does he?*

"Your silence won't deter me, Mister Rook. You see, I've been watching you for several weeks. I've invaded your visions on more than one occasion, and I was there when you saw young Miss Green run for her life. Everything is by design. Her fate was to be nothing but a lure, and it worked just as I foresaw."

"Who are you?"

"I am who I claimed to be. I am Morgan Payne, my job is to analyze, study and report."

"To whom?"

"That doesn't concern you. Not yet," Payne replied. "All you need to know right now, is that you will know pain, you will know suffering, and then you will know death."

"By your hands?" NightVision asked.

Payne gave an insidious toothy grin, and said, "Not by me..."

"Who then?"

Payne's face slacked, emotionless and he said, "When we last met, you spoke of your father. How did that make you feel?"

NightVision stilled his tongue.

"You must answer me," Payne said.

Still, NightVision didn't reply.

"You have to answer me."

"No, I do not," NightVision replied, angling his body to align himself with Payne. *Just come a little closer, you bastard... a little closer.*

"You cannot bait me, Mister Rook."

NightVision relaxed, *no, I guess I won't.* He drew a breath, but before he spoke, Natalie Green stirred on the floor.

Payne turned toward her. "Our guest awakes."

NightVision lunged forward, applying strength to his bindings and pulling them to their zenith. "Leave her alone...!" he ordered.

Natalie turned, and recoiled when she saw Payne, and NightVision. "Who are you?" she demanded. The words tight in her throat.

"You are not in danger, my dear," Payne said unconvincingly. "As long as Mister Rook agrees to cooperate."

Natalie's face wrinkled, and asked, "Mister Rook?"

Again, NightVision relaxed. "State your questions," he said.

Payne wheeled around. His hands aglow, he stalked forward. "Your father," he said flatly. "Your discontent, your torment, your shame."

NightVision studied Payne as the man stalked forward. There was a familiarity about him, something NightVision couldn't decipher, yet clearly, he had some kind of power in him that set him apart from the simple run of the mill street thug. "What are you?" he chagrined. "How are you doing this?"

"Think of me as your conscience," Payne moved around NightVision like a predatory animal. "Your hatred is prevalent. I am here to remind you of it."

"Remind me?"

"You hate him, don't you?"

"Oh, yes," NightVision admitted. Imagery from his childhood flooded his memories. The beatings, the verbal abuse, the constant belittlement. The anguish at seeing his mother bleeding on the floor at his father's hand. "My father disgusts me...!" he shouted. "He was a vile despicable person, and I hate him. But he does not define me."

"You lie!" Payne shouted. The luminosity around his hands intensified. "He made you. Your visions are because of him. Visions I share, visions I can control."

"Huh..." The vision came to Night-Vision, shrouded in the night. *What is happening?* He fought to gain control. Visions never came to him at night, but this one invaded his senses as clear as a summer's day.

Fires burned all around him. The intoxicating heat stifled him, and NightVision knew the place in an instant. *The old foundry, on Cheshire Avenue.* The effervescent glow cast a myriad of shadows causing movement everywhere. Then he saw her. "Lori?" His secretary lived near the foundry. By the disgruntled look etched on her features, she was frightened, confused and in trouble.

She's the second victim, NightVision's stomach tightened when the figures of two men stepped out of the orange glow, and Lori spotted them, she backed away in terror.

NightVision lurched forward, like all his visions, he could not interfere. All he could do, was watch in horror, as she died.

Suddenly, the vision ended, and NightVision found himself back in the warehouse. Gunshots echoed throughout the building. He narrowed his eyes trying to focus, catching the glimpse of... "Atticus...?"

"Yeah, it's me," Atticus called from his hiding place.

Footfalls echoed throughout the building as armed men ran everywhere.

"Your friend can do nothing to help you," Payne said.

"You're wrong about that," Night-Vision replied. "He's a distraction." With a twist of his wrist, the hidden blade slid forth, instantly cutting the rope holding him and NightVision dropped to the floor.

The shimmering glow around Payne's hands subsided, and he tugged a pistol from inside his coat. He leveled it on Natalie. "Take one step toward me, and I swear to God, I'll kill her," he warned.

Natalie recoiled, staring into the end of the pistol.

More weapons fire echoed inside the building. Hammering footfalls scattered all around them.

"Your friend is going to die," Payne said assuredly.

"You'll find him more difficult to kill than you believe," NightVision replied slowly taking another step toward Natalie.

"Your faith in your friend is admirable, *and* you're killing this girl with each step."

NightVision hesitated.

"That's right," Payne said. "There is nothing you can do to stop me."

"Maybe I can't..."

Payne chuckled. An expression of complete control tightened on his face and he said, "You have too much faith in your man. He is no match for my hired men."

Atticus came out of the dark in a quiet fluid motion, positioning himself behind Payne. He drew up the pistol in his hand and cocked the hammer, and said, "I wouldn't say that."

Payne paled, but drew a strong breath and shouted, "Guards...!"

"What guards...?" Atticus snarled. "They're all dead. Drop your pistol."

Unmoving, Payne stood his ground. His pistol hovered over Natalie.

Atticus shifted his footing, and said, "I will not ask again. Drop your weapon."

"You won't have time to kill me before I kill the girl," Payne said. "Are you willing to take that chance?"

Atticus didn't reply.

A lilt of a laugh came to Payne's voice, and he said, "I didn't think so."

With Payne's attention on Atticus, NightVision slipped his gloved hand down to his side, reaching into a pouch on his belt.

"You only have two choices," Payne said.

"There is a third," NightVision said tossing the flashbang to the floor – shielding his eyes before it exploded. The instant shock of light brightened the room, and Payne dropped his pistol – his hands went to his eyes. NightVision rushed him, throwing a punch sending the rogue to the floor.

Atticus placed a foot on Payne's chest, and said, "There's always another option."

NightVision went to Natalie, bending down to her on the floor. She held a scream in her throat but recoiled.

"It's alright," NightVision said yanking the mask from his face.

"Mister Rook...?"

"You're safe now. You're safe."

Natalie trembled, her eyes wrenched in their sockets, and she said, "I... I don't understand."

Still poised over Payne, Atticus admitted, "I'm afraid I don't really know what the hell is going on."

"Lori," Rook scattered to his feet, pulling the mask over his face, and heaving Payne off the floor. "Stop your men."

Payne offered a bloody smile," Even if I could stop them, I wouldn't," he said.

NightVision tossed Payne aside, as Atticus kept his gun trained on him.

"He has Lori. She's in the old foundry. Where's the car?"

"Six blocks away, in the opposite direction," Atticus said.

NightVision glimpsed his shotgun propped up in a corner and retrieved it. "There's no time," he said bolting for the warehouse door.

"The foundry is nine blocks away," Payne roared with laughter, "You'll *Never* make it in time."

NightVision darted from the building. Payne's last words ringing in his ears. The thought of Lori's death on his mind. He created his secret persona out of the need to do good. Having lived a life of abuse and tragedy, the idea of saving people, fighting those who would do harm and bringing them to justice was his way of putting his father's pain behind him, and honoring his mother by helping those in need, like she protected him against his abusive father all those years ago.

Lori would not die this night, he swore it to himself, no matter if it meant his own death, she would live... *I swear.*

The night grew long as NightVision came upon the foundry. The immense old factory of rusted metal, and dilapidated infrastructure still produced metal to this day. Perhaps the call to condemn the old behemoth was justified, but the fact it still produced material and kept hundreds of men working was a huge deal in the midst of a great depression.

Huge flames from the stacks at the top of the main building lit up the deep dark sky. A thunderstorm brewed in the distance – streaks of lightning sheeted overhead.

Keeping to the shadows, NightVision leapt over the large stone wall that encircled the compound. The foundry was at full production, and the facility teamed with activity as men labored to complete the quota, completely oblivious that a woman fought for her life under their very noses.

NightVision followed what he saw in his mind, using it as a guide as he homed in on Lori – remembering the look in her eyes when he witnessed the vision.

A flash of lightning exposed him for half a heartbeat, his form nothing but an apparition, and he moved quickly and stealthily before anyone could get a better look at him.

NightVision recognized the outer building from his vision as he approached. The structure leaned slightly and look as if it were ready to collapse. Deep holes filled the walls and pricks of light shot through rusted fissures.

A horrific scream bellowed in the night, masked by the intense drumming sound from the main foundry building. No one would have heard it, even if they were close – yet NightVision was entuned. His stomach sank. *God, am I too late?* He burst into the shoddy building, his shotgun out in front of him.

His vision washed some, but the light inside the building wasn't overwhelming and his eyesight adjusted with the use of the special lenses in his mask. He scoured the interior, and silently went deeper into the infrastructure stopping when he saw movement behind a stack of ceramic piping. He hesitated, and regarded the movement before continuing, unsure who it was ahead – friend or foe.

When a wiry man came out from behind a stack of crates to Night-Vision's right, he turned charging the attacker, stabbing the man with the end of his shotgun. The force of the blunt attack threw the man off guard and he bellied over, long enough for Night-Vision to deliver a swift kick across his face, sending the hood to the floor.

NightVision turned back to the ceramic piping, waiting for another attack. He charged forward and that's when he saw her. Lori came out in the opening. Haggard and disheveled, her blouse was ripped, and she held it, covering herself.

Stunned by NightVision's appearance she faltered. "The Ghost," she said in a whispered breath.

Another man came out behind her. He carried a long knife and Night-Vision called, "Get down."

Without hesitation, Lori did as she was instructed and NightVision pulled the trigger, splattering the man with shot. The force of the blast shoved him back – little specks of scarlet decorated the piping behind him.

NightVision snagged Lori by the arm, and she pushed away. "Don't hurt me," she yelled.

"How many more are there?" he asked.

She eyed him for a few long seconds, and replied in a broken tone, "Two more."

NightVision wheeled around, cocking his shotgun, sending fresh cartridges into the chamber. "Where?" he asked.

"They were here," Lori said, and then asked, "Who are you?"

Masking his voice, Simon said, "I'm no one." He led Lori out of the building into the rain. Intense light flashed across the sky, temporarily blinding him and he stopped.

"It's just some lightning," Lori said.

NightVision grimaced. *This is where it happened,* he recalled his vision. He pulled Lori close, and waited.

"What are we..." the words stuck in Lori's throat when the two forms charged them. The sheeting rain masked their forms, but NightVision saw them clearly in the dimming light. He rose his shotgun to fire, but the first man was quick, and he knocked the weapon from NightVision's hands. The weapon slapped the wet ground. NightVision blocked the attack, and Lori screamed. He wheeled around, slipping a knife out of his belt, he lobbed it through the air, catching the second attacker in the shoulder and sending him to the ground in pain.

NightVision recentered his attention on the first man, but he was gone. Lori came in close to him for protection and asked, "Where did he go?"

NightVision held his answer, waiting for the shoe to drop, but it never did. "Gone," he said. *Can it be that simple?*

Red lights strobed in through the main gate as several patrol cars came in. NightVision turned to Lori, "You're safe now," he said and stepped away.

"Wait," Lori reached out. "Who are you."

NightVision couldn't answer. He refused to answer. Too many people learned his secret tonight. The more who knew of his secret would put him, and them in danger. He touched Lori on the shoulder, and she grabbed his hand, holding it tight, she said, "Wait, Ghost…"

NightVision took her hand in his, aware the police cars were getting closer. Letting go of Lori, he told her, "I'm NightVision…" and with that he ran into the rainy night.

***

The outer cell door opened, and Simon Rook followed the officer down the corridor into the detention area. Rook kept his eyes to the grimy floor, as they walked past a series of incarcerated individuals who stared intently. Passing through another outer gate, the officer said, "I can only give you five minutes before shift change. My Sergeant will be by soon. You have to be gone before he arrives."

Simon reached out his hand, and the police officer placed his hand inside Rook's. The officer wore the all-seeing eye bracelet on his right wrist. "Thank you, Watchman," he said. "This won't take long."

Morgan Payne sat at the back of his cell and offered a wide grin. "You have them everywhere, don't you?" he asked. "I wonder how they would react if they knew you were their benefactor?"

Simon ignored the statement and asked, "I came to ask… who are you. And how are you able to control my visions?"

Payne placed his hands on his knees and simply said, "You don't think you're the only one in the world with abilities like yours, do you?"

"Are you saying you have visions, also?"

"I used to, until I learned to control them. Though I daresay my abilities came to me from a car accident. Where yours came to you by a more dubious manner. Either way, you and I are alike."

"We are nothing alike," Simon said. "I help people."

"And I help myself," Payne said. "It's a profitable profession. You should try it."

"And you were hired to what, kill me?"

Payne stood and crossed the cell, stopping at the bars. "Oh, God no. I was hired to test you. To see if you could live up to the challenge, and my employer will be most pleased to find that the hate for your father burns inside you. You really hate him, don't you?"

"How would you feel about a man who killed someone you loved. Can you love I wonder?"

Payne took hold of the bars and squeezed tight. "This isn't over. You know that."

"No, I think it is. I have pity for the person who tries to hurt those in my life again."

"Are you threatening me?" Payne asked.

"Take it however you like," Simon replied. "But the truth is I'll be waiting, and I will stop you."

"Oh, for me, this is over," Payne said. "I did the job I was hired to do.

Even though I failed, that won't stop him. He's still coming after you. And he doesn't care who gets in his way. He hates you, as much as you hate him."

Simon's heart skipped a beat, and the blood rushed to his feet. He drew a tight breath.

"You asked, who hired me. But you don't need me to answer that, do you?"

Simon forced out, "No."

Payne's lips parted into a wide toothy grin. "Your father sends his regards."

Simon stepped away from the bars, his heart drummed in his chest, and his throat went cottony dry. The man who fathered him, beat him, killed his mother was still very much a part of him, and it seemed that not even prison would stop him from finishing what he started. Either his father would kill him... or *I'll kill him...* Simon thought.

As Simon Rook walked away from Payne, fighting with the revelation that his father was still very much a part of his life, he didn't notice the afternoon paper sitting on the front desk, and the headline that read:

NightVision:
Eyewitness Gives Name to
The Ghost

***

NightVision *will* return...

Charles F. Millhouse is Stormgate Press' Award Winning Publisher and the author of twenty-five books in the Science Fiction/Fantasy/New Pulp genres. A storyteller/dreamer since childhood, Charles published his first book in 1999 and he hasn't looked back. Find him on stormgate-press.com

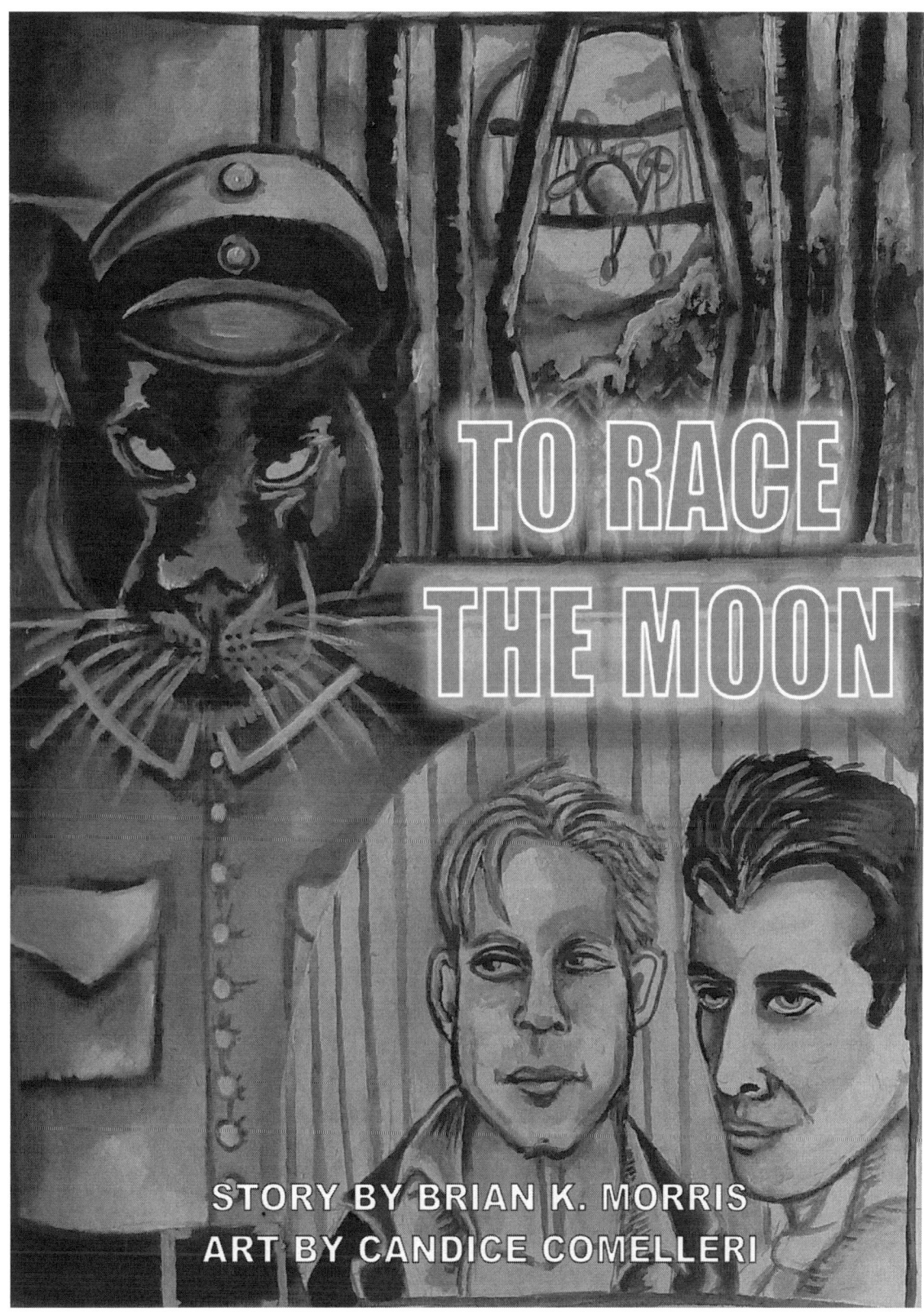

TO RACE THE MOON

STORY BY BRIAN K. MORRIS
ART BY CANDICE COMELLERI

3

TO RACE THE MOON
By Brian K. Morris
A CAPTAIN HAWKLIN &
DOC SAGA ADVENTURE
Based on characters created by
Charles F. Millhouse
& Brian K. Morris

1917: British Army Outpost #56

Corporal James Powell never saw a were-panther before and in three more minutes, never would again.

The thinning rays of late summer daylight gave one final caress to the British Army camp thirty klicks from Nice, France. A sentry kept watch on the western perimeter as Private Willhelm Gottlieb stumbled towards him in his ragged German Army uniform. The barefooted enemy soldier's feet bled from walking over the rough ground. However, the only agony Gottlieb's face showed was the kind that found roots in one's very soul.

As the British Army man called out for reinforcements, Gottlieb looked behind him to see the sun drop below the horizon. Tears of profound regret rolled down his face as he turned toward the full moon overhead.

Troops swiftly poured from their tents, guns at the ready. Corporal Powell leveled his rifle as he shouted, "Halt! Who goes there?" He searched through his memory for the equivalent in German but came up short as he saw Gottlieb grin maniacally.

Gottlieb's arms sprouted thick clumps of black hair. His ears and lips pulled back into a deaths-head grin as his incisors grew longer, glinting in the silver rays of moonlight. Gottlieb's back arched and his speed increased as the approaching soldiers watched the transformation with incredulity.

Without missing a step, Private Gottleib turned into a terrifying blend of man and panther, completing the transformation upon reaching Corporal Powell. The creature snarled at the sentry and reared back a taloned hand.

Following a heartbeat's worth of hesitation, the sentry fired at the man again and again. All of the bullets hit their mark in Gottlieb's chest and stomach. The other soldiers joined in, their bullets mutilating the were-panther in mere seconds.

Losing blood rapidly and half-blinded, whatever used to be Wilhelm Gottlieb howled in pain. With two swipes of his scalpel-sharp claws, Corporal Powell fell to the ground, dying. Without a second's hesitation, the creature launched itself into the thick of the troops. Ignoring the Brits' screams of confusion and pain, the monster moved from soldier to soldier, removing them from this existence.

Two sergeants sprinted from the Commander's abode, with Colonel Abel Forton close at their heels. As the monster turned his face towards the stars to announce his triumph in a blood-chilling howl, the duo buried their bayonets deep into the back of the creature's calves, severing his Achilles tendons. The were-panther twisted to face his attackers, but instead fell to the ground.

Frantically, the two sergeants slashed at the creature as their commanding officer brought the butt of his rifle down again and again and again with all his might upon Gottlieb's skull. After the former soldier hadn't moved in ten minutes, the Colonel told them to stop and to take a step back from the body.

Its brains lay exposed to the night air as his last drops of blood soaked into the dark mud below. Both of Gottlieb's arms bent in foreign directions and the monster's lower legs were all but freed from the rest of his body. Yet still, the creature took in a moist, painful breath and tried to push itself back onto its feet.

Colonel Forton pointed to one of the soldiers and then to his tent. "You, go inside, call the High Command for help and I want it here as soon as possible." He looked down at the body at his feet. "Then bring some rations and that bottle of brandy I keep by my pillow." The Colonel paused. "We're going to be here until the dawn." Forton arched his back, feeling his vertebrae crack in protest. "If it moves, cut off its head. Maybe that'll stop it."

As the private ran for provisions, Colonel Forton lifted his rifle high and drove the bayonet deep into the werepanther's chest. With tears streaming down his face, Forton repeated the action until he could lift his arms no more.

Nine hours, several uneasy breaks, and most of the brandy later, the sun rose in the east and Britain's finest men ended their grisly task as the body resumed part, but not all, of its human characteristics. "Bind this thing," Colonel Forton commanded, "but don't take your eyes off it."

Later that afternoon, a young American Army Lieutennant entered Colonel Forton's office. The exhausted officer lay with his head on his desk.

The soldier cleared his throat, waking the elder military man with a start. The colonel snapped to attention and saluted his visitor.

"Second Lieutenant Steven Hawklin, sir, reporting as ordered."

Colonel Forton stood up painfully and walked around his desk to shake Hawklin's hand. "Thank you for your prompt arrival and thank your commanding officer, Major Fogle. Tell him I owe him a drink, but there's little time for pleasantries. We must move quickly." As he explained the eerie events of the night before, the Colonel led Hawklin to a tent where one of the British soldiers stood by its opening.

The weary-eyed sentry rose to attention when the pair approached, visibly fatigued to the point where he forgot to salute. Colonel Forton acknowledged the man with a nod and held the tent flap open for Hawklin to enter.

Inside the tent a man laid on a cot, swathed from head to toe in gore-stained blankets, bandages, and several lengths of towing chains. The soldier's faint breathing could be heard from the far side of the tent.

Another man rose to his feet from a folding chair at the foot of the cot. He allowed a weathered leather shoulder bag to slide along his arm onto the floor. He extended a hand and offered a faint smile. "Hello, you must be Hawklin. I hear you're such an Ace, you're giving Richthofen some sleepless nights."

Hawklin shook the stranger's hand. "I'm looking forward to that contest. You're a medic? You sound American."

With a brief chuckle, the man said, "I'm attached to the American Army, Dr. Jedediah Sagamore."

"Oddly enough, Dr. Sagamore got here before my man could ask for someone to aid us." The Colonel rubbed his eyes. "Tell him what you told me, Doctor."

"What you see here—" Dr. Sagamore paused to study Hawklin's expression. "Are you all right?"

Hawklin turned his gaze from the gory figure on the cot. "I have a thing about blood. Please continue, Doctor."

"Then it's a good thing you're a pilot and not a medic." Sagamore looked down at the broken figure with sadness. "I had a vision this would happen three nights ago. I was doing a purification ceremony and—"

"You did a *what?*" Hawklin interrupted. "What manner of doctor are you?"

Colonel Forton interjected, "Dr. Sagamore's area of expertise extends beyond the world we know. That's what my own Commanding Officer told me." He studied Sagamore's faintly lined face. "Apparently, the doctor has earned quite a number of favors in his travels in and out of the trenches."

Hawklin turned his attention back to Sagamore. "Okay, why is this person here and what's wrong with him?"

"This man suffers from Bastecanthropy." Sagamore paused to let the word sink into Hawklin's mind. "It's a virus that's activated by the peculiar radiations of the full moon and goes into remission at sunrise. Similar to lycanthropy, but feline-based."

"Like a werewolf," Hawklin stated. "I've heard about those in my travels. So why is this man here?"

Sagamore shook his head. "From his uniform and bloody trail, I suspect this soldier was infected and sent to the Allied lines to cause mayhem." The doctor stroked his chin in thought. "This reminds me of an incident in Skillet Valley, Kentucky back in 1872. A mine owner infected one of his workers with lycanthropy and used the man as a disciplinary tool against his employees. "

"That's a little far-fetched, don't you think, Doctor?" Hawklin turned his head as the figure on the cot moaned and shifted position, re-opening his wounds.

"I guess you had to be there, Hawklin." Sagamore pointed towards the shredded boots that barely covered his patient's lower legs. "Given there was a full moon the last two nights and the damage to his footwear, I'd say he transformed *en route* last night."

Colonel Forton searched his memory. "Twenty-seventh Division Airships report a Prussian outpost about a day from here by foot."

Sagamore's expression turned grim. "Here's my diagnosis, gentlemen. This man, by nature of his illness, will return to full health tonight upon the full moon's rise. I can't guarantee his bonds will hold once the virus activates. We need to return this man to his own camp before he murders everyone in ours."

"Can this bastecanthropy somehow be cured?" asked Hawklin.

The doctor shook his head. "If he was infected and the virus lay unactuated, I could purge it from his system. However, once activated, there's only a handful of ways to end this man's suffering, all of them fatal." Sagamore's eyes narrowed. "And I don't kill my patients. On the other hand, I won't let him murder our allies. Instead, he can be the Kaiser's problem."

Hawklin glanced outside. "I think we've only got a couple of hours' worth of sunlight left. If we wind up attracting the wrong attention, I might have to walk home."

"*We* might," Sagamore corrected Hawklin. "My vision said I was to be in the back seat."

Colonel Forton said, "I've got an F-2 you can borrow, gents. It's a two-seater and I want it back when you're done."

Dr. Sagamore picked up his satchel. "I took some blood samples for later study. I'll get our guest onto the plane while it's warming up."

Twenty minutes later, Colonel Forton and another soldier helped Sagamore tie the injured German onto the space between the two cockpits. In the front cockpit, Hawklin checked the controls of the plane as he ran through his mental list of pre-flight checks.

As Hawklin put on his flight helmet, Dr. Sagamore climbed up beside the pilot and shouted in his ear, "I've found that during combat, calling me by my full name could get us both killed, if only for the time it takes to say it."

Hawklin smiled. "Combat, eh? So, Doctor, what should I call you?"

Dr. Sagamore refused to return Hawklin's smirk. "I'm not a fan of the nickname, but from this point on, call me 'Doc Saga.' Trust me when I say that name saves lives, probably our own." As Hawklin contemplated his passenger's grim words, the doctor dropped onto the ground and made his way to the aircraft's rear seat. Once the doctor secured himself, the airplane taxied to a dry patch of land and powered its way into the skies.

Once at peak altitude, Hawklin glanced over the side of the airplane to admire the patchwork scenery below. He never grew tired of this view and it reminded him why men with courage and talent fought so hard to ensure the freedom and safety of innocents, regardless of their nationality.

Hawklin glanced backwards, past the restrained bastethrope, to see Doc Saga's head bowed in what appeared to be prayer. Hawklin wasn't an expert in reading lips, but the words formed on Saga's lips belonged to no language he knew. So instead, Hawklin focused his full attention to navigating towards the coordinates given by Colonel Forton.

The sun crawled over the clouds as Hawklin located a field a kilometer from what appeared to be a hastily erected German outpost, no more or less permanent than their nearby British counterpart.

As soon as Hawklin brought the aircraft to a halt in a natural clearing at the center of a small forest, Doc Saga called out, "Keep the motor running, Hawklin. I won't be long." No sooner had the doctor finished his sentence, his legs went over the side of the cockpit and he slid to the ground, landing soundlessly.

Hawklin checked his gauges. He had enough fuel to return to base with a little time for any evasive maneuvers needed. *After all*, he reasoned, *the Germans had to have heard the plane's engines as we flew by*. Hawklin's aerial skills were second to none, and he could be as fierce a warrior one could imagine, but he never seized the yoke in the hopes of preventing some young pilot the chance to see his family again.

Saga pulled a small handsaw from his shoulder bag. As he raised his hands to sever the soldier's bonds, several bullets struck the fuselage of the aircraft. Each one landed near the fuel tank and Saga instinctively backed away from the plane, but not before rapidly shredding the soldier's bonds and pulling him roughly onto the ground. Ignoring the enemy soldiers emerging from the forest, Saga shouted, "Bail out, Hawklin."

Without hesitation, Hawklin threw himself out of the aircraft, rolled twice on the ground, then sprinted towards half a dozen German soldiers. Ignoring their drawn rifles, Hawklin pumped his legs frantically until the airplane's fuel tank ignited. The resulting explosion knocked the pilot forward onto his face at the military mens' boots.

Hawklin opened his eyes but it wasn't the soldiers' rifles that drew his attention, but the voices beside the burning airplane. He twisted his head to see Doc Saga rising to his knees, seemingly unharmed. A man in an officer's uniform stood over the doctor and aimed a Luger at Saga's head.

"Put your hands behind your neck," the man commanded in passable English as he waggled his handgun. "Good. Now, rise to your feet." As Saga found his footing, the officer shouted towards his troops in German, "Load these two into the truck." He waved two of his closest men towards him. "Help me with Gottlieb."

Saga and Hawklin gave no resistance as the soldiers herded them towards a waiting truck. Hawklin passively allowed the German soldiers to pat him down, finding no weapons. On the other hand, Saga squirmed in place as his captors ran their palms quickly over his uniformed body.

As they were being searched, Hawklin marveled silently that they allowed Saga to keep his aged shoulder bag, although they eyed it warily. What did they know about it that he didn't?

The squad leader, a Captain if the decorations on his sleeves were to be believed, dropped to one knee beside Gottlieb's body. He studied the bloodied form critically for a few seconds before he rose to his feet. With a snap of his fingers, the two soldiers lifted Gottlieb's body and after three wide swings of the carcass, they hurled it into the blaze that now enveloped the entirety of the British airplane.

Doc Saga gasped and moved towards the cold-blooded murder scene, his face twisted with rage. He felt Hawklin's hand drop onto his forearm. Ignoring the rifles aimed at them,

Hawklin said softly, "Time and place, Doc." Saga gripped both of Hawklin's wrists tightly and nodded.

The Captain followed Hawklin and Saga into the back of the truck, leaving his two men behind to watch the burning bastethrope. Doc and Hawklin sat in silence as the truck turned towards the north.

The truck sped towards the German encampment while the sky's edge turned scarlet as the sun neared the horizon. Looking past a dozen large tents that looked more suited to a circus than a military encampment, Hawklin saw several one or two-man aircraft lying in a straight line at the far end of the clearing. He glanced at Doc Saga who appeared to be silently taking the measure of the troops that marched in formation across the grounds.

One unadorned cinder block building stood beside the makeshift airfield. Iron bars covered every set of windows and the wooden front and rear doors each appeared to be reinforced with steel slats across their length. The truck slowed to a halt and both Americans were shoved to hit the ground, literally. Saga bumped into Hawklin with a muttered apology as the two were herded towards the brig.

The Captain unlocked the front door and motioned for the Americans to enter. Once inside, they saw a man in a Bavarian military uniform on the far side of the room who stood up quickly. The men exchanged swiftly spoken greetings in German. The only noteworthy aspects of the Bavarian were his voluminous mustache and his dark, intense gaze. Once the front door closed, the Captain motioned for Hawklin and Saga to stand and wait.

Steven Hawklin surveyed the interior of the building. Aside from a desk and two wooden chairs, the only rooms in this building were constructed from iron bars, just as any jail might be. A pair of soldiers stood guard at the door, their rifles at the ready in case their new guests decided to leave.

Saga's brow furrowed as he listened to the nearby conversation between the Captain and the Bavarian. He muttered to Hawklin, "It seems the Lance Corporal there also anticipated our arrival quite some time ago, just as I did."

"Maybe he's doing some purifying too." Hawklin looked towards Doc Saga whose grimace shot down the pilot's supposition. One of the German guards cleared his throat to end his prisoners' conversation.

The German Captain approached his prisoners. He came to attention, clicking his back heels together smartly in the process. "Forgive my poor manners, gentlemen. I am *Kapitän* Karl Meier of the German Army and you are both my prisoners." Captain Meier addressed Doc Saga. "So, my friend, the Lance-Corporal, says you understand German?"

"I speak many languages," Saga confessed. He turned towards Hawklin. "Do you speak German?"

"Sorry." Hawklin shook his head, a gesture that brought a gentle smile to his captor's face. "How many languages do you speak, Doc?"

"How many do you need?" Doc Saga asked with a smile.

"Not to worry," Captain Meier stated in thickly accented English. "I speak German, English, and French fluently. I will attempt to make your stay as brief as possible before you are sent to meet the Kaiser."

Doc Saga smiled. "Really? I never get to meet anyone famous." He turned towards Hawklin. "Have you ever met Kaiser Wilhelm?"

"I'm rather hoping to put that off, sorry." Hawklin's neutral expression failed to convey any regret whatsoever, just as the Lieutenant intended.

Captain Meier snapped his fingers and gestured towards the cells. Immediately, Hawklin and Saga found themselves prodded towards, and locked inside separate cells. An empty space separated them, allowing them to make eye contact, but no chance of the physical sort.

Before Doc Saga's cell door slammed shut, two soldiers removed the well-worn leather bag from the physician's shoulder. As the soldiers tugged, Saga maintained a death grip on the strap that his captors couldn't break.

The mustachioed man spoke forcefully to the senior officer as he glared at Doc Saga. Captain Meier stated in German, "If he refuses to release his satchel, shoot the pilot."

Upon hearing that, Doc Saga released the bag. He watched the soldiers carry it to the Lance-Corporal who accepted the carryall with the reverence of a religious icon. The soldiers then left the building as the German tugged at the knot that held the flap shut tight.

"You won't be able to open that," Saga stated evenly in perfect German. "You must know the spell that keeps it sealed and how to counter it. Even if you bypassed the sigils, you might reach into my bag and pull out a bloody stump. You do know what sigils are, correct?"

The Corporal leapt from his chair and barreled towards Doc Saga's cell door, "You will tell me how to open this satchel or your companion suffers." He paused to take the measure of the physician's steely gaze. "I am eager to learn all your secrets, not just how to open this bag...Doc Saga."

"Uh-oh." Without changing his expression, Saga told Hawklin, "He knows who I am."

"That much German, I understand." Hawklin turned towards the Doctor. "So, who is he and why is he so interested in you?" In reply, Saga shrugged, never moving his eyes from the Corporal's.

The man with the mustache smiled as he slung Doc Saga's bag over his shoulder. He glanced at Hawklin, regarding him like something to be scraped from the bottom of his boot before he turned his full attention back to the physician. The Corporal spoke with reverence, "My true name would give you power over me, Dr. Sagamore. Instead, just call me 'Gefreiter Adi.'" The Lance-Corporal grinned. "It is quite the honor to meet you, Doctor. I have followed your exploits as an ageless shaman with rapt fascination." Adi's eyes practically glowed. "I have so many questions. Are you really 150 years old?"

"I shall leave so that you two can become fast friends." Captain Meier clicked his heels together again before he walked quickly towards the front door. Hawklin noticed the man kept his head down, unwilling to make eye contact with his new prisoners, while Adi glared at the man hatefully.

"Why so much interest in me?" Saga asked Adi. "It's not like I'm special."

Adi's glare vanished as he contemplated the worn leather shoulder bag at his side. "You are far too modest, Dr. Sagamore. As for accessing the secrets of your infamous satchel..." Adi's voice dropped in volume as he spoke slowly, ominously. "You will tell me how to gain entry."

Doc Saga shook his head. "Too many drops of blood helped form that sorcerous lock, Lance-Corporal Adi. It'll take a far better man than you to open it because I refuse to help." Saga added firmly, "And don't try threatening my life or my companion's. Remember what I said about better men and take note they aren't here to dispute me."

Adi glared at Doc Saga for several seconds, his jaw clenched and shaking. Unnerved by the American's absence of fear, the Corporal returned quickly to his chair.

Lt. Hawklin now sat on the floor of his cell and whispered to Doc Saga, "Corporal Adi seemed quite intimidated by you, Doc. Any way that reverence translates to an escape?"

"He wasn't impressed, he was terrified." Saga sighed. "There was a time, not long ago, when I would have lived up to, and exceeded, the rumors of my ability." The physician smiled wistfully. "He called me a 'shaman,' Lieutenant. I guess in time, I became more like a wizard."

"You have quite the sense of drama," Hawklin observed as he rubbed his left wrist, his brow furrowed. "Fortunately for you, I keep an open mind, Adi doesn't seem to care we're chatting, and I have some time to kill. Please go on, Doc."

"I know this sounds mad, Hawklin," Doc said, "but it's real." He took a deep breath before continuing. "Over the last century, I have entered into agreements with beings beyond this plane of reality in exchange for...talents, abilities to help others." Doc's voice and gaze took on a thin veneer of fear. "But something's happened that's cut off my connection to those other worlds. I can't access certain abilities anymore, and I don't know why."

With that admission, Doc Saga glanced briefly at Lance-Corporal Adi who tugged and cursed at the leather bag. The tie-down might as well have been constructed of steel for all the resistance it offered. Then without warning, Adi turned his mad eyes towards the prisoners. He glared at them as if trying to peer into the depths of their souls. Then Adi rose from the table and left the building. His oddly compelling voice rose in volume long after the door slammed shut.

Hawklin turned towards Doc Saga. Saga translated, "He's calling for a couple of men, Lieutenant."

Less than a minute later, the two soldiers who guarded Gottlieb's smoldering body entered the building. Adi followed close on their heels with a bundle of white broadcloth clutched tightly in his hands. He aimed his angriest gaze at Lt. Hawklin and barked a command for his men.

"Brace yourself, Hawklin." Saga gripped the bars of his prison tightly as he watched the pilot's cell door be unlocked. Without hesitation, the soldiers each grabbed one of Hawklin's arms, lifted him from the floor none too gently, and held him firmly, despite his struggles.

Adi smiled as he reached into the bundle of fabric and dramatically withdrew what used to be a human hand. However, its flesh was blackened and pulled back at the fingertips, giving the former bearer's nails the appearance of claws.

Doc Saga shouted in German as he thrust his hand past the iron bars of his prison. "No, Adi. You don't want to do this."

Adi's smile vanished as he pulled back his arm and slashed Hawklin's face with the detached hand. Hawklin tried to minimize the damage by turning his head, but to no avail. Three scarlet lines appeared on his face and those wounds suddenly burned like someone poured lemon juice and salt into them.

Doc Saga muttered an angry curse that Hawklin couldn't translate. The pilot felt certain it wasn't in any language meant for human ears. Adi took a step backwards with a smile. "Don't worry, Dr. Sagamore. Your lackey's injuries will heal when the full moon rises tonight and his bastecanthropy blossoms."

"I'm so sorry, Hawklin." Doc Saga dropped his head.

The soldiers tossed Hawklin hard against the back of his cell, stunning him for a moment. By the time he recovered, the door was secured once again, the soldiers departed the building, and Adi resumed cursing at Doc Saga's shoulder bag.

Hawklin heard a distant howling in his ears and something in his blood boiled in response. He turned towards Doc Saga who alternated his gaze between Hawklin and the German who ignored them both.

"What did he do to me?" Hawklin looked at Saga with concern. The pilot pressed gently on his tender wounds.

Doc Saga narrowed his eyes towards Lt. Hawklin's right front pants pocket. Hawklin followed the physician's gaze. He slowly reached into his pocket where he located a small wad of paper. The pilot squeezed it gently, feeling some sort of granulated substance within its folds.

"DER HURENSOHN!"

Both Hawklin and Doc Saga turned towards Adi who threw the leather bag onto the floor in a rage just before he ran to Hawklin's door. The German pulled out a Luger from his belt holster and aimed it directly at the pilot's face. Adi shouted in German and Hawklin raised his hands slowly. "I take it I made him unhappy, Doc."

"Lt. Hawklin," Doc Saga said evenly, "our captor wants to know if the contents of your pocket are worth dying for. It seems he wasn't as distracted as I hoped."

Hawklin shrugged. "You tell me and then we'll both know."

Doc Saga grinned as he spoke to Corporal Adi in German. The taunting tones barely struck Hawklin's ears when the soldier closed the gap between himself and Doc Saga's cell.

With a speed unlike any snake could replicate, Doc Saga dug one hand deeply into his pocket. He raised that fist to his lips, leaped towards the iron bars, loosened his fingers, and blew with all his might, all in one coordinated move. A cloud of yellowish powder flew forward from Doc's hand, striking Adi full in the face.

As he stumbled backwards, Adi clawed with his free hand at the dust that clung to his flesh. Within seconds, his gaze lost all emotion as his arms dropped to his side. Adi's pistol slipped from between his fingers to strike the wooden floor.

"It's a Haitian compound," Doc Saga explained. "Dampens the rational parts of the brain. I'd happily give you the recipe, but we don't have much time." Doc pointed towards Hawklin's trousers. "The packet in your right pocket. I put it there when we bumped into each other. Shape it into a cylinder as best you can without spilling the contents and be quick about it."

Hawklin molded the bag into a more tubular shape. "Then what do I do?"

"Stuff it into the lock quickly." Doc Saga kept a watchful eye on Adi. "And don't spill any of that powder. Once activated, it becomes quite flammable."

"And you keep this in stranger's pockets?" Hawklin asked incredulously.

"Better yours than mine," Doc Saga stated. "So, get busy, Hawklin."

The compound's heat built up rapidly, going from uncomfortable to unbearable in the space of a couple of seconds. Hawklin crammed the paper into the lock's opening as best he could. But the pain generated by the compound swiftly overwhelmed the pilot. He felt a few grains of the bizarre compound slide across his fingertips, but he suppressed a cry of pain as he completed his task.

"Step back from the door," Doc Saga commanded. "It's going to get warm in there quite swiftly."

A wave of intense heat from the lock forced Lt. Hawklin to back away from the cell door. As he watched, the lock liquified and dribbled down the bars to the floor. Hawklin prodded the cell door open with his boot and stepped rapidly down the walkway to Doc Saga's cell. "How did that packet wind up in my pocket?"

Doc Saga explained, "I've spent decades learning how to hide things. I managed to twist to avoid their examinations, but I figured I'd be searched more thoroughly than a mere pilot, so I slipped it into your pocket."

Hawklin pushed Adi's pistol into his waistband. "My ego's taking quite a bruising today, I'll have you know." He quickly searched Corporal Adi's uniform to find the key that seconds later, opened Saga's door.

Saga emerged and laid a hand on Hawklin's shoulder. "Lieutenant? Tell me how you're feeling right now."

"Exhilarated," Hawklin said with a grin that surprised him. "Like I'm baking from the inside out." He looked at Saga with concern. "I think we've got at least an hour before the sunset. Don't ask me how I know."

Saga prodded Hawklin towards the front door. "I know how you know. We need to get back to our camp right now." Saga opened the door just long enough to peek outside. "We're quite outnumbered," Doc Saga stated in a whisper. "We might be able to sprint from the back door to get into one of the airplanes. Are you well enough to do so?"

Hawklin chuckled grimly. "I don't know, but turnabout is fair play, don't you think?"

Doc Saga looked at Hawklin, unable to conceal his worry. "What do you mean?"

"That poor soldier died as a weapon to be used against the Allies," Hawklin said, his voice thick with ill-repressed animalistic fury. "I should stay here until sundown and give this camp a taste of their own medicine." The pilot clutched Saga's upper arm. "Make your way back through the woods. Don't let me catch you."

"No, your job was to get me home, Hawklin. That's not you talking."

"Quiet!" Hawklin said with greater volume than he intended. He pressed his hands against his ears as if shutting off the whispers of the demons inside him. "I won't let this disease take me without a fight." He gestured in the direction of the airfield before snapping his fingers. "Do you have any more of that fire powder?"

"No." Doc Saga reached into Lt. Hawklin's left pants pocket and withdrew another wad of paper. "But you do. I believe in backup plans."

Hawklin smiled. "How are you at distractions?"

Doc Saga grinned in reply. "I've been creating distractions before you were even born. I'm practically a specialist in that field."

With a brief nod, Lt. Hawklin exited the building via the back door. He pressed his back against the outside wall, his senses aflame, sensitive and hungry, taking in every distant whisper, every heartbeat as he wrestled down the savage animal inside him. He glanced towards the west and saw the very top of the sun, orange and especially painful to Hawklin's eyes.

Hawklin took a deep breath, let it out slowly, then cautiously trotted towards the bank of the aircraft at the edge of the encampment. He banked on the enemy's overconfidence, feeling secure so far from the frontlines, to achieve his immediate goal. He risked a look back at the makeshift prison, disappointed to not see his new friend close on his heels.

Only a couple of yards away from the closest aircraft, Lt. Hawklin reached for the first wrung of the ladder that would bring him into the cockpit. But he stopped short as a bare-chested mechanic raised his head from the canopy to meet the American's astonished gaze.

Back inside the brig, Doc Saga searched for some rope to bind Corporal Adi. But Saga's captors filled the room with the barest of furnishings; two chairs, one table, and three buckets in one of the cells that Saga refused to examine. On the far side of the room, Adi remained in the same position he'd held for the last several minutes.

Doc Saga leaned on the table, contemplating his next move when he heard a scraping behind him. He turned to see Adi advancing on him. The Corporal's limbs moved stiffly, and the man's eyes burned with fury and danced on the edge of madness.

"Damn you, Sagamore," Adi snarled, "I have seen the visions. You have no idea of my glorious destiny, one that your power and knowledge will guarantee." Once within arm's length of Doc Saga, Corporal Adi stopped, and his demeanor changed to one of calm. "I will unite the world under my banner. Despite your affiliations to the mongrel races—"

"Enough of that claptrap," Doc Saga said. He raised his right fist. "Remember what happened last time I did this?"

"You can't fool me, Sagamore." Adi smiled evilly as he took a step forward.

Once the Corporal stepped within reach, Doc Saga hurled a punch straight into the German's face. As Adi staggered backwards in confusion and pain, Saga threw an uppercut that knocked the man out before gravity pulled the soldier downward to the floor.

"Oh, yes I can," Saga muttered as he rubbed his knuckles. He concentrated, using a Native American discipline to temporarily sever the link between his nerve endings and his brain. Once he could again move his fingers without wincing, Doc Saga pulled a handkerchief from his back pocket, pushed it into Adi's mouth, then dragged the German to the rear door.

Whether it was due to instinct or sheer stubbornness, Saga felt Corporal Adi's hand wrap around his wrist. He turned and stared again into the depths of passionate insanity. Saga tugged but the German's grip proved too great to break.

Saga dug deep into his pocket and pulled out the packet whose twin gained Lt. Hawklin his freedom. The Messenger's eyes grew wide in recognition, then even wider in fear as Saga tossed the packet with all his might against the back wall. Neither man heard or saw the paper shred upon impact, but the resulting *WHOOMPH* and immediate conflagration were impossible to ignore.

Flames rapidly filled the building, traveling along any flammable material it could locate. Adi released Doc Saga's hand and ran towards the rear doorway and potential safety. As the Corporal whispered, "*Die tasche,*" he felt Doc Saga's fingertips bury themselves into his carotid artery. Seconds later, Adi fell to the ground, unconscious.

Doc Saga pulled the madman outside, beyond the heat of the flames as the camp's population came alive with surprise. Soldiers shouted for buckets and water as they formed a line to a nearby water tank. Then Saga gazed deep into the fire and whispered, "Yes...*die tasche*...'the bag' indeed."

Saga closed his eyes. He began a chant in a low voice before he walked towards, and into, the conflagration without a second's hesitation.

On the airfield, Lt. Hawklin and the German mechanic stared at each other for what felt like an hour. Hawklin knew he couldn't climb up the ladder swiftly enough to pull the man from the cockpit. He also didn't want to pull the Luger free of his waistband for fear of receiving a lug wrench to the skull. The mechanic just stared back in fear and confusion. Hawklin assumed the man was no better prepared for a confrontation than he was.

However, both men soon registered the sound of bewilderment and panic among the barracks. The mechanic turned first to discern the cause of the confusion. He gasped as he saw the jail engulfed in flames and his comrades scrambling to extinguish the blaze.

The mechanic's trance broke when he felt a hand grip the front of his oil-stained shirt. He looked down to see Lt. Hawklin rearing back his fist with a grimace on his face and a lupine snarl on his lips.

With a ruthless strength that surprised both men, Lt. Hawklin yanked the man from the cockpit and threw him to the ground. The feral side of Hawklin's mind urged the lieutenant to finish off this opponent, to bathe in the warmth of the man's blood. "N-no," Hawklin snarled to his emerging savage side, "I'm better than that."

Hawklin dropped to the mechanic's side. He landed on all fours like a cat, unable to take his eyes from the unconscious German. He studied his helpless foe as madness whispered for blood. Hawklin pulled a wrench from the man's tool belt and studied the man's bloodied nose.

A wave of nausea overwhelmed Hawklin and he turned away, once again in tenuous control. He smiled as he looked at the metal tool in his grasp. "I've got a much better use for you."

Hawklin pulled the chocks free of the wheels of his newly acquired aircraft. Then he sprinted from one airplane to the next, silently praying the Germans continued to focus on the jail and not him. He arrived at the closest plane and deftly went to work.

As Hawklin worked at loosening the fuel lines of one engine after another, he glanced over at the jail. The soldiers tossed bucket after bucket of water on the raging fire, but to little effect. Smoke poured from the windows and the open back door and Hawklin knew that a compound that could turn steel molten couldn't be extinguished by such tiny amounts of water.

By the time Lt. Hawklin finished his mission of sabotage, Doc Saga emerged from a cloud of gray smoke that issued from the remains of the building. He wore a look of total serenity and didn't open his eyes until he was several yards past the doorway. With a swift glance around him, Saga broke into a run with one hand holding the strap of his strange leather bag to his shoulder. Hawklin never saw the like of the doctor's peculiar gait, nor did he ever see a man cover as much ground as Doc Saga did in so short a time.

Hawklin shook Doc Saga's hand with a broad smile that resembled that of a panther sending a warning to his potential meal. "Doc, we've got to get in the air quickly. We're running out of sunlight."

Doc Saga tossed his bag into the rear seat just as a shot rang out.

Still lying on the ground, the mechanic's hand trembled as he attempted to aim his pistol for a second attempt on Hawklin's life. But before he could pull off the shot, Hawklin booted the handgun out of the man's grasp. A second kick rendered the mechanic unconscious.

"Sorry, Doc," Hawklin stated. "I guess I should...have...searched him...better..." Hawklin fell into Doc Saga's arms, the right side of his shirt turning dark red with his blood. "Guess...guess you'll have to leave me here," he said weakly, refusing to look at his wound.

"Like hell I will." Doc looked towards the jail. The gunshot drew the soldiers' attention. Several of them pointed at the Americans as they reached for their handguns.

"Time to go, Hawklin. I guess I'm in the pilot's seat."

Hawklin shook his head to clear it. "Doc," Hawklin growled, "you ever fly before?"

Looking at the advancing German soldiers, Doc Saga said rapidly, "No, but I watched someone fly a Sopwith Camel a few months ago and I have an excellent memory."

Hawklin seized two handfuls of Saga's shirt. "My job's to bring you home. Even wounded, I'm a better pilot than you'll ever see. Help me into the cockpit."

Doc Saga took a worried glance at the darkening skies as he pushed Hawklin up the ladder to the cockpit. Hawklin instinctively fastened his safety harness as he started the engine. The machine emitted several coughs that reeked of burned oil before the propellor turned smoothly. As he revved the motor, Hawklin looked up to see the soldiers abandoning their desperate attempt to quench the flames. With guns raised, they swiftly advanced towards the aircraft en masse.

Lt. Hawklin opened up the throttle and the plane moved slowly in a semi-circle, turning away from the approaching soldiers. The pilot gunned the engine as the aircraft picked up speed over the bumpy makeshift take-off strip. Bullets whizzed past Hawklin's head as he waited for the sweet moment when he could pull back on the stick and take to the air. "Hang on, Saga!"

Hawklin's inner demon howled in terror as the wheels lost contact with the ground. The airplane wobbled as Hawklin felt the early effects of rapid blood loss. He listened to the bastethropy inside him scream in triumph as the sun disappeared behind the edge of the world.

"We must survive." The sound of Hawklin's inner voice merged with that of the disease inside his veins. "Leap to the ground and return to the walking meat. Slay them, feast upon their sweet marrow and the terror of their screams."

"N-no," The airplane banked suddenly, pressing the Lieutenant against the side of his enclosure. Hawklin snarled at Doc Saga in the seat behind him, suddenly and irrationally furious at his attempted rescuer.

"Yessss," the disease purred seductively. "You will gorge on the aged human's blood like a fine, sweet wine."

Hawklin's stomach rebelled at the thought of the taste of someone else's vital fluid. His wound burned and his flesh itched as he clutched his midsection and gnashed his teeth. "No...I won't let you take me," he said with minimal conviction. "I have a job to do."

The virus's laughter echoed in every corner of Hawklin's mind. He felt his resolve melt as the early rays of the full moon emerged on the eastern horizon. "You cannot resist, human. You will kill proudly in my name. So, surrender your will. You know I cannot be stopped."

"Ohhhhh," Hawklin moaned as a sly grin crossed his lips, the smile of one hunter outmaneuvering the other. "Let's see about that," he whispered confidently.

As the light of the full moon struck him, Hawklin lifted his shirt as far as the safety harness would allow. He forced himself to look down at his wound, illuminated in bright silver. A terrifying amount of blood covered his torn skin with more seeping from the injury.

Hawklin imagined he could see his vitals through the gaping wound as he gripped the stick and devoted his attention to the eastern skies, just before darkness overwhelmed him and the pained howling of a beast grew silent.

***

Lt. Steven Hawklin sniffed the air upon waking. It smelled of bleach and soap. He slowly opened his eyes and mentally commanded the blurs to take shape.

"Lieutenant Hawklin?" Colonel Forton placed a hand on Hawklin's shoulder. "Just lie back, son. You're in friendly territory again."

"We made it. Intact?" The room began to come into focus as Hawklin relaxed.

Colonel Forton turned his head to hide his smile while Dr. Sagamore cleared his throat. "Um, mostly intact," the physician confessed. "Not one of your smoother landings, I'm sure."

"How long have I been out?" A wave of adrenalin brought the pilot to full consciousness. "Saga! Did I change?"

Dr. Jedediah Sagamore smiled at his patient. "No, sir, you didn't. You must have some kind of amazing willpower, sir, because you held the virus at bay."

"How could you know?" Hawklin asked as he allowed his head to sink deep into the pillow.

"Remember, I am a doctor of more than medicine, Lieutenant." Sagamore smiled enigmatically as he penciled his notes onto a sheet of paper. "After our crash landing, I sedated you and created a cure from the soldier's infected blood. You should be flying again in a couple of weeks."

Hawklin breathed a sigh of relief. "Thank you, Doctor. You staying around to see me back in the air?"

"I genuinely wish I could." Sagamore cleared his throat. "I took it upon myself to leave my squadron when I got the visions. I didn't exactly wait for permission." The doctor smiled softly. "But I'll burn that bridge when I get to it. I look forward to meeting you again, Lt. Hawklin."

"I don't understand what you do," Hawklin said as he raised his right hand, "but I'm glad you do it. Thank you on behalf of all of us."

Dr. Sagamore gripped the pilot's hand firmly. "You're a good man to know, Hawklin." A grin appeared on Sagamore's thinly lined face. "I told you I never met anyone famous. I have a feeling when this war ends, I'll be able to say I did today."

***

Elsewhere, far behind enemy lines, Lance-Corporal Adi examined his orders. "Back to headquarters?" He picked up a pen. "I'm sure your superiors appreciated the swiftness used in filing your report."

"Indeed, as well as its accuracy." Captain Karl Meier's voice carried an arctic chill. "Apparently, someone in the High Command had a history with Sagamore and you let that man slip through your fingers." He paused, "I await my own reassignment with equal trepidation. Now if you'll just sign the paper, acknowledging your part in this base's destruction."

Adi choked back his acerbic reply as he read the paper. "One day, *Meier*, I shall delight in overseeing the destruction of you and your entire breed from the face of this planet. Mark my words, you haven't heard the last of me."

Captain Meier said slowly, "You should have put a bullet into your *verdamnt* idol's brain. Now, you will return to your squad so enjoy your time on the front lines." Meier glared at the German. "Your transportation waits outside so sign the papers. And don't use that ridiculous nickname of yours."

Adi lifted the pen and silently vowed revenge upon his multiple oppressors as he signed, "*Lance-Corporal Adolf Hitler.*"

***

Brian K. Morris is a full-time indie publisher, hybrid author, "award-winning" playwright, occasional actor, and former mortician's assistant. He lives in Central Indiana with my wife, no children, no pets, and too many comic books

LET THE SUMMER BEGIN!

COMING JULY 2021

4

SNOW CHASE
An Abraham Snow Thriller
By Bobby Nash

Abraham Snow crashed through the plate glass window.

He hit the deck hard, felt glass cut into his arm, the snow crunched under the combined weight of him as his opponent, a man he had met not too long before named, Ronald Sheffield. Their conversation had started out friendly enough, cordial even, but as so often happens to Abraham Snow, eventually cordial was replaced by opinionated, then words got heated, and weapons were drawn. It was pretty much downhill from there.

A fraction of a second later, the heavier Sheffield landed on top of Snow, who grunted under the impact, felt the breath knocked from his lungs.

With a little effort, Snow pushed the man off of him and heard the man grunt in pain as his attacker recovered quickly and made a break for it.

Back on his feet in a shot, Snow gave chase.

For a man of his husky size, Sheffield moved fast. He leapt over the banister and dropped from the second-floor landing to the snow packed earth below. Landing with a grunt, he fell forward, off balance, but even that didn't slow him down.

"You okay?" Archer Snow shouted from the broken window.

"Yeah! Call it in," Snow shouted to his grandfather. "I'm going after him!"

"Take this!"

Archer tossed Snow his coat and he snatched it out of the air, already on the run.

At the railing, he saw Sheffield steal one of the snowmobiles that Snow and Archer had used earlier that day to poke around on the mountain trails. Since then, night had fallen and a heavy snow continued to fall down on the Aspen resort, the thick white flakes making it a touch more treacherous to go out at night.

That fact did not seem to faze Sheffield.

With a roar, the snowmobile's engine roared to life and leapt free from beneath the meager protection afforded by the second-floor deck.

Snow leapt over the railing himself and landed nearby, rolling on impact and coming up in a crouch. He popped up just in time to see the snowmobile speed away, sending snow and slush flying.

Pulling on the coat and marveling that there were gloves in the pocket, Snow grabbed the goggles off the handle and slipped them on. Then, he straddled the second snowmobile and fired the engine.

Seconds later, he was in hot pursuit across the frigid mountainside with snow and slush slapping him in the face like tiny ice missiles.

Sheffield had a head start, but Snow could still make out the taillights of the snowmobile and he maneuvered to follow. He kept the snowmobile beneath top speed. Although he had been out there earlier in the day, when the sun was shining, Snow did not know this mountain well. It was going to take speed to catch up to his target but driving off a cliff or smashing into a tree were not high on his list of things to do either.

Where the hell is he going? Snow wondered. Running might help him get away for a little while, but there were still on the mountain and the only way down was via gondola. The way down was treacherous, fraught with steep drop offs hidden by snowbanks, impediments covered by snow, and assorted wildlife looking for its next meal.

The inaccessible nature of the location was one of the reasons it was chosen to host the conference. Keeping the collected assemblage of the world's one percenters, movers and shakers, and decision makers secret was important to Snow Security's clients. They were all willing to pay top dollar to keep the anonymity of those in attendance. The fates and fortunes of many of the world's largest corporations would be decided at the conference. This was not information those involved wished leaked to the media.

Ronald Sheffield might have escaped the chalet, but he was trapped on the mountain. There was nowhere to go. Plus, Snow and everyone at the reception knew his name. Where was he going to go? Did he have a plan? How else did he think he would get off the mountain?

These were all good questions and Snow had zero answers to any of them.

As the snowmobile trudged through the night, Snow wondered how he had gotten himself into this mess.

Then he remembered.

It was all Archer Snow's fault.

***

Then.

It was supposed to be an easy gig.

That's how Archer Snow pitched it. Easy. Snow Security had been contracted to provide their services for a business conference at a private chalet in Aspen, Colorado. The guest list for the conference read like a who's who of the heads of Fortune 500 companies, captains of industry, big wigs one and all, each worth multiple millions of dollars on their own. Together, they made up the top one percent of the top one percent, the so-called movers and shakers of the business world.

They were also some of the most hated men and women in the world, especially in these uncertain times when the people employed by the companies run by these CEOs were losing their homes and struggling to put food on the table while the big wigs discarded table scraps that would easily feed a family of four.

The cultural divide between the haves and have nots had always been wide, but in the twenty-first century, it had yawned into a chasm seemingly too extensive to cross, not that there were many willing to try. There were no longer bridge builders working to pull both sides together, which was a shame.

When Archer Snow had asked his grandson, Abraham Snow to join his security detail for an easy gig in the beautiful Colorado mountains, his first reaction was to say no.

So, he did exactly that and politely declined the invitation.

The thing about Archer Snow, however, and it was a fact that his grandson knew all too well, was that the old man tended to get his way. If he wanted Snow on that detail, he would find a way to make it happen.

And that's exactly what he did.

Archer knew exactly what buttons to push to motivate his grandson into doing what he wanted. Though he would vehemently deny it, Abraham Snow was easy to manipulate. His patriotism and sense of duty and honor were well-known and on full display. No matter how much he protested, Archer knew that his Snow would never knowingly sit by and allow someone to be injured. He would help out in spite of his reservations.

If not, Archer would play the *grandpa card.*

That one worked every time.

The attendees of the conference were no stranger to threats, death and kidnapping related, mostly. Some of the threats were more credible than others, but all of them were tracked down and investigated by Snow Security and each company's own security branch. Archer explained to his grandson that, no matter what any of them thought about their clients personally or professionally, they deserved to be protected the same as anyone else.

"Even rich, entitled assholes like these," he added.

Snow reminded Archer that not every average Tom, Dick, or Harry could afford to hire the high-priced Snow Security Corporation, which started a completely different argument about market value and supply vs. demand.

Suffice to say, Abraham Snow didn't win either of those arguments.

That's how he found himself double-checking security protocols in an Aspen chalet early the next morning. Archer's team was top notch and consisted of ten security specialists on hand and they had security fairly well nailed down, front, back, and sideways. With hours to go before the sun came up, security was covered. He didn't need Snow for that. Snow's job was to profile the threats to see if any of them appeared more credible than others and to weed out any they might have missed. As an investigator and an operative who had spent years working undercover, Snow knew how to spot a phony most of the time.

Archer talked him into joining the advance team with the promise of an easy assignment followed by a ski weekend vacation that they all deserved after the conference's conclusion. Archer reminded his grandson that he hadn't a real chance to relax since returning to civilian life after his time in the hospital after being shot twice and left for dead on a South American airstrip in the middle of nowhere. Snow almost died there, in fact, he actually did flatline a couple of times after his rescue, but the wonderful surgeons and medical professionals working on him not only brought him back but saved his life.

He hadn't come home unscathed, of course. That amount of trauma played havoc with the human body and Snow had taken a tremendous amount of punishment. The heart surgeon informed him that the only thing that saved him from instant death was that the shot to the chest missed his heart by half an inch. Half an inch, the doctor reminded him with each checkup, was all that stood between life and death.

He had to be careful. The damage to his chest was substantial, even if he liked to pretend it was otherwise. Snow's heart had been severely weakened by the trauma. Stubbornly, he ignored the doctor's orders to take it easy, which had already caused a couple of health scares.

The doctor warned that a heart attack was imminent.

Snow knew this but continued on as though he was still as young and healthy as he had been a decade earlier when he ran off to join the Army. It wasn't denial. Snow understood the danger he put himself in every time he leapt into a dangerous situation. He didn't have a death wish either. It was the understanding that, if he stopped moving, stopped doing what he had been called to do, he would surely die. Since death was the logical outcome of every choice available to him, Snow decided to stick with the path that let him live life to its fullest until his heart finally did him in.

Archer thought the trip would be a good way to trick his grandson into a relaxing vacation.

Not surprisingly, things didn't turn out that way.

***

Now.

Snow ducked to avoid a tree branch.

In the dark, it seemingly appeared out of nowhere. He managed to miss the deadly obstacle and kept the snowmobile upright.

Ahead of him, he could still make out the lights from the snowmobile he was chasing.

At least one of us knows where he's going, Snow thought. He was completely turned around. He was unsure exactly which direction would take him back to the resort. He chided himself for leaping into action without a plan. This sort of rash behavior had landed him in the hotseat on more than one occasion.

This time, his recklessness might just lead to his freezing to death in a winter wonderland.

Their snowmobiles were evenly matched, so he wasn't making any ground on the man in front of him. The smart play would be to alter course and try to cut the man off, but there were many dangers to attempting that in the dark. He could drive off a cliff, fall into a ravine, hit a tree, or worse, a tree stump and flip his borrowed ride upside down, potentially having it land upon him. The snowmobile weighed somewhere in the neighborhood of seven hundred pounds, he guessed. Possibly more.

None of these potential dangers were worth the risk. He knew the man's name and could no doubt find him later and have the authorities pick him up. That was a safe plan, a smart plan.

So, why wasn't he turning around and heading back toward the resort?

Snow knew exactly why.

He hated to lose.

It was that single, solitary fact that so often made him leap headlong into danger despite knowing how ill-conceived his actions were. It had only been a year ago that he took two bullets, one to the chest, the other to the shoulder, on a South American airstrip. He had been careless. One tiny slip up and his cover had been blown, his true name exposed.

The man he knew as Manuel Ortega had smiled when he pulled the trigger, reveling in the taking of a man's life.

As he lay there on the hardpacked earth, blood pooling beneath him, Abraham Snow knew he was going to die. He recalled a sensation of floating and remembered with stark clarity looking down on himself dying and feeling surprisingly content to let go of this world and move on to the next, whatever that might entail.

There was just one problem.

Abraham Snow didn't like to lose.

Surrendering to death struck him as the ultimate loss and his contentment turned to self-reflection then to anger. Anger at the man who had shot him. Anger to the job that had put him

there. Most of all, he was angry at himself for not seeing it coming. How had he not seen it coming? He was angry because, as he lay there dying, Abraham Snow had almost given up. He had almost lost the ultimate game.

Life.

I don't like to lose.

Since returning home, his family and friends had each expressed concern about what they saw as his reckless behavior. He thanked them for their concern but assured them all that he was okay, even though he knew he was anything but. The pain in his chest came and went, was gone more often than it was there, but when the pain hit, it hit hard.

Half an inch is all that stood between life and death, the doctor had told him. The bullet that Miguel Ortega put into his chest had missed the heart by only half an inch. Half an inch. It didn't seem real, even when the damage and tiny shards of shrapnel they couldn't fully remove reminded him of exactly how close he came to meeting his maker.

The doctors all agreed on one course of action.

Abraham Snow had been ordered to take it easy and get some rest. The body needed time to heal, he was told again and again.

It was advice he ignored time after time.

Case in point. Leaping off the deck and taking a snowmobile into the cold, dark night with no idea where he was going or what would happen when he got there was probably not his smartest play. He should have stayed put and let the authorities handle it.

The thought never entered his mind until it was too late to do anything about it. Of course, he could have called off the chase, stopped speeding through the unknowing wilderness and the unseen hazards, returned to the resort and waited for daylight to resume the search. All he had to do was agree to lose this one.

Losing was a bitter pill to swallow.

Pushing harder into the engine, he tried to coax more speed out of the snowmobile.

I don't like to lose.

As he bounced through the dark, Abraham Snow's mind raced back to how it all started.

***

Then.

The security arrangements checked out, but Snow and Daniel Sisko gave everything one more once over, just to be on the safe side. Sisko was Archer Snow's driver and bodyguard, primarily, but the old man liked Daniel and was teaching him the tricks of the trade so he could eventually move up in the hierarchy of Snow Security.

Snow had offered to help him out, even though, technically, he wasn't part of the security conglomerate's managerial staff. At best, he was a glorified freelancer who took the occasional security gig at the request of his grandfather, who just so happened to own the company.

Archer Snow was a crafty old codger. The man was as cunning as he was likeable, which said a lot about his ability to be duplicitous one second and utterly charming the next, often without the person on the other end of those qualities being any the wiser.

Sisko was a natural. Snow assumed that he had picked up a few tricks by shadowing Archer Snow on his various consultancy visits. Born in Puerto Rico, Sisko's parents relocated to Detroit when he was a young boy, his father going to work in an automotive plant. Eventually, that lead to a transfer to Doraville, Georgia where his dad worked until they tore down the old General Motors plant and he retired.

Daniel Sisko had been a Marine when his parents relocated the second time. Upon his honorable discharge from active duty, he made his home in Georgia as well to be close to the family. It was there that he met Archer and Dominic Snow at a job fair. They were both impressed with his history and locked him into a provisional contract, dependent on his clearing a background check, of course, which he did quite easily. His Marine training made him the perfect aide to Archer Snow while he learned the tricks of the trade.

As a Marine, he had traveled across the globe, but this job allowed him to see a different side of the world. Archer Snow was a down to Earth man in a business that found him often stepping into high society and big business. The old man's *aw, shucks* outward appearance often threw off his opponents, not to mention clients, who underestimated him based on the way he talked, with his folksy wisdom and southern drawl.

It took a while for Sisko to realize how much of it was real and how much was a performance for those he negotiated deals with. Even now, there were days when he still wasn't certain which Archer Snow was the real deal. He guessed that reality was somewhere in the middle of the two extremes the man showed publicly.

After completing their sweep, Snow and Sisko tracked down Archer to give a sit rep.

"All clear," Sisko said, his bearing still that of a military man, even after all the time he had been a civilian.

It was the polar opposite of Snow, who lost his military frame of mind when he was pulled from active duty and sent undercover for a clandestine U.S. Federal Operation codenamed Mother. After being trained how to be a soldier, it was a curious sensation to then be trained how to not act like a soldier. The differences were jarring, at first, but Snow discovered he was quite adept at shifting gears and compartmentalizing details. It made him good at his job. Not so good with interpersonal relationships.

"Yeah. Everything looks good," Snow added. He pointed toward the reception buffet. "We're still three hours from sunrise. I was thinking about grabbing a snack."

Archer raised an eyebrow.

Snow shrugged. "We need to make sure it's not poisoned or anything," he joked.

"It's not poisoned," Archer deadpanned.

"How can you be sure?"

"Well, I'm still standing here and I already sampled the shrimp puffs," Archer said, serious for about half a second before he smiled.

"Ooh, shrimp," Snow said and rubbed his hands together on the way to grab a bite before the guests arrived.

"Before you chow down, run me through it."

"Yes, sir," Snow said. "We have men stationed next to all entrances and exits here and at both the entrance and exit for the gondola. We have extra staff on the door to check and verify invitations and IDs. They've got all the goodies; hand scanners, portable ID trackers, and a metal detector to make sure no one sneaks anything inside they shouldn't."

"We've also upgraded security cameras with multi-spectrum imaging," Sisko said.

"But no sound, right?" Archer asked.

"No, sir. As per the delegates requests, no sound. There will not be a recording made of the negotiations. The client will be the one who controls how the information discussed here is delivered to the public."

"Sounds to me like you've got all the bases covered."

"I think we're good to go," Snow said. "The first of the guests are starting to arrive. If you'd like to give everything the once over, we can walk you through it."

"Nah. I trust you both," Archer said. "Go grab some shrimp before things get busy in here."

***

Now.

Ronald Sheffield handled the stolen snowmobile like an expert.

It was still an hour before the sun would peek over the mountains and blanket the winter wonderland in warm, fiery tones. Abraham Snow was still hot on his trail, but Sheffield had a slight advantage. He apparently knew where he was going. Snow had no clue where they were, much less where the path would take them. The man leading him on this merry chase definitely had home field advantage. Even if Snow surrendered the chase now, he wasn't so sure he could find his way back to the chalet.

The terrain grew rougher the farther they moved from the chalet. He glanced over his shoulder and could no longer see the lights from the mountainside structure Snow Security's client had rented out to hold their secret negotiations. The only light available to him was the snowmobile's headlight and the bright moon above, which made the snow-covered ground glow against the darkness of the trees and sky.

So far, that glow had kept him from crashing. If Snow saw a dark shadow, he swerved to miss it. Hitting a tree trunk or any sort of large rock would end his chase pretty quick. He had to be careful.

Careful did not seem to be a consideration for Sheffield. He seemed to know exactly where he was going and how to get there.

Though a good twenty or so feet separated them, Snow tried to follow his course precisely.

The lead snowmobile's lights disappeared from view, replaced by dark shadows. Sheffield had turned behind something, though Snow couldn't tell what. It could be trees, a barn, or the edge of a cliff with a long drop to the second step.

He had come too far to turn back now so Snow kept going at full speed along the same course as his target. As he neared the patch of darkness, he could start to make out details of a barn with piles of wood scattered about.

The perfect spot for an ambush.

No sooner had the thought hit him than he caught a glimpse of his quarry. Illuminated by the moonlight, Ronald Sheffield had parked the snowmobile next to the barn and killed the engine, extinguishing the light. What really stuck in his mind was that the man was holding an automatic rifle and he was lined up to fire.

Before he could even wonder where the man had acquired the gun, Snow jerked the steering hard, away from the danger.

Ronald Sheffield opened fire, the rifle's sharp barks piercing the peaceful mountain night and sending shockwaves of scampering wildlife away from the sound.

Sheffield was on Snow's right so he leaned as far left as he could go and remain on the snowmobile as bullets *sparked* and *sparked* along the plastic and metal frame.

Snow left the trail, his snowmobile bouncing wildly across uneven terrain.

He dipped down an incline as bullets danced across the snow above him.

His target out of sight, Sheffield ceased fire and waited.

Snow held on tight as the snowmobile heaved and jerked along the rough incline like a bucking bronco desperately trying to lose its rider. Below him, Snow saw only darkness.

Making a snap decision, Snow leapt from the snowmobile.

He hit the snow, felt the instant chill slice through him as he rolled through the soft, wet slush. Eventually, he grabbed a tree and stopped his descent.

It turns out, not a moment too soon.

Just a few feet ahead of him, the snowmobile made a hard drop and its headlight disappeared from view.

It was almost a minute before he heard the echoed crash as it slammed into whatever terrain waited below. Another few feet and Snow would have joined it in a mangled heap far below.

Careful to keep his footing, Snow pushed away from the tree and slowly started making his way back up the slope, digging for handholds in the ground beneath the snow, small trees, and large rocks for balance.

He was about halfway back up when he heard a noise above.

Snowmobile! He wondered if Sheffield had come to confirm that he went over the cliff or if he already knew that he hadn't and had come to finish the job he started.

Snow ducked behind a boulder; his arm wrapped around it to keep from sliding back down. He made himself as small as possible as a flashlight beam played over the incline. Between the flashlight and loaded gun, Snow was beginning to think the entire situation had been staged. Back at the conference, he had thought Sheffield was just being an ass.

Now, he was starting to rethink that assessment.

He also wished he had a gun of his own to even the odds.

His mind whirled back to the first moment he had met Ronald Sheffield.

It was hard to believe they had only met earlier that day.

***

Then.

Ronald Sheffield did not make much of an impression when he first arrived.

In fact, the man barely registered on Snow's radar when he entered the hall. Aside from his height and stature, he blended in fairly well with the others in attendance, suit, tie, jacket. When Snow did notice him, he assumed the man provided security for one of the groups in attendance.

The conference was a private pow-wow of the leaders of a number of large corporations who worked in similar fields. On the one hand, they were competitors, each trying to get a leg up on the competition, but they were also the ones who help set the trends for their respective industries. Conferences like this were designed to strengthen the infrastructure and keep the market stable while still leaving room to be competitive rivals.

Archer explained that these sorts of informal meetings went on from time to time.

"Strictly speaking," he said. "There's nothing illegal about what they are doing here. As long as they are careful not to leak sensitive information or commit insider trading, this is all on the up and up."

"I guess only senators get to do that and get away with it," Snow joked.

From the stern look his grandfather gave him, Snow decided that the old man wasn't the right audience for his political jab, no matter how much truth there was in it.

Snow waved the comment away and they got back to work. Archer detailed the players as they mingled and worked the room. Before the meeting, which was scheduled to begin as soon as the sun rose, everyone was friendly and joyful. It was a party after all. Once they took their seats around the table, the tension would build.

"Despite the reason this cooperative exists, there's still millions of dollars riding on each of these CEO's backs. They can't afford to give their competitors any advantage."

"Do you meet with other security firms like this?" Snow asked.

"No. Thank God," Archer said. "There are trade shows where distributors show off the latest wares and there are panels and demonstrations. That sort of thing. We also set up at some business trade shows to offer our services. It's not the same thing though."

"That's good to know," Snow said.

"What time does the meeting begin," Daniel Sisko asked.

"We still have time. They'll mingle another hour or so until one of them signals everyone toward the meeting."

"I think I'll do another sweep," Sisko said.

"Good idea," Archer said. "We should all mingle a bit ourselves."

And that was all it took for Snow to find himself in a conversation with a small group of businessmen whom he had absolutely nothing in common with including Ronald Sheffield. Topics of conversation ran from travel to the conference, where they usually spent their winters, books they've read, how business was going, stocks, bonds, and whether or not the weather would hold out so some of the guys could hit the slopes before business shuffled them back home.

Somewhere in the middle of the discussion, Snow noticed the gun beneath Sheffield's jacket. It was pretty well concealed, if you didn't know what to look for, but he had spent a lot of time working deep under cover, had infiltrated drug cartels and criminal enterprises where noting details was often the difference between life and death. Snow had been careful back in his deep cover days.

Then he got shot.

Now, he was even more attentive to detail because, even after all this time, he still had no idea what had blown his cover. Had he slipped up? Was it his fault? Had someone sold him out? It was a question he still did not have an answer to and that haunted him.

It also made him a little paranoid, but in his job as an investigator and part time security specialist, paranoia was an asset.

Ronald Sheffield was armed and no one inside the building was supposed to be armed.

How did he get a gun through security? This was the main question running through his mind. Disarming the man was key but disrupting the party would not look good for Snow Security. Archer Snow was more than Snow's grandfather. He was an inspiration. He was also his landlord and the first in his family to welcome him home after the hospital released him back into the wild.

He looked around the room for Archer so he could signal him to join the conversation. Together, the two of them could diffuse the situation calmly and collectively.

When he caught Archer's eye across the room, Snow gave a slight motion with his fingers, the universal signal for *come over here a minute.* Okay, so maybe Snow's signal had a little southern twang on it. He had noticed the old familiar southernisms he had long thought buried creeping back to the surface. He wasn't quite sure how he felt about that.

"What's up?" Archer asked once they were together.

"I don't know how he got it passed security, but that guy's carrying," Snow whispered.

"You sure?"

"Trust me."

Archer took the lead and headed over to the group that was talking and laughing.

"Excuse me, sir. I'm Archer Snow. Can I speak with you for a moment?"

"What's this about?" the big man asked.

"Just a minor security matter," Archer said, motioning him away from the group.

"Fine."

They headed to the window over-looking the upstairs deck. There was a light dusting of snow on the deck and the weather report warned of more fresh powder falling overnight with a possible freeze to follow. Snow in the Colorado mountains was a beautiful sight. Not like they got back in Georgia where it was only snow until it hit the ground and instantly transformed into ice. Thankfully, it didn't happen often.

"What's the problem?"

"What's your name?" Archer asked.

"Ronald Sheffield."

"I'm Archer Snow. This is Abraham. We're in charge of security."

"Yeah. So?"

"I'm sure it's an oversight," Archer said, pouring on the diplomatic charm. "But there are no weapons allowed at this event."

"Why are you telling me that?"

"Because you're carrying a weapon," Snow said, eyeing the slight bulge in the man's jacket.

"If you hand it over, that'll be the end of it," Archer said. "We're not look-ing to hang anyone up. We'll put it in a lock box. It'll be safe. You can have it back when you leave."

"I don't have time for this non-sense," Sheffield said and turned his back on the security experts.

"Hey," Snow said and grabbed the man's arm.

Sheffield jerked free of Snow's grip, his face reddening in anger.

"Do not touch me," he said through gritted teeth.

"No need for this to get rough, sir," Snow said. "But I cannot allow you to keep the weapon."

"You think you can take it from me?"

"Oh, no," Archer muttered.

"There's no need to start a scene," Snow said, even though they were already drawing more unwanted attention than he wanted. "Come on Let's take this outside."

When he saw the big man's smile spread, Snow realized he should have rephrased that.

Before he could say another word, Abraham Snow crashed through the plate glass window.

***

Now.

Snow made himself as small a target as possible.

Above him, at the top of the rise, stood Ronald Sheffield. He was armed with a gun and a flashlight. Snow knew where the gun had come from. The flashlight was a new acquisition. What had started out as a simple breach of security suddenly felt like a premeditated plan.

Sheffield played the flashlight beam across the snowy slope, looking for any sign that the man who had been chasing him had accompanied the snowmobile over the edge to a certain doom.

Snow played the angles in his head. Could he sneak up on the man, take him by surprise? Possibly, but Sheffield had height and weight on Snow. He knew how to use them too. He had tossed Snow through a plate glass window without so much as a grunt. If Snow got his hands on him, there was no guarantee that Sheffield would go down easy.

No choice, Snow told himself. *It's either move now or freeze to death.*

Once convinced, he started to move from cover and slowly crawled through the freezing wet snow toward the rise. He was halfway there when another voice cut through the silence of the crisp winter night.

"What's the problem?" the new voice asked.

"I was followed," Sheffield said.

"Are we discovered?"

"Somehow, one of the security guards noticed the plastic gun. There was a confrontation, a little bit of a scuffle."

"You obviously escaped."

"The security guy came after me."

"Where is he now?"

Sheffield gestured to the bottom of the slope where Snow's snowmobile had gone over the edge only a few moments earlier.

"Anyone else follow you?"

"No," Sheffield said. "We're still in play."

"Good," the new arrival said. "I've planned too hard for this to fall apart now."

"Are you certain?"

"It's all right, Ronald. We were going to create a diversion and evacuate the building eventually. This simply expedited the timetable a bit. Everything is still on schedule. If it hasn't already, the gondola will begin ferrying people off the mountain in groups. Our target will be among them. Come. We should get into position."

As soon as he heard the snowmobile growl to life, Snow started up the rest of the hill, careful not to lose his footing in the slick snow. The sun would be up soon, the dark already turning a shade of purple in anticipation for the dawn of a new day.

Snow overheard enough of Sheffield's conversation with the mystery guest to know they had plans for the gondola. All of this, the entire thing, was a hit. Sheffield and his unnamed partner were targeting one of the people attending the conference. Attacking the conference wouldn't work because there would be too many witnesses, no way for whoever was masterminding things, if they were in attendance, which Snow believed was likely, to get to safety.

The gondola, on the other hand, had a limited seating capacity. They would have to make multiple trips to get everyone down the mountain. This would effectively split the target, and a small group of collateral damage bystanders off from the others. A sharpshooter could take a shot, he thought, but quickly dismissed the idea. The security company would have no doubt proofed the gondola against such an attack.

So, what does that leave us with? Snow asked himself.

Then it hit him.

They've set a bomb!

If he was right, the bad guys, probably Ronald Sheffield's partner, had placed an explosive device on the gondola.

Now that he knew the conundrum, Snow only had to solve a few outstanding problems.

He had to find his way back to the chalet, find Sheffield and his partner, then find and diffuse a bomb.

"Piece of cake," he deadpanned.

***

Then (almost now).

"A decision needs to be made," Archer Snow told the assembled crowd.

Once he was able to secure everyone's attention, the head of Snow Security laid out the entire scenario to his clients and their plus ones. He started with the basics.

"A man named Ronald Sheffield smuggled in a gun. We do not know for what purpose, but as soon as we discovered the weapon and moved to disarm him…"

He pointed to the now boarded up window.

"Well, you all saw what happened."

"How did this man manage to smuggle a weapon past your security," Tolliver James asked. James was the head of a conglomerate of corporations ranging from textiles to banking to home electronics to weapons manufacturing. Archer found the man smarmy and fully expected to eventually hear that he was being sued for some form of assault or another. The man's appetites were legendary, and he was good at covering up the facts that proved his less than legal proclivities.

"The gun he had on him, which is now in my possession, was 3D printed. All plastic. It wouldn't show up on the metal detectors and, when disassembled, does not resemble a gun."

"How does a plastic gun fire?" Silas Cain asked. "A gun requires moving pieces." Like James, Cain was a perverted old man, although he had a good twenty years on James. They were men unaccustomed to being told "no" and used to getting their way.

Archer also thought they were both assholes, but he kept that opinion to himself.

"It was printed and brought here in pieces and assembled. This is not a simple case of wanting to be protected. You only go to this much trouble to smuggle in a gun if you intend to use it. Until we know the full extent of the gunman's plan, it is my recommendation that we adjourn. I know this throws a big monkey wrench in your itinerary, but we are all alone up here and until we have the perpetrator in custody, I recommend we head back down the mountain where our options are not so limited as up here."

Archer looked around the room.

"Objections?"

There were none.

"Then we'll start heading out in groups. This is going to take a few trips, but we'll get you off this mountain safely. That's a promise."

Daniel Sisko sidled up next to his boss.

"I thought you told me never to make promises like that to the clients."

"I did and you should never do that," Archer said. "But always remember, you're not me."

"Yes, sir."

"Now, let's move these folks out."

***

Now.

It turned out to be anything but a piece of cake.

By the time the sun started to glow behind the mountains to the east, Snow was completely and utterly lost. At first, he had tried to follow along the tracks carved through the snow during the snowmobile chase, but the wind and additional snow fall had wiped away all traces of his treacherous run across the darkened landscape.

Hoping that he had guessed the direction correctly, Snow set off in what he hoped was the right way to return to the gondola. Heading back to the chalet would have taken him too far in the wrong direction.

If his assumption was correct, one or more of the delegates on hand was in serious jeopardy, whatever was going to happen would have to go down at the gondola.

It took some time to find it, but eventually Snow saw the first of the towers reflecting the early morning rays of sunlight. There were several towers making up the cable car's path. The cable was stretched tight along the corridor and offered a smooth ride.

87

Taking out one of the towers or the cable itself would eliminate the target, but also the entire cable car system.

Overkill, in Snow's estimation.

There were three cars on the cable system at any given time. All three were loading at the top and would descend with space between them. The smartest move would be to blow one of the cars, taking out the target and their associates, but still leaving the gondola system functional, if not damaged, for everyone else to get off the mountain.

The tower was the quickest way to get close to the cars. He was too far down the mountain to stop them from getting on the gondola and starting down, but if he could climb up so they could see him, Snow could stop any additional cars from leaving by using the radio in the cable car itself.

He could already see the first car begin its descent from higher up the mountain. At this distance, they would never see Snow, so he ran to the tower and started up the ladder. It was a long, steep climb. His fingers ached from the cold, but he continued as quickly as he could.

When the shot rang out, he heard it before he saw the impact only a few inches away.

Snow looked down and saw a man with a rifle taking aim at him again from the tree line.

"Aw, crap!" Snow muttered, making his frozen limbs climb faster.

A second shot was too close for comfort, but also missed.

Snow looked down and saw that Ronald Sheffield, the man he had tussled with earlier, was at the bottom of the tower, climbing up after him. The morning had started out with Snow chasing him. He found it rather odd that now the bad guy was chasing him.

The first cable car was approaching so Snow kept climbing. Once he reached the tower, he tried to get the attention of the car's attendant. They saw him and he tried to let them know to either slow or stop the car so he could climb aboard through the roof access panel.

The first car began to slow their descent and the others followed suit.

Before Snow could move, Ronald Sheffield caught up to him and attacked.

Snow rolled with the punch and fell onto the grated catwalk. It was a long way down and he suddenly felt a tremendous fear of falling. One of the least fun side effects of his heart issue was the occasional bout of vertigo.

Seeing the ground so far below through the floor amplified the feeling.

He tried to push the feeling away. There was too much at stake to succumb to the dizziness and confusion the condition brought on. Instead, he tapped into some hidden reservoir and pulled himself back up and fought back.

Sheffield had height and weight on him, but in the confined space of the catwalk, that worked to Snow's advantage. He could move easier than his opponent. One wrong step and it was a long way down to the second step.

Snow's aggressive assault staggered the man, which bought him time. He had to find out which car had the bomb attached.

When Sheffield crashed to the catwalk, dazed, Snow did not move in for the kill. Instead, he turned, grabbed the icy cold safety railing, and vaulted over it.

He dropped ten feet to the roof of the swaying gondola car where he slipped and fell on his backside but somehow managed not to fall over the side.

Snow opened the service access panel and stuck his head inside, finding Daniel Sisko.

"What are you doing?" the security man asked.

"There's a bomb on one of these cars!" Snow shouted. "We need to get these people offloaded! Can we head back up to the chalet?"

"Do it," Sisko told the attendant. "I'll inform the other cars."

"We've also got a sniper near the tree line," Snow said. "My ten o'clock."

"I'll call it in," Sisko said, already making the call.

Snow felt the gondola car's motor activate and it swayed as the car started a slow ascent.

He took a moment to smile.

He should have known better.

With an angry shout, Ronald Sheffield leapt off of the tower the same way Snow had earlier. He landed on the roof, his feet slamming down hard where Snow had been only a half second earlier.

Snow was on the move, rolling out of the way. He had to be careful. The roof was still slick with wet snow and one simple slip and it was a long way down.

Snow got to his feet and blocked a punch.

He grabbed the attacker's wrist and forearm and gave it a jerk, sending the man falling forward, off balance and with an injured arm. He heard the elbow pop and Sheffield screamed.

A bullet popped against the metal, close, but not close enough to hit its target. The sniper's shot echoed off the mountains.

Snow and Sheffield dropped to the roof, each facedown.

The big man got to his feet faster and kicked his opponent in the side.

Snow grabbed the leg and, repeating the same maneuver as before, sent the man flying off balance.

Another shot echoed all around them.

This time, it hit flesh and bone instead of metal.

Ronald Sheffield's face went slack as he looked down and saw the big red stain on his chest, a victim of friendly fire. His sniper had hit him instead of Snow. Or did the partner see that the assassination attempt was not going well and decide to take out Sheffield before he could be captured? The first rule of assassination, Snow reminded himself, was kill the assassin.

Either way, it was the end of the line for Ronald Sheffield.

He fell backward, the light gone from his eyes as he toppled over the edge and dropped to the snow-covered terrain below. If the shot hadn't killed him, the fall would finish the job.

By the time the cable cars were returned to the summit, Daniel Sisko informed Snow that the security detail he dispatched had caught the sniper. He was in custody.

Once the cars were cleared, Snow, Sisko, and Archer checked the undercarriage of each car. When they found the bomb under the first car, they quickly removed it. Snow was thankful that it was a fairly remedial device. A block of explosive like C-4 with a remote detonator. Archer had already put in a call to the authorities and, once they arrived and took possession of the explosive device, he was going to find whoever held the detonator and they were going to pay.

By the time everyone had been questioned and searched, no such detonating device had been recovered. Everyone carried a cell phone, which could have been used to trigger the bomb. There was no way to check them all. Whoever was behind it was going to get away.

This did not sit well with Snow. Neither did catching a cold from his time running around in a winter wonderland. "Seems to be the only thing I caught," he groused.

"You caught Sheffield," Archer reminded him as they watched the last of their clients climb into the gondola and start their descent. "If nothing else, this has managed to convince them to work together on some of the issues they came here to discuss. I guess the thought of dying for their business made them realize how important it was to do the job right."

"Stranger things have happened," Sisko said.

"Name one," Snow said.

Sisko grimaced.

"Yeah. I can't think of one either." Snow looked to his grandfather.

"Any idea who was behind this?"

"None," Archer said, his irritation growing.

"At least the attempt failed," Sisko added.

"Did it?" Snow said. "I wonder."

"Wonder what?" Archer said.

"Nothing. Never mind."

"No. No. Speak your mind," Archer said.

"You said it yourself. They're working together after this scare. It sounds like you weren't expecting cooperation."

"I wasn't," Archer admitted. "These conferences usually devolve into threats and arguments. Personally, I don't see why they keep having them. Except, of course, for the more successful CEOs to rub it in the faces of their competitors."

"Is it possible the bomb threat was just that, a threat?"

"What do you mean?"

"That me finding out about the bomb was what they wanted all along. If I hadn't noticed Sheffield's gun and he hadn't ran away then there would have been no need to leave so early. The bomb on the cable car wouldn't have done much good, would it?"

"If you hadn't noticed the gun, would something else have happened to force an early departure?" Sisko said.

"I'd almost be willing to bet money on it," Snow said.

"We'll see what the cops say when they interrogate your sniper," Archer said. "Other than that, there's really not much more we can do."

"That's not true," Snow said.

"Oh?"

"You promised me a ski vacation, grandpa," Snow said around a big, toothy smile. "And, as luck would have it, we suddenly seem to have the day off work. Why not take advantage of it?"

"Smart," Archer laughed. "I like the way you think, kiddo."

"I must have learned that from my grandfather," Snow said as he waited for their ride down the mountain to return.

***

Bobby Nash is not a man of action like Abraham Snow, but he loves writing about these amazing heroic characters. Bobby is an award-winning author of novels, comic books, short stories, screenplays, and more. He is a member of the International Association of Media Tie-in Writers and International Thriller Writers. On occasion, he acts, appearing in movies and TV shows, usually standing behind your favorite actor. From time to time, he puts pen to paper and creates art.

For more information on Bobby Nash and his work, please visit him at www.bobbynash.com, www.ben-books.com, and across social media. Learn more about SNOW at www.abrahamsnow.com

PATENTLY FALSE
B-MAN RETURNS
by Clyde Hall
Art by Stephen Burks

"My Shelly," the young man with a goatee fringe breathed, gesturing at a girl sitting front table, stage left. Mirroring the audience's internal response, the microphone screeched. Adjusting for feedback, the beat poet continued, "No mother to monsters, unless I count. Not abalone down by the seashore, my Shell."

Criswell Speakes winced watching the coltish, lank-haired brunette fumble her sunglasses into place. If the Kava Kove 's interior lighting had a shade, it was Charcoal Murk. The shades were added barrier between muse and artist.

Undeterred, the poet continued, "No barnacled conch sold there by Sally, my Shell. I serve only as her bewitched apostle; on the leagues of our love my heart does not waffle."

As Shelly sank further into her chair, Cris used a sip of scalding coffee as distraction from the final stanza. Based on crowd reaction, the maneuver was worth every blister. There was no booing or catcalls, but neither was there more than extremely brief and tepid applause. Coffee house crowds found investment and camaraderie in shared cynicism, disillusionment, usually at the hands of parents or insufferable straights. Adoration expressed well was acceptable, but the youth on stage pushed his luck.

Worse, he mistook audience politeness for approval and not the implied velvet Vaudeville hook it was. The youth picked up a travel-worn acoustic guitar and began strumming as Shelly groaned. The kid tried all possible opening chords and eventually Cris recognized it as a butchered cover to Donovan's current chart-topper. Some mixed pop, rock, folk pastiche about a solar-powered superhero, but a choice sabotaged by an undercurrent of obsession.

Hearing enough, Shelly dropped a crumpled dollar beside her mug and stalked to the exit, shoulders square, shades as shame-concealing curtains. Her hopeful paramour promptly leapt off the stage, more a hop as it was a four-inch raised platform, in pursuit. The audience responded with genuine applause, displaying greater acceptance for themes of unrequited love and artistic suffering than for talent-free, blind devotion.

Cris drained his cup and signaled lone waitress, Elise for a refill. Kove's house band, Turquoise Turnpike, began cleansing everyone's ear canals with an original song, "Bunker Wine".

At a table behind him, two college students debated the merits of television science fiction. Both dismissed a 'vapid space family castaway' show as drek, while one listed merits of a new program, the title of which rhymed with 'drek'. Cris flipped open his small notebook and jotted a reminder to check local listings.

Several cinema and drive-in owners he'd met since buying the Strand Theater bemoaned the growing quality and variety of television programming. Now even small independent stations aired syndication packages, luring more viewers away from movies. Most theater owners suspected it was part of a Commie plot to ruin them, the bigger movie houses feeling especially pinched on nights when the highest-rated TV shows aired.

Cris, less dependent on huge crowds because his film selections were b-movies and second-tour features, fared better. In fact, tracking student tastes guided his mining popular genres. Irwin Allen was having a science fiction field day on the small screen. Now someone else was doing zap-gun stuff, so why not show a Lawrence Woolsey potboiler like *Brain Eaters from Dimension X*? A screening of 1924's Soviet silent *Aelita: Queen of Mars* could be a double draw of film students and poli sci majors interested in Soviet film industry propaganda.

"Dria says meet her at Original Readings," Elise startled Cris from his notetaking as she poured a refill. She smirked at his jump, eyes reflecting the warmth and hue of hot cocoa.

"Now? The shop's closed. In fact, I expected her here after locking up. Did she say why?"

"Nope," Elise answered, smirk becoming a gentler smile. "But it sounded important. Like maybe she wanted you to join her instead of the other way around. Without a crowd."

"Yeah? Huh." Cris glanced down at his casual attire and rubbed stubble on his chin. He'd finished splicing two Coming Attractions trailers together when he noticed the time and rushed over from the Strand's projection booth. Suddenly he was aware how much he needed a clean shirt and a shave.

"Here," Elise dropped his ticket on the table and continued her rounds, "she said bring that. I wrote it down."

Cris read the scrawled ticket, boyish thin face adding years with concentration wrinkles. "Pickets? Pickers?" he asked, but Elise was already four tables away. He sighed and left a tip, heading for the Strand.

The last few weeks, Dria'd helped Cris explore the range of his new abilities. She was present the night four bikers broke into the cinema after a drug deal turned deadly, and she witnessed a supernatural event: Cris transformed into living, breathing versions of silver screen heroes. The gang was subdued and turned over to authorities, though the b-movie heroics were Cris and Dria's secret. Secret, too, was keeping the biker drug money, a windfall funding several repairs at the Strand.

Dria's study of the supernatural for telling fortunes at her Original Readings shop led to her theory that the theater was built atop a convergence of powerful ley lines in 1916. Soaking up potent magical energies for a half century, the building attained a consciousness and defended itself by powering a champion using films shown there as a source.

It was beyond Cris's understanding, but he trusted Dria's insights despite her chicanery when it came to telling the future. She wasn't a psychic but had studied mysticism extensively. Now she convincingly portrayed a medium for her customers, the extra cash supplementing her salary as a Kove waitress.

Together, the movie buff and the fortune teller tested her theory while pushing the boundaries of Cris's powers. Initially, transformations lasted only about the length of a trailer. With practice, Cris called up a seeming for the length of a serial chapter now. Changing was easier in the Strand, but manageable outside, the nearer merging ley lines the better. Concentrating on a film character, he literally became that person. And while he looked like

the actor in the role, he amazingly possessed the fictional character's abilities. Gumshoe Gherkin, private eye, picked a lock in seconds. The Sable Scarab merged with shadows and manipulated darkness, just as in his film exploits.

Dria helped him practice transformations as B-Man, their codename for Cris when he used the ley-power. They canvased the neighborhood most nights, twice conjuring B-Man. Witnessing a purse snatching, Cris channeled the Western hero Lash LaRue, snagging the juvenile thief's feet with his signature bullwhip. Purse recovered, 'Lash' let the youth flee.

In the second instance, Cris became Heracles from a 1920's silent film by Essanay Studios, *The Twelve Labors*. The star was former heavyweight contender Fitz Barlow, dressed for the role in a lion's mane cloak and bearing a studded wooden club. It seemed ideal for a tavern lot brawl they drove upon, but Cris broke a knife-wielding combatant's arm with even a subdued swipe. It illustrated the difference being Barlow, former boxer, and Heracles, a demi-god. Clearly, practice was needed before channeling superhuman characters from screenplays.

Cris finished his shower still considering his and Dria's relationship as it had progressed. By the time he staunched hasty shaving nicks with toilet paper, he'd donned his best black turtleneck and drainpipe trousers and was out the door. He slowed on passing a flower vendor near Dria's shop. Why not? Friends gave each other daisies, right?

Bouquet in hand, Cris quietly tapped on Original Readings' front door though the shade was down, and the sign turned to the 'Sorry, we're closed' side. Then he noticed the car parked just off the alley. A sleek, golden Studebaker Avanti was strikingly out of place along the scruffy storefronts dotting Rock Island Way.

Dria flipped the locks and opened the door, ready with a greeting. Instead, the words died on her lips and she stood there, her Lady Alexandria 'seer' attire of flowing silk dress and scarves shifting in the gentle breeze. Her hazel gaze travelled deck shoes up, stopping at the fistful of flowers.

"What are you doing, Cris?"

"Uhm, Elise said you needed me?"

"No, I need the pickle guy. I specifically told her, 'Bring pickles.' Like a code you'd understand." She grabbed the daisies and glanced over her shoulder quickly before stashing them behind floor-length window curtains.

"Pickle gu---oh! Gumshoe Gherkin! What do you need B-Man for?" Cris lowered his voice.

"Get in here," Dria grabbed his shirtfront, pulling Cris into her shop. "I called an hour ago, where've you been? Why is there bloody tissue paper on your neck?" He was still deciding which to answer first when the faux psychic secured the door and leaned against him, speaking in frantic whispers. "Look, this is a chance to make half a year's rent with one client, OK? She's been here a few times for tea leaf readings, spiritual guidance. Today, she's looking for a missing item, a valuable

one. Guessing isn't an option, so maybe your P.I. can find it."

"Ah, I get it. We're on a case," Cris answered in matched whispers, feeling his cheeks warm. Recalling the lovesick bard at the Kove, an overwhelming sense of 'deja-you' drifted across him; that feeling you've witnessed the suffering of another, only to experience it firsthand soon after. He concentrated, reaching out to the mystic lines coursing beneath the neighborhood, and his vision blurred like a projector threading film clips.

"Her name's Catarina Baker-McGuffey," Dria shared, glancing back again to the reading room. "I told her I knew a private investigator; someone I'd worked with and who had full confidence in my 'gift'."

"Say no more, dollface. Gumshoe Gherkin's on the job. Where's our pigeon?"

Dria turned back, looking straight into the tall man's striped tie knot. This was necessary because Gumshoe was a foot taller and more heavily muscled than Cris. Waggling a match tucked into the corner of his mouth, the lantern-jawed P.I. suppressed an amused grin. His double-breasted suit was long out of style, his fedora the wide-brimmed affair preferred by Humphrey Bogart, and both were varying shades of gray.

"Do *not* call me dollface," Dria said quietly, but with a half-smile. It was an expression mixing amused and amazed to Cris's quick transformation. "And her name is---"

"Catarina Baker-McGuffey, gotcha. Lemme guess. Between that hotrod outside and a missing dingus, she's a kitten with a pending trust fund burnin' a hole in her mink coat. The sort they write about in high society columns but use small words 'cause her names eat up all the column space. How'm I doin'?"

Dria suppressed a laugh and shook her head. "She comes from a very wealthy family, yes, but now she's all alone after the death of her husband, F.E. McGuffey."

"McGuffey?! Say, isn't he that brain trust inventor guy?"

"He was. He hid his last project notes in preparation for filing a patent. McGuffey claimed this idea was revolutionary, worth tons, but he suffered a fatal heart attack two weeks ago and never submitted his work. Catarina's financial future depends on finding those papers."

"Tick tock, darlin'," Gumshoe crooked a smile and tapped his shiny Marlin wristwatch. "Lead on."

The Widow McGuffey sat at a table before a large crystal sphere, her black tulip cocktail dress and pearl necklace more fashion statement than mourning attire. She was in her low thirties judging by the barely discernible crow tracks on the pale snowscape around her eyes. Those, by contrast, shone bluish gray, like skies above a wintry vista of placidity. Medium brown hair with professionally coaxed curls was parted left of center, waves held in check by antique Spanish combs.

"This is the associate I spoke of," Dria said in her most professional Lady Alexandria timbre. It always struck Cris as a throaty, modulated Mid-Atlantic

affectation akin to Vincent Price's and nothing like her conversational voice. "Mr. Gherkin, this is our client, Mrs. McGuffey."

"Gherkin? Like the cucumber," Catarina said while taking stock of Cris's avatar. Gumshoe removed the matchstick from his mouth and doffed his hat lightly.

"Sure, but don't let that throw ya. I make my rep gettin' people *outta* pickles."

"How are you at solving puzzles, Mr. Gherkin?"

"I keep up with the Times crossword until Thursdays. Friday if an assistant editor's in charge," Gumshoe shot back, taking the reins fully from Cris. The P.I. was in his element.

"What about secret codes? Ciphers? My late husband *was* a riddle in every sense of the word. Oh, he was brilliant, of course, but not personable. He had few colleagues, fewer friends. He never spoke of it, but I always assumed his was a traumatic childhood. When you're four years younger but smarter than everyone in your class, including the instructor, well. People are cruel."

"Mmm," Gumshoe replied. "Musta helped his self-image, landing a wife so young. And a looker."

Dria started to protest, but Catarina cut her off, unfazed.

"Our marriage was more an arrangement. Daddy's funding attracted Effie. His genius attracted by father. I was a means to their ends," the young widow admitted. "Investors preyed on Effie's naivete regarding business. His inventions made fortunes for backers, not for him. He was famous as an innovator, but you can't eat fame. Father would fund his patents as a simple loan, Effie would own all the rights, and it would make a good living for us. Having me taken care of also a relief for my parents. They had me late in life, and as they grew elderly, I tasked them. May I smoke?"

"Not in the shop," Dria said quickly.

It was the first time Catarina exhibited unease, and Cris prompted Gherkin. "We'll make an exception. Here." He offered the client one from an open pack and struck the matchstick he yet held with his thumbnail. She lit her cigarette and took a deep draw.

"No filter. You enjoy living dangerously, don't you Mr. Gherkin?"

"If the flavor's rich enough, I'll take a chance. Go on."

"There isn't much else. Daddy's attorney, Victor Chadwick, practiced intellectual property law early in his career. With his help, Effie filed half a dozen patents and began seeing significant profit, most reinvested back into research for new products as my parents' health faltered and their own fortunes declined. They both passed last year."

"I'm sorry."

Catarina shrugged. "They were elderly, and it wasn't unexpected. Effie's heart attack, though, that was a shock. He always worked hard, driven to prove his theories, but the months before he died, he was obsessed."

"He ever spill about what he was up to?" Gherkin asked.

"Only the name," Dria interjected.

"He called it 'superior silica'," Catarina said as she drew a small leather-bound journal from her purse.

"Sand?" Gumshoe chuckled. "How's sand, even better-than-average sand, a moneymaker?"

"I haven't the faintest, but he claimed it would set us up for life. He had Vic draw up patent papers. I feel certain he finished them along with a comprehensive filing folio. He kept this notebook with him always, its contents protected by his own coding system. The secret location of Effie's last patent is in here. I hoped we'd bypass the code using Lady Alexandria's psychic ability. Now it seems I need a private investigator, too."

"My powers, along with Mr. Gherkin's skills, will lead us to that portfolio, Mrs. McGuffey," Dria said confidently.

"I'm counting on it. My poor Effie died securing our future, and I won't let his work be in vain," Catarina said. "You should also know, someone else is after the paperwork."

"Yeah? Who'd know about it?" Gherkin asked.

"I suspect his former business associates. We've caught them sifting through our garbage before. Some may have had organized crime connections. Even Mr. Chadwick, the lawyer, could be involved. The way he looks when I bring up that patent gives me chills," the young widow said as a visible shiver crossed her shoulders. "Now, how much will this cost?"

"A case o' good whiskey and $50 a day, plus expens---owww!" Cris winced for Gumshoe, Dria's kick under the table challenging how 1943 rates compared with 1966 renumeration. "I mean, Lady Alexandria sets the fees."

"You offered a $500 retainer," Dria said, "and another $500 when the item's found. Given he serves as both investigator and my personal bodyguard, a $500 share for Mr. Gherkin seems fitting."

Catarina placed the journal on the table as they finished the business details, while Cris-as-Gumshoe felt himself slipping into overtime. He idly tapped his watch as if it had stopped. Holding it to his ear, he fixed Dria with a meaningful stare. She gave a subtle nod and quietly wound their session up, collecting the retainer and notebook before escorting Catarina out.

Gumshoe stood, scratchy film frames crossing his vision and signaling his 'reel' fast running out, when Dria's voice rose in protest from the outer room. Cris retained Gherkin and hurried into the greeting room where Dria struggled with a stranger holding the door open from outside.

"I said we're closed!"

"Don't be like that," the man forcing the door further open chuckled in a mockingly patient tone. He was young, beefy, and full of face. Only a brief tuft of hair showed where a forelock once sprouted, leaving him bald except for reddish frill above his ears. That hc'd grown shoulder length and, combined with small round spectacles planted over a walrus mustache, he reflected youth culture. His suit, however, was conservative pinstripes of an expensive Brooks Brothers bent. Cherubic cheeks shook with mirth at Dria's struggles. A second man loomed behind him, obscured by the first man's bulk.

Cris sensed Gumshoe's assessment: This man made a living by intimidation and he enjoyed the work. Behind him was likely an equally unpleasant partner because these professionals travelled in pairs. Control slipping, Cris compelled Gherkin to defuse the threat quickly.

Dria's shoes slid on the slick tile, the intruder shouldering past. Gumshoe grabbed his tie, jerked it tightly into his double chin, and yanked him inside. Sudden forward momentum was halted by Gherkin's Detective Special flattening his bulbous nose.

"Welcome to Original Readings, Chipmunk," Gumshoe grinned and watched the flushed, round cheeks drain pale. With his free hand, Gherkin found the gunman's shoulder holster and freed a wheel gun from it, then spun his captive toward the lurker outside. "If this development's a shock, gents, now you know the value of a psychic adviser. For the record, I got your buddy's gat pointed at his liver. Mine's trained on you." He waggled the snub beside Chipmunk's waistline as proof. "Real slow, open your coat, show me your roscoe, and fish it out. Two fingers only."

The second man was shorter and considerably thinner than Cris's captive, a full pageboy mop of chestnut hair above sharp, clean-shaven features including a strong, dimpled chin. Chipmunk found his work perverse fun. Pageboy was a calculator, figuring odds. He was also careful because he followed Gumshoe's directions pre-cisely.

"Now gently put it on the floor. Slide it here with one foot. Keep those hands up," Gumshoe said, beads of sweat dotting his forehead under the fedora. "Lady Alexandria, get his gun. If either of 'em moves, plug 'em some-where they'll have trouble explainin'. Now, what's your business and who sent ya?"

Pageboy produced a perfectly con-descending smirk. "Asking such things wastes our time and yours."

"That case, I'll assume you're a cou-ple cheap triggermen shaking down a dukkering dame for lettuce. Turnin' you over to the cops'd be a waste o' manpower." While Dria covered Page-boy, Gherkin traded his snub for a set of high tensile handcuffs, slapping one on Chipmunk's wrist. The large re-volver still digging into the man's back, Gumshoe barked, "Drop your drawers to your ankles. You too, pally."

"Wait a damn min---," Chipmunk sputtered until he heard the clear, me-tallic sound of a hammer cocking. Two seconds flat, Cris and Dria witnessed boxers not as fine as the suits covering them.

Gherkin relinquished guard duty on Chipmunk as he covered Pageboy and brought out his second set of cuffs. He snapped one bracelet on Pageboy's left ankle, then ordered, "Waddle over here, big man. Now lean down." In short order, Pageboy had the other bracelet attached to his right ankle, and Chipmunk was secured with a set on his wrists threaded between his part-ner's legs at the knees. Motivating

down the sidewalk would prove chal-lenging with trousers down, gait hin-dered, and one nearly piggybacking the other, but that's what Gumshoe di-rected once he emptied their pockets.

"Scram," Gherkin said, two guns leveled at the contortion twins. They carefully stepped down onto the side-walk while leaning heavily against the door frame. A passersby gawked openly but quickly decided a pair of pants-less men being held at gunpoint while forming a handcuffed human pretzel was none of his business.

"We'll meet again, friend," Pageboy smiled despite his situation. Chipmunk was less subdued.

"You're a dead man! A d---," he frothed spittle as Gumshoe slammed the door shut.

Maintaining the visage of Gumshoe past his limit drained the final reserves of Cris's willpower. As Dria threw the lock and the duo tottering unsteadily away, Criswell Speakes reappeared. Then promptly collapsed.

***

Cris dimly recalled Dria catching him and easing him onto the cool, mo-saic flooring of her shop. He didn't re-member her helping limp him back to the Strand, nor how she shepherded him up to his office. The cracked vinyl couch with aluminum legs was a hide-ous fairway green, thinly padded and uncomfortable, but a bundle of Lady Alexandra's frocks under his head helped. Cris was so drained, he could've slept soundly on porcupines. Live ones. Waking, he panicked 'til catching sight of the window over the marquee. Daylight yet, time enough for the evening show. He was still experiencing an odd mixture of buzz and hangover, numb fingers and prickly feet.

"How're you feeling?" Dria came into view bringing a damp washrag for his forehead. She traded it for a dried one and he noticed she'd exchanged fortune teller fashion for dark cigarette pants and a clever black sweater, rhinestone cat pin on the collar.

Cris said in a quiet voice, since loud sounds made funny white stars shoot across his vision, "Day I mustered out of the Army, I downed a bottle of swill bourbon. Woke up the next morning in underwear not my own, hugging a balsam on a Christmas tree farm. This isn't so bad. Thanks for getting me back here."

"I knew you'd rather throw up at home," Dria deadpanned, then added, "Thanks for ejecting the creeps. Think those 'interested parties' Catarina mentioned sent them?"

"Maybe. Or maybe the family lawyer, wanting her journal."

"It's safe," Dria hooked her thumb at Cris's desk. "For something called 'super sand', someone's taking serious interest."

"The widow didn't bat one false eyelash at your price quote," Cris said.

"I noticed! That payday keeps my doors open, and the Strand can always use your part," Dria returned, expressive hazel eyes wider and greener than usual. "Tell me you have a B-Man character who'll break McGuffey's code."

"I've got the perfect someone."

"Good, because it'll take several transformations. Codebreaking's not easy."

"Professor Eldon Arkwright'll get it in one session," Cris predicted.

Dria stiffened. "That's not humanly possible, Cris. I've read about World War II codebreakers. It's slow, tedious work."

"True," Cris attempted sitting up. His daisies were in a water-filled coffee mug on the windowsill. "But remember, my manifestations don't embody human potential. They possess the skills and powers of their screen characters."

"So, who's this Prof?"

"Played by Martin Grogan in the 1939 Metropolitan serial, 'Undercover Invaders'. Arkwright was part of Bandy Bohannan's Planetary Defense Bureau. He smashed enemy codes and eventually translated an alien language after discovering interplanetary alliances between fascists and Venusians."

Dria's expressive eyes narrowed. "You made that up."

"With serials, embellishments unnecessary. Remind me to tell you about the singing cowboy and the Lemurians."

"Your Professor Arkwright did all that in twelve reels?"

"No, he did it in ten reels. He's the best."

Dria smiled, demure. "Gherkin's a hoot, but seeing you smart? That'll be novel."

"You're a riot," Cris stood shakily. "Let's get him on the case before showtime."

"You're still wobbly," Dria said, taking his arm in support. "Here, lean on me."

She eased Cris into his squeaky office chair next to the journal. "I didn't realize funds were so tight," he said, looking at coded pages instead of his confidante. "Dria, there's cash left over from those bikers, and you stopped them as much as B-Man did."

Her bearing unchanged but tone more guarded, Dria answered, "The offer's appreciated but I've traveled that road before. No thanks."

"What road?"

"The one where a guy takes care of me forever, until he doesn't. Now I plot my own course and pay my own fare." There was no room for 'what abouts' in the quiet strength of her reply. "Having a magic friend help me turn a profit for his cut, though? That's kosher."

"Time for work, then," Cris gestured to the seat across from the desk and Dria settled after pouring them both a mug of fresh coffee. He turned back to the first page of the journal and studied a complex diagram while his mental 'film' wound across the light beam of his soul.

"Fluff and tut," the older gentleman sitting where Cris had been moments previous growled in a rich, British baritone. "He dares challenge Professor Eldon Arkwright, the Thoth of the Thames?"

"People actually call you that?" Dria asked, smile half-hidden behind her coffee quaff.

"No," Arkwright admitted, perching a pair of pince-nez spectacles on a prominent proboscis and casting deep shadow across his pencil moustache. Luxuriously thick, dark hair topped with iron gray waves hinted at Old-World sophistication confirmed by his Shetland wool cardigan, proper shirt and bowtie beneath. The scholar's thatched eyebrows were tufted white, his cheeks slightly hollow. A slender frame indicated an intellectual who regularly forgot meals while solving conundrums. "But repeated often enough, it might catch on, what?"

Cris watched from an operating theater perspective, away from the workings of what he sensed as a vast, powerful intellect. The film buff caught equations and formulae zipping past but understood none of it. The nosebleed seats were just where he belonged.

"This," Arkwright breathed softly with obvious delight, "is elegantly wrought." Instead of using the pens in Cris's holder, the scholar slowly withdrew a Waterman eyedropper in mottled red and black and uncapped it. Of more use was Cris's legal pad, the scholar writing furiously with his left hand while turning pages with his right and rhythmically scanning each one.

Dria observed the machine-like way he worked, his almost typewritten lettering.

Without slowing he softly shared, "At the top of my notes I've placed a codex. I shall translate the most vital passages, but others may be distilled using it. Mr. McGuffey's constructed a Playfair and Rot hybrid cipher, combined with a grid encryption. Viewing another's work seldom produces envy pangs, but there it 'tis."

"You're saying you've cracked it?"

"Indubitably," the Professor replied, still without looking up or slowing his transcription. "Did your young man not tell you I was the obvious choice for this task?"

"He's not my young man."

"No? Fluff and tut if human hearts are not the most challenging puzzles." Arkwright's brow shelves gathered, and he made a slow tutting sound while translating a final passage. "Hullo. Someone has been naughty."

"What? Who?"

"All here in my notes," Arkwright replied, finishing and tearing out a ten-page sheaf. He turned it and the journal over to Dria after carefully replacing his pen. "See to it Criswell refers to them for guidance. His attention to detail is often inconsistent."

"Sometimes. He knows more about movies and film than anyone, though. Plus, he always remembers a half squirt of butter on my medium popcorn, hold the salt."

Smiling quietly, Arkwright fished a worn tobacco pouch from his sweater pocket, loaded a cherrywood pipe, and lit it. Puffing contentedly, he considered the equation of the young woman sitting across from him. "Indeed, she likes him very much. She's also quite fond of you."

"She?"

"The Silver Lady of the Strand. She admires your... what was the word? Ah! Your moxie, that's it."

"She *does* have a name, then!"

"Certainly," he said, blowing a long plume of smoke upward and away from Dria while she fanned the air

clear, "and while Criswell may be her knight, you, Lady Alexandria, are her court magician."

"Tell me about her."

"Some riddles, my dear, *you* must solve," the scholarly codebreaker gave an enigmatic nod. "Mind you, review my notations together regarding the journal. Until next we meet, adieu dear lady. I am ready, sir knight." Arkwright addressed the last upward to the ceiling before Cris released his chimera and returned.

He pulled out the Imperial whiskey along with two shot glasses, filled one and downed it, gasping, "Forgot about that stinkweed he smokes. In Chapter Four: The Captive Gambit, Arkwright engineers an escape from Venusians using a magnifying glass and a lump of Dunmill standard mixture. Guards thought the tarpaper roof caught fire."

Dria traded the Professor's information parcel for her own draught of spirits and cracked the office window. "He translated parts of the journal, claiming someone 'misbehaved'."

"I sensed that, yeah," Cris agreed, "but he worked so fast I couldn't read it."

Three pages in, the duo lingered on a passage and turned together onto Page 4 for the remainder.

"Wow. Misbehaving's one word for it," Cris said, flopping back in his chair.

"No wonder Catarina accused the lawyer."

"If we want justice served up along with our tidy profit, treading lightly's required."

"Does B-Man have access to anyone in sneakers?" Dria asked and poured another round.

***

Meeting arrangements were made for two days hence, Dria requesting it take place at the McGuffey home with the journal's secrets revealed on completion of their transaction. Pleasantly surprised by the quick turnaround, Catarina arranged transportation for Dria and an associate. The inference was Gherkin the bodyguard, but Cris had settled on going himself.

"The address she gave's a half hour from here. My time limit would end before we got there. Besides, your ley line pattern shows sizeable ones a block east, easy range for summoning B-Man."

"It's not an exact science!" Dria had countered. "What if I'm wrong?"

"We have these," Cris said and doled out Chipmunk's revolver, slipping it into a leather satchel which also held journal notes, and Pageboy's small automatic pistol, a good fit for Dria's purse. They were the most useful things the gunmen carried, their wallets devoid of anything save $5 each and a coffee coupon.

"It's risky," she said, chewing her lower lip.

"We've planned as best we can, and the other alternative's calling the cops, turning over the journal and our notes. Then hope they make a case that'll stick. But-"

"No payday."

"Nope. But if we stick to the plan and get a confession, justice is the house special."

When Catarina's driver pulled up the following night, Cris and Dria were ready; she the exotic, silken-robed soothsayer Lady Alexandria, he's the bookish clerk with a button-down white shirt and dress slacks, carrying the satchel.

The driver, a tall man with shoulder and hip dimensions perfect for a former College Frat President, wore his raven hair short, his male model profile closely shaven, and his expensive suit expertly tailored. He matched his blue LeBaron in stylish sophistication. More surprising was his easy manner and convivial approach as he climbed out, greeted the duo, and opened the back passenger door.

"Good evening! Lady Alexandria, I've heard a lot about you," he offered his hand as she took a seat. "I'm Catarina's attorney, Victor Chadwick." He turned and shook hands firmly with Cris. "You must be Mr. Gherkin. Pleased to meet you."

"Likewise, Mr. Chadwick," Cris said, but didn't correct him.

"Please, call me Vic," he said as the two settled in. He peered around the block, catching sight of the Strand. "I love these older neighborhoods. Wonder if that neon still lights up."

"It does," Cris replied regarding the marquee. Very shortly it would, in fact, when the college kid Cris hired began a showing of Screen Classics' *The Laughing Cadaver*. As F.E. McGuffey's notes claimed, Chadwick was a decent sort and an ally solely responsible for the inventor's change in fortune the final years of his life.

Vic made polite conversation during the ride, mostly questions about the fortune-telling business, before finally pulling into the long driveway of a story-and-a-half brick bungalow. Like other Wickerton homes, the basic design was personalized with awnings and landscaping. Unlike the others, an attached garage crowded against the property line. McGuffey's workshop, Cris surmised, based on pasteboard boxes filled with beakers and flasks. Someone was making room for Catarina's Avanti currently sitting outside.

"Was Mr. Gherkin unable to join us?" the widow asked as Cris and Dria followed Vic into the home's study. Shelves filled with reference materials, science journals, and catalogs lined the walls. Seated behind an antique carved desk, Catarina sported travelling clothes, with an emerald pullover sweater and tan capris. "Or is this the cryptographer you mentioned?"

"Mr. Criswell's responsible for cracking your husband's code," Dria inferred more than affirmed.

"Then we're in your debt," Catarina produced a shimmering smile and held her hand in a manner for clasping or kissing. Cris chose the former.

"Delighted. Not to give the matter a razor tip, but we'd appreciate payment being the first order of business."

Leaning against a nonfunctional grandfather clock, Vic gave Catarina a considerate expression, then a half shrug. "You'll forgive us being skeptical of your solution. Proof, then payment, is more equitable," the widow said.

"We propose a compromise," Dria said in her best Lady-esque tone.

"Produce the cash and leave it on your desk, in view. Then we shall produce your papers before collecting our fee."

"Agreed," Vic nodded and pulled a thick envelope from inside his suit jacket. Opening it, he fanned ten c-notes for Dria's consideration before placing them on the desk edge.

In response, Cris removed the Arkwright notes from his satchel and oriented himself before the banks of shelves. He counted off measured paces, pivoted left of the entryway, and reached for bound volumes of 'Mechanix Today'. Sweeping along the spines, he plucked a tome marked "August 1937 – December 1938". Cris opened the oversized volume to the back cover, carefully removed a false section of binding, and liberated a thin sheet of velum.

Vic and Catarina both craned their necks for a better look at the swatch of onionskin, the lawyer finally asking, "What's that?"

"A safe combination," Dria answered.

With a wry twist of perfectly painted lips, Catarina replied, "Effie had no safe."

Cris returned her knowing smile, added a waggle of brows, and replaced the volume, consulting his notes again before crossing the hallway and entering the lavatory. The medicine cabinet was original to the home, built directly into the wall. Cris opened it, running fingers along the side above the middle shelf where a nail head painted a matching shade of cream jutted slightly. Cris pushed it. The deep click of a released catch sounded, and he raised the entire interior like a pulley window. Steel of a recessed safe gleamed once the cabinet shelves and contents were elevated into the wall. Cris reached inside, carefully spun the combination lock, and opened the well-oiled door silently.

"Here's your husband's final invention, ma'am. Everything you need regarding 'superior silica'," he said, removing the completed patent forms and a folio of supporting notes. He relinquished them to Catarina before pulling the cabinet back into place.

"That's great!" Vic beamed, leading them back to the study. "Soon we'll know exactly what he had in mind and how we can market it."

"That was in his journal," Dria said. "Superior silica is waveguide fibers spun from fused silica in a refining process his patent describes. It'll carry 60,000 times more information than the best copper wire, using light beams."

"It's gonna revolutionize communication," Cris added. "Globally."

"Good lord. Effie, you poor, brilliant, wonderful man," Catarina murmured, clutching the papers tighter as the implication of its worth took hold. Switching the parcel for the payment envelope, she handed Dria her fee and gestured to the threadbare sofa. "This calls for a celebration. Please, join me?"

Cris returned the journal and notes to the leather satchel and situated it between himself and the arm of the couch for easy access. Dria settled next to him, envelope disappearing into her robes.

"I hope Scotch suits everyone," the widow said, tone light as she opened the liquor cabinet revealing a silver tray with four cut glass tumblers. Hearing no objections, she poured the drinks and served her guests. "To Effie," Catarina said, hoisting her tumbler. All parties joined in, but only Vic and the widow drank. Cris swirled his Scotch slowly before putting the glass down, while Dria sniffed and pretended to take a small sip.

"It's a shame, him not seeing his greatest triumph," Cris shared.

"Lady Alexandria," Catarina said after a second sip, "do you think, in the afterlife, Effie knows?"

"Absolutely," Dria replied, arching an eyebrow. "In this life, he suspected you were trying to kill him, Catarina." The widow choked on her drink as Dria went on, "He wrote about it in his journal and I'm sure his spirit's watching your downfall now."

"H-how dare you!"

"It's all here," Cris said, patting the satchel. "The sawed-through basement step he nearly fell down. Penetrating oil residue in his shower. He suspected you'd try poison eventually; equally certain you'd use a common form since no inquest was likely. That's why he wrote it down, counting on Vic finding it and seeing justice done."

Catarina slammed her glass onto the desk, pacing now like a caged lioness. Dria continued, "You he trusted implicitly, Mr. Chadwick. You'd been a friend and a confidante, and the journal should help in filing charges."

"Ma'am," Cris kept an eye on the fraught Catarina, "we're turning the journal and key over to the police. If you'll turn yourself in it may lessen your sentence."

Catarina looked pleadingly at Vic who said, "It wasn't a common substance. In fact, no medical examiner would detect Columbian dart frog poison. Native hunters carefully collect it and coat their darts with the poison. A doctor discovered it this year and I've filed his patents for pharmaceutical applications. He was kind enough to provide me with a sample for analysis. It paralyzes your muscles, eventually stopping your heart for perfect, simulated cardiac arrest. The glass of your tumblers? Sharpened to make tiny cuts, a layer of the toxin spread onto it."

"I *told* you we should have killed them and searched their bodies afterward. Idiot," the widow pointed her manicured fingernail at Vic.

Cris and Dria blinked in unison. McGuffey suspected his wife, but apparently it was tandem homicide. The lucrative fee was a carrot, the gunmen a stick for hurrying them along. Dria's glass bobbed as her equilibrium wavered, contents spilling onto the carpet. The glass followed.

"Hey...what's..." Cris felt it, too, and tried reaching out to his partner as she toppled onto the floor. His arm moved loosely, erratically, and he missed.

Vic shot back, "What if they'd only brought part of the solution?"

The murdering pair argued as Cris tried rising but instead only bent over at the waist, propped against the satchel and couch arm. The stuff acted fast. Cris wondered how long before their systems shut down, and what B-

Man character could be immune to toxins? Even Heracles was half human. He felt a tug at his hair and looked up into Chipmunk's grinning face.

Vic came into view. "We're loading up, reservations out of town. Dispose of the remains where they won't be recovered."

"Our pleasure," Pageboy joined them before Chipmunk let Cris' head drop. "I know of a hog lot, sows that'll eat...anything. Everything. Where's that P.I.?"

"Don't know, but if you hog lot him, we'll add a ten-grand bonus. Thirty total for tying up loose ends, plus the satisfaction of settling old scores," Vic chuckled.

"Perks of the profession," Chipmunk gloated. "Getting paid for getting even."

"Have fun, gentlemen." Vic's footfalls receded down the hall.

"We could save time, feed them to the hogs still alive, then find our detective," Pageboy mused, idly twirling Dria's blonde locks.

"He might even be at the fortune teller's shop waiting for his cut," Chipmunk chortled.

Cris felt Chipmunk grip his shoulder and heft him up when inspiration arrived. Lex Freeman was British prop master on Postern's 1953 children's film *The Whizz-Kid*, an adaptation of daily comic strip "Justin Page, Boy Genius". As with most Postern projects, the budget was laughable. Still, it was decided the hero needed a companion, a walking, talking robot of his own making.

Digging through studio storage, Lex uncovered a suit of plate armor, a mannequin for leaning in a corner during castle scenes. Cannibalizing old recording circuitry and welding the metal shell into a jointed suit, Freeman created Sir Sterling, the Robo-Knight. Cartoon veteran Milton Brake's voice-over gave the 'platinum paladin' personality and Postern posted a rare profit.

The projector bulb glared across Cris's vision, instantly blotted by a scratchy film strip.

"What's up with the lights?" Chipmunk called out, beefy hand on Cris's shoulder. The act of drawing power from the ley lines buzzed the bungalow's wiring and the gunman suddenly jumped back, a bright flash of static electricity jolting his stubby fingers.

"Anow! Declare thyself!" a stout, echoing voice rolled from metallic depths. "Be ye blackguards, scofflaws, or ne'er-do-wells? For assuredly one doth apply." An iron footfall rang across the study, then another. Amidst the flickering lamps, a stylized knight faced them, halberd in hand. Pageboy's eyes narrowed. He pulled his handgun while Chipmunk backed into shelves, further retreat impossible.

Cris felt no ill effects from the poison now but found the automaton a one-speed wonder, slow as he'd been onscreen. Chipmunk finally unlimbered his pistol, both gunmen taking aim at the atomic surcoat insignia painted onto Cris's chest plate while the robot lumbered toward them. They fired and slugs ricocheted off impervious robot armor, one shattering a window, another puncturing Chipmunk's neck.

"Unwise, using slings 'gainst me," Sir Sterling's mechanical voice reverberated. "Have at ye!" The last was levelled at Pageboy as Chipmunk fashioned a doily tourniquet for his neck.

A heavy oaken end table stood between Pageboy and Sir Sterling, Cris imagining how long circumventing it would take. Instead, the Robo-Knight brought his halberd down hard, axe blade splitting the table in twain with a thunderous crack. Exposed, Pageboy emptied his gun at the knight's visor and reloaded. Behind the grille, the glowing armored golem almost seemed to smile at him.

The hired killer stuffed the pistol into his waistband and closed with his attacker, grabbing hold of the halberd to wrench it from Sir Sterling. It didn't budge. "What, ho! Is that thy best, villain?"

Pageboy snarled, gripped the haft tighter, and pulled again. This resulted in Cris yanking the halberd upward, bringing Pageboy onto his tiptoes. The hitman's eyes bugged at the gleaming axe positioned overhead to strike. Instead, Sir Sterling drove the lower part of the haft between Pageboy's demi-pointe legs. When he bent forward in blossoming agony, Cris met him halfway with the halberd's wooden handle, breaking his nose and dropping him to the floor.

Sir Sterling made his cumbersome way to Dria, putting down his halberd and lifting her to her feet. She leaned heavily against the robot in a precarious balancing act and slung her neck back enough to look at the Robo-Knight.

"Hosp-i-tal?"

"Aye, m'lady. We both be in dire need of hospitalers, forsooth. But e'en St. Joseph's, the nearest source o' succor, lies a league distant."

Most b-movie heroes had automobiles, yet most were also poison-susceptible. There must be a faster alternative, Cris reasoned, just before settling on an inordinately chancy one.

"Mayhaps a mad possibility I've devised, yet one with method in't."

Dria's breathing grew labored and she nodded, forcing out, "Glass."

"Brilliant," Sir Sterling answered. "For the alchemists' consideration." He held Dria with one arm, collected her glass, and slipped it into her blousy silken robe. Chipmunk, tying off his makeshift bandage and searching for his gun, was unceremoniously cudgeled by a mailed fist atop his bald head. Stepping over him, Cris and Dria made measured progress to the exit.

Sir Sterling and Dria stepped through the open outer door and onto the stoop as the little gold Avanti sped away. Sharing the stoop were several abandoned suitcases, and Cris surmised Connivers, Inc., upon hearing the gunfire, had fled. Seeing a metal man and one of their victims exiting the house gave them third thoughts; the little coupe, Vic at the wheel, hung a u-ey and pulled back into the drive. Cris pushed his robotic form ahead, taking a position in the middle of that driveway while recalling everything he could about a 1952 Principal serial entitled *Defenders of the Jetstream*. Its hero,

test pilot Rance Rockwell, donned a prototype Turbo-Pack of his own design and became Captain Stratosphere, bane of BEMs and Cold War comrades.

Cris ignored the car sitting at the head of the drive and mentally prepared for Captain Stratosphere. Switch characters, cope with the poison, blast off for a very brief but exciting flight to St. Joseph's. He could do this, he told himself, and he mostly believed it.

Before Cris could change, Vic floored the Avanti and aimed it right for them. "Base dastards!" Sir Sterling's metal larynx reverberated. Balancing Dria, he slung a short sword from his scabbard, flipping it with machine precision toward the oncoming car. Steel severed sidewall, causing an explosive blowout which jerked the auto head-on into a shade tree. Both motorists went through the windshield, Vic impacting the maple limply while Catarina arced over the lawn, then tore across rose bushes a foot short of the house's foundation. She collapsed, moaning through tangles of raw flesh.

Leader film crossed Cris's vision, and Captain Stratosphere replaced the Robo-Knight. Jack Winterbauer, the actor playing Stratosphere, was a gymnastics contender in the 1924 Paris Olympics, and nearly twice Dria's size. Cris felt this work in his favor, felt the poison lessened as he channeled a larger, heavier, and younger world class athlete. He pulled Dria against him, finding the pack's control dial where most belts had buckles. She roused, seeing a flight helmeted fellow in form-fitting black bodysuit with cerulean patterns, a comet emblem blazoned across his chest.

Dria focused, lifted an arm weakly and managed a glancing blow against the comet. "Hanndsss!" she slurred as he fumbled the control dial.

"Sorry! Dria, it's me." Cris slipped the helmet off, forgetting that Jack Winterbauer's profile wouldn't assure her much. Her attention drifted to the tri-tanked apparatus on his back, eyes registering her understanding: This was a Chris chimera, one with a jetpack, and that was his mad plan.

"Noooo..."

"We've gotta get to the hospital, PDQ," he replied, "Have a little faith, willya? Here. You wear the helmet." No sooner was it in place than a gun went off behind them, an incoming bullet deflected by Dria's new accessory. Cris willed Stratosphere's glance back as he flipped two toggles and took hold of the propellent dial. Pageboy held onto the door frame, blood running down his stylish shirt from a broken nose, his pistol leveled at them. Chipmunk almost fell down the stoop, swaying recklessly, but also raised his handgun. With no idea how vulnerable the Turbo-Pack was to hot lead, Cris twisted the dial full throttle and held onto Dria.

Exhaust and flames shot out catching both hitmen in a blistering backwash. Careening upward, Cris worked small gyros made into his gauntlets and looped back, the setting sun's twilight glowed his compass. He last saw the gunmen engulfed in flame, Chipmunk collapsing, Pageboy stumbling blindly into the house.

Cris steered Captain Stratosphere directly toward the hospital, gaining altitude. Dria, once unsure about flying, now hung on with all possible might, Cris's free arm circling her waist. But he felt hinderance, like a film strip jammed, one frame suspended before the projector bulb as its heat melted the celluloid. He was suddenly Cris, nearly unconscious, then Stratosphere again, jetpacking. His control wavered.

He'd never considered the ground flashing by beneath them until he felt the ley power falter. Dropping lower, Cris found proximity helped stabilize his power, but ahead was the expressway, and passing over it so low meant courting vehicular disaster. He reached out mentally, desperately seeking the magnetic pathways below while adjusting his flight path. It was indistinct, intermittent, and then... did he smell popcorn? The force of the Strand's power surged up from the ley lines like a high-pressure hose, tearing through clots of dirt and grass, toppling trees across an empty lot before encasing him. He steadied, shooting Captain Stratosphere higher into the air before the moment passed. The energy bolt tethering him to the magic lines remained, but no longer causing damage and now invisible.

Screeching brakes sounded far below as they came into view of the highway. Altering course again, Cris cut across residential areas, then a suburban ballfield where both teams dropped gloves and bats while watching a flying man rocket overhead. Cris felt the adrenalin and the power surge wearing off, the poison's influence harder to shake. Even gripping the accelerator knob proved difficult. He blacked out for a second, lulled by the shared warmth beside Dria, the fragrant incense of her Lady Alexandria silk scarves. A brush with the top of a stately oak brought him back for two panicked hops over the hospital parking lot and a hard touchdown in shrubs twenty yards from the Emergency Room entrance. Captain Stratosphere replaced his helmet and let go the last frames of the high-flying hero, toxin making Cris's and Dria's final stagger to the ER uncertain. An orderly exiting for a smoke spotted them and called for help. Cris drew the tumbler from Dria's pocket, the one with

■■■■■■■■■■■■■■■■■■■■■■■■■■■■■■■■■■

which, applied in large doses, rendered the amphibian secretion inert. Two days after arriving, Cris and Dria sat in the hospital snack room enjoying their first solid food since the attempt on their lives.

"We need Turquoise Turnpike playing the room," Cris observed, "if their coffee's gonna be as bad as the Kove's."

"That's my workplace you're demeaning," Dria fixed him with a glare, starting on her second cracker packet.

"Both of 'em. You take left-over coffee from the Kove and reheat it at Original Readings, right?" Which earned him a friendly smack on the arm. "Physical violence is not denial."

Dria nibbled a saltine and studied a photo from today's newspaper. The caption read, 'Motorists Report Mystery Flyer' with a short article about a

UFO over Wickerton. The picture was smudgy and dark, snapped quickly by a parent at a Little League game. Without the witness descriptions in the brief article, it was hard telling what it was. With them, it might resemble two humanoid figures. Or not.

"They didn't even get my good side," Dria pouted.

Dr. Leonida Harris drifted in from the nurse's station raising the snack room occupancy to three. Taking a seat at their table, she shared a handwritten note. 'We need to talk,' was printed in the cursive of Detective Captain Harold Siska, watching them impatiently from the hallway. They'd seen his writing before. He held up a knife for them, one with an evidence tag, before stalking off. It looked like a Medieval short sword. Or a movie prop.

"He won't tell me what about, so I say he can wait 'til my patients are released," Dr. Harris said, chuckling good naturedly as ringlets of her salt-and-pepper afro bounced around horn-rimmed glasses. She turned to Cris, dark brown eyes making a slow, non-medical assessment of him. "Wonder why he's in such a snit."

"Policing's a hard job?" Cris offered, taking a sip of retched coffee, now cold.

"He's got a murder case solved, partly thanks to you, but not in a way he understands. He's got one contract killer deceased. Another in the burn ward, under arrest on outstanding assault warrants in California. He's got a de-coded book telling how a recently deceased inventor didn't die from a heart attack but was poisoned. The same poison his suspects, the widow and a lawyer, used on you. She'll stand trial, the lawyer'll spend the rest of his days comatose, staring at ceiling tile. And our Detective Captain believes you're both involved up to your eyeballs."

"What about the Flying Highwayman?" Cris asked, holding up Dria's newspaper. "We've gotta be behind this too, right?"

Unfazed, Dr. Harris pinioned Cris with her intent, intelligent gaze. "He wants notified when I sign your release forms. That'll be in the morning, and I'll tell him. But not until the day after. Sound good?"

"Very good," Dria said. "Thank you."

"Don't thank me too fast. You two may be the only ones not playing someone patently false in all this, but you bug that man."

After she continued her rounds, Cris and Dria exchanged amused looks over Dr. Harris' wording, mostly played against their nervousness.

"She's right, Cris. He won't just accept our story like last time."

"Maybe we'll tell him the truth. Someone he trusts giving him the facts might ease his mind," Cris answered, Dria's expression skeptical. The chimera suddenly replacing Cris was a stony-faced man with short cropped black hair, 1950's suit, and business-like police bearing. "All he wants are the facts, ma'am." Dria snorted and smacked Cris Friday with her newspaper. "Hey, it was a movie, too."

***

∙∙∙∙∙∙∙∙∙∙∙∙∙∙∙∙∙∙∙∙∙∙∙∙∙∙∙∙∙∙∙∙∙∙∙∙

Clyde Hall was raised a TV addict, a comic book fan, a movie buff, and a monster kid. He's worked as a comic shop employee, a snow cone peddler, a cashier, a reporter, a news director, a security officer, and a 911 operator. But he's always been a writer. For writing fun things, he used to rely on Game Mastering RPGs, staffing MUSHes, contributing to APAs, and scripting fan fiction. Then he retired and became a comic book reviewer at www.DoomRocket.com and a contributing writer for Stormgate Press. He's also submitted a story to Brian K. Morris's Doc Saga series.

He and wife Ginny live in Illinois. No, in the southern part of Illinois. No, further; further south than most people think the state goes. He and Ginny cosplay many heroes but raised a daughter who now is a health care hero, a Nurse. They're currently teaching their dog, Quill, to master canine sign language while they train their cat, Casper, not to murder him in his sleep.

6

THE LEGEND OF THE FANCY CAT
By Amy Hale

My footsteps slowed as I approached The Fancy Cat. "Is this the right address?" I whispered as I checked the text message on my phone for the third time. I glanced the building over. It was in rough shape and appeared deserted. A flash of something white in the glass doorway caught my attention and it brought to mind a story I'd once heard. It was something about a figure in white that supposedly haunted places like this. I couldn't remember all the details, but after a while these kinds of folklore blended together. Every town had its legends and ghost stories, and I was sure this one was no different.

I tried the door, relieved to see it was unlocked. I entered and quietly shut it behind me. The inky blackness enveloped me like a blanket. I allowed my eyes to adjust to the dark as much as possible before stepping farther into the building. A blast of cold air rushed past me as if I'd just walked into a commercial freezer.

"What the hell?" I whispered as I rubbed the goosebumps on my arms.

Nothing made sense here. From the outside this building appeared completely abandoned, but from the way my newest client talked this was a thriving club.

My other senses took over, trying to get a reading of any kind from the

spot in the entryway. I couldn't hear the air conditioner or the whizzing of a fan, despite the oppressive heat outside. I detected no humming of electronics. Complete silence rounded out the eeriness of the room.

I groped for my flashlight, concerned that my somewhat frantic client did not meet me at the door as I'd expected.

"Christine?" I called out as I swept my flashlight around the large room. Chairs, tables, a small dance floor, and a stage all revealed themselves under the beam of light. I moved my focus to the bar and a small lamp flickered on, making me jump.

"Hi, you must be Alana March." The woman put a cigarette to her lips and struck a match. It flared brightly before it died down to a small flame. She put the match to the end of her cigarette and took a deep draw before shaking out the flame and releasing a large puff of white smoke.

"Yes. Are you Christine?" I kept my light trained on her and couldn't help the small smile that played on my lips. She looked the part for a place called The Fancy Cat. A blue and white polka dot halter dress hugged the upper half of her curvaceous body like a caress. Her bright red lipstick, rosy cheeks, and dark lashes spoke of freshly applied makeup. She'd fashioned her fiery red hair in a fabulous pin-up style that curled around her face, framing her delicate features. I'd guess she couldn't have been over thirty years old, at most.

She smiled and took another drag. "Yes, thank you for coming so quickly."

She placed the cigarette in an ashtray and moved to the wall, flicking a switch that illuminated the bar area.

I put my flashlight away. "Well, you said it was urgent and you're paying me well." I stepped up to the bar. "Tell me about your problem."

She leaned across the scarred wood and scrutinized me. "You have the signature March eyes – dark and broody."

My eyebrows raised in surprise. "You know my family?"

"I met a relative of yours once. He went by the name of Shorty back then."

I frowned. "I don't recall anyone using that name."

She shrugged. "It's not important. I'm just glad I have a genuine March legacy helping me with this. Ghost hunters with your talent are scarce."

It was my turn to shrug. "It seems to be in my blood. I can't imagine doing anything else."

She shook her head, short red curls swaying with the movement. "I think you're all coo-coo, but right now I'm thankful for it." Her gazed swept over me. "I'll say, it's refreshing to see a woman doing a job that most men can't handle."

I crossed my arms across my chest; one much less ample than the buxom woman in front of me. "I was born with the gift. It's silly to waste it simply because I wasn't born with a male appendage."

She barked out a laugh. "Oh my. I do like you, doll. You say what you think. We need more women like you in the world."

I was about to remark that there are plenty of outspoken women in our day, but she cut me off with a wave of her hand.

"The stage is one of the hot spots."

I turned and faced the area I'd only glimpsed in the dark.

"I'll get the rest of the lights for ya." Christine made her way to the panel on the wall, and I heard the metal clang as she opened an access door. With a few audible clicks, a neon and fluorescent glow bathed the entire club.

I walked up to the edge of the stage and placed my hands on the worn wood planks that made up the floor. I felt an odd vibration that was unlike the normal readings I get when investigating a supposed haunting. It was strong and left an ominous awareness in the pit of my stomach. This would not be an ordinary investigation. But that was fine, because I wasn't an ordinary investigator. The universe had gifted the March family with a keen perception of the paranormal, and it manifested itself in many forms. Previous generations had the ability of sight or even communication with the dead. Some could feel their emotions or experience the trauma once suffered by the spirits. Genetics, or the powers that be, endowed these abilities to future generations; some singularly and others in combinations of some sort or another.

I could feel their trauma. Often it started with the vibrations and as I got closer to the source of the pain, I could sort out what happened. Feeling the trauma itself sucked, but it helped me lead each spirit peacefully to some kind of peace. It wasn't always simple or easy, but I'd always figured out what

they needed. My father had similar gifts. He'd only hunted temporarily, and he hated that I had taken up the family business. His father, Grant March, disappeared when my father was a baby. My grandmother always felt it was the paranormal that took him, though she had no proof. Dad had a close call of his own once and after learning my mother was pregnant with me, decided it was time to retire. My following in the March family footsteps was a constant worry to him.

I focused on the vibrations under my hands, which were overpowering, and I needed a moment to reconnect with myself. I had to push out everything that wasn't me and get grounded before I moved forward to whatever I would soon face. This was going to be powerful, and I'd need my wits about me.

I stepped back and rubbed my now sweaty palms against my jeans. "Christine," I took a cleansing breath. "I need a moment to collect my thoughts. Is there someplace less…"

"Buzzy?" She supplied the word I was looking for.

I smiled. "Exactly. I just need a minute or two."

She waved me to follow her and led me down a dark hallway. She pushed open a door that said OFFICE and ushered me inside. "This room is relatively uneventful in the scope of things."

I smiled. "Thank you."

She stood in the doorway, her perfectly manicured hand on the knob. "Let me know if you need anything else. I have incident reports on the desk, if you want to look through them."

I picked up a folder as I took a seat behind the desk. "Great."

She began to close the door when I called out to her. "Christine, I just wanted to say that I love how retro this place is. I rarely notice these things, but your club feels authentic."

She inclined her head in thanks. "I appreciate that. We've tried to keep it in the style of the original owners."

"Would there be any original artifacts in the building? Anything I can pull a reading from, possibly?"

She smiled widely. "Absolutely. A good portion of this building still holds the original club furnishings that were used when it opened in 1949."

"Perfect." I looked at the paperwork in my hand as she closed the door behind her. My mind reeled with the possibilities. Any original objects could hold energy from their previous owners. Was this poltergeist attached to one or more items in the club? To stop the haunting, I'd first need to know the source of the problem.

The pages before me held eyewitness accounts of activity. Items disappearing, objects being thrown across the rooms, patrons being touched or shoved, and a few accidents being blamed on the ghost or ghosts. But at the bottom of the stack were the truly disturbing facts. Several people had gone missing, last seen coming into this club. If it'd just been a certain type of clientele or during a specific time period, I could chalk it up to human foul play and shady characters. But these files showed disappearances that were spread out over decades, with no obvious connections between them. It was bizarre at the least.

There were twenty-two missing: the most recent just last year. The earliest noted was in 1951.

A loud thump on the door startled me. I bolted out of the chair and dropped the files back on the desk. "Christine? Is that you?"

All was silent for a moment, then another loud thud against the door, this time shaking it on its hinges. Something slid down the wood on the other side, followed by dragging sounds that disappeared down the hall. A chill ran up my spine. That didn't sound paranormal. It sounded like someone being hit and hauled away.

"Christine?" I called again, louder this time. Still no answer.

"Damn it." This was why my dad always nagged me about carrying a gun. Not all threats that I'd hunted ended up being paranormal, although they were usually harmless, but this time I wasn't so sure.

I looked around the room for something, anything, I could use as a weapon. A wooden baseball bat sat on a shelf, a signature scrawled across it I didn't recognize. I sighed. "It's probably valuable, but it'll have to do."

I removed it from its resting place, then gripped it firmly in my hands and swung it a couple of times for good measure.

With one hand on the knob, I slowly turned and pulled the door open. It was no small wonder I didn't have splinters in my palms considering the death grip I had on the bat.

beam down the hall and into the primary room. It was dark, just as before I'd entered the building and Christine was nowhere around.

"Christine! Where are you?" I took a couple of tentative steps toward the front of the building. "Christine?"

I saw a faint glow emanate from the dancehall and then grew in intensity, as if someone were slowly turning a dimmer switch to high. The light was blinding for a moment, and I had to cover my eyes with the crook of my arm.

When the blinding flare died down, I lowered my arm and tucked my flashlight into its case once more. The sound of voices pierced the silence. A lot of voices.

I quietly made my way to the growing ruckus, surprised to find a room half full of people. Bodies occupied the bar, the dance floor, and the tables. There was a band on the small stage, and they were taking up their instruments. Within moments they were in the first strains of a song.

I stepped into the room and took a moment to register what I was seeing. Christine was behind the bar, serving drinks as fast as she could make them.

I pushed past a small group and slipped behind the bar. "Christine. I've been yelling for you. What is going on?"

She smiled. "Sorry, doll. Business for the night is just ramping up."

I looked around. "When did all these people arrive?"

She poured a beer in a glass. "While you were studying in my office."

I cautiously peered into the hallway, looking in both directions before I stepped onto the polished wood planks of the floor. I released the door and reached for my flashlight, sending a

I frowned. "How is that possible? I was only in there a few minutes."

She shook her head as she slid the drink to a patron. "That's something else I forgot to warn you about – time slips. We have them often in here."

Time slips? I'd heard of them but had yet to experience one. Well, until now, I guess.

I hitched my thumb behind me, indicating the hallway I'd just left. "There was a loud bang on the door, then another and some other weird sounds. I called out to you, but you didn't answer. I got a little worried."

She turned to face me. "Thumps and bangs are part of the trade, right? You got spooked by one and you call yourself a ghost hunter?"

I chuckled. "You would have a point if this were normal bump in the night sounds, but this sounded very human. I was afraid someone had hurt you." I handed her the bat.

Christine smiled as she placed it on a shelf near the floor, then faced the bar once more and took some money from a guy in a pinstripe suit. She winked at him as she tucked the cash into a small box under the counter.

I turned and studied the patrons. They were all dressed in 1950s attire. "Wow." I looked back at her. "You guys take this theme seriously."

She downed a shot of something and then smiled at me once more. "Indeed, we do. In fact, you are the only person in this bar allowed to break the dress code right now."

I ran a hand through my short brown hair. "I appreciate the leniency. It's kinda hard to do my job in a dress.

Speaking of hard to do my job, how am I supposed to investigate with all these people in here?"

She shrugged. "It'll calm down soon."

"I should have come on a night when you are closed."

Christine shook her head. "We're never closed."

"After hours then." I replied.

"This bash will slow down soon enough, and you'll be free to explore all you like." She poured a drink of something amber in a shot glass. "In the meantime, have a drink. Get to know the locals a bit."

"You're kidding, right? I need to keep my head clear. I can't drink on the job." Her offer shocked me.

She shook her head and pushed the drink at me. "One shot."

I took the glass and peered inside. "What is it?"

"Bourbon." She poured herself another shot. "Take your shot and then maybe go meet some regulars. Do some interviews. Everyone in here has a story to tell."

I gazed around the room, unsure this was the wisest course of action. But I knew I couldn't investigate with a building full of people, so I might as well get all the information I could until things calmed down.

Christine must have noticed my hesitation. "Don't be a square. They won't chat with you unless they think you're one of us."

I frowned, looking down at the glass. "This is against my better judgement." I tossed back the drink, the bourbon burning my throat as it slid down and warmed my stomach. I felt like I could breathe fire.

"Wow, that's some powerful stuff." I muttered.

A man with an expensive watch and gold cufflinks raised his glass to me. "Indeed, it is. That's how you know it's the good stuff." He looked at Christine. "She's a fuzzy duck." He looked me over and whistled. "But what a classy chassis."

I glanced down and my skin-tight jeans and white tank top, then narrowed my eyes at him. "Excuse me?"

Christine motioned for me to lean into her. "Play along. Like I said, this is a themed club, and we are one hundred percent authentic in every way."

I sighed and resigned myself to some misogyny for the evening. "Okay, who should I talk with first?"

Christine smiled and addressed the man who'd just talked about me as if I were a piece of meat. "Hey Charlie, this cookie wants to ask you a few questions about the club."

He smiled widely. "This should be a gas! What would you like to know?"

I sat on a stool next to him and reached out to shake his hand. "I'm Alana."

His palm touched mine, and the very room spun before settling down around us. It was unnerving. "Charlie. Charlie Branch."

Something nagged at the back of my mind. Where had I heard that name before?

I tried to shake it off. "So, tell me Charlie, how long have you been coming to The Fancy Cat?" I studied his face as I set a tape recorder on the bar.

He looked at the recorder, then at Christine before finally settling his gaze on me once more.

"Feels like I've been here forever." He chuckled. "But I guess I've been coming to this club every night since I was nineteen."

The rest of his words faded into the background as I remembered why he seemed so familiar. He had a case file in the office. He was the first missing person in 1951.

***

I stood so fast I knocked the bar stool out from under me. It clattered to the floor loudly and all eyes turned on me. Even the band had stopped playing.

"Are you okay, doll?" Christine asked.

I shook my head. "This isn't right." I murmured and trained my eyes on Charlie. "You can't be here. You haven't aged a day since..." I choked on the year I meant to say.

Charlie smiled and straightened his tie with pride. "Why, thank you. You're a bit of a looker yourself."

I rubbed a hand over my face and whispered. "He must be a spirit."

I turned to talk to Christine, but she had moved. I searched the room and found her chatting with another customer near the stage.

I looked at Charlie. "Will you stay here so we can communicate more? I just need to speak with Christine a moment."

He inclined his head and raised his glass to me.

"Thank you." I hurried across the room to where she stood.

She smiled down at a couple sitting at the table, and I heard her say my name. "Ah, here she is now."

I flashed the couple a quick smile, but far too preoccupied by my thoughts to do more. "I really need to chat with you."

She placed a hand on my arm. "Sure thing, just give me a moment."

The band began to play once more, and I jumped at the sound. I stood to the side of the stage and leaned against the wall. I've communicated with ghosts before, but never in such stark three dimensions. It was truly as if Charlie was sitting there in front of me. Christine saw him too, so what did that mean? Was she gifted too? Or was he that insistent on making his presence known?

She interrupted my thoughts. "Okay, I'm free now. I was just telling Fred and Macy why you were here. What can I do for you?"

I grabbed her hand and led her out of the busy room and down the darkened hallway.

"You know about Charlie, right?" The words pushed past my lips so fast I almost stumbled over them in my excitement.

She glanced behind her at the busy room. "Charlie?"

"You know he's one of the missing, don't you? He's the first name in the file, missing since 1951."

"You're pulling my leg." She laughed.

"I'm not. Not at all. I'll show you." I took a few more steps into the hall and opened the office door. The light was still on inside, so I waved her to follow me.

When I reached the desk, the files were still where I'd dropped them. I shuffled through the folders until I found the one that contained Charlie's information.

I held it out to her. "See?"

She took it from my hands and opened it slowly, as if she feared what she might see. Her eyes widened as she scanned the information. She paled slightly, then swayed a moment.

I rushed to her side to steady her. "Are you okay?"

She nodded and tossed the file on the desk. "Yes, I'll be okay. I'm just a little... surprised."

"It's understandable. I mean, holy cow! We have a class A EVP and a full-bodied apparition working in tandem to communicate using only the power in our surroundings. No equipment required. Can you believe that!" I know my excitement was probably over the top for most people, but this was pretty much unheard of in the parapsychology community. I needed to capture it on video, if at all possible.

Christine still appeared shaken up by the revelation.

"Do you think Charlie would object to my videoing our conversation?"

She frowned.

I jumped in to assure her. "I would be totally respectful. Nothing provoking or upsetting if I can help it."

She backed out into the hall; her eyes still trained on me. "I need some air. I'll be back soon."

Before I could ask her more about Charlie, she'd gone. It then dawned on me; how could Charlie have been a regular patron for so long without her noticing? It made little sense. She'd said he was one of her regulars.

I grabbed Charlie's folder and tucked it under my arm, then grabbed my cell phone and hit record. As I walked down the hall toward the noisy club, I added commentary.

"I'm making my way to the active part of the club. The owner, Christine, has been regularly serving and communicating with a man named Charlie, who disappeared from this club in 1951. All this time she did not realize he was a spirit. This is unprecedented."

I reached the room and looked around at the active club patrons. I put the phone to my mouth so the mic could easily pick up my voice over the music. "It amazes me that Charlie makes himself so visible during such busy times during the club. He seems to enjoy joining in the festivities. I'm going to talk to him now."

I approached the bar and sat next to him once more. "Hey Charlie, do you mind if I record you on this?"

He moved his eyes to mine. "Record?"

I'd forgotten that he lived in a time where phones still required landlines and bulky camera equipment were integral to filming. "I have a small device right here…" I held up my phone. "This allows me to record audio and video of you… like a movie." I grabbed the digital recorder I'd left in my haste. "This one is audio only." I turned it off.

His eyes narrowed as he leaned in close to the phone. "I suppose."

I propped it up on the bar using a small stand I carried with me and made sure I focused it on him.

"Please tell me your name." I asked.

He smiled at me. "Charles Branch, but my friends call me Charlie."

I glanced down at the screen to assure the video was clear. "And when were you born, Charlie?"

He wagged a finger at me as if I were a naughty child. "Such a question. Would you like it if I asked you that?"

I chuckled. "Good point. How about this, tell me what year it is now?"

He swirled his drink in his glass, the amber liquid sloshing up the sides of the expensive-looking crystal. "Look around you, Doll, it's 1951."

I nodded. "Of course." I straightened in my chair. "And what is the last thing you remember, before coming here tonight?"

He opened his mouth, then closed it again. "I… I remember nothing before tonight." He frowned. "I only remember here."

He looked down at his drink, then back up at me. With eyebrows drawn together, and lips pressed in a tight, disapproving line, he disappeared right before my eyes.

I picked up the phone and switched to the forward-facing camera. "Did you see that? Simply amazing!" I couldn't contain the elation at catching such a unique spectral image.

I stopped recording and turned to study the rest of the customers in the club. How many others sitting here amongst the living were actually spirits reliving their glory days? But I still didn't understand one thing. If the spirits were like Charlie, why did Christine need someone to fix her problem. It all seemed pretty innocuous, to be honest.

Then I remembered the noise I heard outside the office door, that ominous feeling in the pit of my stomach, and the unusual vibrations that radiated from the stage. This situation might appear harmless on the surface, but my gut told me something sinister was behind it all. I'd allowed myself to get wrapped up in the excitement of the hunt and forgot my place. I was here to do a job, and I needed to focus on that purpose.

I scanned the room for Christine, but she was nowhere in sight. She'd mentioned getting air. My bet was, she'd stepped out the back door for a moment. I quickly made my way down the dark hallway, my flashlight leading the charge. When I saw the door with the exit sign, I gave it a shove.

It didn't budge.

I shoved again, but nothing.

I put my shoulder into it while simultaneously pushing against the bar. It was as solid as a brick wall. Not a hint of movement.

"Christine," I shouted. "Are you out there?"

I worried maybe she'd gotten locked outside.

No reply from the other side, or elsewhere for that matter.

I gave the door one more shove, then walked back to the office. I pushed it open to find Christine sitting at the desk, her face in her hands. Her shoulders shook as deep sobs racked her body.

I softly closed the door behind me and I once again tucked away my flashlight. "Christine? Are you okay?"

She raised her eyes to mine and dark lines of mascara had marked a trail down her cheeks, giving her the look of something out of a horror movie. She shook her head slowly, but her eyes were unfocused, as if she were lost in thought.

"I loved him. My husband, Aikyan, is a brute and a tyrant. But Charlie.... He gave me a reason to smile, ya know? I can't believe he's dead."

I stepped closer and put a hand on her shoulder. "I know it's hard to fathom. He's so very... lifelike."

She sniffled loudly, and I reminded myself that this was a delicate situation. Weird, but delicate. She needed kindness in this moment.

"Well, if it helps any, I think he was kinda sweet on you as well." I wasn't sure if that was the right thing to say, but it seemed to cheer her up a little.

Her smile trembled, but it had replaced the frown she wore moments earlier. "It is nice to think that maybe I brought him some happiness, too."

I leaned against the filing cabinet. "I have to ask you a couple of questions."

She nodded as she reached for a tissue box on the desk.

"Do you think there are more like Charlie out there?"

She shrugged. "It's certainly possible."

I chewed my lip and took a moment to figure out how to best phrase my next question. "Christine, you have at least one friendly spirit. I've yet to see anything malevolent, despite these weird sensations I'm picking up on. Outside of the missing persons cases, why did you bring me here?"

She looked up at me, and her red-rimmed eyes were pleading. "Make it stop. Make it all stop. Set them free."

"You mean help the spirits move on?" I was still a little confused.

"You can't really help them do that. Only a psychopomp can do that. But you can convince him to take them!" She grabbed my arm with both her hands and she frantically clutched at my skin. "You have to make him see reason."

I pulled from her grasp. "Him? Who are you talking about?" I stepped back. "Why are you talking about mythology? Psychopomps ferry the dead from this world to the next in stories and fables. Surely you aren't suggesting they are real."

She stood. "Why do you doubt it? You just saw Charlie and that defies logical explanation."

"True." I countered. "But our bodies are energy, there's some science to back up the possibility of ghosts." I shook my head. "I've never heard of someone encountering an entity from mythology."

She chuckled sadly. "You are in for quite a night, doll." She lit a cigarette and looked at it before taking a second drag. "Not everything you see tonight will be explained by science or logic."

I released a humorless laugh. "No kidding. So, who is this psychopomp you think I need to deal with?"

She blew out a puff of smoke and opened her mouth to speak, but quickly snapped it shut.

"Christine!" A menacing, deep voice called for her from outside the door.

She quickly snuffed out her cigarette. "My husband is here."

The door flew open with a force that caught me off guard.

A large man loomed in the doorway. His frame filled the space and his eyes were dark, like pools of ink. His perfectly slicked hair parted on the side, not a single black strand out of place. "Who is she?" His eyes narrowed as he looked me over.

"Aikyan, this is the girl I was telling you about. Alana March." Christine offered him a shaky smile. "She's gonna help with the troublemakers in the club."

He looked me up and down once more. "This wisp of a thing?"

I flashed him a confident smile. "I'm much stronger than I appear."

He smiled, but his mouth forgot to tell the rest of his face to relax. "Well, you are a March. I guess we'll see how you hold up."

He walked out and Christine blew out a shaky breath. "Sorry."

I waved it off. "I can handle tough guys." My voice didn't sound as confident as I'd intended. Aikyan instantly made me uncomfortable, and I wasn't sure if it was because he was such an intimidating figure or because I suspected he treated Christine terribly. Maybe it was both.

"He knows of my family as well?" I asked.

She nodded. "He also knew Shorty."

I shook my head. "This is without a doubt the weirdest case I've been on."

She briefly put a hand on my arm as she stepped past me and out into the hall. "Probably, but I believe in you."

She disappeared down the hall, and I took a moment to piece it all together in my head. Overbearing husband, emotional affair, and Charlie's death are obviously just scratching the surface of the negative energy in this building. Those things could feed something darker. Possibly the psychopomp, if Christine is to be believed. But how do I know who this mysterious ferryman is?

I walked back into the busy primary room. Couples were dancing on the small floor space, while others looked on and chatted animatedly. I studied a few of them, hoping to see some hint of who is human and who is spirit. There appeared to be no difference, just as Charlie had presented no hints. It was baffling.

A tap on my shoulder alerted me to a young blonde woman in a flared skirt and tight shirt. She had big blue doe eyes that would have looked ridiculous on anyone else, but on her they seemed to fit perfectly.

She smiled shyly. "Are you the investigator?"

I nodded "I'm Alana March."

Her smile broadened. "I'm so happy to meet you. My name is Patty." She looked around. "Can we talk a moment?"

I nodded and motioned for her to have a seat at the table next to us. Once we were both comfortable, I pulled my phone out of my pocket and set it to record. She looked at me with alarm.

"No, don't worry. I'm just recording so I can make sense of all these events once I get home."

"That's what I need to talk to you about. You aren't going home. None of us are."

"What?" She came across as a little melodramatic.

Patty waved to someone across the room, and he approached the table. He wore slacks and a long-sleeve shirt that spoke of blue-collar work. His attire didn't fit in with the rest of the classy customers in The Fancy Cat.

The man sat down, never taking his eyes off of me. Of average height, with dark eyes and hair, he had slim, sharp facial features. He looked vaguely familiar to me, but it wasn't from the files in the office. This was a recognition that I felt in my bones. He reached across and took my hands in his. I couldn't seem to pull from his grasp. I didn't really want to.

"I bet you look just like your mother." He sighed. "Although I certainly see dominant March features."

I frowned. "I'm sorry. You two aren't making much sense to me right now. How do I know you?"

He released my hands and for the first time I realized that my skin had been freezing under his touch. I rubbed my hands to bring the warmth back into them.

"I'm sorry. I'm being so rude. It's just... I never thought I'd see you face to face." He rubbed a hand over his stubble. "Although this is the last place you should be, Alana."

I scoffed. "Now you sound like my father."

"I'm glad to see he grew up with some sense then." The man frowned at me. "Patty told you everything?"

Patty shook her head. "I didn't really get to," she said. "I thought it'd be better coming from you. You are her grandfather, after all."

Taken aback, I stuttered, "You can't be. You're far too young. And my grandfather disappeared in 1958."

My hands shook.

"It's nice to finally meet you, Alana. I'm Grant March, but folks used to call me Shorty."

Grant March was born in 1934. He married my grandmother, Alice Brown, in 1956. In 1958, while my grandmother was carrying their first child, Grant disappeared. That child, my father, Austin March, grew up without his father and blamed Grant's extracurricular activities on that absence. My father hated ghost hunting. It's why he was so disappointed I'd picked up the family business once I realized I had the March family gifts.

I sat stunned for a moment. "Did you disappear after coming here?"

He nodded. "They called me to investigate, just as you were. I wish I'd had a way to warn you beforehand, but there was no way. We are kept on a tight leash here."

"What happened to you?" I could hardly believe my eyes or ears.

"I can't remember. None of us can. And that's part of the rub. We know we are dead, and we know we should move on, but we can't."

"The psychopomp?" I struggled to believe it.

"Exactly. He won't show us the way. He won't take us across."

I rubbed my temples. This was all too much.

"I don't know why," his voice was full of remorse. "But I never left his club. And I'm afraid that you won't either unless you can fix this mess."

I held up a hand. "Wait, so you are saying they tricked me into coming here?"

The band stopped playing. The instant silence was palpable. Then a low roar began to build. It traveled on the tips of a wind that rushed through the club and slammed into my chest. I felt his presence before I saw it. A dark, looming figure that grew as it moved.

I stood as it migrated closer, its presence filling the room with a heavy sorrow. I realized I was the only person surprised by this entity. Everyone else sat quietly, almost in reverence. Then I realized: everyone in this club was likely a spirit. Charlie and Grandpa Grant never aged, and they likely died in this club. They appeared as real as any person you'd meet on the street as real as all the other patrons who looked at this entity as if it were a regular part of their night. They'd all seen it before. They'd all lived with it for decades.

I scanned the room and my eyes met Christine's. She looked terrified, and it made me wonder what part she played in this nightmare.

The roar died down and the entity settled in front of me, hovering just off the floor. The voice that I heard was familiar. Deep and growling. It was Aikyan.

"You are now one of my subjects, Alana. Accept your fate and use your skills as a guardian from those who would seek to destroy all we have built." He changed into a human form and reached his hand out to me.

"Are you nuts?" I shouted. "I'm not here to be one of your henchman or slaves. I do not agree to this, and I'm guessing none of these other souls did either."

His dark eyes transformed into an inferno, the irises roiling like the sun. "You will not defy me." His voice boomed as it echoed off the walls.

Christine stepped forward. "Could we give her a few moments to take it all in?"

He turned his face to hers. "You like this one?"

She nodded. "She'll be a gas to have around. But this is a lot to swallow, even for a ghost hunter."

Aikyan stared me down. "Think before you speak again, girl." Then he vanished.

I grabbed Christine by the arm and pushed her into a chair. "You have a lot of explaining to do."

She wiped away a tear. "I'm so sorry. He... Every couple of years he makes me lure someone here. The new life force rejuvenates his powers. Kind of like getting your coffee topped off in a I." She cleared her throat. "This time he wanted someone unique. Someone that could not only give him extra energy but also have the skills to help Grant here fight off anyone that would try to change the order of things. We've had a couple of teams come in before,

without permission, trying to clear the place."

I turned to my grandfather. "You help them?"

He shook his head. "Not at first, but when Aikyan threatens to consume the souls of those you've grown to love, it's harder to say no."

I glared at Christine. "You should have been an actress. Those tears for Charlie back in the office were very convincing."

She shook her head vigorously. "No, those weren't fake. Aikyan wipes our memories every night. We forget we are dead. We forget how we died. We forget almost everything but who we are allowed to be right now. I had honestly forgotten that I'd lost Charlie in 1951."

"So it's true. Everyone in here is dead?"

All three of my tablemates nodded in unison.

"Well, I'm not dead and I'm going to get us all out of this." I did not know how, but I couldn't give up.

Christine glanced at Grant and Patty, a look of guilt and remorse crossing her features.

Grant cleared his throat. "You aren't completely dead... yet. But you're very close."

I whirled on him. "Excuse me?"

He grabbed my hand. "Let me show you something." He pulled me through the crowd of tables and down the hallway. There was a supply room at the end of the hall, near the exit door. Grant pushed it open and flipped on the light.

I gasped and stumbled back into the wall behind me. There, on the floor, was my own body, covered in dried blood from an injury. I was breathing, but barely.

"How is this possible?" I shouted.

Christine stepped close to me. "That thump you heard when you were in the office? That actually happened before we walked through that door. Aikyan hit you over the head, then dragged you into the supply room. The bleeding stopped some time ago, but you haven't eaten or drank anything in almost two weeks. It won't be long now."

"Two weeks? I've only been here a few hours." I stared at my mostly lifeless body.

Christine put a hand on my shoulder. "I told you, time passes differently in here."

My eyes closed. I had to figure out how to save myself, release the others, and get out of this building. I was running out of time.

My heart raced as I pushed past them and shut myself in the office. I scanned the bookshelves for anything that might be helpful. Not that I expected to find a grimoire or other such tomes on how to defeat a mythological entity, but I'd hoped I might see something that sparked an idea. There was nothing.

Then I remembered my phone. I dashed from the office and ran to the table where I'd sat with Grant. Patty was still there, staring at the stage as if the musicians enthralled her. They'd once again started their show. I snatched the phone and sat in the chair next to her.

Frantically, I pulled up the search engine and felt relief that it still worked. At least I hadn't been gone long enough to have my phone and internet turned off. I typed in the address of a secret website where many paranormal investigators shared information. If there were information on something as off the wall as a psychopomp, they'd have it.

I typed what I was looking for in the search bar. The little wheel spun in circles and I prayed I'd find something that helped.

Patty leaned over to see what I was doing. "What's that?"

I glanced at her before studying the screen again. "It's the internet. Kind of like an encyclopedia where you can look up anything, except it's not always accurate."

Her eyebrows rose in surprise. "Really? That's amazing."

I saw a post made by a guy named Raymond Hartness. He was a demonologist, but he'd spent some time studying mythology in college. He shared random, unsubstantiated stories that had been passed down to him through the years, but there seemed to be no concrete answers there. As I scrolled down the posts, one caught my eye. A girl fairly new to the trade had come in contact with a spirit that was domineering, not allowing other spirits to pass on. It turned out that the entity was simply lonely. She didn't have an answer, but she had a cause. Maybe that issue was in play here as well. It was something to consider.

I thought about Christine. She'd said Aikyan was her husband. I needed her to explain that relationship to me.

I left the table and approached the bar where Christine was again slinging drinks and looking distracted. I noticed then that she looked tired. She was doing her job, both at the bar and for Aikyan, and it seemed she didn't want the responsibilities anymore.

"I need to speak with you. Now." I gave her a pointed look.

She nodded, passed a scotch across the bar and then followed me as we went back to her office. As we approached the door, I faintly recalled being hit on the head. It was odd how those little bits of memory were popping in now.

We entered, and I shut the door behind me. I turned to face her and leaned against the desk. "You said Aikyan is your husband. He's not human, so how does that work?"

She took a deep breath and cleared her throat. "Well, technically he's not, but he inhabits the body of the man who was my husband. To save his soul from the underworld, I had to agree to Aikyan's plan. The form Aikyan is wearing is Hank. He's not much better than Aikyan, to be honest, but he's still my husband, ya know? I couldn't refuse. Does Hank deserve paradise? Probably not, but I couldn't make that call."

I understood. My father could be overbearing, and we didn't really get along, but he was still my dad. I'd do what I needed to save him.

"So Aikyan sends your husband to paradise as long as you agree to his plan?"

She nodded.

Why does he need a body? Why does he want to keep people here? Why is he so determined to build his own community here?"

She shrugged. "He likes to go out in the actual world, so he uses Hank. As for the others, he's never said."

I chewed on a ragged fingernail as I processed what little information I now had. "Do you think he's lonely?"

She looked up suddenly. "You know, that would make sense. When he first showed up here, he masqueraded as a customer, wearing some other body he got from who knows where. He always wanted to talk. Said he had no family. That kind of thing. And to be honest, I think he cares for me, in his own way."

"So, he's building his own community or family." I shook my head. "But he's a ferryman. He's supposed to be helping people crossover. You'd think that job would keep him busy."

"Only for moments at a time." A voice softly interjected.

Aikyan materialized before us. His deep voice was soft and sad. "Time doesn't work for me the way it does for humans. What seems like days to you is years to me." He frowned. "Those seconds when a person passes from life to death are quick and fleeting. I'm tired of being an errand boy for the gods. I'm choosing my own path. I'm making my own kingdom."

"Aikyan," I began. "I understand it has to be lonely. I also understand that it sucks to be forced into servitude. But what you are doing to these souls is no better. They need their freedom. They have loved ones who have long passed that miss them and expected to see them when they crossed over. None of us are yours to enslave this way."

He shook his head.

"Let us go, then you can choose whatever existence you want without guilt."

"I cannot. I not only require you all for companionship, but I need the life-force to exist on this plane. With each new soul, I gain more strength and the ability to stay on this side of death."

"Please, Aikyan. You must let us go." I begged.

"No. Never!" He roared. "I warn you now, human. Do not make this worse for yourself. If you meddle in my affairs, I will send you to the underworld! Remember your place!"

I swallowed hard. He was scary and immortal. I didn't know how to fix this.

He glared at me, then disappeared.

Christine frowned. "I guess that ends that discussion."

"No, it doesn't." I regained a little of my courage once he left. I stomped out the door and down the hall. "We can change this. We have to change this."

I gathered Charlie, who was once again at the bar, with Christine, Patty, and Grant.

"If we want our memories and our freedom, we have to fight back." I stated.

"Fight back? How?" Patty looked uncertain at the idea.

"You. I mean we." I corrected myself. "We are what feeds his strength.

We keep him going. If we confront him and take back what is ours, maybe we can weaken him enough to send him back."

Christine spoke up. "I've lived with him for a long time. You are correct. Souls are his strength, but also his weakness."

I thought a moment, then smiled. "I have an idea, but we have to get everyone in on it."

Grant nodded. "Whatever you need. I have no doubt everyone here will be willing to help."

I explained the plan, then we set to work.

I moved to the stage and examined the curtain that hung behind the musicians. I grabbed the rope attached and pulled the fabric up and out of the way. Christine brought me a can of white spray paint from my bag and I shook it violently before removing the cap.

The musicians beside me all nodded in recognition of the plan, but never stopped playing. I worked behind them, using one of their stools as a ladder, to paint a large sigil on the brick behind them. It was a seal I remembered seeing in an old book a friend of mine had. He said it could trap almost any spirit, if the circumstance were right. I prayed he was correct. We had little to lose by trying.

I lowered the outer curtain once more to hide the seal and then slowly enacted my plan.

I started with Charlie. We walked down to the hall where my body lay, and I kneeled down close. I looked myself over, praying this would actually work. Then I touched my head, and it all went black for a moment.

My eyes flickered open and my head throbbed. It felt as if I had sand in my throat. Every muscle in my body felt like mush. I weakly pushed myself up on my elbows and looked at Charlie standing over me.

He smiled at me. "It's been fun, doll, but I do hope to never see you again."

I grinned. "I hope so too, Charlie."

He put both hands on my shoulders and slammed into me, knocking me back to the floor.

I gasped in gulps of air, then sat up straight. I felt stronger.

I could hear Charlie in my head. "I've never possessed anyone before. It feels... weird."

I laughed. "You think it's weird, try being on this side of it."

"Go get the rest and make Aikyan pay." His words reverberated through my body.

I stood on trembling legs and shuffled my way down the hall until I reached the bar. I leaned against it and looked around the room.

Christine nodded and handed me a small glass of water. "Sip it slowly. Your body is struggling right now."

I did as she said, resisting the urge to gulp it all down in one swallow. I was so thirsty.

Patty approached me next. "Thank you." She grabbed me and held me close, her spirit absorbing into me.

My body once again felt a small surge of strength.

The other spirits began to casually line up in front of me, each taking a moment to thank me before possessing my frail frame.

Twenty-four spirits possessed me, and I was almost as strong as the moment I walked through those doors. We had four left. Grant and Christine wanted to be last in case I needed help.

"What are you doing?" Aikyan's voice boomed. It seemed to come from everywhere. A young lady named Sara ran to me and without hesitation took her place with the others as I gripped the table to steady myself.

Aikyan appeared before me. His expression thunderous. His form not quite solid, but not all spirit. "You dare defy me!" Icy wind whipped around me in a gale to rival the darkest storm.

Once again, his gaze turned to fire and I could feel heat coming off him in waves. He moved closer, and I pushed a table over to put a small shield between him and I, should I need it.

"I told you, Aikyan. You have to let everyone go." I shouted above the noise. "This isn't right!"

He growled, and it sounded like something from the pits of hell itself. "I am an immortal. You have no hope of winning this battle. Give up now or you will be punished!"

Another spirit named Jack slipped up behind me and wrapped his arms around me, quickly joining his friends. My body jolted in response. I opened my eyes to a rush of power I'd never experienced before.

When I opened my mouth, it wasn't my voice, but the voice of all of us speaking at once. "We are tired of your enslavement. We take back the power you stole from us, and we banish you to an eternal torment."

He laughed, the wind stopped, and the entire room went dark. "You have no power. You are puny, pathetic human souls with no value."

Anger welled up inside us. It spilled forth, the violence of it creating a scream unlike any mortal had ever made. "Our souls, human souls, are the most valuable thing in existence and you do not own them anymore."

Grant rushed Aikyan, hoping to distract him while Christine attempted to merge, but Aikyan was too fast. He grabbed Grant by the throat and held him high in the air.

"I will consume your grandfather, right before your eyes, Alana." Aikyan's mouth opened wide as if to follow through with his threat.

"Aikyan, darling!" Christine called. "Please come to me." She stood on the stage, now empty of everything but her and the instruments, that had been pushed to one side. "I know the lack of souls weakens you, but let me help you. Together we can defeat her. Like in the beginning."

He lowered Grant and looked at Christine. "You have always been a faithful servant. When we destroy these Marches, we will rebuild anew."

"Yes, my love. We will start over and build an even better kingdom for you." She held out her hand to him.

That's when I realized he was truly in love with Christine. I could use it. While he looked at her, I made my move, grabbing grant around the waist and dragging him with me to the floor. I didn't have time to say goodbyes, but

I could hear him in my head, his voice a soothing balm. "You have this, Alana. You have already won. Just get him on the stage."

Realizing he'd lost Grant, Aikyan moved quickly to Christine. But I could see that he was losing steam. For all his bluffing, Aikyan was weaker with each soul I stole from him.

When he reached the stage, he moved to touch Christine. She jumped back and let go of the rope she'd been holding behind her back. The outer curtain fell, revealing the sigil I'd painted on the wall behind it.

Aikyan howled. "You can't do this!"

I moved in front of the stage for a front-row seat of his demise. Christine jumped from the platform and stood next to me.

"I hate you, Aikyan. I've always hated you for the things you made me do." Then she merged with me, the last piece of the puzzle complete.

He lunged at me but couldn't move from the radius of the circle. While I merged with souls, Grant had painted a second sigil under a rug on the stage. Aikyan wasn't going anywhere. He tried again, but with each attempt it only weakened him further.

We laughed. And if anyone alive had witnessed that laugh, it would have chilled them to the bone. It was the laugh of twenty-nine angry, vengeful souls who had finally found redemption.

It tired me. I found a comfortable seat on a small sofa facing the stage. Then I took a deep breath and released them all, giving them the chance at real freedom.

A woman in a black, flowing dress appeared in the hallway, her smile bright and her skin glowed. "Come my children, I'll take you home." She whispered.

I somehow knew the gods had sent her to do the job Aikyan refused to do for almost seventy years. My soul felt it.

My eager new friends rushed her, disappearing into the most wonderful warmth that emanated from her presence. All but Grant. Before he left, he turned to face me. "I'm proud of you, kiddo. You coming?"

I shook my head. "No. I still have a job to do here."

He nodded. "Understood." He blew me a kiss, then disappeared.

The mysterious woman smiled at me, and an understanding passed between our glances. We both knew what I had to do.

I watched her back away, her light fading as she evaporated from sight.

Aikyan mocked me. "You fool. You should have gone with her."

I sighed and leaned back. "No, I have important work here." I closed my eyes and leaned my head back, releasing my soul from my far too battered body. The exertion from the possession had depleted what life I had left.

My spirit stepped away from my body, content in the fact that I'd chosen a comfortable spot for my place of permanent slumber. Then I walked to the door and flipped the open sign to say closed. I turned to face Aikyan. I crossed my arms in front of me and glared at him.

"You're permanently closed for business and I will be here to assure you never leave that trap."

So be warned, wayward traveler. If you ever try to enter an old building called The Fancy Cat, the ghost of a determined young woman will meet you. One who will never allow another living being to enter her domain. She protects and defends it at all costs. It's the only way she can keep you safe. The only way I can keep you safe. That flash of white you see just out of the corner of your eye, is me. I am the legend of The Fancy Cat.

•••••••••••••••••••••••••••••••

Amy Hale is a mother and wife living in Illinois, but fondly remembers her roots growing up in a small town in Oklahoma. Her husband and kids are the center of her universe, although her cat believes otherwise. She loves reading, writing, and photography. Amy believes that happiness comes from surrounding yourself with those you love and being content with your current place in the world

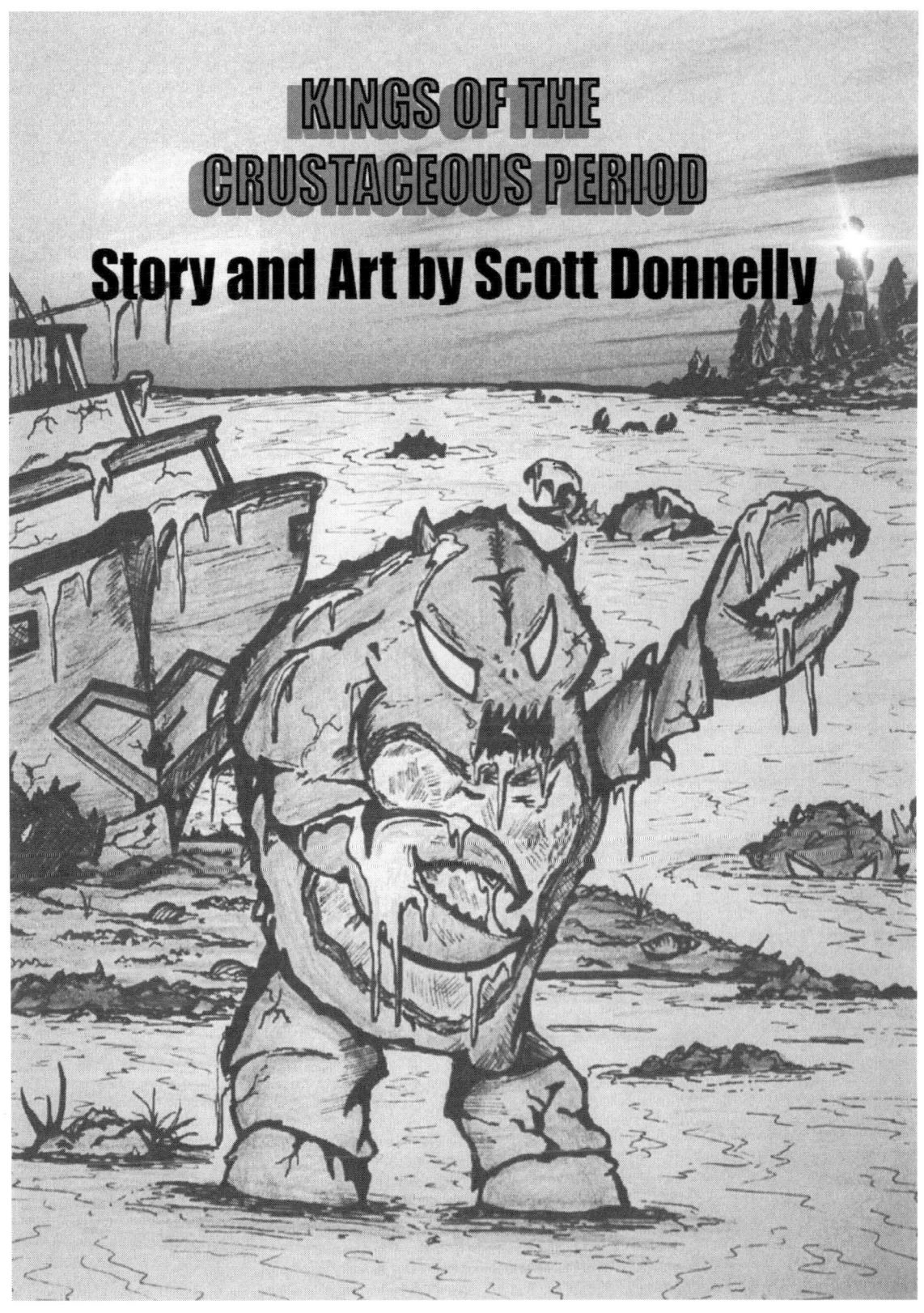

KINGS OF THE CRUSTACEOUS PERIOD:
The Clamoring of the Crabs
By Scott Donnelly

It started as a one-off sighting on a secluded beach in Maine in 1945. A fisherman witnessed *it* rise from the icy waters during a holiday fishing trip. The sighting was abnormal...*unbelievable*. Something like this had never been seen before.

It was kind of a crab. But like, a humanoid man crab. It stood on two shell-armored legs, was burgundy in color, and nestled on either side of its head, were two glowing eyes. Between them, was a ferocious mouth. The fisherman rushed back to the village and reported it to the papers, and *then* to law enforcement. The police didn't believe a word the fisherman said, but the papers, however, ran the story on the front page.

Crab-Men Invade New England!

The story detailed the account of the fisherman but decorated the story to sell. It described an army of crab-people that had been released from the sea after an earthquake. But there *was* no earthquake, and there was only *one* man-crab.

Another paper ran the story as well, claiming the fisherman was killed and dismembered by the bulbous claws of the deep-sea monstrosity:

Fisherman Killed by Mutant Crab Monster! Who's Next?

The New England papers had fun with the story for a while, months, really. That was until an American family of four vacationing in Nova Scotia reported a similar sighting. They had been hiking a ridge near Sambora when they noticed unusual activity on the beach below. Curious, the father led his family down the ridge and onto the sandy beach. There, they all witnessed two of the crab-men feasting on a dead moose.

When their glowing eyes spotted the family, they snapped their claws together in a way that felt threatening. The family fled.

Demon-Crabs Terrorize Americans in Canada!

The Canadian papers had a field day, and it didn't take long for the Sambora and Maine incidents to be undeniably connected. The two seaside sites became tourist attractions. People flocked from all over to try and catch a glimpse of the elusive humanoid crustaceans, and some of them got lucky.

The sightings began to increase over the coming months, and the crab people started to pop up all over the eastern seaboard and throughout eastern Canada. As the number of crabs grew, run-ins with humans became frequent, and often violent. The crabs were declared an international threat, and bounties went out. *"Kill a crab, make some money."*

But the number of crab-men quickly topped that of humans on the east coast. People were being killed by the crabs, and they only kept rising from the depths of the sea in large numbers.

Society fell, and a worldwide fallout occurred as the crabs began to take other countries such as China, Russia and Scotland. The modern world was no more, and the Crustaceous Period was ushered in.

People continued to survive, but struggled in the fight against the crabs. Mankind moved inland, hoping the crabs wouldn't begin a systematic migratory behavior. As the decades went on, many groups of people tried to eradicate the deep sea threat but failed miserably. You could kill a crab, but four more would make landfall. Most people, set on *only* killing crabs, did not think of the larger issue at hand. But, *some* did...

In 1990, three men rose to the occasion and succeeded in crab mutilation more than any others that had come before them. The trio was known as *The Kings of the Crustaceous Period*, a self-proclaimed moniker won by a 2-1 vote in the group. Made up of three childhood friends brought together years later by the destruction of their hometown under a crab attack, they swore to "Find the origin of the crab invasion, eliminate its source, and give birth to a new, better world, without crabs."

Finding the source was the key to survival, and ultimately man's reclaiming of their own planet.

Individually, the Kings were known as Brimstone – a former welder who wielded a homemade flamethrower. "The only good crab is a cooked crab," he'd always say. The second King was Dillinger – a former mail carrier who came into possession of a Tommy Gun formerly owned by his namesake. "I deliver the *pain* now," was tattooed on his arm. The third and final member of the Kings was a tall, lanky fellow named Kyle, Kyle Mumford. He was a Debbie-Downer if there ever was one, but he was an unstoppable beast with a bow staff. You wouldn't want to be hit upside the head with his wood. "Cracking shells, taking names," was his forced catchphrase. Kyle, obviously, was the sole contrarian to the trio's moniker.

The world had deteriorated, and stunk overwhelmingly of raw seafood. Approaching a coastal ghost town on the southeastern coast of Maine, were The Kings. They had become nomadic after the gasoline supply dried up, forcing them to abandon their vehicles in favor of military-grade boots. Their boots, belts, backpacks and weapons were constant attire. Another item they each devotedly carried were jewel en crusted antique forks which dangled from their belts. These were for a very specific tradition. The clothing would change as needed to adapt to the changing seasons and *blowback* factor. It was a summer day, high in the upper 80s, which elevated the powerful fish-stink to unbelievable new levels. They made it a priority to move up and down the eastern coast of the United States, trying to keep the man-crabs at bay, but also looking for clues as to where they were exactly coming from, and why.

The majority of the crabs seemed to be attracted more to the New

England area, which is where the King's focused most of their attention. They hadn't been down south in months, convinced their answer was more local.

The Kings arrived in Majestic Harbor, the ghost town in question. Majestic Harbor was once known for its heavy supply of rare, blue lobsters. More blue lobsters had been caught in Majestic Harbor's waters than anywhere else in the entire world. The sign that welcomed them even had a large painting of a smiling blue lobster frolicking in rippling water and holding a bouquet of seaweed.

"Lobster would be good for a change," Dillinger said. He was dressed for the weather: shorts, t-shirt, and a backwards ball cap. He wore ski goggles over his eyes to help block the sun, and also to protect his eyes from any blowback of crab guts. When he unloaded his Tommy Gun into a crab, he made sure it counted, usually making his clothes just as much of a victim.

"I'll tell ya what sounds good," Brimstone chimed in, "a burger."

"Ooh, yes, definitely a burger," Dillinger agreed. "Kyle, can't you see yourself eating a burger right now?"

Kyle shrugged. "Burgers are the love child of human cruelty and special seasonings."

They were used to Kyle's comments, but were still always shocked by how fast he could kill a mood.

A small crab, a normal one, suddenly scurried across the sandy road they walked on. It skittered right in front of Kyle, clicking its tiny feet on the road. Without hesitation, Kyle squashed it like a bug beneath his boot.

"Cripes, Kyle! Why did you have to do that? That thing was harmless," Dillinger exclaimed. He bent down to examine the shattered remains, mourning the sudden and needless death of the small animal.

"Hey!" Kyle exploded defensively. "That thing could turn into one of those giant mollusk suckers one day."

"You don't know that," Dillinger said. He was clearly bothered by Kyle's malicious crab stomping. "We don't know *anything* yet."

"Yeah, it's been years," Kyle said. "That's the problem. We're no closer to finding out anything about the invasion. All we do is slaughter crab monsters. We're just like the dopes that tried before us."

Brimstone stood there and looked around. Not every town had met an unfortunate fate like Majestic Harbor, here. Most of them were still somewhat habitable. It was only the ones where supplies and food ran out that would be abandoned. A ghost town like Majestic Harbor wasn't a daily discovery, but they'd definitely come across the likes of these before. And these poor, vacant towns, that once thrived with life and energy, is what fueled Brims. He wanted these towns to live again. He wanted people to return and have street festivals, parades, and thriving tourism. Eliminating the source of the crabs would be the starting point to bringing society back from the dead.

A screech from a nearby dwelling caught their attention, and they all took a defensive stance, holding their signature weapons out. The screech was unmistakable—it was a crab-man. This one sounded distressed. The Kings began to slowly move around, trying to locate the crab.

Brimstone, who wore an old welders' mask on top of his greasy, untamed apocalypse hair, held the nozzle of his flame thrower as he crept to the edge of a nearby alley. The tip of the nozzle had been fixed with an ignition trigger, and a hose connected it to a small weed-killer tank on his back, which was instead filled with propane. One pull of the trigger would expel a nice, steady stream of crab-roasting fire. He looked down the alley, but nothing seemed out of place.

Across the street, Dillinger fixed his hat to face forward, a quirk he had when he was about to go into battle. It made him feel "ready to go", like business was about to happen. He held his Tommy Gun out in front of him. He had an itchy trigger finger, and was always ready to deliver the pain.

Kyle slowly encroached on Majestic Harbor's Maritime Museum. The windows had been long shattered, and the inside was dark; electricity was a thing of the past. He moved in closer, crunching the old glass beneath his boots, and squinted as he peered into the museum. All was quiet.

The *screech* erupted again, and Kyle snapped his head to the right. Just beyond an overgrown patch of grass, was an embankment that sunk down into a small swampy area. A rickety old boardwalk went through the swamp and ended up at the beach on the other side of it. In the swamp, apparently stuck, was the screeching crab monster.

"Guys! Over here!" Kyle shouted. The King's all gathered by the corner of the museum and studied the swamp. The crab seemed to be immobilized. The top half of its body was out of the water, but it made movements indicating its lower extremities may have been stuck in some thick mud. Brimstone smirked.

"That guy's not going anywhere," he said. "I got this one."

Brims stealthily shuffled through the tall grass and onto the boardwalk. He walked slowly along the creaky wooden boards, trying not to draw attention to himself. The crab had its back to him, and Brims wanted to keep it that way. He paid close attention to his surroundings, making sure this wouldn't be an ambush. The crabs were known to execute coordinated attacks. They were smart, and seemed to become smarter as the years went on. But this one in particular, seemed to be legitimately stuck in the mud.

As Brimstone made his final steps toward his target, he unlocked the safety switch on the side of the flamethrower's grip, which made a very audible *click*. The crabs' glowing eyes dipped into anger and zeroed in on Brimstone. The crab growled and spun around with ease, snarling at the lone King. Brims' eyes widened. "Trickery!" he screamed.

Dillinger and Kyle sprang into action, dashing relentlessly toward the boardwalk. The crab reached out, viciously snapping its claws at Brims, creating a similar sound of two razor-sharp swords clashing. Gooey saliva splashed from its mouth as it roared.

Brimstone huffed with staunchness as he lowered

his welders mask and held the trigger down on his weapon. Out of the nozzle, an unstable flame exploded, instantly engulfing a crab. The beast screeched as its shell cracked and splintered, and then finally burst. The succulent meat from inside the monster showered the swamp and boardwalk. Brimstone lifted his mask, revealing a satisfied smirk.

"Ooh," Dillinger jokingly cringed as he and Kyle arrived on the scene. "He's been signed, *seared*, and delivered."

"Anyone got butter sauce?" Brims quipped.

Kyle was on it. He pulled a squeeze bottle of butter sauce from his pack, and the Kings all unlatched their jewel-encrusted forks from their belts. They each pulled off a chunk of crabmeat and Kyle generously drizzled each forkful with the butter sauce. Not only was this a traditional big middle finger to their salty enemies, but it was also an elegant food source in a post-apocalyptic world.

The Kings chewed their crabmeat, and Kyle just happened to glance up at the beach as he swallowed his chunk. Dark clouds were forming over the sea, and the gulls that littered the sky called out loudly. Down the beach, a boat caught Kyle's eye. He wiped his saucy mouth with his sleeve and looked closely. It was a yacht; white with a blue trim, and it looked to have forcefully made landfall at some point. Possibly from one of the recent squalls. A giant hole was punctured into its hull.

"Guys, look," Kyle pointed. Brimstone and Dillinger looked. Seagulls crooned above the wrecked yacht, and in the distance, thunder softly rolled. "Should we check it out?"

Brimstone stabbed and ripped one more forkful of crabmeat, slurped it up, and wiped his mouth. "Better make it quick. Weather's coming."

The Kings made their way across the beach. The beach itself was crunchy, made up mostly of rocks and seashells. Seaweed had been strewn about and wrapped around larger rocks due to the ever-changing tides. The darkening sky brought a cooler wind from over the ocean and chilled the beach by at least twenty degrees.

"This aint right," Dillinger noted. The atmosphere changed as soon as they hit the beach. As they approached the yacht, they didn't know what to expect. Was it a crab bunker? Someone in need of help? They were about to find out.

As they got closer, they noticed there was a name on the side of the yacht, *The Haven*. The hole ripped in the hull of the boat was a fatal one. The interior of the ship could be seen plain as day through it, and it wasn't pretty. This definitely did not end up a safe place, as its name ironically suggested.

"Stay cautious, Kings," Dillinger calmly commanded as he took lead on this one. With his gun in front of him, he crept closer to the dead sea vessel. Water created an eerie *drip, drip, drip* from inside the opening, only slightly quieter than the thunder rumbling over the ocean.

"Friend, or foe?" a small voice called from up above. All three of the Kings stopped abruptly and looked up. On the bridge of *The Haven*, was a young girl no more than eight years old.

"She's a little young to own a yacht," Brimstone joked quietly, trying to ease the mysterious tension that had suddenly cropped up on that rocky beach.

"It's probably not hers," Kyle boringly said, murdering the mood in cold blood

"Friend, or foe?" the little girl repeated from behind the handrail up top. An emotional urgency was apparent this time in her voice.

"Depends," Dillinger called back. "What are you up to?"

The little girl scowled. "I'm not up to anything. We're shipwrecked."

"I see that," Dillinger agreed. "How long have you–" He was stopped when Brims nudged him. "What?" Dillinger asked.

Brimstone whispered closely to his ear. "She said *'We're'* shipwrecked."

Dillinger faced the girl again, now unnerved by the possibility of more people than just her. How many were there, and why had they not shown their faces?

"Where have you come from, little girl?"

Dillinger questioned her. She hesitated, and then reluctantly said: "Joe Batts Arm."

"Who?" Dillinger squinted. Kyle leaned in. "It's in Newfoundland." "Who else is with you?" Dillinger asked

the girl, ignoring Kyle's geography lesson. "My dad. He's trapped below."

The Kings had every right to be cautious. As with any end-of-the-world scenario, there were always groups of people who were just out for themselves. Whether they were in need of food, supplies, weapons, or just something to do, no one could be trusted at their word. Especially with the Kings, trust needed to be earned.

"What's wrong with your pops?" Brimstone called up to her.

"Pirates shoved him in a barrel and sealed the lid," the little girl said. It was so matter-of-fact, that it completely caught the Kings off guard.

"Pirates?!" Kyle exclaimed with a partial laugh. The girl nodded. "No way guys," Brims said, shaking his head. "I don't do pirates." "What do you mean by that?" Dillinger questioned.

"Pirates freak me out," he said. "I saw a movie when I was little where some kid flew to a pirate ship. It scarred me for life."

"Modern pirates aren't like the old stories, Brims," Kyle said. "They're just thieves and criminals who ride boats and steal from other boats."

Dillinger laughed. "There're no hook hands, man. No peg legs or parrots either." He looked at Kyle for confirmation. "Right?"

"No," he confirmed.

Dillinger then turned back to the girl. "We can help your dad. What's your name?"

"Wendy," she called down.

Brimstone's eyes widened. "I don't like the sound of that," he said. "*Wendy* flew to that pirate ship too."

"We're coming in Wendy," Dillinger announced. He made sure his hat faced forward and his goggles were on. Brimstone pulled down his mask again, and Kyle did nothing cool at all to prepare. Gray clouds filled most of the sky at this point, and those clouds started to spit down rain as the Kings left the salty air of the beach. They entered *The Haven* through its gaping side.

It was dark and drippy in the hull, like a cave, with the only light coming from outside through slivered cracks in the wall. And even *that* light was dull due to the approaching storm. The skeletal structure of the boat was severely battered and broken in too many places for it to ever be operational again; at least in the world's *current* state.

The Kings slowly made their way through. The entire boat was so fragile, that even the slightest wrong step could bring a beam crashing down, and then the rest of *The Haven* on top of that, which would crush them, and that wouldn't have been ideal.

The air inside the hull was warm and damp. Through the foggy little window on Brimstone's welders mask, he saw three barrels lined up against the side wall. They were blue plastic drums, and not the wooden barrels Brims had pictured in his mind. Only one of them was sealed with a lid. There were two other barrels on the opposite wall. They were black, steel, and had *flammable* printed on them in red. The Kings wisely converged by the blue barrels and then Dillinger, leading

this particular campaign, knocked on the lid.

"Wendy's dad? You in there?" he called out. After a moment of nothing but silence, the muffled voice of a man spoke from within the barrel:

"Yes. That's me. I'm Wendy's dad. Who are you? Are you with the pirates?"

"Absolutely not," Brimstone shuttered.

"We are The Kings of the Cretaceous Period," Dillinger said. "You may have heard of us."

"N-no..."

"Or maybe you haven't. But you have now," Dillinger added.

"We're *not* superheroes," Kyle groaned. Never had he been okay with the name they'd chosen. He didn't even see the point of a name to begin with. And when he thought of that, he thought of how Brimstone and Dillinger were not necessary either. Kyle went by his real name, and he continued to survive just fine.

"Ok, Wendy's dad, we're gonna get you out of there," Dillinger said. He pulled a fillet knife from a small sheath on his belt and used it to pry the lid off. After its suction-ized seal was broken, the lid popped right off and hit the floor. The Kings helped the man to his feet.

He was a man of average height, a striking dad-bod, sandy blonde hair and glasses that were cracked on both lenses, making them look like little kaleidoscope windows. He stretched his back, creating an audible crack, and then extended his hand to the three men. After the Kings officially introduced themselves, the man did as well:

"Name's James," he said, climbing out from the barrel.

"Pirates put you in there, James?" Dillinger questioned.

"Yes. A group of them."

"What did they want with you?"

"They took our food, my gun, my *hope*. They set sail for Gull's Beard. I think they have a camp there."

"Gulls Beard? Where's that?" Brimstone questioned.

"About six miles out to sea. We were fishing nearby there, and they came in hot, boarded our yacht and had their way with us...materialistically, of course." James then looked at the trio, hopeful. "Can you help us get our stuff back?"

Kyle cringed, and hated to disappoint James and Wendy. But it was just too dangerous of a task to tackle. Pirates on top of the crabs? It was going to be a hard no from–

"Absolutely!" Dillinger happily accepted the job. Kyle slapped his friend on the arm.

"Are you nuts?"

Brimstone then slapped Dillinger on the other arm. "I hate pirates!"

Dillinger was stunned. He was only trying to help a struggling father and daughter. He tossed his arms up in a 'well, excuse me' kind of way, and then Wendy's small voice screamed from above:

"*Crabs!*"

The Kings armed themselves appropriately and all instinctively stood in front of James to protect him.

"They're coming up the beach!" she frantically added. Dillinger hustled through the hull of *The Haven* and to the gaping hole in its side.

The rain was starting to come down ferociously outside, and the trees that separated the beach from the Majestic Harbor forcibly waved back and forth in the savage winds, teasing the risk of just snapping in half. Mud started to pool sporadically throughout the coarse surface of the beach, and the waves were violently crashing down.

But looking straight out, Dillinger realized Wendy was right. He could hear her screaming from up top as his eyes witnessed what appeared to be a throng of bipedal crabs tearing through the rocks and shells on the ground, and coming straight for *The Haven.*

"Brace yourselves, Kings!" Dillinger shouted. He lifted his Tommy Gun and gallantly walked out onto the beach. His boys followed, and the three of them now stood just outside of the shipwreck, rain hammering down on them. The clamoring of the crabs sent chills through their bodies like a nervous electrical current. This was something they hadn't seen before. Never had the crabs merged into larger groups. It was always just one or two together, and rarely three. So, for a troop of what appeared to be at least a dozen, it could have only meant one thing:

The crabs were evolving...

Brimstone released the safety from his flamethrower, and Kyle grit his teeth as he gripped the carefully positioned duct tape on his bow staff. Dillinger glowered at the incoming crabs.

It was their jobs as the Kings to protect the innocent, and annihilate any and all decapods. The dozen or so crabs rushed in, growling louder and snapping their jaws and claws.

"Brims!" Dillinger shouted, shuffling to the side. Brimstone knew what to do. He was usually the first line of defense. He stepped up and pulled the trigger, spraying fire like a fire hose. The dim beach lit up in reds and oranges as the crabs collided with the flames. They screeched, and most of them fell back to wait out the roaring stream of fire. One of the crabs ignited and ran for the crashing waves. Another, a bold 'big-man-on-campus' crab, powered through the flames. Brimstone let go of the trigger, baffled by the fiery crabs massive cojones. The monster went berserk as the flames danced off its body. It didn't take no for an answer, and continued straight for them. A respectable warrior, but one that needed to be put down.

Brims was stunned by the sight. He lazily lowered his weapon and took a small step back.

"What are you doing?!" Dillinger screamed as he leapt in front of his zoned-out frontliner. He dropped to his knees and fired the Tommy Gun. The bullets blew a hundred different holes into the crab's shell, claws and legs, and it smacked down hard on the rocks where it continued to burn as it died.

Dillinger turned back to Brims, completely astonished. "What was that? You froze!"

Brimstone didn't have time to answer. He looked over Dillinger's right shoulder to see a crab spring from the ground and soar toward him. "My God..." Brims uttered. Dillinger swung around just in time to jump out of the way and avoid the crabs landing. Kyle jumped into action and cracked his bow staff

over the crabs head. It dropped to its knees, and Kyle smashed it across its side. The crab collapsed to the ground, and Dillinger loomed over it. He aimed his gun down, and fired, tearing the crab apart.

"Look out!" Wendy screamed, warning the Kings that the crabs had made their way around the lingering fires. The Kings all stood their ground, and Dillinger nudged Brims. "Stay sharp, alright?"

Brims returned to a cool and collected focus and lifted the nozzle of his weapon. Ten man-crabs closed in and surrounded them. Dillinger lifted his gun and started to fire a barrage of shell-piercing rounds at the monsters. Crab shell pieces began to fling and fly every which way. One of them charged Kyle, but he was quick to force his staff into the beast's stomach and helped it to the ground. Brims finished it by squashing its head into a meaty pulp.

The crabs kept coming. Kyle gave each one that came his way, a *thwack* and a wallop with his bow staff. Brimstone continued to ignite the stormy beach, and Dillinger pounded out round after round of loud pops and bangs from his gun. Crabs fell, crabs screeched, and the Kings were winning the attack. Thunder resounded from above as the rain continued to drown the rocks and shells on the beach. It wasn't letting up; instead, the rain became *more* forceful.

Lightening wriggled across the sky above the fierce waves, bringing brief flashes of light that illuminated a second wave of crab-men galloping towards them; their eyes glowing boldly on the darkened beach.

"Christ!" Kyle shouted as the new wave caught his eye through the pummeling precipitation. The others took notice.

Dillinger made a decision quickly, "Retreat! Into the ship!"

The Kings fell back into *The Haven*, and quickly worked together to block the ships gaping cavity with the flammable barrels, and then began to stack the empty plastic ones on top of them. James was in full panic mode, pacing frantically around the hull. "Those won't stop them!" he cried. "Nothing will!"

"Shut up, James!" Dillinger snarked as he tried to work at full tilt, but in the end, James was right. Crabs blew against the barrels from the outside, knocking the plastic ones back into the hull. The Kings jumped back defensively as the crabs all tried to squeeze in through the hole at once.

"Up here!" Wendy's tiny voice shouted. Dillinger turned and saw James working his way up a broken ladder and toward an open hatch.

"Come on guys!" Dillinger ordered. The others followed Dillinger to the ladder, and once James had cleared through the hatch, Kyle went up first. Brimstone was second, as Dillinger aimed his weapon back at the crabs pounding into the underbelly of the yacht. He aimed and started firing. The pops and bangs from the gun were about on par with the loudness of the rain and thunder outside. It all just blended together into one unintelligible, deafening noise.

The crabs all wailed in gut-wrenching harmony, but just as Brims cleared in through the hatch, one crab in particular powered through the cascading bullets. As it roared and pounced for Dillinger, the final King in the hull lifted his gun higher and fired heavy rounds at the crab's foul-looking face. One of its white eyes ripped and shredded upon impact, and it screamed as it stopped in its place. Dillinger took advantage of the delay and swung around, facing the ladder.

As he wrapped a hand around the side rail, he felt a whoosh of air behind him, and then a sharp pain erupted in his glutes. He cringed and swallowed what would have been an angry and painful cry. He looked back and saw the one-eyed crab snarling at him. It's claw was clamped down on his buttocks, and Dillinger didn't like it one bit. He stared into the crabs one good eye, and barked, "This ain't over, crab!"

In one swift motion, Dillinger let go of the side rail of the ladder, ripped his knife from his belted sheath, and slashed at the joint just below the beast's claw. The crab screamed and released Dillinger's butt from its grip. The King hurried up the ladder just before it collapsed down into the hull, disappearing into the surging population of crabs.

Dillinger joined the rest on the bridge. The rain continued to pound the beach, and the swarm of crabs beneath them thrashed about angrily. Brimstone and Kyle stood in front of James, who held Wendy tight. Dillinger looked around, desperate for their next move – whatever it was, it was going to be crucial. It could very well determine life or death for the group. Just down the beach, he saw a boat shack. He wasn't sure if it would be safe, but he knew that they were definitely *not* safe in their current position.

"To the shack!" he commanded. He rushed to the rails along the bridge and looked down. The water was tossing about violently below, but it was better than jumping down onto the sharp rocks and shattered shells on the beach. "Come on!"

Dillinger led by example and hopped over the side of *The Haven*, dramatically splashing down into the ocean. Kyle was next. "Here comes Kyle!" he needlessly exclaimed on the way down. Brimstone turned to the frightened father and daughter.

"Come on, guys. This is our chance."

"Do we have to?" James stuttered.

"Do you want to become fish food?" Brimstone sarcastically quipped. James and Wendy rapidly shook their heads. Of course, they didn't. "Then jump." They did, and Brimstone followed.

The water was rough, and with the rain hammering down on the surface, it made visibility extremely difficult. The five of them worked their way through the crashing waves and fought against the undertow. Wendy was not a good swimmer, so she held onto her

father's back as he swam as efficiently as he could. He followed Kyle, who was quick to surpass Dillinger. He was also the first to make landfall.

Once he regained his composure, he looked out to the sea with his hands over his eyes like little awnings. Closely watching, he was able to spot each and every one of them. He counted to himself as he spotted them. He saw Dillinger, James and Wendy first. "One, two, three..." He then spotted Brims on the tail end of the group. "Four...five..."

Wait, he thought, *I'm five!* He struggled to look closer, trying to defy his bodily capabilities by zooming in with his eyes. He spotted a fifth figure quickly approaching Brimstone from behind. It was darker, so it was harder to make out through the rain.

"Brims!" Kyle called out. "Behind you!" His fellow King couldn't hear. The rain, thunder, and crab squeals from inside *The Haven* were just too loud. Then, another dark mass popped up from the ocean. And then another, and another. They were dark bulges just breaking the water's surface. Kyle was nervous. Something about those ominous bulges didn't sit well with him. And it was only seconds later when his nervous fear was granted merit. On each of the bulges, glowing white eyes all ignited at once.

"Crabs!" Kyle screamed. "Crabs in the surf!"

Dillinger hit the beach and briskly crawled to Kyle before standing. He too saw the demon crabs rising from the depths. "Hurry! Hurry!" Dillinger waved in James and Wendy. He helped them out of the water and then looked back out for Brims. He couldn't see him anymore. The crabs stood upright as they hit shallow water. Algae and slime dripped from them. They snarled and their eyes glowed a blinding white; it was like looking directly at the sun.

"Brimstone!" Dillinger called out. "Brims!" There was no answer, no sign of him at all. Dillinger, now worried sick, then screamed, "Leopold!"

Kyle was shocked. Neither Brimstone nor Dillinger had gone by their real names in years. Dillinger must have been truly worried about his best friend.

"You know better than that, Dillweed!" a booming voice shouted from a short distance away. Dillinger and Kyle turned in the direction of *The Haven*. Brimstone stood on the beach, soaked to the bone, and dripping with green algae. "Leopold doesn't exist anymore!" he smirked. Brims then lowered his welders mask again, aimed his flamethrower at the gaping hole in the hull of the smashed yacht, and pulled the trigger.

James covered Wendy's eyes as the heavy rush of fire from the nozzle lit up the beach once again. The fiery stream reached the flammable barrels just inside the hole and wrapped all around them like snakes from hell. The flames flickered against the shells of the crabs seething inside. The wails and cries of the crustaceans abruptly ended as the barrels blew, sending the entire shipwreck into a bursting detonation that made the ground explode and the sky glow a striking red-orange.

A smoke cloud rose high into the sky, spinning with flames, and everyone hit the deck. Even the crabs emerging from the sea stopped momentarily to admire the explosive spectacle exploding before them. But after the steamed crabs from inside *The Haven* spilled out onto the beach in pieces and chunks, the sea crabs wised up. This was war. They all focused malevolently on the humans and attacked suddenly.

Kyle swung his bow staff and cracked one of them across the head. The shell splintered and Kyle reached in with both hands, peeling the shell open to expose the moist, white meat inside. Kyle finished the crab off with a kick to the groin, and the creature collapsed.

Dillinger unloaded his Tommy Gun on the stampeding crabs, ripping and tearing them apart as they advanced. He mowed them down like an overgrown lawn, and then turned to a second batch running up the beach. His bullets pierced their shells with ease, and they began to drop like flies.

Brimstone watched as the smoke plume from the yacht diminished, leaving only the smoking carcass of *The Haven* nestled on the beach. Any crabs that had miraculously survived the blast, crawled out onto the rocks, and sizzled the rest of the way to their deaths.

Kyle beat a few more crabs to a salty pulp, and Wendy cried in her father's arms. The rain began to let up, and out at sea, sunlight started to delicately burn the clouds apart. Dillinger reloaded from his pack and picked off the final few crabs. His gunfire then fizzled out. Kyle leaned on his bow staff to catch his breath, and Brimstone watched *The Haven* crackle and pop in a fiery death.

Almost in unison, the Kings removed their forks from their belts and all approached the closest crab. Kyle knelt down and pried a claw back until it cracked, spewing salt water like a geyser. The meat spilled out onto the beach and the Kings all dug in, ripping out chunks and chewing like there was no tomorrow. James cringed, and covered his daughter's eyes from the awkward ritual.

Once their ceremonious bites were over, the Kings converged with the Canadian father and daughter. With steaming crab carcasses surrounding them, James thanked the trio of heroes. "I really don't know what to say, except thank you."

"It was our pleasure," Dillinger responded.

James looked on at the three men, mystified by their heroic appearance and perfectly-timed arrival.

"Who *are* you guys?"

"Just a few guys who—"

"We're the Kings," Dillinger proudly interrupted Kyle.

"The Kings of the Crustaceous Period," Brimstone added with a playful wink.

James nodded and smiled. "The Kings," he said. "I like that. This world needs more heroes like you all."

"The world sucks right now," Dillinger said. "We want to correct it."

"How are you going to do that?" James asked, caressing his daughters

head as she latched onto his side for comfort.

"Killing crabs is one thing. Finding their origin, the source of this shell-ish nightmare, is a whole 'nother ball game," Dillinger said.

"If we can eliminate the source, we can start to rebuild the world," Brims added.

"That's a tall order," James said. "The world has been in a state of decay for many decades now."

"We're up to the challenge. There's a lot to learn, a lot to discover out there," Dillinger said. "We will restore order to our planet."

James nodded and smirked again. Something about The Kings gave him hope. After watching them in action, he honestly believed in them. He trusted that they would make good on their promise to the world. He wanted to *help* them.

"I wish I could give you something," James said. "A good luck charm to help keep you safe on your mission. But the pirates took it."

"The pirates," Brimstone nervously uttered, forgetting all about them.

"They went to Gulls Beard, you say?" Dillinger asked, looking out to sea as the storm clouds sizzled away. There was a hazy visual of an island on the horizon; a tall lighthouse seemed to emerge up from the trees that covered the land. It was Gulls Beard, an old trading post for sailors, and now the alleged hide-out of the thieving pirates.

"We can get your things back," Dillinger assured them. Kyle exploded:

"What? We don't have time for missions like that. We need to stay on our own course. We have our *own* mission."

"Our mission is to restore the world to its pre-crab infested condition, which includes showing mindful humanity," Dillinger said directly to Kyle. "We *will* sail for Gulls Beard."

"With what, genius?" Kyle argued.

Dillinger pointed behind Kyle, and at the boathouse down the beach. Just beyond the boathouse, bobbing in the water by the dock, was a brittle rowboat. Kyle rolled his eyes.

"I am the owner of an incredibly valuable item," James said. "An heirloom, or sorts. It's been with my family for generations."

"What kind of item?" Dillinger asked.

"The Seafarer's Scabbard."

The Kings fell into silence; an obvious reaction that they knew exactly what James spoke of. Kyle stepped a little closer. "The actual Scabbard? Or a replica?"

"The actual."

"The Seafarer's Scabbard is said to have mystical powers," Brimstone said, astounded by the information that was just unshackled before them. The thought of even just seeing it excited him.

"Yes," James said. "You wouldn't believe its powers unless you witness them yourselves. It's quite the spectacle."

"We'd love to see its powers, James," Dillinger said. "All in favor of recovering the stolen goods, and said Scabbard, say aye!"

Dillinger and Brimstone lifted their hands, and both gleefully shouted "Aye!" Kyle left his arms dangling like a bored ape and made sure his repulsed facial expression was seen by everyone.

"Cheer up, bucko!" Dillinger smacked Kyle on the back. "Let's give those pirate-wannabes a flogging they'll never forget!"

Dillinger and Brimstone cheered, excited for a new mission. Sure, it wasn't their main priority, but the chance to help others in need was too good of an opportunity to ignore. Not only did the world need rid of crab monsters and playschool pirates, but kindness and comradery were in desperate need of a comeback as well. They would be the staples of building a new society and civilization.

Across the rippling waters of the Atlantic, scattered around Gulls Beard, were the bodies of the pirates. They were contorted and stuffed in bushes, mangled on the sharp rocks, and bobbing lifelessly in the foamy surf. They were all dismembered and decapitated; the sharp cuts being the results of monstrous crab claws.

Deeper in the jungle of Gulls Beard, a row of bipedal crab monsters lay in the mud. They had all been cut in half at the waist. Succulent meat poured out from the fresh cuts, attracting bugs, snakes and other vermin.

A pair of yellow, glowing eyes opened in the darkness of the overgrown environment. And then another pair. And another. On the island of Gull's Beard, surrounded by dead pirates and dismembered crab creatures, the sea of yellow eyes watched and waited for the bait to be taken. ***The Story Will Continue in Pulp Reality #3.***

Scott Donnelly is an indie author based in Grove City, Ohio, where he lives with his wife, three children, and labradoodle, Maxwell. Scott writes in a variety of genres to keep his ideas fresh and different; they range from horror, to science fiction/adventures, and action thrillers. Scott is known for "The Scout Brooks Saga" (a soon to be 7-book science fiction adventure series), "Unheard Of" (an alien thriller based in his hometown of Grove City), "The Red Echo Series" (an action/thriller series that calls back to the action movies of the 1980s and 1990s), and his latest horror novella, "The Whool."

8

THE WIND-UP KID

STORY BY RON FORTIER
ART BY ROB DAVIS

THE WIND-UP KID
By Ron Fortier

Ten-year-old Cesar Ramirez had been pestering his father, Manuel, from the second they had opened their stables at the southern end of Main Street early that bright and sunny Wednesday morning. Manny, as everyone knew the likeable, hardworking smithy, owned and operated the only blacksmith shop and public stables in the small northern Texas town of Sandy Creek; population two hundred and twenty.

Holding a red-hot horseshoe over his blazing forge, Manny held his heavy hammer in his hand so as to pound the heated metal the second he set it on his massive, scarred black anvil. A red bandanna was tied around his forehead keeping the sweat from rolling into his brown eyes as the rising flames continued their fiery dance.

Out of the corner of his eye, he could see barefoot Cesar, moving from one pen to the next carrying armfuls of hay and scoops of grain to feed the seven horses currently being housed under the big open building's red roof. In between seeing to each animal as his father had taught him, Cesar would take every opportunity to stop by the open entrance and stare at the townspeople marching past, many of them in their Sunday best all heading for the big field beyond the cattle stockades.

It was here that Professor Phineas Proctor and his Traveling Show of Wonders had set up their two canvas tents and were now preparing to dazzle the good people of Sandy Creek with more stupendous miracles than anyone could ever imagine. Or so said the flyer that had been handed out on the street the previous evening after Prof. Proctor's three cloth-topped wagons had rolled in from out of the hills and set up camp, much to the delight of the town's children.

Professor Phineas himself had stopped by the stable with his crew boss, a tall lanky black fellow named Wallace Duprai, to see if Manny would help fashion new shoes for several of their horses. Phineas was dressed in an all-black outfit crowned with an old stovepipe hat that would have done Abe Lincoln proud. He had an angular, clean face and a lopsided smile Manny liked from the second he shook the showman's bony hand.

But it was Cesar who had been enthralled by the flamboyant entertainer, having never in his young life seen anyone dressed so somberly and yet be boisterous in nature.

"So, will you be attending our premier tomorrow afternoon, young sir?" the distinguished looking Phineas asked the mystified lad.

"I do not know, senor," Cesar replied truthfully casting furtive glances at his father while doing so. "Does it cost money?"

"Not a red penny, my boy," Phineas smiled happily. He looked at Manny to explain. "The local merchants are only too happy to recompense my little troop when we attract the farmers and ranchers from all over to come and watch our performances. While in town, they generally spend time at local eateries and other establishments."

"Yes, I could see that," Manny nodded. "There is so little in the way of entertainment in a place like Sandy Creek."

"Then the lad...." Phineas stopped. "Forgive my manners, young man, I did not inquire as to your name."

Cesar's chest swelled. "I am Cesar Luis Alonzo Ramirez, senor."

"Then it is a genuine pleasure to meet you, Cesar." The tall man leaned over and shook the boy's hand. "As the flier indicates, I am Prof. Phineas Proctor at your service. I do look forward to seeing you at one of our shows."

"What are you going to have there?" Cesar was unable to contain his curiosity.

"A fine question." Phineas reached into his jacket and pulled out one of the folded fliers and opened it. "There will be Antoine the Fire Eater, Madame Mabel Higgins, the world's strongest woman, the amazing Chin brothers from San Francisco, acrobats."

Of course, Cesar had no idea what an acrobat was but the way Prof. Proctor said the words implied it was most important.

"Ah, let me see," Phineas touched his pointy chin looking at the paper with a puzzled expression. "I believe there was one more act. Now what was it?" Then his eyes lit up and he snapped his fingers, "Of course, how could I possibly forget the most spectacular being ever created by science?"

With a dramatic sweep of his hand, Phineas turned the flier over and held it up in front of Cesar's face. There,

beautifully drawn over most of the flyer's surface was the picture of a very strange looking man. Cesar blinked. The man was covered with metal!

"Cesar, my boy, I give you the Wind-Up Kid, the one and only mechanical gunfighter!"

Manny thought about the exchange as he continued to pound the heated horseshoe. Before departing, he and Wallace Duprai had agreed he would make and fit four of the company's draft horses with new shoes while at the same time providing for their shelter and care during the troop's stay in town.

Delighted with the arrangement, Duprai had promised him double his usual fare and wouldn't take no for an answer. When Manny had told his wife Dolores that night, she had clapped her hands and hugged him for several minutes. Although Manny made a decent living for the three of them, it was going to be nice to have some extra money for a change. All during supper, Dolores had gone on and on about possibly purchasing new bolts of dress cloth from Waginer's Mercantile from which she could make them all new clothes. It had been a long time since he had seen her so happy.

All of which brought him back to the present and his fidgeting son still hovering by the open doors.

"Cesar," he said, exasperated, while dunking the hot shoe into the bucket of water next to the anvil.

"Yes, Papa?"

"Have you taken care of all Prof. Proctor's horses as I told you?"

"Yes, Papa."

"Then what are you doing just standing around here?"

"Ah…" the boy stammered awkwardly.

"Go on," Manny said waiving his hand towards the street. "Go see the metal man."

"I can go?"

"It's better than having you underfoot all day," Manny smiled. "Go on, get out of here."

"Si, Papa." Cesar took two quick steps out the door then stopped, turned and beaming ear to ear said, "Gracias, Papa."

Then he was bolting down the dirt street as fast as a scared jackrabbit.

"Hey, don't be late for supper," Manny called after him, but the boy was long gone in the crowd making their way to the stockades.

Manny chuckled and started to work on the horseshoe again.

• •

"If Dolores is making her chicken Tamales, can I come to supper too?"

Manny recognized the voice before the town sheriff, Tom Hancock, walked around him, his brown Stetson tilted back on his head, his thumbs hitched into his gunbelt. A man in his late forties, Hancock was stout with a round belly; his dungarees held up by two hard working suspender straps. Pinned on his blue cotton shirt was his tin star.

"I'm sure Dolores could find enough to fill another plate," Manny grinned. "Though that may not be enough for a man with your…ah…appetites, Sheriff."

Hancock patted his stomach and laughed. "It's a real curse, Manny, loving good vittles like I do. Can you believe when I was starting as a deputy down in El Paso, I was thin as a fence rail."

The blacksmith studied his longtime friend and shook his head negatively. "I could try all day, my friend, and never believe such a tall tale."

"So, what do you think of these show folks?" Hancock asked changing the subject. "I see you're taking care of their horses."

"Si," Manny nodded. "They seem like good people. Why? Do you think otherwise?"

"No," the lawman said pulling off his hat and fanning himself. "That Proctor fellah stopped by my office soon as they rode into town yesterday to see if there were any legal restrictions to their putting on a show. He seemed courteous and even likeable."

The blacksmith dunked the iron U shoe into the water again, causing it to hiss. "And yet you seem concerned, my friend."

"Well, not so much about them," Hancock waved his hat towards the streets where several wagons were rolling past slowly to avoid families walking in the street. "It's that crowd they've pulled in to see them. We ain't had so many people in town at the same time since last year's Fourth of July shindig."

"Tom, they're all our ranchers and farmers from around here."

"Not all of them, Manny. I've spotted a few strangers here and there."

"Well, I'm sure word about the traveling show got around is all. And we always get a few drifters coming through here."

"True enough," Hancock conceded, putting his hat back on. "I just like to keep on top of things is all."

"Ha, it is your job after all," Manny chuckled putting down the finished horseshoe in the bucket with the others he had finished.

At that, Sheriff Hancock walked over and slapped him on the arm. "Hey, I'm gonna stop over at the saloon and wet my whistle. How'd you like me to bring you back a small can of beer?"

The sweating Manny smiled. "That would be most kind of you, amigo."

"Good enough, I'll be back in a little while then."

Cesar Ramirez had never seen so many people in his young life. It was as if the town's only street was going to burst like an old worn seam from the press of the crowd moving towards the open field. There, two huge tents had been erected and in between one of the three wagons had been unhitched and placed to act as an impromptu stage.

With so many people gathered together, Cesar knew immediately if he attempted to push his way through them, he still wouldn't be able to get close enough to see above the adults. They were forming an impenetrable human wall. Some men had hoisted their young'uns up on their shoulders. Biting his lower lip, Cesar looked about and then spotted several of his schoolmates across the road. They had smartly solved the viewing problem by climbing atop the huge wooden railings that surrounded the cattle stockades.

Cesar ran to them and scampered up one of the gates to sit between Jack Braddock and Nancy Waginer; the cute blonde whose family owned the general store.

"Hi, Cesar," she greeted. "You got here just in time, the show's about to start."

"Hey, be quiet," Jack snapped. "I want to hear what they're saying."

Cesar whispered hello and then turned all his attention to the tents and wagons. He watched in anticipation as the tall, lanky figure of Phineas Proctor stepped out of the tent to the left and hoisted himself onto the back of the wagon. Then the showman tipped his top hat to the assembly and bid them welcome.

"Ladies and gentlemen of Sandy Creek, I am Professor Phineas Proctor and I welcome one and all to our humble presentation. Today you will see some of the most amazing sights ever conceived and brought to you solely for your entertainment."

A round of applause answered Phineas' proclamation. With a flourish he donned his hat once more and then nodded his head towards his assistant, Wallace Duprai, who stood before the entrance to the tent on his left.

"But before we welcome you into our tents and begin we felt it only fitting to give you a small taste of what is in store inside.

"Mr. Duprai, if you please."

At that the slim foreman pushed back the canvas flap, leaned inside and called to someone. Then he stepped back quickly, still holding the sheet wide.

Out of the tent walked a seven-foot-tall mechanical man covered in gold paint from the top of his dome-like head, to the massive thick blocks at the ends of his legs. The crowd gasped as if it was one singular organism, each and every one of the onlookers simultaneously awestruck.

The harsh, mid-day glare of the sun struck the metallic skin and glimmered off it as the artificial being walked forth. He turned, his limbs making a soft whirring sound like that of a steam engine and he moved to stand in front of the wagon. There he faced the crowd, his arms stiff at his side. Some of the people in the front nervously eyed the giant metal effigy and pushed back slightly, not yet sure if they should be afraid of it or not.

Though its physique was solidly constructed, and rivets and bolts were visible along its entire frame, the head had been shaped smoothly, the jaw long and pointed with sharp cheek indentures under two depressions in which were set eyes made of red glass lenses. The automaton had no mouth, only a thin rectangle in its stead. There was no nose and the ears, if that's what you could call them, were two small cones welded to the sides of its smooth, shiny head.

The chest was massive, at its center a circle surrounding a black slot. Its arms seemed well shaped, and its hands possessed five human-like fingers.

As if all this wasn't enough of a marvel to cause the faint hearted to keel over, strapped low around the man-like machine were twin holsters, each filled with a silver-plated brand-new Colt .45 Peacemaker.

"Ladies and gentlemen," Phineas cried out loudly. "I give you the Wind-Up Kid!"

Silence followed and then a few brave souls began to clap until everyone followed suit nervously still not knowing what to expect next.

Prof. Proctor raised his hands to silence them and then moving to the edge of the wagon he bent down slightly and said to the seven-foot-tall man-machine, "Say hello to everyone, Kid."

"Hello," the tinny voice emerged from the mouth-slit. It had a cold, echoing quality to it.

The showman straightened up and with a flurry of hand motions, once again addressed his captivated audience. "The Wind-Up Kid will now give you a small demonstration of his uncanny shooting skills. Be aware, my good people, he never misses."

With that Phineas looked over at Duprai. "Mr. Duprai, if you will please."

Next to the dark man was a small burlap bag. He picked it up and from it withdrew four brightly painted plaster balls. He lowered the bag to the ground and then held up his hands so all could see that he held two balls in each hand.

"When you are ready," Phineas said.

Duprai pulled back both his arms and then threw all of four balls high into the air above the assembly.

"SHOOT THE BALLS!" Phineas commanded the golden man.

The Wind-Up Kid's head looked up slightly and then in a blur both his pistols were in his hands and firing. Four shots rang out loudly and a second later all four flying spheres exploded in mid-air, showering plaster dust down on the startled townspeople.

A loud cheer went up and across the road, young Cesar nearly fell off his fence perch screaming, "Wahoooo," at the top of his lungs.

"Want to see more?" Prof. Proctor inquired of the now delighted throng. He was answered with more applause and cheers. "Very well, good people. Let's see how the Kid fares against six balls."

Wallace Duprai was once more digging into the burlap bag at his feet when the Wind-up Kid turned around and looked up at his creator. "I am winding down, Professor," he said in his odd voice.

"Aha," Phineas chuckled, again waving his arms to the crowd. "Then let us wind you back up." And with that he reached into his fancy coat and from an inside pocket pulled out a black key approximately five inches long. He held it up for all to see. "We can't have a proper show if our star is incapable of performing now, can we?"

He casually jumped off the edge of the wagon and went over to the Wind-Up Kid who had now turned to face

him. Reaching up, the flamboyant Proctor inserted his key into the chest slot at the automaton's center and then proceeded to turn it clockwise. His actions created a clanking sound reminiscent of a grandfather clock being wound tight.

"How long does such a winding last?" a comely young woman in the front of the line dared to ask as she watched in fascination.

After finishing his task where he could no longer turn the key, Phineas pulled it out and turning to the lady replied, "Each full wind up allows the Kid to function for a full twelve hours before he slows down to a stop." He pocketed his key and then signaled Duprai that they were ready to continue with the demonstration.

Sheriff Hancock had heard the gunfire while emerging from the Broken Wheel Saloon and rightly assumed it came from the traveling show down by the stockades. As he stood in the shade on the saloon's boardwalk, he could just make out the huge crowd gathered there and then he heard them cheer loudly.

Must be a hell of a show, he thought, glad that his friends and neighbors were enjoying themselves. In his right hand he held a small two-pint tin bucket filled with beer. He stepped down onto the dirt street doing his best not to spill a drop. He wanted to make sure Manny got all of it. He walked slowly balancing the bucket of brew very, very carefully.

Just then several more shots rang out. But these were different. They seemed to come from his left down the other end of the main drag. Hancock stopped in the middle of the road and looked back towards Waginer's Mercantile just in time to see four men with bandanas covering their faces leap onto their horses and pull away from the store. Two of them appeared to be holding guns and firing them up in the air.

Sunofabitch! As the four riders galloped down the street towards him, he saw the front door to the shop slap open and out came Dan Waginer, his old single barrel shotgun in his hands.

"I've been robbed!" the apron wearing Waginer yelled as he lifted his weapon and took aim on the fleeing horsemen. He fired and the recoil sent him flying back into the store, his shot going wide as the scattered buckshot was sent harmlessly into the sky.

But Tom Hancock wasn't going to be so lucky. Not with four armed desperadoes charging right down upon him. In that infinite second of halted time, the dedicated lawman did the only thing he could do; he threw away the bucket in his hand and drew his six-gun from its holster on his hip.

Having spotted him, the robbers all began shooting at him, most of their shots tearing up the dirt before him. Whereas Hancock turned his body sideways, hoping to diminish his own vulnerability as he raised his gun to shoulder length and fired away. He missed and fired again.

The horsemen grew larger before his eyes and suddenly he felt a stabbing pain in his left thigh and then another in his shoulder. He cried out and fell over, his gun falling from his grasp. Then the riders were racing past him as he lay on the road bleeding and in pain.

At the same time everyone gathered around Prof. Proctor's presentation had also heard the gun battle between the escaping hombres and the sheriff, but few had been able to see the action itself. Amongst those few were the children across the street atop the stockade fences, including Cesar and his pals.

Upon witnessing the shooting, the boy had stood tall and, waving his arms at the still confused gathering, yelled at them at the top of his lungs, "THOSE RIDERS SHOT THE SHERIFF!"

At that, several women screamed and some of the men started moving away from the field to get a better look down the town's central artery.

Whereas Phineas Proctor, upon hearing Cesar's cry, looked down at this amazing invention and gave it new orders. "KID, STOP THOSE RIDERS COMING DOWN THE ROAD!"

And just like that the seven foot tall, gold painted Wind-Up Kid moved through the crowd like a scythe through a field of wheat; people backed out of his way in fear of being trampled by his humungous feet. Straight on he marched until he stood in the middle of the road and there turned to face the oncoming outlaws.

Although each of the four villains must have been shocked at the sight of the shiny, giant man-shaped machine that blocked their exit path, none of them hesitated for a moment. Each directed his shots at the Kid.

Several slugs hit the Kid but only ricocheted off his metal skin, whizzing off into nowhere. As for the Wind-Up Kid, he merely did what he had been directed to do. He whipped up his Colts and holding both hip-high, began blasting away at the oncoming varmints. Each of his shots hit their targets and all four men were hit with his first volley. The two on the left fell back out of their saddles, their horses suddenly rearing up in fright from the loud gunfire. One of them collided with the horse still carrying a masked shooter and toppled him to the ground, where he lay stunned.

The final rider managed to stay atop his horse as it reared up although he was wounded in the arm. As soon as the horse's hooves touched the ground again, he started to aim for the Kid, only to be hit by another bullet from the mechanical gunslinger's smoking gun. This one nailed him in the heart and he folded over his horse's neck dead. The skittish animal ran a few more feet until the corpse slid off its back.

Within twenty seconds three of the men who had robbed Waginer's Mercantile lay dead in the street and the fourth, rolled up clutching his side was in no condition to continue the fight.

The Wind-Up Kid walked past the nervous horses and stood above the hurt outlaw whose gun had fallen beside him. When the masked man looked up and saw what was standing over him, he feebly rolled onto his side and frantically tried to reach for his gun.

The Kid took a step forward and brought his foot down on the gun with a massive crunching sound.

The aftermath of the main street gunfight began as a chaotic stampede as the people of Sandy Creek all flocked to the site pushing and shoving each other to see whatever there was to see.

Manny Ramirez, upon hearing the first few shots, had run out of his shop and witnessed the entire confrontation, from Tom Hancock's brave stand and fall to the incredible prowess of the giant golden Wind-Up Kid. Now he was doing his best to make himself heard above the din of anxious people.

"Please, everyone get back!" he implored. "Here comes Doc Anderson. Let him get by, please!"

At that, folks started backing away from the bodies, both dead and wounded, laying stretched out on the ground, allowing the small bald-headed man with the rimless eyeglasses to push his way through to Hancock, still on his side and moaning from his two wounds.

"Get the hell back!" Doc ordered, holding up his familiar bag. "Give us some damn room! All of you."

Now having cleared an area around the fallen lawman, Anderson dropped to both knees, gently touched Hancock's arm near the bloody spot and began to examine how severe he was injured. "Take it easy, Tom," he assured his lifelong friend, "it don't look too bad."

"Yeah, maybe," gasped the sheriff, "but it sure hurts like hell."

While the town healer continued to examine his patient, Manny kept pushing the onlookers back. Several were around one varmint who appeared to be still breathing.

The other three were clearly dead. The Wind-Up Kid continued to stand guard over the injured man.

When Manny spotted Cesar and his young friends, he called him over loudly. He pointed to the outlaw's four horses still milling around the outer edges of the huge crowd. "Cesar, you and your friends round up those horses and take them into the stables. Get them taken care of and wait there for me. Understood?"

"Si, Papa, we'll do as you say."

As the boy signaled his friends and they ran off to get the four skittish horses, Manny heard Doc Anderson again. "Some of you men help me get the sheriff and that other fellow to my office."

Considering Tom Hancock's bulk, the blacksmith knew that wasn't going to be a pleasant task. Several local ranchers were moving forward to volunteer when they were all stopped short by Phineas Proctor and his foreman, Wallace Duprai.

"Gentlemen, please." The showman approached Doc Anderson, who by then had tied a tourniquet around hancock's left arm and another around his left thigh. "Allow us to be of assistance."

Doc looking up at the fancy dressed stranger, pushed his tiny glasses up his round nose. "Huh, what d'yah mean?"

"Only that my machine is better suited to moving Sheriff Hancock in a manner that will cause him the least amount of suffering." He pointed to the mechanical Kid.

Doc Anderson had seen many strange things in his long career of ministering to the sick in Sandy Creek but this had to be one of the strangest. Still, his only concern was his patient's care. "Alright, mister, go ahead with it. But make sure that thing is careful with him."

Phineas nodded, turned and with a few hand motions, directed people to open a path for his machine. Then he clapped his hands loudly and said, "KID, COME HERE AND PICK UP THE SHERIFF."

The Wind-Up Kid turned, walked over to its creator in three long strides. He looked down at Hancock, and then dropping heavily to one massive knee, he brought his hands down and under the wounded man.

"BE GENTLE WITH HIM," Prof. Proctor cautioned.

"Yes, sir," the Kid replied in his tinny voice. Then he stood slowly, holding Hancock safely cradled in his powerful arms as if he were as fragile as a newborn babe.

"This way," Doc Anderson said as he too got to his feet. "Some of you other men bring the other one."

Manny waved to the doctor and then proceeded to recruit two of his neighbors to help him. As he did so, he looked at the lifeless bodies and knew the undertaker, Silas Wilson, would be along quick enough to deal with their remains.

Thus the odd procession began its way back down the main street of Sandy Creek.

With the principle players having departed, the gathering soon dispersed. Many of the single men headed for the Broke Wheel while most of the country folks packed up their families in their buckboards and began their journeys back to their farms and ranches.

None paid any particular attention to the lone cowpoke who, upon seeing the surviving bandit hauled away, rushed to find his own horse, mounted up and galloped out of town hurriedly. He was a shiftless drifter named Walt Calhoun and he was on a mission. One he hoped would prove highly profitable

∙∙∙∙∙∙∙∙∙∙∙∙∙∙∙∙∙∙∙∙∙∙∙∙∙∙∙∙∙∙∙∙∙∙∙∙∙∙∙

It was almost sunset when Sheriff Tom Hancock swam up through a deep pool of pain to regain consciousness. He felt the aches in his thigh and arm, his senses still woozy from whatever medicine old Doc Anderson had administered while he was unconscious. He attempted to lift his head only to have the room start to spin. He sighed and lowered his head to the soft pillow beneath it.

Doc Anderson had three rooms from which he conducted his practice. The first was the parlor where his patients first entered his small home and had to await his presence. There were two doors opposite the front door; one led into his examination room and the other to a large corner room filled with two comfortable beds. It was here that recovering patients could rest and heal properly until it was time for them to go home.

It was in this room that Hancock found himself; a small candle on the table between the two beds provided a soft light as darkness set in outside the window to his left. He heard snoring and turned his head to look at the sleeping fellow he shared the room with. It took the sheriff only a second to recognize the grizzled face of the wounded robber.

Holy Jehosophat!

At that precise moment the door opened and Doc Anderson walked in, his shirt sleeves rolled up to his elbows and a tired expression on his face. As he approached the bed he saw that Hancock was awake and smiled. "Well, glad to see you're all done your napping, Tom."

"Yeah, right. Thanks for patching me up, Doc? How bad am I hurt?"

"You're a lucky man, Tom. The bullet in your arm didn't hit anything but muscle and I got it out clean while the one that hit your thigh went clean through so all it needed was a good washing and bandages."

"Good. How long before I can get out of here?"

"Whoa, hold on a second there, Tom. I said you were doing fine but you still lost a good deal of blood before I could get you sewn up properly. And you ain't gonna be walking on that leg, at least not without a crutch, for at least a good month."

Tom started to sit up again despite the dizziness behind his eyes. Anderson went over, put his arm behind his shoulders and propped him up with the pillows against the bed's head-post.

"Jesus, Mary, Joseph, Tom, why are you so all fired up anxious to get up for? That fellow in the bed over there is the only one of the varmints who survived the shoot-out with that crazy tin man." Doc pointed to the sleeping man's wrist to show it had been hand-cuffed to the bed frame under him. "And as you can see, he ain't going no-where once he heals up from some busted ribs."

"You don't understand, Doc," the sheriff explained. "It's who that fellah is that has me spooked."

"What?"

"I recognized him from wanted posters I got back at the jail."

"So, who is he?"

"Doc, that there is Billy Faro; Butch Faro's kid brother."

▪▪▪

Understanding the full importance of that revelation, Doc promised to alert several of the leading merchants. As Sandy Creek was so small, they had no mayor or actual ruling civic organization. Most matters dealing with business were handled by a loose coalition of entrepreneurs led by Dan Waginer and Manny Ramirez.

Doc was happy to find the two of them, along with Prof. Proctor and Wallace Duprai, seated around a table at the Broken Wheel saloon celebrating the dramatic defeat of the outlaw robbers. In fact both Phineas and Duprai were hailed instantly as heroes and Chuck Larkin, the owner proprietor of the tavern announced their drinks would be "on the house" for the remainder of their stay in Sandy Creek.

This was a fact that sat well with Waginer because all his hard-earned money had been recovered from the bodies of the three dead men. Thus there was much cause for celebration among all the patrons that night. Phineas had even stationed the now famous Wind-Up Kid to stand outside the saloon where he was admired for several hours by passing citizens, especially their children, until night fell and they were shooed away home.

Upon entering the boisterous saloon, Doc spotted the quartet through the thick haze of cigarette and cigar smoke at the center table, about to start imbibing on yet another round of drinks, and he proceeded over to join them. He found an empty chair along the way and pushed it in between Waginer and Ramirez.

"How's Tom?" Manny asked immediately.

"Just woke up and as cantankerous as ever."

"That's Tom alright," the shop-keeper said holding up his whiskey glass. "Here's to Sheriff Tom, a truly courageous soul."

"Here, here," the others chimed in lifting their own glasses.

"Well, that's only half the news I got," Anderson continued watching the four of them carefully. "There's more. And it ain't good."

"How do you mean, doctor?" Phineas inquired curiously.

"Well, after he come to, Tom identified the varmint resting up in the next bed." He paused to see if he had all their attention. Ramirez's eyes were a bit glassy from the alcohol, which he wasn't used to at all.

"So," the blacksmith prompted, "who is he?"

"According to Tom, he's Billy Faro; Butch Faro's baby brother."

And just like that a somber pall fell on the merry makers.

"Butch Faro?" Phineas was holding his top hat in his hand and now scratched the top of his head. "I seem to recall hearing that name before."

"Boss," the tall skinny black man had put down his empty whiskey glass. "They're talkin' about Butcher Faro, the cold-blooded killer who's wanted in three states. He and his gang have laid waste to half a dozen towns from here to Waco in the past few years."

"The one and the same," Doc nodded. "Last I read the Texas Rangers had chased them south into Mexico and that was the last anyone heard of them."

"Oh, my God," Dan Waginer's face was white, the color draining from it quickly. "If that's Butcher Faro's brother we caught, then he's got to be in these parts somewhere and ...and..." He gulped down the last of his drink unable to say anything else.

Manny Ramirez picked up the thread. "And that means once he hears we got his brother, he'll most likely be coming here to free him."

"That's how Tom figures it," Anderson added. "That's why he sent me here to find you all and let you know what trouble we got coming our way."

"But what does he expect us to do about?" Waginer's nerves were getting

the best of him. First he had been robbed at gunpoint and now was being told one of the most notorious outlaw gangs was about to ride into town any day soon. "We're just clerks and such. None of us is any good with guns and there's no way we can defend ourselves against the likes of the Faro gang."

"So, what do you suggest we do, Dan?" Manny wiped his lips with the back of his hands. "Just go get Billy Faro, untie him and let him loose?"

"Why not? I mean, once he rejoins his brother, there'll be no cause for them to come here. Right?"

"You're forgetting we already killed three of their gang this morning," Doc reminded the babbling Waginer. "I really don't think letting Billy go is going to satisfy a mad dog like Butcher Faro. Do you?"

And so the discussion had gone full circle and brought them all back to the same dilemma they had begun with and no apparent solution. Which was when Prof. Phineas Proctor put his top hat back on his head and coughed lightly.

"If I may, gentlemen, I am correct in hearing that Sheriff Hancock has no deputies to rely on?"

"Town's too small to afford any," the Mexican smithy confessed. "Some months we can barely scrape enough to pay Tom's salary. But he never complains. Says having a roof over his head and a place to call home is all he ever needed."

As the words tumbled out of Manny's mouth, he thought of his amigo and how bravely he had faced the four banditos. All because he loved

Sandy Creek and its people. Manny was suddenly ashamed of himself.

"Then perhaps I might be able to offer you kind people a viable solution to this perilous situation you find yourselves in," Proctor suggested with a lopsided smile on his angular face.

"Cut out the flowery lingo and speak plain, will yah?" Doc barked, now feeling the strain of the past few hours. "If you've got an idea, out with it!"

"Well, you gentlemen all witnessed how efficiently my mechanical gunfighter stopped those miscreants. What if I were to offer you his services for the next few weeks as Sheriff Hancock's temporary deputy? Do you think that might help?'

Four sets of eyes widened, and Phineas mentally congratulated himself for coming up with such a brilliant strategy.

Then Wallace Duprai kicked him in the shins under the table.

• •

It was dark when Walt Calhoun rode into the hill country just south of the Snake River. He'd been in the saddle all afternoon since leaving Sandy Creek and had only stopped once to relieve himself and then eat a few pieces of beef jerky before continuing his journey. Having ridden the outlaw trail often enough, Calhoun had heard Butch Faro maintained a hideout in one of the dozens of caves that pockmarked the area. It was Walt's hope that if he just rode through them in a roundabout course that eventually he would make contact with the gang.

Riding at night was never a wise course, what with gopher holes dotting the trails or even worse, mountain lions roaming hills for their next meal. But luck was on the cowboy's side this night as a full, yellow moon had come rising out of the east and was lighting up the countryside like a giant lantern hang directly overhead. Still, he kept his horse walking at a very careful pace and his right hand firmly on his gunbutt.

He guessed it was nearing ten o'clock when, upon descending a slight ravine between two hills, a man's voice suddenly rang out above him to the right. "Hold it right there, partner!"

Calhoun pulled back on his reins to stop his mount and then raised both his hands in the air. "Don't shoot." He directed his comments to the rocks from where the warning had originated. "My name's Walt Calhoun and I got a message for Butch Faro."

"Is that so?" the voice said. "Keep them hands where I can see 'em."

Then there was silence and Calhoun sat quietly not knowing what to expect next. After a few minutes a rider came around the rocks in front of him. In the moonlight Calhoun could see he was holding a rifle and it was pointed at him.

"You keep your gun hand up in the air," the stranger said, "and move on up the trail ahead of me. When you come to the small fork, turn to the left. You got that?"

"I got it."

"Good, then move out. And remember, you even sneeze wrong and I'll put a bullet in your back. Now get riding."

For the next few minutes Calhoun rode silently as he had been ordered. When they reached the split in the trail, he went left and then coming around a steep slope, found himself riding up to the front entrance of a cavern dug into the side of the hill before them. Through the gray of the night, he could just make out a tiny spark of flame from way back inside the cave.

There were several other men standing outside the hideout smoking. Upon seeing the two riders approach, one dashed back into the bowels of the cavern while the other stepped forth to meet them.

"Fellah says he needs to talk to Butch," the rider behind Calhoun informed the other man.

The mean faced guard looked up at Calhoun and examined him for a second. He was holding a Winchester and its barrel also was lined up with Calhoun's chest.

"Get off your horse, mister."

Calhoun did as he was told, keeping his right hand high.

"Now, hand me your six-shooter nice and slow and remember, Henry back there has still got you in his sights."

Once off his horse, the one called Henry also dismounted, walked up behind him and after removing his pistol from its holster, told him to lower his hand. Then he nudged him in the small of his back with his rifle and the three of them marched into the rock walled hideaway.

The cavern was so big that one section had been set aside as a corral to keep the gang's horses together. The blazing campfire was burning against the opposite wall and there were clustered another five men all stretched out lazily; a few were sound asleep.

As the three men halted in front of the fire, Butch Faro, seated with his back against the hard rock, cocked his red sombrero back on his head and looked up at them. Faro was a man of average build, but it was his face that made people pause. It was swarthy with a square jaw buried beneath a dirty gray beard. He had a bulbous nose and a livid pink scar stretched from his left cheek up to the corner of his left eye. He wore a bullet heavy bandolier across his chest and twin pistols butt forward on each hip for a fast cross-body draw.

"What's this?" he growled. "We got us some uninvited company."

"He said he had a message for you, Butch," Henry Slater answered. "Said his name was Calhoun or some such."

Just then one of the men to Faro's side sat up and peered up over the fire. "Well, I'll be! If it ain't old Walt Calhoun." The man, named Chester Welman, turned to the gang leader. "I can vouch for him, Butch. Walt and me used to work for the Circle B Ranch up in Abilene before we decided to rustle us a few dozen head for our own profit."

"Is that right," Butch Faro pulled a pouch of tobacco from his calico shirt pocket and a piece of cigarette paper. He licked one side of the paper, then folded it expertly and started to drop tobacco onto it. "So, what's this here message you got for me, Calhoun?"

The moment of truth had arrived and Walt Calhoun's mouth had suddenly gone dry. Though not a religious man by any means, he suddenly praycd the outlaw wouldn't blame him for the bad news he was about to impart.

"Your kid brother...ah...Billy...ah.."

Having finished rolling his smoke, Faro had caught it in the corner of his mouth and was in the process of lighting it with a glowing branch from the fire. "What about Billy?" He puffed on the cigarette and tossed away the burning stick.

"He got shot trying to rob the mercantile store in Sandy Creek this morning."

"What?" Butch Faro jumped to his feet and moved around the hot fire to confront Calhoun. "Is he dead? Tell me!"

"Ah...no...Butch," Calhoun exclaimed. "He was only wounded. The doctor there patched him up."

"What about the boys that was riding with him?"

"They wasn't so lucky. They all got killed."

Butch Faro grabbed Calhoun by the shirt and pulled him up close. The glowing tip of his cigarette was almost touching Calhoun's face and burning him.

"How da hell did it happen?" Faro barked, his brown eyes filled with rage. "You tell me everything that happened...right from the start. And do it fast!"

Walt Calhoun gulped. "Right, Butch...right. It was just after that

traveling show had started up on the south side of the town. Some fellah named Prof. Proctor was showing off his mechanical shooter..."

"Have you gone plum loco?" Wallace Duprai asked his friend and employer, Phineas Proctor, as they walked back to their tents after leaving the Broken Wheel saloon. The massive Wind-Up Kid followed behind them by a few yards, his heavy feet thumping into the ground with every step.

"Please, Wallace, lowci your voice." Prof. Proctor indicated the darkened shops to either side of the street. "You'll awaken the dead shouting like that."

"Dear Lord, I'm gonna do more than shout if you don't come to your senses!"

Realizing his associate was not about to cease his ranting, Phineas simply increased his pace as they moved along.

"Well, I don't see what has you so all riled up," Phineas went on in his own defense. "All I did was offer our services to these good people who were kind enough to welcome our little family into their town."

Wallace, whose dark chocolate skin was nearly invisible in the dark, sighed and shook his head in resignation. "How long we been working together, Professor? What, going on almost ten years now?"

The two had met in New Orleans months after the end of the Civil War. Phineas, a native of South Carolina, had quit his teaching position at the beginning of hostilities and gone to the port city to devote his time and genius into creating something positive. The horrors he had witnessed on his trip to war ravaged communities had only strengthened his resolve to invent something truly special. Something that would rekindle the spirit of people and help them forget the years of the conflict.

Wallace Duprai, a recently emancipated slave, had come to Proctor's attention as a hardworking, honest individual with a talent for tinkering with machinery. Upon their first meeting, each had recognized in the other a like soul and their bond had been struck instantly. In fact, once the Wind-Up Kid had been built and proven reliable, it was Duprai who had come up with the idea of putting together a traveling circus and gone out to recruit the others. For the next ten years they had traveled the southwest visiting hundreds of small communities and entertained thousands.

It was a good life and neither ever regretted their partnership.

"They've been very, very good years, my friend," Phineas agreed.

"Then why you wanna go spoiling it all now?"

"I am doing no such thing."

"Look, Professor, what you are doing is putting us, and everyone else in our troop, smack in the middle of a fight 'tween these folks and the gang."

"What other recourse did I have, sir?"

"Recourse? Why you could have just kept your mouth shut, is what. You could have just had another drink, said

good night to them fellahs and we could have gone on our way.

"Professor, this ain't our fight and I'm afraid you is gonna get us all killed for sure. Don't you see that?"

They had reached the end of the road and their tents and wagons were silent before them. Lantern light peeked out through one of the enclosures indicated some of their colleagues were still up and most likely awaiting news of their immediate fate.

Phineas stopped and turned to address the mechanical man. "KID, RETURN TO YOUR PLACE IN THE TENT AND TELL THE OTHERS WE WILL SOON BE THERE."

"As you command, Professor." The Kid walked between Proctor and Duprai and continued on to the nearest tent.

Watching him walk off, the Professor said, "I'm truly sorry if you believe I've somehow endangered you and others, Wallace. That was not my intent. Ever."

"Then why'd you go and do what you done?"

Phineas pointed at the retreating figure of his greatest creation. "Look at him, Wallace, a true marvel of scientific achievement. And yet all we do with him is parade him around like a dancing dog, making him do silly tricks for the masses."

"So, ain't that why you built him fer?"

"Perhaps...in the beginning." Phineas looked at his oldest friend and pleaded his reasoning. "But here, in this place and this time, I suddenly realized he could be so much more than a mere toy to be displayed for peoples' amusement.

"Don't you see, if he can protect this town and its citizenry, the Wind-Up Kid will become something more; something truly historical and no one will ever forget him...or us."

"What in darnation are you talkin' about, Professor? What do you think he's gonna become?"

"A legend, Wallace. He's going to become a legend."

■ ■

By the time Walt Calhoun had finished his tale, Butch Faro had finished his cigarette and was in the process of rolling another one.

"If that ain't the biggest crop of horse apples I've ever heard, I'll eat this hear sombrero," the bandit boss said, blowing a puff of smoke from his dirty lips. "I oughta shoot yah just for being a liar."

"But it's all gospel truth," Calhoun protested, his eyes doubling in size as he saw Faro's right hand falling to the butt of his pistol. "I swear it is! I done saw it with my own eyes, I tell yah!"

"Butch, he ain't lying," Henry Slater interrupted. By now all the other members of the gang were gathered around the fire and most had heard Calhoun's amazing report.

"I seen this gold-colored shooting monster in Arkansas a few years back. It's just like he said; big, shiny and when it shoots at something' it never misses."

"I seen it too," Chester Welman joined in from his place by the fire. "I think it was in Waco. This Professor dude brought it out for all to see then had it put on this shooting exhibition. It was the strangest thing I ever seen. Just like Henry says, the damn thing never misses a single shot."

So now Butch, the Butcher, Faro found himself in a quandary. He scratched his thick gray beard while still holding the cigarette in his lips. His eyes narrowed and he tried to mentally assess the problem that confronted him.

"Then how the hell am I suppose to ride in there and free Billy," he voiced aloud, "if'n we have to come up against some giant shooter thing that never misses?" His gaze went from man to man, hoping against all odds that one of them would have an answer. "Seems like what you boys sayin' is there's no way to beat this Wind-Up Kid."

"Well, there might be on way," Walt Calhoun said softly, hoping not to sound too boastful. He was still nervous being around the Butcher.

"Oh, and how's that?" Faro barked.

"Well, just before this Professor feller sic'ed his machine on your brother and his pals, he had to wind him up with a key."

"Huh? A key? How so?"

"Well, as I recall, the Kid...ah...the machine, after taking a couple of shots at those colored balls, told the Professor he was gonna wind down. So the Professor pulls this key out of his pocket..."

"What kind of key?" Faro again put his face right up to Calhoun's.

"Ah...it looked like any other key, Butch. You know, like a house key that opens your front door if'n you got a house."

"Okay. Then what did he do with it?"

"Well, he put it in the mechanical feller's chest and cranked him up. It was like he was boosting him up with new strength and all."

Butch Faro took a step back and now adjusted his thinking. "Do you know how often this Professor has to use this key? Did he say?"

"Well, I think some woman at the show asked that very question, Butch, and the Professor said each wind-up was good for twelve hours."

"Hmm, so if'n this shooting machine don't get wound up after twelve hours it just up and what? Does it die?"

"Gosh, I don't rightly know, Butch. Maybe it just stops."

At that Butch nodded and then his eyes shined with a gleam from the campfire and he slapped Calhoun on the arm. "That's right, partner. It just stops!"

He looked around at his men and then motioned all of them to move in closer. "Alright you mangy varmints, listen up good. Here's what we're going to do. First thing tomorrow we're gonna ride out of here for Sandy Creek and…"

• •

The following day, Prof. Phineas Proctor made sure his troop put on their regularly scheduled afternoon show. Although the audience wasn't as large as it had been the day before, those assembled were clearly appreciative of their efforts and applauded soundly after each act. Madame Mabel Higgins even received a few wolf whistles from some of the men in the audience when she crawled under one of the empty wagons and then, flexing her knees, managed to stand erect holding the wooden construct off the ground for over ten minutes. Some even called out proposals of marriage after she stepped away from the wagon and struck a pose as the World's Strongest Woman.

Antoine Boulanger, the French fire eater dazzled everyone with his sword-swallowing routine and then had them cheering when he put flaming sticks in his mouth with no visible ill effects. And lastly the acrobatic Chin brothers spent a good half hour tumbling all over their platform stage in tent number two, much to the delight of the good people of Sandy Creek.

Still, it was the Wind-Up Kid they had all come out to see; especially after the word of the previous day's gun battle with the outlaws had spread throughout the community and even to neighboring towns. Prof. Proctor was delighted with the Kid's reception and made sure no one went home disappointed.

After the performance, Phineas left Duprai in charge and went off to visit Sheriff Hancock to discuss how he wished to utilize the services of his mechanical gunfighter.

"Well, Professor, I think the best thing would be to simply have that …machine of yours station itself outside the jail and stand guard," Hancock said as he hobbled around Doc Anderson's front room. He was leaning on a wooden crutch tucked under his right arm. His left arm was wrapped up in a sling which made using two crutches impossible.

"The fool wants to move back to his office and bring the Faro kid with him," the doctor elaborated. "He's always been a stubborn cuss."

"Well, the town don't pay me to stay in bed all day do they?" Hancock fired back. "Besides, I'll go stir just sitting around here a minute longer. I'll rest lots easier once I'm back in my office and Billy is locked up in a cell."

Thus, it was decided that at the end of the day, when all their performances were concluded, that Prof. Proctor would deliver the Kid to the sheriff's office at the other end of town across from the general store and leave him there to stand watch during the night.

Nightfall came quickly as the remainder of the day seemed to speed away for everyone. With the last show of the day completed, Prof. Proctor and Wallace Duprai left their people to clean up, and with the Wind-Up Kid in tow, started north on foot. Duprai wanted to stop off at the stables and see how Manny Ramirez was coming with the new horseshoes.

As they neared the smithy's open front doors they could hear Ramirez's hammer pounding away and the light from two lanterns hung on support posts spilled out onto the street. "I'll see you back at the camp," Duprai said as he headed for the stable. As he was about to enter, a small, speedy figure darted out of the shop and ran to Proctor and the Kid. It was Cesar Ramirez.

"Hello, Senor Professor," he said breathlessly.

"Good eveing, Senor Cesar." Phineas smiled at the boy.

"Where are you going with Senor Kid?"

"To deliver him to Sheriff Hancock. Would you care to join me?"

"Si! Yes, please."

"Then come along."

Proctor and the automaton continued walking northward with Cesar following in-step with them. He was totally mesmerized by the Wind-Up Kid and kept glancing up at him in sheer wonderment.

Neither paid any attention to the two cowpokes who rode past them on the other side of the street. In the gloom of twilight, they appeared to be just another two roving saddle tramps making for the saloon.

"What does he eat, Professor?" the boy wanted to know.

Phineas chuckled. "He doesn't really eat at all, Cesar. Oh, no. He just requires oil to lubricate his gears and joints. As long as they are properly maintained, he will continue to function perfectly."

"Oh."

They were both surprised to see Sheriff Hancock seated in an old rocking chair on the jailhouse porch smoking a cigar, his hands folded comfortably over his round belly.

"Good evening, Sheriff." Proctor tipped his hat. "Here we are as promised."

"Evening, Professor. Hello, Cesar." The boy smiled and returned the greeting. Hancock pointed to the Kid. "So what next?"

"Please watch my method of commanding him," Phineas said before turning to face his tall, golden machine man. "KID, YOU ARE TO STAND BEFORE THIS OFFICE AND ALLOW NO ONE TO PASS EXCEPT MYSELF OR THE SHERIFF."

The tiny glass eyes of the Kid seemed to sparkle as he replied. "I hear and obey, Professor. No one shall pass save for you and the Sheriff."

"HOW ARE YOUR COILS?"

"I will wind down in approximately twenty-minutes," the Kid replied.

Professor Proctor reached into his jacket and pulled out his key. He stepped up to the Kid, inserted the Key and turned it several times clockwise until he could no longer move it.

"There," he said to Hancock, as he pocketed the key, "he will remain active for the next twelve hours."

"And what if I need him to move or some such?"

"Simply speak to him in the loud manner you observed me doing and call him Kid, nothing else. He will respond to your commands."

"Then I guess we're all set here." With that Hancock rose up out of his rocker, taking up the crutch that had been resting against the wall. With it under his arm, he tipped his hat to Phineas and Cesar. "I'll bid you both a good night, gentlemen."

After the sheriff had disappeared into his office and locked the door behind him, the Professor and Cesar started back down the street, their mission accomplished.

They were passing the saloon when suddenly a cry rang out from the alley next to the tavern. "Help me somebody!"

Phineas looked towards the alleyway, trying to see what was happening in its inky well of blackness. He heard men scuffling and again another plea for help.

"Cesar, run and fetch your father and Mr. Duprai."

"Si, Senor!"

"Hurry."

As soon as the boy was gone, the Professor ran for the alley. As he approached, he could just make out one figure on his knees while another stood over him pounding him with his fist.

"Stop that!" he called out. Rushing up behind the attacker, he shoved him off his victim. "Leave that chap alone!"

"Oh, yeah, well let's see how you like it,' a gruff voice retorted. Then a powerful fist connected with Phineas' chin, propelling him backward. A hand pressed up against his arm to stop him. It was the supposed victim. But now he wielded a pistol in his other hand and, grasping it by the barrel, brought the butt down on the Professor's head.

Phineas collapsed to the ground, his eyes suddenly crying. He felt two pairs of rough hands toss him on his backside and then someone one was digging into his vest pocket.

"I've got it!" the rough man sang out and immediately the hands left him alone. As he sank into unconsciousness, Phineas Proctor heard feet rushing away to be followed by the sound of galloping horses.

Then he gratefully passed out.

••••••••••••••••••••••••••••••••••••

A few minutes later, Manny Ramirez and Wallace Duprai, led by the boy, Cesar, found the unconscious inventor in the alley. Seeing that he was still alive, Manny told his son to run and fetch Doc Anderson. Then he and Duprai carefully picked up the Professor. Duprai picked up his friend's hat off the ground before they proceeded to carry him back to the stables. There they sat him up on a bale of hay stacked against an empty pen.

By then Phineas had started coming around, though he was groggy and confused as to where he was and what had happened. Manny took one of his many ladles and, going to the well behind the shop, filled it with cool water from the bucket there. He handed it to Phineas and told him to drink it.

"What happened to me?" the injured showman asked as his vision began to clear and he recognized his friends.

"You were robbed in the alley next to the saloon," Wallace informed him, still clutching Phineas' top hat in his hands.

At that point Doc Anderson came hustling into the stables along with Cesar. He saw the Professor and went over to him. There he set his bag on the ground and bent down to examine the back of the man's head. His stubby fingers explored the top of his skull.

"Ouch!" Phineas cried out. "That hurts."

"No doubt," Anderson said. "You've got good size goose-egg here. Somebody really walloped you hard, Professor."

"But why would anyone hurt Senor Proctor?" Cesar asked innocently.

Which was when Phineas recalled his final thoughts after having been assaulted. He reached into his dirty coat and his fingers fumbled around in his vest pockets.

"It's gone!" he suddenly realized aloud. "They stole the key to the Wind-Up Kid!"

"Aw, hell," Wallace cursed. "If you can't rewind the Kid come sunup tomorrow morning, he ain't gonna be no better than one of them cigar store injuns back in New Orleans."

While listening to the exchange, Doc Anderson had sat down beside Phineas and, digging into his medical bag, had removed a small envelope with granules of white powder in it. He reached over, took the ladle out of the inventor's hands and dumped the medicine into it. "Here, stir that stuff in the rest of the water with your finger and then drink it down."

"What is it?"

"Laudanum. It will help with your headache."

As Phineas complied with the doctor's wishes, Manny looked from him to Duprai trying to fathom the gist of their words. "I don't understand by what you mean about winding up the mechanical shooter?"

"Imagine him like a clock," Professor Proctor said, after swallowing the pain medicine and making a sour face at its bitter taste. "That's how the Kid works. If he isn't rewound when he runs down tomorrow morning, we won't be able to use him to help defend the jail."

"I'd wager it was some of Butch Faro's men who attacked you, Professor," Doc guessed, putting the pieces together. "Someone must have told them about the key and Faro sent them here to steal it from you."

"But do you not have another key?" Manny asked hopefully.

"Sadly, no, my friend." Phineas started to shake his head and then thought better of it. The throbbing inside it was as a loud as a kettle drum. "A foolish negligence that we are now going to suffer for, it would seem."

"Perhaps I can make you a new one?" the blacksmith offered.

At that the Professor sat up a bit straighter, his eyes narrowing. "Can you do that?"

Manny waved his muscular arms about and smiled. "Senor, look around you. Making things is what I do."

"But you don't know what the key looks like, Papa." Cesar was caught in the possibility like the others.

"No, I do not," Manny told his son, "but if the Professor can draw it for me, then I can make it. All I need is a good picture and from that I can shape the iron. It may not be a perfect key, but if it is close enough, it may still work on the machine man."

"Can you do it?" the boy inquired of the inventor. "Can you draw this key so my Papa can make it for real?"

It was a desperate plan, of that there was no doubt. When the sun rose the next morning, all of them knew Butcher Faro and his killers would ride into Sandy Creek to free his brother and there would be lots of bloodshed. Realizing there was no other solution,

Professor Phineas Proctor closed his eyes for a second and attempted to visualize the small key he had owned for nearly a decade.

"By Jove!" he exclaimed as his eyes snapped opened. "I do believe I can!"

The four men together decided on what courses of action were required. Doc Anderson thought it best not to bother Sheriff Hancock as he still needed all the rest he could get. As they did not suspect any attack from the Faro gang until the next morning, Doc told them he would be up before the dawn and go about warning the local residents of the impending danger; to include Sheriff Hancock as well.

As for Phineas Proctor, he agreed to spend the night with the blacksmith and offer what help he could in the fashioning of a new key for the Wind-Up Kid. He ordered Wallace Duprai to return to their people and inform them of what had happened. They were to prepare themselves for whatever the next day would bring.

After Anderson and Duprai had departed, Manny told his son to go home and tell his mother he would be working throughout the night and not to worry. Cesar, not wanting to leave, tried to argue, but the blacksmith was adamant and upon the threat of the seat of his pants being warmed, the lad reluctantly bid them goodnight and exited out the back door.

"So," began Phineas once he and Ramirez were alone. "What now?"

"I need to measure the slot in your mechanical man so that I may gauge the proper size to make this key you will draw for me."

"But of course, let's get on with it."

Using a lit candle, the two men once again went out and hurried through the nearly deserted street. It being early, the Broken Wheel was open for business though there didn't appear to be too many patrons inside. Once at the jail, the Professor held the candle up to light the slot in the Kid's chest so that Ramirez could take his measurements. The smithy used a ruler to determine the length of the aperture and then carefully extended a charcoal pencil into the hole. It went in as far as six inches. Quickly Manny jotted these numbers on the back of an old piece of newspaper he'd folded into his torn, heavy leather work apron.

"It is good," he told Phineas, who then blew out the candle and the two hurried back to the stables.

Once there, Manny closed the big double doors behind them and dropped the securing post onto their braces, locking them in and unwanted guests out.

Manny then started stoking the fire in his forge with more wood while Proctor, now holding the charcoal pencil and scrap of paper, stood beneath one of the two hanging lanterns and did his best to draw the stolen key. When he was done, he handed the scrap to the blacksmith.

"That's my key...as well as I can remember it, Mr. Ramirez."

"Please, Professor, we are amigos. Call me Manny." He took the paper, studied the detailed drawing and then nodded. "I think we are ready to begin."

As the long night wore on, so did Manny Ramirez's frustration. He had never attempted to craft anything as delicate as a key from iron. His first attempts at sculpting the heated bars he'd shaped from old horseshoes proved disastrous and he was clumsy with his hammer and chisel. Too many times he'd knocked off a chunk of the key's head when trying to fashion the two tines that jutted out of the body.

By midnight he'd failed eight times and was cursing under his breath as the Professor worked the bellows to maintain the heat in the brick encased forge. Most likely the tired blacksmith would have given up entirely if not for the unexpected visit of his lovely wife, Dolores, at that exact moment. She had brewed a pot of coffee and brought it to them along with a few sugar cookies to help keep their energy up. Seeing the tiredness in Manny's eyes, she embraced him lovingly and planted a kiss on his scruffy cheek.

"You can do anything you put your mind to, Manny." The look in her brown eyes was all he needed.

After Dolores had gone, Phineas, munching on a sweet cookie, said, "You are truly a lucky man, Manny."

"Si, Professor. Now, let's do this thing."

Thus, they went at it again. As the hours passed, Manny's hands learned to hold the chisel just right and soon he had shaped a serviceable key. But his euphoria evaporated the second he picked it up with his tongs and submerged it into his water bucket only to see it snap in two.

"What happened?" Phineas asked. "Why did it break like that?"

Manny held up his tongs, now only pinching the remaining bottom half of the key. Steam hissed off the still hot metal. "I believe it's too thin and fragile to endure the extremes of the heat and then the cold of the water."

His assertion proved true as the next few keys he produced all broke apart the second they were put in the water.

"If you can't cool them off, what then?" Phineas was looking at all the pieces on the ground next to the water bucket. Dawn was only a few hours away and they were running out of time.

"There is only one thing I can do," Manny explained. "We make another and then we set it on the bricks and let it cool without the water. I can't think of anything else that will work."

Phineas pulled a silver-plated timepiece from his vest, popped open the cover and looked at the time. "It's almost five, Manny. If my calculations are correct, the Kid will shut down in two hours. Will that be enough time to make another key and let it cool as you suggest?"

Manny put down his tongs, reached out with his gloved hand and grabbed another iron bar. "Well, there's only one way to find out."

▪▪▪▪▪▪▪▪▪▪▪▪▪▪▪▪▪▪▪▪▪▪▪▪▪▪▪▪▪▪▪▪

Butcher Faro and his seven men rode to the top of a small hill south of Sandy Creek just as the sun began to fill the sky to the east. Its purple and pink rays fought the blueness overhead, signaling the oncoming new day.

From their position atop the rise, the outlaws could see the rooftops of the town in the distance.

Faro leaned back in his saddle and twisted back to motion Walt Calhoun forward.

"Are you sure it was seven o'clock when that fellah cranked up that machine shooter?"

"You bet," Calhoun confirmed. "Jake and I had just walked past the saloon and I looked inside. There's a big clock over by the piano and it was just seven o'clock before we ducked into the alley and waited for him to come by."

Faro looked at the lightening sky. He'd never owned a timepiece and never needed one. He had always been good at deducing time. Now his instincts told him that they still had at least thirty minutes before the appointed hour.

"Alright, we'll wait here for a bit," he told his men, "just to make sure. Check your guns and carbines. In thirty minutes, we get Billy and tear that town apart."

▪▪▪▪▪▪▪▪▪▪▪▪▪▪▪▪▪▪▪▪▪▪▪▪▪▪▪▪▪▪▪▪

Professor Phineas Proctor heard the loud banging and thought it was his head still causing him grief. But the noise just got louder until it forced him to open his eyes. He'd fallen asleep on the floor, with his back against a bale of hay. Sitting up, he saw Manny Ramirez also slumbering, only next to his forge, his head cocked at an angle.

Phineas tried to remember when they'd both nodded off as he pushed back against the hay and managed to get to his feet. The banging was coming from the barred front doors and he started for them.

Ramirez's head moved and he too came awake, rubbing his eyes with the back of his hands. "What is it?" he mumbled half-asleep.

"Get up," Phineas said as he reached the doors. "It's morning." Sunlight filtered through the slats of the double doors.

"Who's there?" he questioned before lifting off the restraining post.

"Professor, open the doors!" Wallace Duprai said. "It's me and the others. Hurry."

Phineas pulled the post up and set it against the wall. Duprai pulled open the door and he and the members of the traveling show all rushed in. All of them were armed with one kind of weapon or another and the Professor could see fear in their faces. "What is it?"

"The outlaws," Duprai replied, pointing outside. "They're here!"

Phineas stepped out the door and glanced down the street. There he saw the horsemen riding boldly up the middle of street. Their leader wore a large, red colored sombrero. Phineas dashed back into the stable and pulled the door behind him.

"Damn!"

"What are we going to do?" Duprai wanted to know. He was clutching an old Remington repeating rifle.

"Is it the bandidos?" Manny Ramirez had gotten to his feet.

"Yes," Phineas said. "They're coming up the road as if they already own the town."

Manny looked down at his forge. The last key he had made was lying beside his gloves. He reached down and carefully touched it with his fingertips. It was cool to his touch and he picked it up in his hand to hold it up for all to see.

"The key, it is finished."

"Then one of us has to take it and get to Wind-Up Kid before the outlaws do," Phineas said.

No one had heard the backdoor opened until a small voice spoke, "Please, Senor Professor, let me do it." All eyes turned to see Cesar Ramirez standing behind his father.

"You?" his father reacted. "No, it is too dangerous. The bandidos have come, Cesar. They are outside in the street. It is too late now."

"No, Papa," the boy claimed. "Give me the key. I will run to the jail from behind the stores, Papa. They will not see me until I am there. Then I will use the key and wake up the Kid."

Phineas walked over to Manny. "It would appear the lad is our only remaining option, Manny. But it is your decision to make."

Manny nodded, understanding what was being asked of him, and grateful Dolores wasn't present. He patted the Professor on the arm. "Si, I know this." Then he went to the boy and handed him the precious key.

"Listen to me carefully, Cesar. Stay behind the buildings until you reach the jail and then come around from behind it. Do you understand me? Do not come out onto the street so that the bandidos can see you. Come around the jail and go to the machine man in that way only."

"Si, Papa," the boy said with all the seriousness he could muster. "I will do exactly as you say."

"Then go...now. Hurry, and God be with you." Manny reached down, kissed his son on the top of the head and then moved to open the rear door for him. "Go, before I change my mind."

Cesar held up to key to Proctor and grinned. "I will not fail you, Senor Professor."

Then he was gone, leaving the adults behind to wonder if they had done the right thing or not.

"Look, they are moving past," Wallace Duprai spoke in a whisper while standing by the doors. He'd cracked them open by a few inches so he could see the riders as they approached.

Phineas and Manny joined the others and peeked over Duprai's shoulder as the tough looking bunch trotted past the stables. The outlaws appeared nervous as they weren't prepared to find the town deserted. Phineas assumed Doc Anderson had achieved his own mission in rousing the townsfolk before dawn and warning them to stay off the streets no matter what happened.

Phineas counted eight men, all of them rough looking characters whose savage histories were etched in their dirty, hard faces. What would happen next was anybody's guess.

∎∎∎∎∎∎∎∎∎∎∎∎∎∎∎∎∎∎∎∎∎∎∎∎

Cesar dashed behind the shops of Sandy Creek like a racing fox, moving in and around rain barrels, piles of trash and other discarded items left by the merchants over the years. He was totally familiar with this winding path as he and his young companions had spent countless hours playing in and out of the alleyways and back yards few adults bothered with.

As he moved further along, he caught a glimpse of the riders via a narrow alleyway and that only spurred him to run faster. He had to reach the jail first or all would be lost.

He grasped the key tightly as he leaped over a mound of junk like a jackrabbit in flight.

∎∎∎∎∎∎∎∎∎∎∎∎∎∎∎∎∎∎∎∎∎∎∎∎∎

Butch Faro was worried, although he made sure to conceal that fact from the men riding behind him. The quiet, empty street was not what he had expected when they rode out of the hills and into town. Apparently, the people who owned the machine gunfighter had reasoned it was his men who had stolen the operating key and so were prepared for his arrival.

But even if they were foolhardy enough to set a trap for him, he couldn't believe simple shop keepers would have the gumption to fight it out with them. Years of subjugating similar towns with his cold-blooded savagery had proven to him that such spineless men were no threat. Still, their absences gave the town an eerie, graveyard atmosphere that was felt by all his men and none of them had spoken a word since coming into Sandy Creek. Now they rode slowly, all of them watching the windows and doors around them, wary of a possible strike, if such a thing were possible.

"Look, there's the jail...and the golden man!" Henry Slater announced suddenly.

Butch Faro pulled back on his reins and his horse stopped. In the glare of the morning sun, he saw the machine gunfighter for the first time, though he had to squint as its golden skin was sparkling brightly. The thing was huge, just as he'd been told. It was also creepy just standing there, its long arms stiff by its side. He could just make out the twin holsters and re-membered his men's stories about how deadly the monster was with them.

But now it was just standing there, oblivious to anything including their presence. Faro felt his confidence ris-ing. His plan was working out just fine.

He started to nudge his mount for-ward when he spotted something dart out from the corner of the jailhouse. It was a young boy with a mop of brown hair and wearing cheap homemade clothing.

What the hell? Faro thought per-plexed until he saw the boy run up to the golden giant and reaching up on his toes, insert something into its chest.

It was another key! The damn kid had a second key! In disbelief, the out-law boss watched as the boy began to crank the key.

"NO!" Faro cried out, seeing his grand scheme being foiled before his eyes. "Stop that kid from winding it up!" He pulled out one of his pistols and started shooting.

Hearing the gunfire, Manny Ramirez pushed past the others in the stable and bolted outside. "They've seen Cesar! We must stop them!"

Manny could have save his breath for even as he spoke, Phineas, Duprai and the others all came up beside him and began firing their weapons at the outlaws. Maybe they couldn't hit any of them, but that wasn't the intent; to distract them from firing at the boy was.

Faro's horse reared up as bullets suddenly whizzed all around them. Twisting his head, he saw the door to Waginer's Mercantile was open and man was standing in it firing an old shotgun at them. On the other side of the street, other rifle barrels poked out from nearby windows, belching their own hot lead.

At the same time the gang was com-ing under this assault, Sheriff Hancock had opened the front door to the jail and leaned his head out. From his front window he had seen Cesar rush up and start to wind the mechanical gunfighter

"KID," he yelled to be heard over the roaring gunfire. "PROTECT THE BOY!"

The Wind-Up Kid's head shifted slightly and then looked down at Cesar Ramirez. Although the boy had only turned the key a few revolutions, it was enough for the Kid to comply with Hancock's command. Smoothly the Kid reached down, picked up Cesar and holding him to his chest, pivoted around. Now the lad was shielded from the gang's bullets, and he continued to turn the key as fast he could.

Bullets spanged off the automaton, but Cesar continued to crank the key his Papa had made. Then it was done turning.

"Cesar," the sheriff called out, again poking his head from behind the door frame. "Get your butt in here now!"

"Si, Senor Sheriff."

Cesar, looked up into the polished face of the Wind-Up Kid, directly into the machine's glass eyes. "You can put me down now, Kid."

Somehow the machine understood the boy and taking a step up onto the porch, it set him down in the open doorway while bullets continued to fly all around them.

Once on his feet, Cesar gave his new friend one more command, "Now go and save my town, Senor Kid, and defeat the bandidos."

Having said that, Cesar was suddenly yanked out of sight by Tom Hancock. "Fool, kid, you're just as crazy as your father."

"Si, Senor, I am." And the boy smiled mischievously.

Having been given his marching orders, the Wind-Up Kid stepped off the porch and facing the gun blasting outlaws, began walking towards them. He drew his two revolvers and opened fire with deadly accuracy.

One rider was knocked off his horse, followed immediately by two others as the Kid got closer and closer.

Butch Faro, struggling to keep his horse from bolting, fired at the unstoppable golden gunfighter and though his bullets hit the Kid, they had no

noticeable effect. Faro's worst nightmare was at long last coming true; he was fighting something he couldn't beat no matter how hard he tried. The Wind-Up Kid continued shooting while coming closer, until half of Faro's men had been unhorsed and were lying in the dust.

Frantic to escape, Butch yanked his reins to bring his horse about. "Get out of here!" he cried out to the men still fighting. He kicked his horse in the side and bent low in the saddle hoping to get away before a bullet with his name on it found him.

As the gang tried to turn their horses around, two more were hit and toppled to the ground. Then the others were racing down the street, desperate to escape the lethal trap they'd so brazenly entered.

Only now their path was blocked by Professor Proctor and his performers. Wallace Duprai fired his rifle and the rider bearing down on him was struck in the chest and fell backwards out of his saddle. The runaway horse nearly collided with Duprai and would have, had Phineas not grabbed his arm and pulled him out of its path.

Meanwhile, Madame Mabel Higgins, wielding a huge block of firewood, swung it around like a baseball bat and hit Walt Calhoun squarely in the stomach. The outlaw doubled over and also fell off his horse.

Butch Faro was almost clear of the chaotic congestion in front of the stables when he felt something hit him in the back. He yelled out in pain and jerking upwards in his saddle, was then hit with two more rounds from the Wind-Up Kid's guns.

As the dead outlaw chief slid off his horse, the last two of his men realized the futility of their predicament and threw their guns away, raising their hands up to the sky in defeat.

The entire contest from the opening shot to the last had lasted four minutes. When it was over, Butch Faro and four of his men lay dead, two were wounded and two had surrendered.

When the dust, kicked up by the frightened horses, cleared, the amazing Wind-Up Kid stood in the middle of the scene, his gun barrels smoking, while back at the jail, Sheriff Tom Hancock had emerged onto the porch, leaning on young Cesar Ramirez, a pistol in his hand. The lad was grinning from ear to ear.

Phineas Proctor looked around him, at his companions, all standing strong and proud. The Chin brothers then began to move amongst the wounded outlaws, relieving them of their weapons, while Antoine Boulanger, sword in hand, had gone up to Mabel Higgins and taken the large woman into his arms.

"Ma belle, you were magnifique!" Then he kissed her soundly on the lips, much to her surprised delight.

As the others started laughing, Phineas turned to see Manny Ramirez standing before him with his hand outstretched. "Thank you, Professor."

Phineas shook the smithy's hand soundly. "No, amigo, thank you!"

Ron Fortier is an American author, primarily known for his Green Hornet and The Terminator comic books and his revival of the pulp hero, Captain Hazzard. Early in his career he also wrote short stories and co-authored two novels for TSR.

9

GHOST FROM THE PAST
A CAPTAIN HAWKLIN TALE

By Charles F. Millhouse
Summer 1920

The Hawklin Island estate sprawled along the cliffs of Seal Rocks, near San Francisco. The home's massive window overlooked the Pacific Ocean. Thomas Hawklin made sure there was an ocean view from every part of the home. He often said, "the closer I am to the sea, the closer I am to God." Thomas was a man of the ocean. He came by it naturally. All Hawklins were – since before the United States was born. His family-built ships to cross it, chart it and explore it. Hawklins were people of the sea with a long bloodline. Saltwater ran in their veins. Each generation contributed something to the Hawklin legacy, everyone that is, until Steven Thomas Hawklin decided to become a man of the air.

When Steven left home at twenty to become a pilot, harsh words were exchanged between him and Thomas, damaging their relationship. Thomas could not understand Steven's desire to go to the air and not the sea.

Headstrong, Steven refused to backdown, and he joined the Army Air Service when the United States entered the war in 1918. Though his dream and

thrill of flying was subdued by war, Steven was an ace among the clouds. Only Eddy Rickenbacker himself was more famous than Steven, yet Steven hated the notoriety that accompanied his time in the service. He wanted to be known for other accomplishments besides a soldier.

Steven returned home to San Francisco, after more than seven years away. He hoped to reestablish his relationship with Thomas, only Thomas, didn't make it easy.

"You were out late last night," Thomas said when Steven came out onto the terrace. The mid-morning sun placed a spotlight on Steven when he came through the ornate French doors and stepped into its bright tinder. He winced, blocked the glow with his hand and focused on his father.

"You look like something the cat drug in. Too much to drink last night?" Thomas asked sternly.

Steven rubbed his eyes. There was an enormous pounding at the back of his head. "That's just it, I didn't," he said trying to remember just what happened the night before.

"Sit down and have some breakfast," Thomas said. "It will come back to you."

Steven scratched the top of his head, yawned and pulled out a chair at the patio table. He dressed in white and blue pajamas and he shifted them an sat down. His blonde hair was in a tussle, and sleep was still in his eyes, but he managed to find the pitcher of orange juice and filled the empty glass in front of him.

He forgot he carried the morning paper folded in his armpit and placed it on the table in front of his father and took a long drink of the juice. The hammering behind his eyes caused black blotches to form in his vision. The alcohol flowed freely the night before, but he didn't drink to excess, yet his head told him otherwise.

"You didn't drive home drunk, did you?"

Steven eyed his father. Usually, his interference in Steven's life led to confrontation, but after thinking about it for a long time, Steven wasn't sure what to say.

A butler placed a fresh baked croissant in front of Steven, and said, "If I may, Master Steven's car is not in the garage where he usually parks it.".

"Thank you, Samuel," Steven said taking another sip of juice, the orange was incredibly sweet. "I must have taken a cab last night."

"Very probably, Sir," Samuel replied.

Steven blinked a couple of times, drew Samuel into focus and asked, "Could I have some scrambled eggs and bacon. Oh, and some of that orange marmalade for my croissant."

"Of course, Sir," Samuel said upon retreat.

"What was it this time?" Thomas asked unfolding the newspaper. "Drinks until dawn."

"If I had," Steven said with groggy tone, "I wouldn't be up now." He cut open his pastry and laid it open on his plate. "If you must know, I was out with Jeffery Morse and his sister, Gretchen on their family yacht until midnight." Then it dawned on Steven, the last thing he remembered was Gretchen crying. His blood chilled when everything went blank after that. He couldn't even remember returning to the dock. "Maybe I got a little seasick last night."

Thomas peered out from the top of the newspaper, before disappearing behind it without a word.

"I know what you're thinking, Thomas. Just because I chose to be an aviator doesn't mean I've given up the sea. I just think..."

"I know what you think," Thomas said from his hiding place. "You think air travel will replace sea travel. You're kidding yourself you know."

Steven grimaced, and his vision blurred again, assured of his consumption. Maybe at one time Steven could drink the next man under the table, but that was before the war.

Samuel placed a plate of food in front of Steven. The smell abled him to focus. Taking a bite of the bacon, he pointed the half-eaten strip at his father focused his thoughts, and said, "People said the same thing about the car when it was feared it wouldn't be as reliable as a horse and buggy. You see what happened. Why are people so afraid of change?"

Thomas manhandled the paper, almost rolling it in a ball before dropping it to the floor at his feet. "Leave it," he scolded at Samuel. The butler hardened his jaw and stepped back into the house. "I'm not against change, when that change benefits mankind. How will air travel do that?"

Steven's brow furrowed. He and Thomas had this conversation many times, and it always ended the same way. He turned his attention to his scrambled eggs forgoing anymore debate.

Lifting the weight from his voice, Thomas asked, "What's on your agenda today?"

"I've been home nearly six weeks. I think that's enough time to recoup from my trip back from Europe. *Though this headache is telling me otherwise.* "So, I thought I'd take a drive up the coast to Crown City. It's been a while since I've been home."

"This is your home," Thomas said.

"This is *your* home, Thomas. I grew up on the docks of Crown City while you were wheeling and dealing, preparing to move us here. I have ties there, that I really don't have here."

"It's your own fault. If you..."

"Hadn't ran away. Yes, well – you never made it easy on me, did you?"

"Did I ever boss you, or punish you, God knows, I should have. But no, no I didn't do that. And how did you repay me?"

"I repaid you, the same way you paid me. I didn't pay you a bit of attention. I went out and made my mark on the world."

"The morning mail, Sir," Samuel said and passed a stack of envelopes to Thomas. "It's a letter from Orman Wintergreen." Thomas said with a bit of admiration in his tone.

"I thought you and Orman were rivals," Steven said.

"We are working on a project together. He just recently remarried, by the way. To a girl half his age, too."

"The heart wants, what the heart wants."

"The heart has nothing to do with it," Thomas said. "It's what she does for his other parts."

"I'm sure she's a nice girl," Steven said.

"Here is one for you," Thomas said passing the envelope over to Steven.

Steven glanced at it for a second, but sharpened his eyes, and he said, "It's from Hardy."

"A fellow pilot, no doubt," Thomas shuddered.

"Hardy Miller can fly, I taught him myself. But he didn't fly in combat. He was my mechanic, and a damned good one."

"Language," Thomas scoffed.

Steven ignored Thomas and opened the letter. He skimmed his eyes over the single paper. His face slacked.

"Bad news?" Thomas asked.

"Seems his grandfather died last year, and he just found out about it. Damned mail."

Again, Thomas reminded, "Language."

"He was close to his grandfather. Taught him everything there was to know about engines. He must be devastated, especially after what happened in France."

Thomas glowered at Steven, but Steven clamped his jaw tight. He said too much already. The story was Hardy's to tell, and no one else's. The death of Bennie shook Hardy's world to its core. It would haunt him until he got a chance to settle the score with Tony Bordello.

"Are you alright, son?" Thomas asked. He rarely called Steven, son, nor care how Steven was feeling. "You're white as a ghost."

Steven woke on the floor. Thomas hovered over him, and Samuel was holding a cold compress on his forehead. "Thomas?"

"You alright?" Thomas asked.

"That depends," Steven replied. "Why am I on the floor?"

"One minute you were talking to me, and the next you toppled out of your chair. Are you sure you didn't have too much to drink last night?"

"I'm beginning to wonder," Steven replied holding up his hand to Thomas, who scooped his hand into Steven's and hoisted him up off the floor.

"I called for the doctor. He will be here soon, until then I want you to take it easy."

A maid came out onto the terrace and cleared her throat. The distraught look on her face was sharp and concerning.

"Yes," Thomas said standing close to Steven.

"The police are here," the young lady said. "They wish to see Master Steven, Sir."

Steven and Thomas shared a look. Thomas' glare was concerning, but nonjudgmental. "Is there something you want to tell me?"

Steven steadied himself. The room spun in a slow steady turn and he reached out for Thomas to steady himself.

"I'll go see what they..."

"No," Steven interrupted. "They're here for me, so I'll go.

Steven followed his father through the spacious house. His feet sunk into the thick carpet. The house was opulently decorated, with fine works of art, priceless antiques, and gifts from heads of state. Thomas always liked to show off.

They came down a hallway and into the main living room and crossed out into an entryway to find two uniformed officers, and a plain clothes detective, accompanied by Jeffery Morse. Jeffery was a tall slender man, with sinewy fingers and lanky arms and legs. Haggard, he wore a, wrinkled blue blazer and matching trousers. Dark circles ringed his eyes, and his hair look as if he combed it with his fingers.

"I'm Detective Abernathy of the San Francisco Police, and..."

Steven pushed forward, offered a friendly smile, and said, "Jeffery, what brings you..."

Jeffery bolted forward, and threw a wild punch, his fist made meaty slap across Steven's jaw, sending Steven to the floor.

"What the devil is going on?" Thomas demanded, stepping in between Steven and Jeffery.

"Please, Mister Morse," the hefty balding Detective Abernathy said. "Behave yourself. Don't make me regret that I brought you along."

"*Yes*, why are you here in my house Detective Abernathy?" Thomas said helping Steven up off the floor.

"That was a pretty good punch there Jeffery. I always thought you were a feather-weight," Steven said righting his footing, his vision blurred as he tried to fight off the effects from last night.

"Don't pretend to know why I didn't slug you, you son of a..."

"Now, that's enough of that," Thomas interjected.

"Please," Abernathy barked. "Will you keep calm Mister Morse, until I've had a chance to hear from Mister Hawklin."

"He knows what he's done. I *want* him arrested... NOW."

"Can someone please tell me what I am supposed to have done?" Steven asked.

His voice level and professional, Abernathy said, "Misses Morse drowned last night."

"Drowned?" Steven said downtrodden. "How, when?"

"As if you don't know," Jeffery's voice was sharp and rancid.

"You keep saying that, as if I know," Steven snapped. "I don't."

"*You* pushed Gretchen off the back of the boat... her head struck the engine, and there was blood, God there was so much blood."

The image of Gretchen crying flashed through Steven's mind. The room around him became topsy-turvy but he kept his footing, and asked, "What would be my motive in killing your sister? Gretchen and I were friends."

"I'd like for you to come downtown with us Mister Hawklin and give a statement," Abernathy said.

"I'll bring him in my car," Thomas said.

"I'm sorry, Sir," Abernathy replied. "That wouldn't be proper."

"Look at him," Thomas interjected. "He's still in his night clothes for God sake."

"We are willing to wait until he's had a chance to change."

Before Steven could remind everyone, he was standing right there, Thomas snapped, "My son happens to be a war hero."

Abernathy cleared his throat, and spoke into the floor, "If you could have him there within the hour."

"I don't believe this," Jeffery grumbled. "You're going to risk him running, because he fought in the war?"

"I'll make sure he is there, detective," Thomas said with a side glance at Jeffery.

After the door closed behind the police, Thomas took hold of Steven's arms, squared him and said, "Think son. It's imperative that you remember everything from last night, if we are going to clear your name."

"Thomas, you never asked if I did it or not."

Thomas' eyes glassed, and he said with certainty, "Well, of course you didn't do it. You're a Hawklin."

Even though Steven and his father didn't always agree, a sense of pride swelled in him that his father trusted and believed him.

"You need a bath, and clean clothes," Thomas said ushering Steven upstairs as he shouted, "Samuel... coffee and lots of it. We need to jar your memory."

"Who would want to kill Gretchen, and why?" Steven asked as he topped the stairs.

"I wouldn't put it past that pipsqueak, Jeffery," Thomas said as Steven closed the bathroom door. He's always had a devious side."

"We were just kids then," Steven said through the bathroom door.

"He tried to get you expelled."

"Just because he failed to get me thrown out of school, is hardly reason enough to frame me for the murder of his sister, now is it?" Steven asked filling the bathtub with hot water. He perched over the tub. The cold porcelain chilled his blood.

"So, you don't think he did it?"

"No, I don't," Steven replied immersing himself in the bath. "None of this makes any sense."

"How could accusing you of murder make any sense?" Thomas asked.

With washcloth in hand, Steven paused. Memories of last night flashed through his mind, yet the only image he transfixed on was Gretchen. Clearly, she was upset, but over what, Steven didn't know. The night was a jumble of sounds, smells and undefined images that Steven couldn't mentally digest. He focused on the engine of the yacht, the clack clack clack clack sound stirred something in him he couldn't process and for an instance the roar of tri-motor blades clamored in front of him and for the span of several heartbeats he was at the controls of his bi-plane in combat the BAM of a single gunshot

traumatized him, and the image of a weeping Gretchen filled his memory.

"Son, you alright?" Thomas asked pounding on the bathroom door.

Steven stirred, the relentless pounding at the bathroom door brought him back to reality. "Yeah, yeah," he called, "I'm here." His hands were petrified as he gripped the side of the bathtub, unable to move. He sat there for a long minute. Thomas said something to him, but Steven didn't register what his father said.

Dragging himself from the water, Steven let his father talk without offering any replies to his endless prattle. Everything Thomas offered didn't ease Steven's mantic mental state. Clearly something happened last night, but the images flashing through his mind only added more confusion.

At his father's insistence, Steven dressed in a sharp black pair of trousers, a crisp white shirt, tie, and jacket. "Dress to impress," Thomas said. "You have nothing to hide, and Steven admitted to himself, the bath and clean clothes helped, but not as much as the gallon of black coffee. It sharpened his resolve and prepared him to face what was ahead.

Forgoing his chauffeur, Thomas elected to drive his Nash Touring sedan, himself, as he and Steven set off into San Francisco nearly an hour after the police visit.

"You're quiet," Thomas said several miles up the road.

"I'm being accused of killing someone, wouldn't you be quiet?" Steven replied.

"I'd be mad as hell is what I'd be," Thomas snarled.

Steven relaxed in his seat, gripped his temple, and said, "I keep getting these flashes of memories."

"You want to tell me about them?"

Steven chuckled, and said, "That's just it, they don't mean a damn thing to me."

"Well tell me what you do see."

"Gretchen for one."

"Crying?"

"Yes," Steven replied. "It all comes back to her crying."

"Go on, son. What else?"

The engine of the yacht. I can hear it echoing, grinding behind my eyes, and then I'm back in the war, in the cockpit, at the stick. The clatter of the yacht engine becomes machinegun fire, followed by a single gunshot."

"A gunshot, what kind of gunshot?"

Steven threw his hands up in the air and growled.

"Alright. Let's take it one image at a time. Start with Gretchen. How well do you know her?"

Steven thought back to school. He, Jeffery, and Gretchen were in the same classes in High School. They hung in the same circles. "I remember having a bit of a crush on her when she was a freshmen and I was a junior."

"Her crying could mean she felt jilted and..."

"No, no, no," Steven said. "My crush never went further than private infatuation. I don't think she even knew I kind of liked her."

"Why did you not pursue her?" Thomas asked.

"The same reason I stopped hanging out with Jeffery," Steven said. "They were anti-Semitic. Their father was even a member of some hate group against Jews. They both resented the fact that I didn't share their belief."

"Yet you went to their yacht last night," Thomas said.

They knew I was home from Europe and asked me to come visit. Jeffery sent a note along with the invitation saying how sorry and wrong they were and wanted to make amends."

Thomas narrowed his sights on the road and didn't offer a reply.

"What?"

"I'm going to play devil's advocate for a minute and say that's suspicious in itself. Do you still have the invitation sent to you?"

"I didn't keep it," Steven said. "I suppose I could have left it back at the house somewhere."

"Alright. So, Gretchen crying could have meant she was sorry for how she acted all those years ago," Thomas said.

"Yeah. I guess so," Steven said with a shrug.

"Alright. But why the flashback of the bi-plane, and the dogfight?" Thomas drew a hard breath and said in a reserved tone, "Son, don't get mad when I ask this but..."

"I'm not shellshocked," Steven said flatly. "That thought occurred to me too. But since the end of the war, this is the *only* time I've had any kind of memory."

"Then, what happened last night must be related to your service," Thomas said.

Steven eyed his father. It was the first time in a long time that he even remotely acted like a father, and that he really cared for what was happening to him. It was a change from the arguing they usually had when it came to flying. He offered a thin smile, and Thomas offered a smile of his own.

Suddenly the car went out of control. The next several seconds happened so quickly that neither of them had time to say or do anything except hold on as the car careen off the road, and down a steep embankment. The front in of the car hit something and stopped with an unexpected jerk. Steven flew forward, ending up under the dashboard. Dazed he regarded his father.

Thomas' forehead was bleeding, and a steady stream of crimson ran down his face.

"You, alright, Dad."

Thomas grinned deeply, and replied, "Yes, I'm alright son."

Steven offered a peculiar stare, and he realized that was one of the few times he called Thomas, dad. He heaved himself out from the floorboard. Steam hissed out of the front of the car and sounded like a pressure cooker. "What the hell happened?"

Thomas drew a breath to speak but dropped down into the seat when a whiz-ding ricocheted, and the back window shattered.

"Someone is shooting at us," Steven said.

"What the hell did you get yourself into?" Thomas asked.

Steven reared his head to peek out the door. The area on his side of the car

was flat except for two trees, and then the ground stopped. Steven grimaced. Another twenty feet or so and the car would have gone into a chasm. "No escape this way," he said.

Another gunshot ripped through the canvas top and hit the front windshield, splintering glass everywhere. "There," Thomas shoved a finger toward a large rock less than five feet from the car. "If we can make it to that."

"I'll slip out my side of the car and draw their fire. When I do..."

"Are you out of your mind?" Thomas snapped. "You'll be killed for sure."

"We both can't go out your side. They'll pick us both off for sure."

Thomas nodded, understanding the logic in Steven's plan, and said, "Maybe I should draw..."

"No," Steven snapped. "Look, Thomas. Take no offense, but I'm younger and quicker. It makes more sense if I draw the fire. Besides, whoever is shooting at us, I'll lay a bet, I'm the one they're after."

Thomas chagrinned, and nodded.

"You ready?" Steven asked.

Again, Thomas nodded.

Steven threw open the door and dove for the ground when he sprung from the car. Another gunshot filled the air and hit the ground next to him. Dashing haphazardly, Steven found cover behind one of the trees, being mindful of the sheer drop-off just beyond it.

Justifying his footing he called, "Thomas, you make it?"

"Yeah, I'm here," Thomas said. A bullet grazed the rock and echoed in the distance.

"Well, keep down."

"Thanks for the advice," Thomas sarcastically replied as another shot splintered the tree. "Jesus."

"Steven, language," Thomas scolded.

Locking his jaw, Steven peeked out around the tree. Dense thickets lined the other side of the road – a good hiding place for an assassin.

"What do you see?"

"Nothing," Steven replied. Again, another shot whizzed by Steven – its wake ruffled his hair. Startled he aligned himself with the tree trunk. His memories flashed back to the previous night and he drew a staggering breath. It all came back to him. Everything. *Damn it.*

Peeking around the tree again, Steven surveyed the car, the ditch, that ran several hundred yards along down the road, and a cropping of bushes along the embankment. "Humm," he muttered and said, "Thomas..."

"Yes, I'm still here," his father replied.

"Are you up to being a distraction?"

"And get shot at ...?"

"I don't think you will."

"You don't think?" Thomas held a laugh deep in his throat.

"It's me they want," Steven said. "I need to get to that ditch over there and come around behind them."

"If you think it will help," Thomas replied. Steven heard the tightening in his throat.

"Are you ready?"

"No. But let's get this over with."

Steven dug in his footing. His plan would be to count to three and they both react. Before he could utter his intentions, Thomas bolted from his hiding place and Steven didn't have any other choice but to go. He winced when another shot rang out, only this time he wasn't being shot at. He glimpsed Thomas for a split second. Dust plumed at Thomas' feet. Evidently the shooter didn't want to shoot his father, merely scare him.

Thomas darted back to his hiding place, but it gave Steven enough time to make it to the ditch, with hopes he wasn't spotted.

Navigating down the narrow causeway, Steven's feet were drenched in the standing water in the channel. Another gunshot rang out, and Steven didn't pause, speculating it was Thomas giving the shooter something to see. It wouldn't be long before they realized he'd gone.

Crossing the road, Steven maneuvered into the bramble along the street edge, he froze when another gunshot went off, hoping that wasn't the shot that got Thomas. He chose his footing with precision. One snap of a twig, one crunch of dry leaves and the shooter would hear him coming.

Steven caught sight of a dark form ahead of him. Cloaked in a hunter's jacket, and brown bill cap. Steven studied him. No matter how he approached, the shooter would hear him coming.

When the shooter rose his rifle again and fired ahead, Steven dashed forward but stopped when the shot faded.

From a pouch at his side, the shooter reached a gloved hand the bag and took out another round. *Single shot.* Steven rushed forward not taking care what was under foot and balled his fist. Startled, the shooter turned, and Steven released his punch, slugging the gunman square in the face. He went down and the hat flung off his head unfurling a long blond mane.

Steven's brow knotted, but he didn't back away, and he said, "Gretchen... Gretchen Morse?"

Gretchen scrambled for her rifle and Steven kicked it away. There was a long silence, and then Steven said, "It's over Gretchen.... It's over."

***

An hour later, Steven and Thomas delivered Gretchen to the police station downtown. Her unexpected appearance let Steven off the hook for a murder that never happened.

Detective Abernathy spent an hour questioning her, with little results. "She won't talk, says it was her own business as to why she faked her death."

"What about Jeffery?" Thomas asked.

"I sent a patrol car out to the Morse estate, but he was nowhere to be found. In fact, the entire family was gone, the house sealed up as if they weren't coming back for a while." Abernathy said.

"I doubt they will ever be back," Steven said.

Thomas, and Abernathy glared at Steven. "You want to explain that?" Thomas asked.

"It all came back to me, when I was behind the tree trying not to get shot," Steven said. "I went to their yacht last night under false pretense. Jeffery and Gretchen claimed they wanted to apologize for how they acted when we were in school together. But it wasn't like that at all."

"Explain," Abernathy said.

***

The wine poured freely on the *Parthenon*, but Steven drank little. Stating that alcohol and the sea never agreed with him. Despite his refrainment from the wine, the night became an unexpected blur. There were conversations about high school, and the pressures of young adults, especially those who were part of prominent families.

Jefferey and Gretchen kept the conversation going, while skirting around the real reason they asked Steven to their yacht. Gretchen hung close to Steven. Her arm interlocked in his. She threw her head back, laughing at Steven's jokes. Her ruby red lips flashing him smiles as she hung on every word.

Steven instantly remembered why he had a crush on her all those years ago. She smelled of dandelions. Her long cornsilk hair blew steadily in the sea breeze and her long blue dress clung to her form in every detail. If it hadn't been for her prejudice beliefs, their relationship might have prospered.

Steven loosened his bow tie and undid the top three buttons of his shirt. It got hotter as the night went on, and his mind became clouded with each passing moment. When the conversation turned to the war, the laughter faded, and things turned darker.

"You're a big, damned war hero," Jeffery said facing Steven as they stood at the back of the ship.

"I did my duty," Steven said, unsure why Jeffery's tone had changed.

Gretchen let go of Steven's arm, and joined her brother at the back of the boat. "You shot down a lot of planes during combat?" she asked.

"My fair share," Steven replied honestly.

"Did you ever come face to face with any of them, instead of just in the air?" she asked.

Steven grimaced, unable to focus, he replied, "Yes, once." His voice sounded distant, as if he stood in a tunnel.

"You shot him at point blank range, didn't you?" Jeffery said.

The face of the pilot blurred in his memory, though Steven wasn't sure he ever knew what the enemy pilot looked like. "We shot each other down on the outskirts of No Man's Land," Steven explained. "We were left to finish the fight on the ground. I got lucky is all."

"So lucky, you killed our uncle," Gretchen said as the tears flowed down her face.

"Your uncle? I thought you were American," Steven said amazed.

"We are of German descent," Jefferey explained. "Germany asked for those of us loyal to our homeland to go back, and fight for it. Our uncle was one such man."

"And you killed him," Gretchen sobbed.

Steven touched his forehead, trying to remain coherent. "How is this even possible?"

"Ironic, isn't it. That a man who turned his back on us, those years ago would be the instrument of our uncle's death," Jeffery seethed.

"It was war," Steven explained. "He was trying to kill me. That's what you do in war. Kill or be killed."

Gretchen came at him, and Steven wasn't ready for her quick movement. She slapped him across the face with an open palm and screamed, "You're going to pay for this, Steven Hawklin."

"What... what did you put in my drink?" Steven asked. The next thing he realized, he laid – face planted into the deck of the yacht. Gretchen still cursing him, "You're going to pay for this dearly, Steven Hawklin."

Steven lay there, his head swimming, listening to Jeffery and Gretchen spell it all out for him. The information unfolding like some cheap pulp novel, and the realization that it was all true.

***

"If you check, you'll find that Gretchen Morse is Gretchen Müller. Her parents, along with other members of their family moved to the United States before Jeffery and Gretchen were born and slipped through the system. They're no more American than the Kiser," Steven said. "They held me responsible for more than just the death of their uncle. Seems after I turned my back on them in school, they lost a number of friends and their status in certain circles. Who knew I had that much influence?"

Abernathy looked back toward the door of the interrogation room and said, "So, her parents and brother..."

"Are on their way to Germany now," Steven said. "To help rebuild their homeland, after the allies left them with nothing. They probably think I'm dead by now."

"Why would they leave her to try and kill you?" Thomas asked. "*And* not Jeffery."

"And why not just do it that night on the yacht... make it look like an accident?" Abernathy said.

Steven shrugged his shoulders. "Maybe they didn't want to be implicated in my murder, so they could come back to the United States one day. I don't know. She was a rather good shot with the rifle. Maybe that's why she was picked to kill me."

"That's true," Thomas said. "She had some pretty clear shots of me, and she chose to shoot around me, waiting for you, son."

"Too many loose ends, for my liking," Abernathy said.

"What's going to happen to her now?" Thomas asked.

"I can't charge her with faking her own death. She didn't try to do it for insurance fraud, so there's no crime, except attempted murder."

"*I'm* not pressing charges," Steven said.

"What?" Thomas asked.

"I can do that right, Detective?"

"If you don't charge her, I can't hold her," Abernathy said.

"Then let her go," Steven said.

"What's to stop her from coming after you again?" Thomas asked.

"She won't," Steven said assuredly. "She'll be on the next ship for Germany."

"I don't agree with you, Mister Hawklin," Abernathy said. "But if you're washing your hands of it, I'll release her in the morning, to give you some time in case you change your mind." He turned, took several steps, and glanced back at Steven before continuing on his way, shaking his head in disbelief.

Steven turned, with his father in tow and said, "I would have never in a million years believed something like that would have happened."

Thomas took Steven by the arm, and pulled him to a stop, and said, "Son, you'll realize, with every decision you make, the past has a way of catching up with you."

***

10

ACE ANDERSON AND THE CURSE OF DOCTOR ATOMIKA PART II

STORY BY
KELLIE LYNN AUSTIN
ART BY
ERIKIUS CASTRO

ACE ANDERSON AND THE CURSE OF DOCTOR ATOMIKA
Part Two
By
Kellie Lynn Austin

RECAP OF PART ONE: Professional adventurer and scientist, Ace Anderson is summoned to the office of England Prime Minister Morris Mapleleaf to discuss Ace's involvement in tracking down the grounded atomic sub, the *U.S.S. Thresher*. Briefed by Agent Huck Finn, along with Dr. Mason Moreau, it is revealed that the *Thresher* contained dangerous, radioactive ore from the ancient continent of Atlantis, called orraculum and that Ace's former lover, Professor Valerie Vickers was behind the mysterious death of a colleague and the missing golden ore from a military installation. Under the guise of Doctor Atomika, she was arrested after her attempt to steal the strange material, that caused the deaths of many Americans.

Doctor Atomika was placed on board the *U.S.S. Thresher* being transported to an undisclosed location to pay for her crimes against America. However, the *Thresher* was lost with all hands.

Charged with finding the *Thresher*, Ace and his crew were attacked by agents of evil, killing Prime Minister Mapleleaf in the attempt. Escaping unscathed, Ace and his crew rendezvous with his great submarine, the bio-organic ship called the *Kraken* – a product of Atlantean engineering.

Picking up on the *Kraken's* radio signals, three Nazi submarines locked in on its position. As the *Kraken*, under the command of Ace's daughter Kenzie, prepares to send the Nazi infiltrators to their doom...

PART II
Through the *Kraken's* intercom, the cries of the German sailors resonate throughout the massive vessel.

"GOTT, HILF UNS!" THEY SHOUTED. "GOTT, HILF UNS!" (Translated) "God help us... God help us!"

"DER TEUFELSFISCH!" More Screams followed: "DER TEUFELSFISCH IST AUF UNS! (Translated) "The Devil Fish... The Devil Fish is upon us!"

Ace watched through the telescope – spotting the dimming skyline of a dying day as he bore witness to the onslaught of terror thrust upon the Nazi triad. Ace heard the endless cries, aggressions, prayers, and felt the fear that the enemy was experiencing. *What they so richly deserve*, he thought.

He walked the metal plank over the fleshy interior floor of his great *Kraken*. Each step methodical and without remorse upon those who had transgressed the peaceful but troubled waters of the North Atlantic. His arms crossed in strength and defiance, Ace held his own fears and vulnerable anxieties to himself. *"A Captain must be strong, and vigilant, at all times of war and peace,"* he said to himself in a faint whisper.

"Quod erat demonstandum..." Ace said, and added, "Thus it has been proven."

"Latin, for proving your point," Kenzie said. "Is that apt?"

Ace eyed his daughter. She had grown into a fine woman, much like her mother. "Your mother thought so when she won an argument with me, which happened more regular than it should of," he said with a wan smile. He placed a hand at the small of Kenzie's back.

"Look at them Kenzie," Ace said pointing to one of the *Kraken's* bio scanners. "They're small ants playing with big boy toys." He coughed. "I must be catching a cold," he mused.

Kenzie closed her eyes, as she took in the death of an entire Nazi crew. The *Kraken's* coiled fleshy metal tentacles constricted themselves around the enemy submarines and ripped them apart like tin paper. Like a boa constrictor attacking its prey, the bio-sub ripped the Nazi ships from the water and high into the sky, until the wrenching sound of metal upon metal fractured and.... SNAP!

Kenzie's role as First Commander on the great *Kraken* always took her to the strangest places and the most implausible situations. She knew of death and the dreams of madmen and world conquering schemes, but to watch in horror as people died without mercy, well, it sometimes took its toll on her. Just fifteen years into life, childhood was but a dream. Thrust into adulthood and the fantastic, Kenzie tried to live up to the role her father required in these times of uncertain futures.

She closed her eyes, but Ace reached over to her chin and gently moved her head back to the eye bubble. Her eyes opened.

"Watch." Ace told her... "And remember this is how fools die.

The remaining two sub fled, as the fragments from the other U-boats began falling, raining large chunks of debris upon the fleeing sub.

"The enemy will always speak of superiority and the technology that sets themselves with dreams of grandeur. That way of thinking will always be their downfall. The vanities of the enemy are your greatest strength against them." Ace smiled and coughed again.

"You'd better have that coughed seen to," Kenzie said, gazing at her father.

"The doctor is busy with the crew right now. The crew, our family always comes before me. You know that. The *ship* comes before me. You know that too."

"As you say, father," Kenzie said returning to her duties as First Commander, and ordered, "Prepare torpedo."

"Torpedo room reports standing by," an officer replied.

"Standing by Captain," Kenzie said. "You are patting yourself on the back, aren't you?" Kenzie asked as she turned to her father.

Ace's brow furrowed, and he asked, "Meaning what, exactly?"

"You pride yourself on super technology, your self-induced pride and honor that sometimes hinders those under your command. You're not known for pleasantries with outsiders you understand. Someday, the odds will be against you and someone will die." Said Kenzie, a concerned look about her.

"You mean your Mother?" he responded.

"I wasn't thinking about mom or what happened. I was thinking in general to the family we have here on the *Kraken*. We're alone in society, but together in what makes us unique and special. Can't we just forgo everything and just explore the seas, maybe make a life somewhere sheltered away from the bad things?" Kenzie asked.

Ace looked away from her, and watched the carnage taking place outside the ship. His heart swelling. He glanced at Kenzie, "You're young. I sometimes forget that. Your mother was as smart and vibrant as you, Little One, but she didn't understand either. I guess age isn't a factor after all. Still, a dream like yours in the middle of a Great War isn't a bad one, but being adventurers is part of our lives."

"First Commander," Ace said formally, "fire the torpedo."

Kenzie walked slowly over to the center of the great grand staircase that made up the upper part of the viewing platform. Placing her hand into a fleshy orifice, a metallic periscope dropped from the high ceiling to where she was standing. Her hands grasped tightly upon the brown bars as she took a moment to lock in on her target. A hesitation deep within her began to emerge, but pushing past the nervous stomach and emotional reasoning, abled her to give the final command to fire upon the last sub as it attempted to dive out of sight. Her eyes closed, holding back an emotional outburst she stood there defeated.

"I'm not a child. I'm a soldier in a great war..." she said in a whisper. Kenzie knew her father heard her but stood fixated against the periscope's viewfinder. The sight of the torpedo scorching throughout the water toward its intended target, made Kenzie grip the handlebars tighter as the German sub was ripped asunder.

The mighty ship caught the feedback, causing some of the crew to fall from their positions, including Ace. Kenzie held on for dear life. The enemy sub lost its engine room with the hit and began taking on water.

"Damn! Didn't see that coming!" exclaimed Ace, hoisting himself up and with hurried state towards his daughter.

"Are you alright?" he asked. Shaking her head in acknowledgement, Ace looked outside the giant eye to witness the sub's distress.

"Stay there, I got this." He said, going over to another orifice and manipulating the controls which caused the great ten mechanical tentacles to coil themselves around the enemy vessel and suffocate any who still lived. He watched as the submarine's outer metal was crushed like tin foil and survivors jumped into the freezing depths.

One by one, each survivor slowly began sinking into the depths of the ocean, lifeless bodies bouncing in and out of the water like "bobbers" tied at the end of a fishing pole. Kenzie kept stern sight on those struggling to stay above the water.

"As I feared." She said out loud, turning towards her father.

"Meaning?" Ace asked.

"A survivor. We should take him aboard," Kenzie said. Hoping she could keep the German alive by using reverse psychology, playing on her father's conservative nature.

"First Commander, you know I don't take prisoners, but in this case, you're right to assume that doing so would be prudent. We can interrogate him and see what can be found out about his mission and if it's connected to the *U.S.S. Thresher's* demise."

"Ace once more entered the command code for the *Kraken's* tentacles to attach themselves to the lone survivor. Pulling the sailor from certain doom.

"Good job." Ace said, turning toward the ship's navigator, and said, "Have you determined a probable location of the *Thresher*?"

The young navigator, in his mid-twenties, turned toward Ace, and said, "Our best estimation, using last known coordinates and the boat's intended course, we've surmised, its somewhere near the Davy Jones cliff in the middle of the mid-Atlantic ridge. Sonar detects a large vessel or natural formation there, half on and half tilting towards the great mid-Atlantic "blue hole". The navigator continued to say that the location was dangerous due to the "blue holes" strange magnetic influence on vessels travelling over or near it. Many a ship has been lost to this anomaly.

"What about coordinates?" asked Ace, motioning to a yeoman to bring him some coffee.

"Coordinates are as follows: 576.09.00214. South west, forty-seven minutes to penetration of area at maximum motor control."

"First commander, set course on those coordinates maximum speed. Initiate thermal thrusters to penetration area." Ace grabbed his coffee from the yeoman, and took a sip while Kenzie repeated the orders and typed in the information on the ear shaped red console.

"First Commander, you have the watch," Ace said making his way out of the command center.

"Where are you off to?" Kenzie inquired.

"First I'm going to check on the others, to see if Mister Finn has gotten over the shock of this fine vessel. Then to the brig." He stopped and turned, adding, "Have the German sailor properly seen to. Dry clothes, that kind of thing. I may not be in the habit of taking prisoners, but I won't mistreat one in my charge."

***

Inside the medical area, Doctor Moreau continued his examination of Huck Finn, whose lungs were reeling from the consumption of too much salt water.

"You'll have to rest, you know." Moreau said. He opened up his right hand to reveal two pills.

"Swallow two of these and call me in the morning," he muttered, smiling and said, "I took some blood while you were unconscious. Why didn't you say your blood was tainted? Are you aware you have the curse of the wendigo?"

"I knew. Was hoping to keep it all to myself, save my superiors." Replied Huck, coughing.

"This Factor Four you belong to, I would say, is something of a "creature companion" group. Doctor Moreau continued to say "You see, any name with the word factor in it is usually a sign of an agency which isn't official, but official enough to be a non-conformist type of group. Examples being, "Medusa and her Monster Society of Justice, perhaps?" Doctor Moreau grabbed Huck's blood vile and stared at it for a moment, and said, "This vile, in the wrong hands could be disastrous. Luckily, I'm one of the good guys."

"Yeah, lucky for me," Huck said glibly.

"You rest for a bit," Moreau said. "I'll be back to check on you in a while."

***

Ace stopped short of the medical bay and diverted to his room. *So much in little time*, he thought. He opened the door and went in, pulling the chair from his desk and sitting down. He grabbed the silver and jade pocket watch that was an anniversary gift from his deceased wife, Maria.

"Twenty-three years it would be next week Maria. How I do miss you..." he whispered, catching a glimpse of Moreau standing in the open doorway.

"Pennies for your many thoughts my friend." Moreau said leaning on the doorframe.

"Only bad memories, I suppose," Ace said regarding the doctor.

"It wasn't your fault Ace. I was there, remember. Maria knew the risks of going into the underwater cavern. She knew what time she had, and well... sometimes things don't work out in the end."

"I remember?" Ace said opening the watch face. The seemingly ghost-like picture therein contained her image. It stared and smiled back at him. It gave Ace comfort.

Mason walked into the room and sat on the corner of the bed, opposite Ace. "You blame yourself for Maria trying to disarm the Axis bomb. You blame yourself so much that you've taken your great mind and turned it into a hate machine in which all those around you are swept up in a whirlwind of a revenge tale. You have those here that care for you and will die at your command my friend... how long before you realize that like your mentor, it is only a matter of time before there is something more terrifying than yourself. When do you realize when you've destroyed innocent lives to satisfy your lustful vengeance, all in the name of mom, apple pie, and God Bless America?" Doctor Mason Moreau was a calm and rational man. His insanity was his own, and he understood Ace's personal demons.

"You have a point, Mason?" asked Ace.

"Yeah, I do. I just made the point to you. You're a time bomb ready to go off. You love Maria to this day. You loved Val, and she betrayed you in the end. She betrayed all of America. Even you could not have known Val was a Nazi agent born and living on American soil. The world is full of surprises."

"Look what your vengeance has done to Kenzie. She's a child who needs to be doing childlike things, dating, playing with dolls, whatever...you've turned her into a soldier, and she shouldn't be." Mason waited for Ace's anger to emerge. Discussing his daughter was a "no no" on the ship, but Mason waited.

"If it were any other person, I'd knock you on your ass for how you're talking to me," Ace snapped.

"Yes, you could. See... Ace Anderson is more human than he likes to believe. That's equal hope for your soul, and unlike your predecessor, lies within you. Inside your tortured soul, lies the redemption for your anger." Mason hopped up and straightened his long silver hair. Smoothing out his suit, he walked towards the door.

"Answer me something Mason." Ace said upon standing.

"Alright," Replied Moreau.

"Will there ever be a day when you will betray me as well?" Ace asked.

"Today, no. Tomorrow... maybe. One never knows what the future will bring.

Ace replied with an awkward grin and glanced at his pocket watch before replacing it in his pocket. Thirty-nine minutes from the *Kraken's* intercept point, to the remains of the *U.S.S. Thresher.*

***

Doctor Atomika wandered the darkened corridors of the downed *U.S.S. Thresher* dazed and confused. *Am I still alive... why am I still alive?* She wondered as she navigated through the remains of the crew inside the sunken submarine. All eighty-nine souls were killed in the crash, and Doctor Atomika considered herself indestructible. Yet she knew her time was fleeting. Hairline cracks enveloped every inch of the *Thresher.* The sunken, tin can would implode at any time. *Though I don't know why it hasn't.*

Throughout the darkened command area, Atomika navigated through the dead – and she wondered if the methane from the decomposing bodies would kill her before the sea would. *Maybe this is how I am to be executed... the Americans will get their pound of flesh after all.*

Goose flesh crawled over Atomika skin, the icy temperatures of the Atlantic absorbed into the skin of the vessel, yet she was running a fever, the scorching heat of a blast furnace reddened her body. For a brief moment she wondered if she was dead? A walking thinking corpse. She felt like this once before, as a child when she had yellow fever.

Catching her reflection in the radar screen, she froze. She looked older... older than her years. Her skin was leathery and like the old crow that used to live down the street from her as a girl. *What is happening to me?*

Her stomach wrenched, and she begged for a drink. Surrounded by ocean and not a drink of water in sight. She grimaced.

Maddened with a ringing in her ears, Atomika lost all sense of what was real, and what was illusion. Her body exhausted she forgot common sense. *Water, I need water.*

Cupping her hands, she allowed a steady stream from a crack in the bulkhead to drop into her hands. But spat the salty liquid from her mouth, shocked back into normalcy. The rusty taste of blood invaded her senses. *What is wrong with me?* She questioned her actions. *I have an IQ of 153, genius level, yet I resort to acting like a barbarian.*

"What's that?" She cried. Catching the glimpse of someone moving among the dead. She drew a hesitant breath as she watched the ghostly form of one of the crew. *Am I going mad?* she questioned her faculties. *And* then it occurred to her… "The orraculum…" she swallowed in a dry throat. "Could it be doing this to me? Driving me insane?" She thought about that for a moment. The strange matter could play havoc with ones DNA, alter their perception or… her hand went to her mouth, and she drew a tight breath. *Bring the dead back to life,* she thought. *Create walking zombies…*

"Am I like that?" She said in a dry voice. "Am I dead, and only now finding out? I need to get off this boat. She stopped to consider, "Perhaps I'm something more than a zombie."

Atomika would have to wait for answers. First she needed to get rescued. Soon the Americans would be looking for the *Thresher. I have to hurry.*

Pushing a dead crewman out of the way, Atomika sat at the radio controls, surprised the transmitter still functioned. Manipulating the controls, she began sending a signal… *must signal… call for the nearest U-Boat. I must be rescued.*

***

The Kraken, twenty-two minutes to the *Thresher…*

Ace and Mason picked up Agent Finn from the med bay as Java joined them. The dog-man had been Huck's constant companion since they arrived on the monster sub.

They made their way to the brig, where the German sailor had been kept since his arrival on the *Kraken.* "Can we have the shackles removed from him?" Huck asked.

Ace complied, having two guards stand nearby, though the German sailor looked like he couldn't fight his way out of a wet paper bag. He was beaten, the disposition on his face proved that.

"Do you understand English?" Ace asked in a commanding tone.

The sailor looked down at the floor.

"Do you understand English?" Ace asked again. "You won't be hurt if you answer some questions for me. It isn't my intention to hurt you, but if you don't talk to us, I can't promise your continued safety."

Huck gave a wary glance, but Ace kept his voice dark and firm.

"I speak English." Answered the prisoner.

"Do you have a name?" Ace asked.

"Gunter, Klaus Gunter, serial number…."

Shh, shh, shh, Ace said. "I have a straightforward question for you. Do you have a family? Would you like to see them again? I will personally take you to them if you answer my questions. Do you understand this?" Ace asked.

"Family, yes. A son of two years I haven't seen," Klaus said. By the dulled expression in his eyes, he was tired, weak and scared. "I want to go home."

"You can go home. I will take you home. Despite our differences, I understand family. Answer me this question. "Were you part of a unit whose mission was to take down the *U.S.S. Thresher*, or detain and board the vessel? Did you know about the subs cargo or its prisoner Val Vickers?" Ace asked intently.

"Envoy to intercept you. All I know." Said Klaus.

"How did you know I was at the governmental office or in this distinctive area?" asked Ace.

"Sleeper agent in office, I think. Many rumors in kitchen." Replied Klaus.

"I see." Ace commented.

Klaus added to his story. "Please don't kill me."

Ace whispered, "I am a man of my word. You will go home to your family."

Ace eyed his compatriots, and said, "We have a mole in parliament... I think we know who it might be."

The Kraken's telephone buzzed, and Moreau yanked the receiver off of the wall and said, "Hello, yes? Understood." He turned to Ace. Kenzie reports we are seven minutes from the last known coordinates of the *Thresher*."

Ace crossed the room and took the receiver and said, "Daughter. Have the mini-servant prepared for launch. Finn, Java and I will be taking it out in an attempt to locate the American sub. In the meanwhile, contact our friend in Parliament and tell them to look out for a sleeper agent. Her name is Miss. Marshallholly. Maintain position here and load all salvos. Two torpedoes locked and ready... just in case."

Ace replaced the receiver, and said, "Mason, I need you here. Your medical specialties might be required. Besides, if the Kraken needs assistance, you know what to do."

Ace, Huck and Java made their way to the submarine bay, where the mini-servant sub was housed. An offshoot piece of technology from the *Kraken* – in the form of a hunk of clay.

"What is that thing?" Huck inquired.

"Technology beyond your understanding, young Finn," Ace said.

"It looks like a huge mass of nothing."

"It was a product from my mentor, Captain Nemoc, or as you know him, Nemo."

"How then..."

Ace raised a finger. "Another time, Huck. Another time. Quickly... into one of those," he said pointing at a cropping of pressure suits. "We will need them to survive the amazing pressure outside the *Kraken*.

Footfalls drew Ace's attention, and he turned to find two crewmen. One of them, was a rather attractive woman, and Huck quickly took notice.

The crewmen threw a salute, and the woman said, "Crewmen Kammy and Peyton reporting as ordered."

Huck shot her a smile and wink, trying to get Kammy's attention."

Java snarled, "Give me a break."

Kammy batted her big brown eyes, and offered a thin smile.

"Who sent..." Ace choked on his words. "Seems Kenzie is watching out for us. First Guard?"

"Of course," Peyton replied.

"First Guard?" Huck inquired.

"Hand-picked crewmen from the half-pint on the bridge, to protect Ace," Java growled.

"Quickly, everyone. Into the compression suits, and let's get to work," Ace said.

The group quickly donned their compression suits and at Ace's beckoning, they entered the small vessel.

"Reminds me of old science fiction stories about going into space." Commented Huck, as he stepped into the small vessel.

"No science fiction here," Ace said. "Just science fact that'll kill you if you're not paying attention."

Sitting next to Ace, Huck clicked in. "How deep will this thing go," he asked.

Ace shrugged, "Unknown. But we are about to find out."

"Super," Huck said with a less than enthusiastic voice.

"Just sit back and let the dog worry about all the important stuff," Java said from the pilot control.

The docking bay door slowly opened, and the crew saw the water begin to rise around them. The steel railroad like track moved them outside

the *Kraken* like a rollercoaster ready to drop...

"SWOOSH!

The crew felt the jolt of being released straight downward, the G-forces unbearable. Java leveled the submersible and brought the speed under control.

"How are we even sure the *Thresher* is here?" Huck said.

"It's here," Ace said with confidence. "The problem is finding it. But find it we will."

The servant's long-range lights came on. The murky waters made it difficult to make out what was outside.

"This could take us ages," Huck said.

"We begin at the beginning and in the end we will find it," Ace said. "Have confidence."

Sonar began to go wild. "There is something close," Java said.

"Turn us toward it," Ace commanded.

The small craft made a turn. Huck let out a silent whistle, "I'll be damned," he said.

"Being damned is for Sunday School and fools," Ace said. "Though I believe them to be the same."

There in front of them, perched topside on the mid-Atlantic cliff sat the submarine.

"Identification lists this as the *Thresher*. We're here. A short slingshot effect and we're right on top of it". Java took a sip of coffee before confirming the *Thresher's* serial number.

"SSN-593 U.S.S. *Thresher* is confirmed, Java said.

The servant moved under half power up to the *Thresher's* side and slowly made its way to the stern where the most damage had been done. The lights illuminated a hole at the back of the craft.

"The stern looks pretty bad," Huck commented.

"Atlantean ore. I recognize it's glow," Ace said in amazement. "It must have been blown from the sub, and onto the ledge, Ace said, punching a series of buttons to begin auto photography and audio recording.

"And what about that?" Huck shoved his finger at the huge opening on the seabed. "Is that natural?"

"It is, but I daresay, I don't want to know what's in it," Ace said, and asked Java. "Are you detecting life signs on the *Thresher*?"

"I'm detecting no life. But it could be because of the glowy stuff," Java said finishing his coffee.

"The sub looks good on top, and the bow seems strong, but it looks like she's taking on water though. Slow and steady flooding. We don't have much time to get in there." Huck said, checking his guns.

"Expecting trouble?" asked Ace.

"You never know Captain," Huck replied.

"Java. Take us to the stern. Huck, Peyton, Kammy and I will drop down the edge and go in from there. Everyone... Java opened a small compartment and took out a box of pills.

"Take two and put your helmet on. You have about sixty minutes of protection against the ore's radioactive content. Be wary of your time and surroundings. Val... Doctor Atomika, is the priority. She is to be retrieved if deceased or captured if alive."

"We will bury the mineral ore as we leave," Ace said. "It's best if no one ever knows where it is."

The crew was silent for a moment, and Ace said, "Java, maintain position until radioed."

"Got it boss." Java said, lighting a cigar as Ace opened the floor hatch, and the group plunged into the icy depths.

The descent downward was slow and steady, and Ace felt like a weight at the end of a fishing net.

"Stay sharp people." Ace landed first, followed by Peyton, Kammy, and then Huck on the stern's ledge. A blinding light from the impurities of the Atlantean ore enveloped the crew. "We have to hurry,' Ace said. "This much exposure to the ore is not safe." He assisted each one into the *Thresher's* shredded cargo bay.

"Watch it everyone. Feel your way around, but gently. The metal is ripped apart and these suits aren't designed to be invulnerable to damage.

"Peyton, you and Huck head for the bridge. Kammy and I will take this section.

Huck and Peyton nodded and turned away, and Ace reminded them to use the suits recording devices to document everything. Huck gave a wave before disappearing deeper into the sub.

"Easy child," Ace warned, as Kammy got too far ahead. "Keep away from that substance. Open exposure to it in small amounts is fine but standing in a pile of it isn't being careful, it's being stupid."

Kammy froze, and Ace took her hand and pulled her away from the ore.

"Where are the bodies?"

"There wouldn't be any down here, the commander of this boat wouldn't want to take chances." Ace squinted and activated the lights on the top of his helmet. "There, that's better. What concerns me is the lack of bodies in the hallway. As cramped as subs usually are, there are no bodies in the adjoining rooms."

"Let's try getting to the crew quarters. The authorities were keeping Doctor Atomika locked up with guard. Room 2e from what I read in the file folder. The format of American subs are pretty much the same, so let's go this way."

Ace saw a ladder and motioned with his index finger saying, "Up."

***

Huck and Peyton made their way toward ship operations and both men noted the immense damage and twisted metal leading up towards the operations section. There was a foreboding sense lurking about the wrecked boat. One that kept Huck on his toes. "Wait," he said. "Did you see that?"

Peyton turned toward Huck, and asked, "You see something?"

"Thought I saw someone move," Huck said. "We should go see."

"Now wait a minute, the Captain wanted us to go to the command area," Peyton protested.

"Yeah, well in case you didn't notice, I don't work for Anderson."

"Regardless, I'm going on ahead and..."

Huck spun around to look for Peyton, but he was... "Gone." Huck raced ahead, the beams from his helmet light bounced off the narrow walls in front of him.

"Peyton...? Peyton...?" but the crewman was nowhere to be seen.

Damn it! Huck swallowed. *How could he just of vanished?* he wondered.

Suddenly, without warning a hand came to Huck's shoulder. His heart leapt into his throat and he turned to find... "Peyton!" Huck exclaimed. He grabbed Peyton by the arms and squeezed. "Dear God man, you know how to give a man a fright."

Huck gasped. The figure before looked like crewman Peyton, but he had changed... had become disfigured in some hideous way. Peyton snarled at Huck, producing sharp incisors.

Huck pushed Peyton away from him. "Stay back!" he shouted; his hands out in front of him.

Peyton charged him, and Huck had no other choice but to pull both revolvers from his holsters and began firing back at whatever Peyton had become.

Blam! Blam! Blam!.... he fired three times and Peyton only snarled in reply. Again, Huck fired, the blasts sent him to the floor. Satisfied Huck replaced his pistols but took several steps back when Peyton got back up.

Huck fumbled for the communicator in his helmet. "Ace," he said taking steady steps backward. "Ace... it's Peyton. Something has happened to him."

He drew his pistols, one at a time reloading. "He's changed into something..." Huck drew his guns in front of him and fired. This time unloading every shot into the beast, until Peyton went to the deck, scarlet pooled around his body mixing with the salt water.

Huck's throat tightened and he studied Peyton. His helmet had been smashed, but the lack of oxygen wasn't necessary as the zombified remains of Peyton returned to his feet.

Deciding not to hang around, Huck raced ahead, putting some distance between him and the dead crewman.

Huck's call didn't go unnoticed, but Ace and Kammy encountered the zombie-like navy men minutes before Finn radioed them.

"RUN!" Ace exclaimed.

"What's happening?" Kammy asked.

"It must be the orraculum that has altered the crew," Ace theorized.

"Why isn't it effecting us?" Kammy asked.

"By the sound of Mister Finn's voice, I'd say one of us has succumbed," Ace replied.

"Java," Ace called, but there was no reply. "Java?" he desperately called again.

"Communications must be down," Kammy said.

"But why?" Ace questioned.

The duo bolted down the corridor, the slurs of the zombies close behind.

A dead sailor dropped down from a ladder above. Without missing a beat, Ace caught it in mid-air and slammed it to the wet floor.

"I'll lead them off," Ace said. "You get to the control room, go now.... help Finn!"

Kammy bolted in the opposite direction – her heart thrumming in her chest. Fear consumed her, but she pushed ahead.

Inside the control room, Huck was surrounded by dead crew members, his gun working on overtime, but the zombies kept coming. They attacked from all sides – when his guns went quiet, he closed his eyes and awaited, then he heard Kammy scream. She swung a spanner tool like a cudgel, striking the undead upside the head.

Huck rolled himself away under a console to get his bearings as Kammy continued to move back and forth swinging at whatever moved, keeping the undead at bay. As he got up to join the battle, the form of a woman came out of the watery shadows. In an instant he knew her – but she was different from the pictures he'd seen of her... changed.

"Doctor Atomika!" Huck exclaimed, swinging toward her. "Kammy, Kammy, get out of here...!" But it was too late.

***

Outside the control room, Ace was backed in a corner surrounded by five dead sailors. It wasn't a place he fancied, but the zombies were encircling him. He stripped himself of his pressure suit finding it cumbersome. When the time came, he would hold his breath. Even at this depth, he could survive for a short time due to the air pressure and compression experiments he endured as a youth.

Taking a knife from his belt, Ace drew a breath. If he was going to fall this day, he would do so fighting for his life. Since his wife's death he had slowly been going down that rabbit hole of despair and regret. Yet there was so much to live for. *Kenzie,* he thought.

When the zombies charged him, Ace went into action, striking first, dropping to his knees and slashing the tendons of the zombie's legs, preventing them from walking.

One of the creatures attacked from behind, driving him under water. He sliced it and jabbed, bobbing up for air, keeping himself away from their mouths, preventing them an afternoon meal

***

Bloody, but not defeated, Ace entered the operations room. He saw Kammy's body in the water floating in a pool of red and Huck laying near her. He took a step further inside, and knelt down next to Huck, and checked for a pulse. *Alive,* he exhaled. He slapped Huck awake.

"Atomika, she's alive, and she's not normal." Huck coughed.

"Where?".

"Here, I'm here," Doctor Atomika said as she came up behind Ace.

Ace went to his feet, bringing Huck up with him. "Finn, get out NOW! No questions, no buts, nothing. Get out!" he exclaimed.

Huck turned toward Kammy, but Ace grabbed him by the scruff of the neck and shoved him, saying, "She's dead damn it... she's dead. Now GO!"

Huck drug himself from the control room, as Ace turned toward Atomika. He stood motionless as he witnessed the radiation damage done to the woman he once loved.

Her body was decaying. Her face peeling away to the muscle tissue below.

"I knew they would send you after me," Atomika said.

"You brought it all upon yourself Val. You spied for the Nazi's. You're an agent of chaos against the Allied Forces. You tried to use an unstable alien ore to create a super weapon that would destroy nation after nation, country after country."

"The bell. Die Glocke', was the only way to secure the power for the Fatherland over those who are undeserving to live," Atomika replied. She staggered backward, but the wall supported her.

"Val..."

"THAT is NOT my name...!" she exclaimed. "I am Doctor Atomika."

"Then the woman I once loved is dead," Ace said.

"And *I* possess the super weapon of the Gods. Rightfully given to us by our Atlantean ancestors, given to us by birthright to decree this planet for the perfect race."

"Your quite mad..."

"Nothing but propaganda darling. You believe your own falsehoods so much you've grown accustomed to the lies."

Ace took a step closer, but stayed out of arms reach. Horrified by her decay... her once golden hair falling out as they spoke.

"Do you even remember who you are anymore?" Ace asked.

"Yes, I remember. But Val Vickers is dead and the ever so clever scientist, is now Atomika."

"You're dying, Val," Ace said.

"Death is nothing. Only the death of America is all that matters."

"It will never happen... never," Ace assured her.

Great chunks of flesh dropped from Atomika's body, falling like a leaf in the fall. "Why am I sweating so much?" she asked.

"There isn't much time," Ace said. "If you want to say something, show some remorse for what you did."

Atomika cackled, "Never," she said. "Never. I am indestructible. Does that make me a God?"

"No Val, you're not a god. You're a victim of madness. I'm not sure when it happened to you... but the Nazis are doomed to fail," Ace said. "Sadly, you won't survive to see their downfall. Your time is over Val... it's over."

Atomika raged with laughter. "It's over for all of us, I think. You see I called for help. The might of the German navy will be here soon, if they already aren't.

"Kenzie...!" Ace cried as he raced from the control room. The water had risen considerably as he fought to get back to the mini sub.

"You're too late...!" Atomika shouted as Ace raced for his life.

***

"How many?" Kenzie asked.

The sonar officer reported, "One Corsair class German sub, crew compliment of thirty-nine, command and crew. It's on a direct course for the *Thresher* Commander."

"Standby to intercept," Kenzie said.

The *Kraken* made a wide turn, cutting along the path of the Corsair,

"Is this the right course of action?" Moreau asked.

"Maybe not," Kenzie said.

"Then if you're not sure, then why..."

"Because I'm in command," Kenzie snapped.

***

The *Thresher* was doomed. Nothing could save it, and sooner or later the ocean would claim all inside, including Ace Anderson.

Without warning, Doctor Atomika attacked him from behind. They fell into the water, both going under. They toss and turned and if Ace didn't know better, he would have sworn that Atomika was stronger than him. Which was impossible. Suddenly she let go.

Breaking the surface, he drew a deep breath of fresh air. Time was up, and Ace knew it. *I need to get back to the mini sub,* he thought as he drug himself through the water, unsure what happened to Atomika.

***

"The German sub has launched torpedoes at the *Thresher,*" the sonar officer reported.

"Launch counter measures," Kenzie ordered.

"Counter measures away," another crewman reported.

"The enemy torpedoes are deflected," the sonar man reported triumphantly.

"Now's not the time for celebration," Kenzie snapped.

"No, commander," the young officer replied.

"The corsair is coming around for another attempt," sonar reported.

"Standby with another round of counter measures," Kenzie said.

"Torpedoes away."

Counter measures... and lock onto that bastard and send him to his doom!" Kenzie snarled.

The *Kraken* fired torpedoes, but the sonar man reported, "Our torpedoes are going to hit the target true... but..."

"What?" Kenzie asked.

"So are theirs," the sonar man said downtrodden.

***

Huck pulled Ace through the hatch and sealed it, as Ace commanded, "Go Java... get us out of here!"

The mini sub broke away, but without warning, the *Thresher* exploded. The blast rocked the mini craft, and Davy Jones cliff broke away.

"The pressure is pulling us down!" Java screamed.

"Down... down where?" Huck asked as he held on.

Ace leaned forward and peered out the front window. "Into that," he shouted.

Huck leaned forward. "My God!" he shouted. The ocean floor broke open, to produce a gaping hole, sapphire blue, and as big as a city. "You said you didn't know where that goes...!"

Ace held on tight... "I don't... it's a mystery! But if I had to guess..."

"Save the physics lesson for another time Ace... because we are going into it...!" Java howled.

***

"Java... Huck... dad?" Kenzie tried multiple times, but nothing.

"The blast must have took them," Moreau said.

"I refuse to believe that..." Kenzie said.

"Then where are they?" Moreau asked.

Before Kenzie could answer... *This is Captain Ace Anderson...*Ace's voice came over the intercom.

Trust me daughter... fix onto my signal and bring the Kraken through. I repeat... bring the Kraken through.

Kenzie pressed the com button, and asked, "Through to where father?"

Ace's laughter filled the intercom, and he said, *To the next great adventure!*

COMING
FALL
2021

PULP REALITY 3

Printed in Dunstable, United Kingdom